A Cowbo

A Texas Christmas

Two enchanting stories from

DIANA PALMER

AND

LINDA LAEL MILLER

A Texas Christmas

DIANA PALMER

LINDA LAEL MILLER

First published in Great Britain 2012
by Mills & Boon, an imprint of Harlequin (UK) Limited, Eton House,
18-24 Paradise Road, Richmond, Surrey TW9 1SR

A TEXAS CHRISTMAS © Harlequin Enterprises II B.V./S.à.r.l. 2012

True Blue © Diana Palmer 2011
A Lawman's Christmas: A McKettricks of Texas Novel
© Linda Lael Miller 2011

ISBN: 978 0 263 90245 7

010-1212

Printed and bound by
CPI Group (UK) Ltd, Croydon, CR0 4YY

True Blue

DIANA PALMER

The prolific author of over one hundred books, **Diana Palmer** got her start as a newspaper reporter. One of the top ten romance writers in America, she has a gift for telling the most sensual tales with charm and humour. Diana lives with her family in Cornelia, Georgia.

Chapter One

"We could lose the case," San Antonio Detective Sergeant Rick Marquez muttered as he glared at one of the newest detectives on his squad.

"I'm really sorry," Gwendolyn Cassaway said, wincing. "I tripped. It was an accident."

He stared at her through narrowed dark eyes, his sensual lips compressed. "You tripped because you're nearsighted and you won't wear glasses." Personally, he didn't think the lack of them did anything for her, if vanity was the issue. She had a pleasant face, and an exquisite complexion, but she was no raving beauty. Her finest feature was her wealth of thick platinum-blond hair that she wore in a high bun on top of her head. She never wore it down.

"Glasses get in my way and I can't ever get them clean enough," she muttered. "That coating just causes smears unless you use the proper cleaning materials. And I can't ever find them," she said defensively.

He drew in a long, exasperated breath and perched on the edge of the desk in his office. In the posture, his .45 Colt ACP in its distinctive leather holster was displayed next to his badge on his belt. So were his powerful legs, and to their best advantage. He was tall and muscular, without it being obvious. He had a light olive complexion and thick long black hair that he wore in a ponytail. He was very attractive, but he couldn't ever seem to wind up with a serious girlfriend. Women found him useful as a sympathetic shoulder to cry on over their true loves. One woman refused to date him when she realized that he wore his pistol even off duty. He'd tried to explain that it was a necessary thing, but it hadn't given him any points with her. He went to the opera, which he loved, all alone. He went everywhere alone. He was almost thirty-one, and lonelier than ever. It made him irritable.

And here was Gwen making it all worse, messing up his crime scene, threatening the delicate chain of evidence that could lead to a conviction in a complex murder.

A college freshman, pretty and blonde, had been brutally assaulted and killed. They had no suspects and trace evidence was very sketchy already. Gwen had almost contaminated the scene by stepping too close to a blood smear.

He was not in a good mood. He was hungry. He was going to be late for lunch, because he had to chew her out. If he didn't, the lieutenant surely would, and Cal Hollister was even meaner than Marquez.

"You could also lose your job," Marquez pointed out. "You're new in the department."

She grimaced. "I know." She shrugged. "I guess I could go back to the Atlanta P.D. if I had to," she said with grim resignation. She looked at him with pale green eyes that were almost translucent. He'd never seen eyes that color.

"You just have to be more careful, Cassaway," he cautioned.

"Yes, sir. I'll do my best."

He tried not to look at the T-shirt she was wearing under a lightweight denim jacket with her jeans. It was unseasonably warm for November but a jacket felt good against the morning chill.

On her T-shirt was a picture of a little green alien, the sort sold in novelty shops, with a legend that read, Have You Seen My Spaceship? He averted his eyes and tried not to grin.

She tugged her jacket closer. "Sorry. But they don't have any regulations against T-shirts here, do they?"

"If the lieutenant sees that one, you'll find out," he said.

She sighed. "I'll try to conform. It's just that I come

from a very weird family. My mother worked for the
FBI. My father was, uh, in the military. My brother
is…" She hesitated and swallowed. "My brother *was*
in military intelligence."

He frowned. "Deceased?"

She nodded. She still couldn't talk about it. The pain
was too fresh.

"Sorry," he said stiffly.

She shifted. "Larry died very bravely during a covert
ops mission in the Middle East. But he was my only
sibling. It's hard to talk about."

"I can understand that." He stood up, glancing at
the military watch he wore on his left wrist. "Time for
lunch."

"Oh, I have other plans…" she began quickly.

He glared at her. "It was a remark, not an invitation.
I don't date colleagues," he said very curtly.

She blushed all the way down to her throat. She
swallowed and stood taller. "Sorry. I was… I meant…
that is…"

He waved the excuses away. "We'll talk about this
some more later. Meanwhile, please do something about
your vision. You can't investigate a crime scene you
can't see!"

She nodded. "Yes, sir. Absolutely."

He opened the door and let her go out first, noticing
absently that her head only came up to his shoulder and
that she smelled like spring roses, the pink ones that
grew in his mother's garden down in Jacobsville. It was

an elusive, very faint fragrance. He approved. Some women who worked in the office seemed to bathe in perfume and always had headaches and allergies and never seemed to think about the connection. Once, a fellow detective had had an almost-fatal asthma attack after a clerical worker stood near him wearing what smelled like an entire bottle of perfume.

Gwendolyn stopped suddenly and he plowed into her, his hands sweeping out to grasp her shoulders and steady her before she fell from his momentum.

"Oh, sorry!" she exclaimed, and felt a thrill of pleasure at the warm strength of the big hands holding her so gently.

He removed them at once. "What is it?"

She had to force her mind to work. Detective Sergeant Marquez was very sexy and she'd been drawn to him since her first sight of him several weeks before. "I meant to ask if you wanted me to check with Alice Fowler over at the crime lab about the digital camera we found in the murdered woman's apartment. By now, she might have something on the trace evidence."

"Good idea. You do that."

"I'll swing past there on my way back to the office after lunch," she promised, and beamed, because it was a big case and he was letting her contribute to solving it. "Thanks."

He nodded, his mind already on the wonderful beef Stroganoff he was going to order at the nearby café where he usually had lunch. He'd been looking forward to it all week. It was Friday and he could splurge.

Tomorrow was his day off. He was going to spend it helping his mother, Barbara, process and can a bushel of hothouse tomatoes she'd been given by an organic gardener with a greenhouse. She owned Barbara's Café in Jacobsville, and she liked to use her organic vegetables and herbs in the meals she prepared for her clients. They would add to the store of canned summer tomatoes that she'd already processed earlier in the year.

He owed her a lot. He'd been orphaned in junior high school and Barbara Ferguson, who'd just lost her husband in an accident, and suffered a miscarriage, had taken him in. His mother had once worked for Barbara at the café just briefly. Then his parents—well, his mother and stepfather—had died in a wreck, leaving a single, lonely child all on his own. Rick had been a terrible teen, always in trouble, bad-tempered and moody. He'd been afraid when he lost his mother. He had no other living relatives of whom he was aware, and no place to go. Barbara had stepped in and given him a home. He loved her no less than he'd loved his real mother, and he was quite protective of her. He never spoke of his stepfather. He tried not to remember him at all.

Barbara wanted him to marry and settle down and have a family. She harped on it all the time. She even introduced him to single women. Nothing helped. He seemed to be an eternally on-sale item in the matrimonial market that everybody bypassed for the fancier merchandise. He laughed shortly to himself at the thought.

Gwen watched him leave and wondered why he'd laughed. She was embarrassed that she'd thought he was asking her to lunch. He didn't seem to have a girlfriend and everybody joked about his nonexistent love life. But he wasn't attracted to Gwen in that way. It didn't matter. No man had ever liked her, really. She was everybody's confidante, the good girl who could give advice about how to please other women with small gifts and entertainments. But she was never asked out for herself.

She knew she wasn't pretty. She was always passed over for the flashy women, the assertive women, the powerful women. The women who didn't think sex before marriage was a sin. She'd had a man double over laughing when she'd told him that, after he expected a night in bed in return for a nice meal and the theater. Then he'd become angry, having spent so much money on her with nothing to show for it. The experience had soured her.

"Don Quixote," she murmured to herself. "I'm Don Quixote."

"Wrong sex," Detective Sergeant Gail Rogers said as she paused beside the newcomer. Rogers was the mother of some very wealthy ranchers in Comanche Wells, but she kept her job and her own income. She was an amazing peace officer. Gwen admired her tremendously. "And what's that all about?" she asked.

Gwen sighed, glancing around to make sure they weren't being overheard. "I won't give out on dates," she whispered. "So men think I'm insane." She shrugged. "I'm Don Quixote, trying to restore morality and idealism to a decadent world."

Rogers didn't laugh. She smiled, very kindly. "He was noble, in his way. An idealist with a dream."

"He was nutty as a fruitcake." Gwen sighed.

"Yes, but he made everyone around him feel of worth, like the prostitute whom he idealized as a great lady for whom he quested," came the surprising reply. "He gave dreams to people who had given them up for harsh reality. He was adored by them."

Gwen laughed. "Yes, I suppose he wasn't so bad at that."

"People should have ideals, even if they get laughed at," Rogers added. "You stick to your guns. Every society has its outcasts." She leaned down. "Nobody who conformed to the rigid culture of any society ever made history."

Gwen brightened. "That's true." Then she added, "You've lived through a lot. You got shot," Gwen recalled hearing.

"I did. It was worthwhile, though. We broke a cold case wide-open and caught the murderer."

"I heard. That was some story."

Rogers smiled. "Indeed it was. Rick Marquez got

blindsided and left for dead by the same scoundrels who shot me. But we both survived." She frowned. "What's wrong? Marquez giving you a hard time?"

"It's my own fault," Gwen confided. "I can't wear contacts and I hate glasses. I tripped in a crime scene and came close to contaminating some evidence." She grimaced. "It's a murder case, too, that college fresh-man they found dead in her apartment last night. The defense will have a field day with that when the perp is caught and brought to trial. And it will be my fault. I just got chewed out for it. I should have, too," she said quickly, because she didn't want Rogers to think Mar-quez was being unfair.

Rogers's dark eyes searched hers. "You like your sergeant, don't you?"

"I respect him," Gwen said, and then flushed help-lessly.

Rogers studied her warmly. "He's a nice man," she said. "He does have a temper and he does take too many chances. But you'll get used to his moods."

"I'm working on that." Gwen chuckled.

"How did you like Atlanta?" Rogers asked conver-sationally as they headed for the exit.

"Excuse me?" Gwen said absently.

"Atlanta P.D. Where you were working."

"Oh. Oh!" Gwen had to think quickly. "It was nice. I liked the department. But I wanted a change, and I've always wanted to see Texas."

"I see."

No, she didn't, Gwen thought, and thank goodness for that. Gwen was keeping secrets that she didn't dare divulge. She changed the subject as they walked together to the parking lot to their respective vehicles.

Lunch was a salad with dressing on the side, and half a grilled cheese sandwich. Dessert, and her drink, was a cappuccino. She loved the expensive coffee and could only afford it one day a week, on Fridays. She ate an inexpensive lunch so that she could have her coffee.

She sipped it with her eyes closed, smiling. It had an aroma that evoked Italy, a little sidewalk café in Rome with the ruins visible in the distance…

She opened her eyes at once and looked around, as if someone could see the thoughts in her head. She must be very careful not to mention that memory, or other similar ones, in regular conversation. She was a budding junior detective. She had to remember that. It wouldn't do to let anything slip at this crucial moment.

That thought led to thoughts of Detective Marquez and what would be a traumatic revelation for him when the time came for disclosure. Meanwhile, her orders were to observe him, keep her head down and try to discover how much he, or his adoptive mother, knew about his true background. She couldn't say anything. Not yet.

She finished her coffee, paid for her meal and walked out onto the chilly streets. So funny, she thought, the way the weather ran in cycles. It had been unseasonably cold throughout the South during the spring then came summer and blazing, unrelenting heat with drought and wildfires and cattle dying in droves. Now it was November and still unseasonably warm, but some weather experts said snow might come soon.

The weather was nuts. There had been epic drought throughout the whole southern tier of America, from Arizona to Florida, and there had been horrible wildfires in the southwestern states. Triple-digit temperatures had gone all summer in south Texas. There had been horrible flooding on the Mississippi River due to the large snowmelt, from last winter's unusually deep snows up north.

Now it was November and Gwen was actually sweating long before she reached her car, although it had been chilly this morning. She took off her jacket. At least the car had air-conditioning, and she was turning it on, even if it was technically almost winter. Idly, she wondered how people had lived in this heat before air-conditioning was invented. It couldn't have been an easy life, especially since most Texans of the early twentieth century had worked on the land. Imagine, having to herd and brand cattle in this sort of heat, much less plow and plant!

Gwen got into her car and drove by the crime lab to see if Alice had found anything on that digital camera. In fact, she had. There were a lot of photos of people who were probably friends—Gwen could use face recognition software to identify them, hopefully—and there was one odd-looking man standing a little distance behind a couple who was smiling into the camera against the background of the apartment complex where the victim had lived. That was interesting and suspicious. She'd have to check that man out. He didn't look as if he belonged in such a setting. It was a mid-range apartment complex, and the man was dingy and ill kempt and staring a little too intently. She drove back to her precinct.

Her mind was still on Marquez, on what she knew, and he didn't. She hoped he wasn't going to have too hard a time with his true history, when the truth came out.

Barbara glared at her son. "Can't you just peel the tomato, sweetie, without taking out most of it except the core?"

He grimaced. "Sorry," he said, wielding the paring knife with more care as he went to work on what looked like a bushel of tomatoes, a gift from an organic gardener with a hothouse, that his mother was canning in her kitchen at home. Canning jars simmered in a huge tub of water, getting ready to be filled with fragrant tomato slices and then processed in the big pressure cooker. He glared at it.

"I hate those things," he muttered. "Even the safest ones are dangerous."

"Baloney," she said inelegantly. "Give me those."

She took the bowl of tomatoes and dunked them into a pot of boiling water. She left them there for a couple of minutes and fished them out in a colander. She put them in the sink in front of Rick. "There. Now they'll skin. I keep telling you this is a more efficient way than trying to cut the skins off. But you don't listen, my dear."

"I like skinning them," he said with a dark-eyed smile in her direction. "It's an outlet for my frustrations."

"Oh?" She didn't look at him, deliberately. "What sort of frustrations?"

"There's this new woman at work," he said grimly.

"Gwen." She nodded.

He dropped the knife, picked it back up and stared at her.

"You talk about her all the time."

"I do?" It was news to him. He didn't realize that.

She nodded as she skinned tomatoes. "She trips over things that she doesn't see, she messes up crime scenes, she spills coffee, she can't find her cell phone..." She glanced at him. He was still standing there, with the knife poised over a tomato. "Get busy, there, those tomatoes won't peel themselves."

He groaned.

"Just think how nice they'll taste in one of my beef stew recipes," she coaxed. "Go on, peel."

"Why can't we just get one of those things that sucks the air out of bags and freeze them instead?"

"What if we have a major power outage that lasts for days and days?" she returned.

He thought for a minute. "I'll go buy twenty bags of ice and several of those foam coolers."

She laughed. "Yes, but we can't tell how the power grid is going to cope if we have one of those massive CMEs like the Carrington Event in 1859."

He blinked. "Excuse me?"

"There was a massive coronal mass ejection in 1859 called the Carrington Event," she explained. "When it hit earth, all the electrics on the planet went crazy. Telegraph lines burned up and telegraph units caught fire." She glanced at him. "There wasn't much electricity back in those days—it was in its infancy. But imagine if such a thing happened today, with our dependence on electricity. Everything is connected to the grid these days, banks, communications corporations, pharmacies, government, military and the list goes on and on. Even our water and power are controlled by computers. Just imagine if we had no way to access our computers."

He whistled. "I was in the grocery store one day when the computers went offline. They couldn't process credit cards. Most people had to leave. I had enough cash for bread and milk. Then another time the computers in the pharmacy went down, when you had to have those antibiotics for the sinus infection last winter. I had to come home and get the checkbook and go back. People without credit cards had real problems."

"See?" She went back to her tomatoes.

"I suppose it would be a pretty bad thing. Is it going to happen, you think?"

"Someday, certainly. The sun has eleven year cycles, you know, with a solar minimum and a solar maximum. The next solar maximum, some scientists say, is in 2012. If we're going to get hit, that would have my vote for the timeline."

"Twenty-twelve," he groaned, rolling his eyes. "We had this guy come in the office and tell us we needed to put out a flyer."

"What about?"

"The fact that the world is ending in 2012 and we have to have tin-foil hats to protect us from electromagnetic pulses."

"Ah. EMPs," she said knowledgeably. "Actually, I think you'd have to be in a modified and greatly enlarged version of a Leiden jar to be fully protected. So would any computer equipment you wanted to save." She glanced at him. "They're developing weapons like that, you know," she added. "All it would take is one nicely placed EMP and our military computers would go down like tenpins."

He put down the knife. "Where do you learn all this stuff?" he asked, exasperated.

"On the internet." She pulled an iPod out of her pocket and showed it to him. "I have Wi-Fi in the house, you know. I just connect to all the appropriate websites." She checked her bookmarks. "I have one for space weather, three radars for terrestrial weather and about ten covert sites that tell you all the stuff the government won't tell you…"

"My mother, the conspiracy theorist," he moaned.

"You won't hear this stuff on the national news," she said smartly. "The mainstream media is controlled by three major corporations. They decide what you'll get to hear. And mostly it's what entertainer got drunk, what television show is getting the ratings and what politician is patting himself on the back or running for reelection. In my day—" she warmed to her theme "—we had real news on television. It was local and we had real reporters out gathering it. Like the Jacobsville paper still does," she added.

"I know about the Jacobsville paper," he said with a sigh. "We hear that Cash Grier spends most of his time trying to protect the owner from getting assassinated. She knows all the drug distribution points and the drug lords by name, and she's printing them." He shook his head. "She's going to be another statistic one day. They've killed plenty of newspaper publishers and reporters over the border for less. She's rocking the boat."

"Somebody needs to rock it," Barbara muttered as she peeled another tomato skin off and tossed it into a green bag to be used for mulch in her garden. She never wasted any organic refuse. "People are dying so that another generation can become addicted to drugs."

"I can't argue that point," he said. "The problem is that nothing law enforcement is doing is making much of a dent in drug trafficking. If there's a market, there's going to be a supply. That's just the way things are."

"They say Hayes Carson actually talked to Minette Raynor about it."

That was real news. Minette owned the *Jacobsville Times*. She had two stepsiblings, Shane, who was twelve, and Julie, who was six. She'd loved her stepmother very much. Her stepmother and her father had died within weeks of each other, leaving a grieving Minette with two little children to raise, a newspaper to run and a ranch to manage. She had a manager to handle the ranch, and her great-aunt Sarah lived with her and took care of the kids after school so that Minette could keep working. Minette was twenty-five now and unmarried. She and Hayes Carson didn't get along. Hayes blamed her, God knew why, for his younger brother's drug-related death, even after Rachel Conley left a confession stating that she'd given Bobby Carson, Hayes's brother, the drugs that killed him.

Rick chuckled. "If there's ever a border war, Minette will stand in the street pointing a finger at Hayes so the invaders can get him first."

"I wonder," Barbara mused. "Sometimes I think where there's antagonism, there's also something deeper. I've seen people who hate each other end up married."

"Cash Grier and his Tippy," Rick mused.

"Yes, and Stuart York and Ivy Conley."

"Not to mention half a dozen others. Jacobsville is growing by leaps and bounds."

"So is Comanche Wells. We've got new people there, too." She was peeling faster. "Did you notice that Grange bought a ranch in Comanche Wells, next to the property that his boss owns?"

Rick pursed his sensual lips. "Which boss?"

She blinked at him. "What do you mean, which boss?"

"He works as ranch manager for Jason Pendleton. But he also works on the side for Eb Scott," he said. "You didn't hear this from me, but he was involved in the Pendleton kidnapping," he added. "He went to get Gracie Pendleton back when she was kidnapped by that exiled South American dictator, Emilio Machado."

"Machado."

"Yes." He peeled the tomato slowly. "He's a conundrum."

"What do you mean?"

"He started out, we learned, as a farm laborer down in Mexico, from the time he was about ten years old. He was involved in protests against foreign interests even as a teenager. But he got tired of scratching dirt for a living. He could play the guitar and sing, so he worked bars for a while and then through a contact, he got a job as an entertainer on a cruise ship. That got boring. He signed on with a bunch of mercs and became known internationally as a crusader against oppression. Afterward, he went to South America and hired on with

another paramilitary group that was fighting to pre-
serve the way of life of the native people in Barrera, a
little nation in the Amazon bordering Peru. He helped
the paramilitary unit free a tribe of natives from a foreign corporation that was trying to kill them to get the
oil-rich land on which they were living. He developed
a taste for defending the underdog, moved up in the
ranks of the military until he became a general." He
smiled. "It seems that he was a natural leader, because
when the small country's president died four years ago,
Machado was elected by acclamation." He glanced at
her. "Do you realize how rare that is, even for a small
nation?"

"If people loved him so much, how is it that he's in
Mexico kidnapping people to get money to retake his
country?"

"He wasn't ousted by the people, but by a vicious and
bloodthirsty military subordinate who knew when and
how to strike, while Machado was on a trip to a neighboring country to sign a trade agreement and offer an
alliance against foreign corporate takeovers."

"I didn't know that."

"It's sort of privileged info, so you can't share it,"
he told her. "Anyway, the subordinate killed Machado's entire staff, and sent his secret police to shut down
newspapers and television and radio stations. Over-
night, influential people ended up in prison. Educa-
tors, politicians, writers—anyone who might threaten
the new regime. There have been hundreds of murders,

and now the subordinate, Pedro Mendez by name, is allying himself with drug lords in a neighboring country. It seems that cocaine grows quite nicely in Barrera and poor farmers are being 'encouraged' to grow it instead of food crops on their land. Mendez is also nationalizing every single business so that he has absolute control."

"No wonder the general is trying to retake his country," she said curtly. "I hope he makes it."

"So do I," Rick replied. "But I can't say that in public," he added. "He's wanted in this country for kidnapping. It's a capital offense. If he's caught and convicted he could wind up with a death penalty."

She winced. "I don't condone how he's getting the money," she replied. "But he's going to use it for a noble reason."

"Noble." He chuckled.

"That's not funny," she said shortly.

"I'm not laughing at the word. It's Gwen. She goes around mumbling that she's Don Quixote."

She laughed out loud. "What?"

He shook his head. "Rogers told me. It seems that our newest detective won't give out on dates and she groups herself with Don Quixote, who tried to restore honor and morality to a decadent world."

"My, my!" She pursed her lips and smiled secretively.

"I don't want to marry Gwen Cassaway," he said at

once. "I just thought I'd mention that, because I can read minds, and I don't like what you're thinking."

"She's a nice girl."

"She's a woman."

"She's a nice girl. She has a very idealistic and romantic attitude for someone who lives in the city. And I ought to know. I have women from cities coming through here all the time, talking about unspeakable things right in public with the whole world listening." Her lips made a thin line. "Do you know, Grange was having lunch next to a table of them where they were discussing men's, well, intimate men parts," she amended, clearing her throat, "and Grange got up from his chair, told them what he thought of them for discussing a bedroom topic in public in front of decent people and he walked out."

"What did they do?"

"One of them laughed. One of the others cried. Another said he needed to start living in the real world instead of small town 'stupidville.'" She grinned. "Of course, she said it after he'd already left. While he was talking, they didn't say a word. But they left soon after. I was glad. I can't choose my clientele and I've only ever ordered one person to leave my restaurant since I've owned it," she added.

She dragged herself back to the present. "But the topic of conversation was getting to me, too. People need to talk about intimate things in private, not in a public place with their voices raised. We don't all think alike."

"Only in some ways," he pointed out, and hugged her impulsively. "You're a nice mother. I'm so lucky to have you for an adoptive parent."

She hugged him back. "You've enriched my life, my sweet." She sighed, closing her eyes in his warm embrace. "When I lost Bart, I wanted to die, too. And then your mother and stepfather died, and there you were, as alone as I was. We needed each other."

"We did." He moved away and smiled affectionately. "You took on a big burden with me. I was a bad boy."

She groaned and rolled her eyes. "Were you ever! Always in fights, in school and out. I spent half my life in the principal's office and once at a school board meeting where they were going to vote to throw you right out of school altogether and put you in alternative school." Her face hardened. "In their dreams!"

"Yes, you took a lawyer to the meeting and buffaloed them. First time it ever happened, I heard later."

"I was very mad."

"I felt really bad about that," he said. "But I put my nose to the grindstone after, and tried hard to make it up to you."

"Joined the police force, went to night school and got your associate degree, went to the San Antonio Police Department and worked your way up in the ranks to sergeant," she agreed, smiling. "Made me *so* proud!"

He hugged her again. "I owe it all to you."

"No. You owe it to your hard work. I may have helped, but you pulled yourself up."

He kissed her forehead. "Thank you. For everything."

"You're my son. I love you very much."

He cleared his throat. Emotions were difficult for him, especially considering his job. "Yeah. Me, too."

She grinned. The smile faded as she searched his large, dark eyes. "Do you ever wonder about your mother's past?"

His eyebrows shot up. "What a question!" He frowned. "What do you mean?"

"Do you know anything about her friends? About any male friends she had before she married your stepfather?"

He shrugged. "Not really. She didn't talk about her relationships. Well, I wasn't old enough for her to confide in me, either, you know. She never was one to talk about intimate things," he said quietly. "Not even about my real father. She said that he died, but she never talked about him. She was very young when I was born. She did say she'd done things she wanted forgiveness for, and she went to confession a lot." He studied her closely. "You must have had some reason for asking me that."

She put her lips tightly together. "Something I overheard. I wasn't supposed to be listening."

"Come on, tell me," he said when she hesitated.

"Cash Grier was having lunch with some fed. They

were discussing Machado. The fed mentioned a woman named Dolores Ortíz who had some connection to General Machado when he lived in Mexico."

Chapter Two

"Dolores Ortíz?" he asked, the paring knife poised in midair. "That was my mother's maiden name."

"I know."

Rick frowned. "You mean my mother might have been romantically involved with Emilio Machado?"

"I got that impression," Barbara said, nodding. "But I wasn't close enough to hear the entire conversation. I just got bits and pieces of it."

He pursed his lips. "Well, my father died around the time I was born, so it's not impossible that she did meet Machado in Mexico. Although, it's a big country."

"You lived in the state of Sonora," she pointed out. "That's where Machado had his truck farm, they said."

He finished skinning the tomato and reached for

another one. "Wouldn't that be a coincidence, if my mother actually knew him?"

"Yes, it would."

"Well, it was a long time ago," he said easily. "And she's dead, and I never knew him. So what good would it do for them to dig up an old romance now?"

"I have no idea. It bothered me, a little. I mean, you're my son."

"Yes, I am." He glanced at her. "I love it when people get all flustered and start babbling when you introduce me. You're blonde and fair and I'm dark and obviously Hispanic."

"You're gorgeous, my baby," she teased. "I just wish women would stop crying on your shoulder about other men and start trying to marry you."

He sighed. "Chance would be a fine thing. I carry a gun!" he said with mock horror.

She glowered at him. "All off-duty policemen carry guns."

"Yes, but I might shoot somebody accidentally, and it would get in the way if I tried to hug somebody."

"I gather that somebody female mentioned that?"

He sighed and nodded. "A public defender," he said. "She thought I was cute, but she doesn't date men who carry. It's a principle, she said. She hates guns."

"I hate guns, too, but I keep a shotgun in the closet in case I ever need to defend myself," Barbara pointed out.

"I'll defend you."

"You work in San Antonio," she said. "If you're not here, I have to defend myself. By the time Hayes Carson could get to my place, I'd be…well, not in any good condition if somebody tried to harm me."

That had happened once, Rick recalled with anger. A man he'd arrested, after he'd been released, had gone after Rick's adoptive mother for revenge. It was just chance that Hayes Carson had stopped by when he was off duty, in his unmarked truck, to ask her about catering an event. The ex-convict had piled out of his car and come right up on the porch with a drawn gun—in violation of parole—and banged on the door demanding that Barbara come outside. Hayes had come outside, disarmed him, cuffed him and taken him right to jail. The man was now serving another term in prison, for assault on a police officer, trespassing, attempted assault, possessing a firearm in violation of parole and resisting arrest. Barbara had testified at his trial. So had Hayes.

Rick shook his head. "I hate having you in danger because of my job."

"It was only the one time," she said, comforting him. "It could have been somebody who carried a grudge because their apple pie wasn't served with ice cream or something."

He smiled. "Dream on. You even make the ice cream you serve with it. Your pies are out of this world."

"Don't you have an in-house seminar coming up at work?" she asked.

He nodded.

"Why don't you take a couple of pies back with you?"

"That would be nice. Thank you."

"My pleasure." She pursed her lips. "Does Gwen like apple pie?"

He turned and stared at her. "Gwen is a colleague. I never, never date colleagues."

She sighed. "Okay."

He went back to work on the tomatoes. This could turn into a problem. His mother, well-meaning and loving, nevertheless was determined to get him married. That was one area in which he wanted to do his own prospecting. And never in this lifetime did he want to end up with someone like Gwen, who had two left feet and the dress sense of a Neanderthal woman. He laughed at the idea of her in bearskins carrying a spear. But he didn't share the joke with his mother.

When he went to work the next day, it was qualifying time on the firing range. Rick was a good shot, and he kept excellent care of his service weapon. But the testing was one of the things he really hated about police work.

His lieutenant, Cal Hollister, could outshoot any man in the precinct. He scored a hundred percent regularly. Rick could usually manage in the nineties but never a perfect score. He always seemed to do the qualifying when the lieutenant was doing his, and his ego suffered.

Today, Gwen Cassaway also showed up. Rick tried

not to groan out loud. Gwen would drop her pistol, accidentally kill the lieutenant and Rick would be prosecuted for manslaughter...

"Why are you groaning like that?" Hollister asked curtly as he checked the clip for his .45 in preparation for target shooting.

"Just a stray thought, sir, nothing important." His eyes went involuntarily to Gwen, who was also loading her own pistol.

On the firing range, shooters wore eye protection and ear protection. They customarily loaded only six bullets into the clip of the automatic, and this was done at the time they got into position to fire. The pistol would be held at low or medium ready position, after being carefully drawn from its snapped holster for firing, with the safety on. The pistol, even unloaded, would never be pointed in any direction except that of the target and the trigger finger would never rest on the trigger. When in firing position, the safety would be released, and the shooter would fire at the target using either the Weaver, modified Weaver, or Isosceles shooting stance.

One of the most difficult parts of shooting, and one of the most important to master, was trigger pull. The pressure exerted on the trigger had to be perfect in order to place a shot correctly. There were graphs on the firing range that helped participants check the efficiency of their trigger pull and help to improve it. Rick's was improving. But his lieutenant consistently showed

him up on the gun range, and it made him uncomfortable. He tried not to practice or qualify when the other
man was around. Unfortunately, he always seemed to
be on the range when Rick was.

Hollister followed Rick's gaze to Gwen. He knew,
as Rick did, that she had some difficulty with coordi-
nation. He pursed his lips. His black eyes danced as he
glanced covertly at Gwen. "It's okay, Marquez. We're
insured," he said under his breath.

Rick cleared his throat and tried not to laugh.

Hollister moved onto the firing line. His thick
blond hair gleamed like pale honey in the sunlight. He
glanced at Gwen. "Ready, Detective?" he drawled, pulling the heavy ear protectors on over his hair.

Gwen gave him a nice smile. "Ready when you are,
sir."

The Range Master moved into position, indicated
that everything was ready and gave the signal to fire.

Hollister, confident and relaxed, chuckled, aimed at
the target and proceeded to blow the living hell out of
it.

Rick, watching Gwen worriedly, saw something incredible happen next. Gwen snapped into a modified
Weaver position, barely even aimed and threw six shots
into the center of the target with pinpoint accuracy.

His mouth flew open.

She took the clip out of her automatic, checked the
cylinder and waited for the Range Master to check her
score.

"Cassaway," he said eventually, and hesitated. "One hundred percent."

Rick and the lieutenant stared at each other.

"Lieutenant Hollister," the officer continued, and was obviously trying not to smile, "ninety-nine percent."

"What the hell...!" Hollister burst out. "I hit dead center!"

"Missed one, sir, by a hair," the officer replied with a twinkle in his eyes. "Sorry."

Hollister let out a furious bad word. Gwen marched right up to him and glared at him from pale green eyes.

"Sir, I find that word offensive and I'd appreciate it if you would refrain from using it in my presence," she said curtly.

Hollister's high cheekbones actually flushed. Rick tensed, waiting for the explosion.

But Hollister didn't erupt. His black eyes smiled down at the rookie detective. "Point taken, Detective," he said, and his deep voice was even pleasant. "I apologize."

Gwen swallowed. She was almost shaking. "Thank you, sir."

She turned and walked off.

"Not bad shooting, by the way," he commented as he removed the clip from his own pistol.

She grinned. "Thanks." She glanced at Rick, who was still gaping, and almost made a smart remark. But she thought better of it in time.

Rick let out the breath he'd been holding. "She trips over her own feet," he remarked. "But that was some damned fine shooting."

"It was," the lieutenant agreed. He shook his head. "You can never figure people, can you, Marquez?"

"True, sir. Very true."

Later that day, Rick noted two dignified men in suits walking past his office. They glanced at him, spoke to one another and hesitated. One gestured down the hall quickly, and they kept walking.

He wondered what in the world was going on.

Rogers came into his office a few minutes later, frowning. "Odd thing."

"What?" he asked, his eyes on his computer screen where he was running a case through VICAP.

"Did you see those two suits?"

"Yes, they hesitated outside my office. Who are they, feds?"

"Yes. State Department."

He burst out laughing as he looked at her with large, dancing brown eyes. "They think I'm illegal and they're here to bust me?"

"Stop that," she muttered.

"Sorry. Couldn't resist it." He turned to her. "We have high level immigration cases all the time where the State Department gets involved."

"Yes, but mostly we deal with the enforcement branch of the Department of Immigration and Natu-ralization, with ICE. Or we deal with the DEA in drug cases, I know that. But these guys aren't from Austin. They're from D.C."

"The capitol?"

"That's right. They've been talking to the lieutenant all morning. They're taking him to lunch, too."

"What's going on? Any idea?"

She shook her head. "Only that gossip says they're on the Machado case."

"Yes. He's wanted for kidnapping." He didn't add what Barbara had told him, that his own birth mother might have once known Machado in the past.

"He's not in the country."

"And how would you know that?" Rick asked her with pursed lips. "Another psychic insight?" he added, because she had a really unusual sixth sense about cases.

"No. I ran into Cash Grier over at the courthouse. He was up here on a case."

"Our police chief from Jacobsville," he acknowledged.

"The very same. He mentioned that Jason Pendleton's foreman is on temporary leave because of Machado."

"Grange," Rick recalled, naming the foreman. "He went into Mexico to retrieve Gracie Pendleton when she was kidnapped by Machado's men for ransom."

"Yes. It seems the general took a liking to him, had him investigated and offered him a job."

Rick blinked. "Excuse me?"

"That's what I said when Grier told me." She laughed. "The general really does have style. He said somebody had to organize his mercs when he goes in to retake his country. Grange, being a former major in the army, seemed the logical choice."

"His country is Barrera," Rick mused. "Nice name, since it sits on the Amazon River bordering Colombia, Peru and Bolivia. Barrera is Spanish for barrier."

"I didn't know that, only having completed two years of college Spanish," she replied blithely.

He made a face at her.

"Anyway, it seems Grange likes the idea of being a crusader for democracy and freedom and human rights, so he took the job. He's in Mexico at the moment helping the general come up with a plan of attack."

"With Eb Scott offering candidates, I don't doubt," Rick added. "He's got the cream of the crop at his counterterrorism training center in Jacobsville, as far as mercs go."

"The general is gathering them from everywhere. He has a couple of former SAS from Great Britain, a one-eyed terror from South Africa named Rourke whose nickname is Deadeye…"

"I know him," Rick said.

"Me, too," Rogers replied. "He's a pill, isn't he? Rumored to be the natural son of K. C. Kantor, who was one of the more successful ex-mercs."

"Yes, Kantor became a billionaire after he gave up the lifestyle. He has a daughter who married Dr. Micah

Steele in Jacobsville, and a godchild who married into the ranching Callister family up in Montana." His eyes narrowed. "Where is the general getting the money to finance his revolution?"

"Remember that he gave Gracie back without any payment. But then he nabbed Jason Pendleton for ransom, and Gracie paid it with the money from her trust fund?"

"Forgot about that," Rick said.

"It ran to six figures. So he's bankrolled. We hear he also charged what's left of the Fuentes cartel for protection while he was sharing space with them over the border."

"Charging drug lords rent in their own turf?" Rick asked.

"And getting it. The general has a pretty fearsome reputation," she added. She laughed. "He's also a incredibly handsome," she mused. "I've seen a photograph of him. They say he has a charming personality, reveres women and plays the guitar and sings like an angel."

"A man of many talents."

"Not the least of which is inspiring troops." Rogers sighed. "But it has to be unsettling for the State Department, especially since the Mexican government is up in arms about having Machado recruit mercs to invade a sovereign nation in South America while living in their country."

"Why are they protesting to us? We aren't helping him," Rick pointed out.

"He's on our border."

"If they want us to do something about Machado, they could do something about the militant drug cartels running over our borders with automatic weapons to protect their drug runners."

"Chance would be a fine thing."

"I guess so. None of that explains why the State Department is gumming up our office," he added. "This is San Antonio. The border is that way." He pointed out the window. "A long, long drive that way."

"I know. That's what puzzled me. So I pumped Grier for information."

"What did he tell you?"

"He didn't. Tell me anything," she added grimly. "So I had my oldest son pump his best friend, Sheriff Hayes Carson, for information."

"Did you get anything from him?"

She bit her lower lip. "Bits and pieces." She gave him a worried look. She couldn't tell him what she found out. She'd been sworn to secrecy. "But nothing really concrete, I'm sorry to say."

"I suppose they'll tell us eventually."

"I suppose so."

"When is this huge invasion of Barrera going to take place? Any timeline on that?"

"None that presented itself." She sighed. "But it's going to be a gala occasion, from what we hear. The

State Department would have good reason to be concerned. They can't back a revolution…"

"One of the letter agencies could help with that, of course, without public acknowledgment."

Letter agencies referred to government bureaus like the CIA, which Rick assumed would have been in the forefront of any assistance they could legally give to help install a democratic government friendly to the United States in South America.

"Kilraven used to belong to the CIA," Rick murmured. "Maybe I could ask him if he knows anything."

"I'd keep my nose out of it for the time being," Rogers cautioned, foreseeing trouble ahead if Rick tried to interfere at this stage of the game. "We'll know soon enough."

"I guess so." He glanced at her and asked, "Hear about what happened on the firing range this morning?"

Her eyes brightened. "Did I ever! The whole department's talking about it. Our rookie detective outshot the lieutenant."

"By a whole point." Rick grinned. "Imagine that. She falls into potted plants and trips over crime evidence, but she can shoot like an Old West gunslinger." He shook his head. "I thought I'd pass out when she started firing that automatic. It was beautiful. She never even seemed to aim. Just snapped off the shots and hit in the center every single time."

"The lieutenant's a good loser, though," Rogers commented. "He bought a single pink rose and laid it on her desk after lunch."

Rick's eyes narrowed and his expression grew cold. "Did he, now?"

The lieutenant was a widower. Nobody knew how he lost his wife, he never spoke of her. He didn't even date, as far as anyone knew. And here he was giving flowers to Gwen, who was young and innocent and impressionable...

"I said, do you think that could be construed as sexual harassment?" Rogers repeated.

"He gave her a flower!"

"Well, yes, but he wouldn't have given a man a flower, would he?"

"I'd have given Kilraven a flower after he nabbed the perp who blindsided me in the alley and left me for dead," he said, tongue in cheek.

She sighed. She felt in her pocket for the unopened pack of cigarettes she kept there, pulled it out and looked at it with sad eyes. "I miss smoking. The kids made me quit."

"You're still carrying around cigarettes?" he exclaimed.

"Well, it's comforting. Having them in my pocket, I mean. I wouldn't actually smoke one, of course. Unless we have a nuclear attack, or something. Then it would be okay."

He burst out laughing. "You're incorrigible, Rogers."

"Only on Mondays," she said after a minute. She glanced at her watch. "I have to get back to work."

"Let me know if you find out anything else, okay?"

"Of course I will." She smiled.

She felt a twinge of guilt as she walked out of his office. She wished she could tell him the truth, or at least prepare him for what she knew was coming. He had a surprise in store. Probably not a very nice one.

"But I made corned beef and cabbage," Barbara groaned when Rick phoned her Friday afternoon to say he wasn't coming home that night.

"I know, it's my favorite, and I'm sorry," he said. "But we've got a stakeout. I have to go. It's my squad." He sighed. "Gwen's on it, and she'll probably knock over a trash can and we'll get burned."

"You have to think positively." She hesitated. "You could bring her home with you tomorrow. The corned beef will still be good and I'll cook more cabbage."

"She's a colleague," he repeated. "I don't date colleagues."

"Does your lieutenant date colleagues?" she asked with glee. "Because I heard he left her a single rose on her desk. What a lovely, romantic man!"

He gnashed his teeth and hoped the sound didn't carry. He was tired of hearing that story. It had gone the rounds at work all week.

"You could put a rose on her desk..."

"If I did, it would be attached to a pink slip!" he snapped.

She gasped, hesitated and turned off the phone. It was the first time he'd ever snapped at her.

Rick groaned and dialed her number back. It rang and rang. "Come on. Please?" he spoke into the busy signal. "I'm sorry. Come on, let me apologize..."

"Yes?" Barbara answered stiffly.

"I'm sorry. I didn't mean to snap at you. I really didn't. I'll come home for lunch tomorrow and eat corned beef and cabbage. I'll even eat crow. Raw." There was silence on the end of the line. "I'll bring a rose?"

She laughed. "Okay, you're forgiven."

"I'm really sorry. Things have been hectic at work. But that's no excuse for being rude to you."

"No, it's not. But I'm not mad."

"You're a nice mother."

She laughed. "You're a nice son. I love you. I'll see you at lunch tomorrow."

"Have a good night."

"You have a careful one," she said solemnly. "Even rude sons are hard to come by these days," she added.

"I'll change my ways. Honest. See you."

"See you."

He hung up and sighed heavily. He couldn't imagine why he'd been so short with his own mother. Perhaps he needed a vacation. He only took time off when he was threatened. He loved his job. Being sergeant of an eight-detective squad in the Homicide Unit, in the Murder/ Attempted Murder detail, was heady and satisfying.

He assigned lead detectives to cases, reviewed cases to make sure everything necessary was done and kept up with what seemed like tons of paperwork, as well as reporting to the lieutenant on caseloads. But maybe a little time off would improve his temper. He'd talk to the lieutenant about it next week, he resolved. For now, he had work to do.

Gwen had been assigned as lead detective on the college student's murder case downtown. It was an odd sort of case. The woman had been stabbed by person or persons unknown, in her own apartment, with all the doors locked and the windows shut. There were no signs of a struggle. She was a pretty young woman with no current boyfriend, no apparent enemies, who led a quiet life and didn't party.

Gwen wanted very much to solve the case. She'd told Rick that Alice Fowler had found prints on a digital camera that featured an out-of-place man in the background. Gwen was checking that out. She was really working hard on the mystery.

But in the meantime, she'd been pressed into service to help Rick with a stakeout of a man wanted for shooting a police officer in a traffic stop. The officer lived, but he'd be in rehab for months. They had intel that the shooter was hiding out in a low class apartment building downtown with some help from an associate. But they couldn't find him there. So Rick decided to stake out the place and try to catch him. The fact that it was a Friday night meant that the younger, single detectives were trying to find ways not to get involved. Even the night detectives had excuses, pending cases that they simply couldn't spare time away from. So Rick ended up with Gwen and one young and eager patrol officer, Ted Sims, from the Patrol South Division who'd volunteered, hoping to find favor with Rick and maybe get a chance at climbing the ladder, and working as a detective one day.

They were set up in a ratty apartment downtown, observing a suspect across the alley in another run-down apartment building. They had all the lights off, a telescope, a video camera, listening devices, warrants to allow the listening devices, and as much black coffee as three detectives could drink in an evening. Which was quite a lot.

"I wish we had a pizza." Officer Sims sighed.

Rick sighed, too. "So do I, but the smell would carry and the perp would know we were watching him."

"Maybe we could put the pizza outside his door and he'd go nuts smelling it and rush out to grab it and we could grab him," Sims mused.

"What do you have in that bottle besides water?" Gwen asked, with twinkling green eyes.

Sims made a face. "Just water, sadly. I could really use a cold beer."

"Shut up," Marquez groaned. "I'm dying for one."

"We could ask Detective Cassaway to investigate the beer rack at the local convenience store and confiscate a six-pack for the crime scene investigation unit," Sims joked. "Nobody would have to know. We could threaten the owner with health violations or something."

Gwen gave him a cold look. "We don't steal."

Marquez gave him an even more vicious look. "Ever."

He flushed. "Hey," he said, holding up both hands, "I was just kidding!"

"I'm not laughing," she returned, unblinking.

"Neither am I," Marquez seconded. His face was hard with suppressed anger. "I don't want to hear talk like that from a sworn police officer."

"Sorry," he said, swallowing hard. "Really. Bad joke. I didn't mean I'd actually do it."

Gwen shrugged. Sims was very young. "I'm missing that new science fiction show I got hooked on," she groaned. "It's making me twitchy."

"I watch that one, too," Rick replied. "It's not bad."

"You could record it," Sims suggested. "Don't you have a DVR?"

She shook her head. "I'm poor. I can't afford one."

Rick glared at her. "We work for one of the best-paying departments in the southwest," he rattled off. "We have a benefits package, expense accounts, access to excellent vehicles..."

"I have a monthly rent bill, a monthly insurance bill, a car payment, utilities payments and I have to buy bullets for my gun," she muttered. "Who can afford luxuries?" She glared at him. "I haven't had a new suit in six months. This one looks like moths have nested in it already."

Rick's eyebrows arched up. "Surely, you've got more than one suit, Cassaway."

"Two suits, twelve blouses, six pair of shoes and assorted...other things," she said. "Mix and match and I'm sick of all of it. I want haute couture!"

"Good luck with that," Rick remarked.

"Luck won't do it."

"Hey, is this the guy we're looking for?" Sims asked suddenly, looking through the telescope.

Chapter Three

Rick and Gwen joined him at the window. Rick snapped a photo of the man across the street, using the telephoto feature, plugged it into his small computer and, using a new face recognition software component, compared it to the man he'd photographed.

"Positive ID. That's him," Rick said. "Let's go get him."

They ran down the steps, deploying quickly to the designations planned earlier by Rick.

The man, yawning and oblivious, stepped out onto the sidewalk next to a bus stop sign.

"Now," Rick yelled.

Three people came running toward the stunned man, who started to run, but it was far too late. Rick tackled him and took him down. He cuffed his hands behind his back and chuckled as the man started cursing.

"I ain't done nothin'!" he wailed.

"Then you don't have a thing to worry about."

The man only groaned.

"That was a nice takedown," Gwen said as they cleared their equipment out of the rented apartment, after the man had been taken away by the patrol officer.

"Thanks. I try to keep in shape."

She didn't dare look at him. She was having a hard enough time not noticing how very attractive he was.

"You know," he mused, "that was some fine shooting down at HQ."

She beamed. "Thanks." She glanced up. "At least I do have one saving grace."

"Probably more than one, Cassaway."

She shouldered her purse. "Are we done for the night?"

"Yes. I'll input the report and you can sign it tomorrow. I snapped at my mother. I have to go home and try to make it up to her."

"She's very nice."

He turned, frowning. "How do you know?"

"I came through Jacobsville when I had to interview a witness in that last murder trial," she reminded him. "I had lunch at the café. It's the only one in town, except for the Chinese restaurant, and I like her apple pie." She added that last bit to make sure he knew she wasn't frequenting his mother's café just because she was his mother.

"Oh."

"Has she owned the restaurant a long time?"

He nodded. "She opened it a couple of years before I was orphaned. My mother worked for her as a cook just briefly."

Gwen nodded, trying to be low-key. "Is your mother still alive? Your biological mother?" she asked while looking through her purse for her car keys.

"She and my stepfather died in a wreck when I was almost in my teens. Barbara had just lost her husband and had a miscarriage the month before it happened. She was grieving and so was I. Since I had no other family, and she knew me, she adopted me."

She flushed. "Oh. Sorry, I didn't mean to pry. I was just curious."

He shrugged. "Most everybody knows," he said easily. "I was born in Mexico, in Sonora, but my mother and stepfather came to this country when I was a toddler and lived in Jacobsville. My stepfather worked at one of the local ranches."

"What did he do?"

"Broke horses." The way he said it was cold and short, as if he didn't like being reminded of the man.

"I had an uncle who worked ranches in Wyoming," she confided. "He's dead now."

He studied her through narrowed eyes. "Wyoming. But you're from Atlanta?"

"Not originally."

He waited.

She cleared her throat. "My people are from Montana, originally."

"You're a long way from home."

"Yes, well, my parents moved to Maryland when I was small."

"I guess you miss the ocean."

She nodded. "A lot. It wasn't a long drive from our house. But I go where they send me. I've worked a lot of places—" She stopped dead, and could have bitten her tongue.

His eyebrows were arching already. "The Atlanta P.D. moves you around the country?"

"I mean, I've worked a lot of places around Atlanta."

"Mmm-hmm."

"I didn't always work for Atlanta P.D.," she muttered, trying to backpedal. "I worked for a risk organization for a year or two, in the insurance business, and they sent me around the country on jobs."

"A risk organization? What sort of work did you do?"

"I was a sort of security consultant." It wasn't quite the truth, but it wasn't quite a lie, either. She glanced at her watch as a diversion. "Oh, goodness, I'll miss my television show!"

"God forbid," he said dryly. "Okay. We're done here."

"It didn't take as long as I expected," she commented

on the way out. "Usually stakeouts last for hours if not days."

"Tell me about it," he said drolly. "Is your car close by?"

She turned at the foot of the steps. "It's across the street, thanks," she said, because she knew he was offering to walk her to it. He was a gentleman, in the nicest sort of way.

He nodded. "I'll see you Monday, then."

She smiled. "Yes, sir."

She turned and walked away. Her heart was pounding and she was cursing herself mentally. She'd almost blown the whole thing sky-high!

Barbara was her usual, smiling self, but her eyes were sad when Rick showed up at the door the night before he was due home.

"You said tomorrow?" she murmured.

He stepped into the house and hugged her, hard, rocking her in his arms. He heard a muffled sob. "I felt bad," he said at her ear. "I upset you."

"Hey," she murmured, drawing away to dab at her eyes, "that's what kids are supposed to do."

He smiled. "No, it's not."

"Want some coffee?"

"Yes!" he said at once, pulling off his suit coat and loosening his tie as he followed her to the kitchen. He swung the coat around one of the high-back kitchen chairs at the table and sat down. "I've been on stakeout, with convenience-store coffee." He made a face.

"I think they keep it in the pot all day to make sure it doesn't pass for hot brown water."

She laughed as she made a fresh pot. "There's that profit margin to consider," she mused.

"I guess."

"Did you catch a crook?"

"We did, actually. That new face recognition software we use is awesome. Pegged the guy almost immediately."

"New technology." She shook her head. "Cameras everywhere, face recognition software, pat downs at the airport..." She turned and looked at him. "Isn't all that supposed to make us feel safer?"

"No, it's supposed to actually make you safer," he corrected. "It makes it harder for the bad guys to hide from the law."

"I guess so." She got out cups and saucers. "I made apple pie."

"You don't even need to ask. I had a hamburger earlier."

"You live on fast food."

"I work at a fast job," he replied. "No time for proper meals, now that I'm in a position of responsibility."

She turned and smiled at him. "I was so proud of you for that promotion. You studied hard."

"I might have studied less if I'd realized how much paperwork would be involved," he quipped. "I have eight detectives under me, and I'm responsible for all the major decisions that involve them. Plus I have to co-

ordinate them with other services, work around court
dates and emergency assignments... Life was a lot
easier when I was just a plain detective."

"You love your job, though. That's a bonus."

"It is," he had to agree.

She cut the pie, topped it with a scoop of homemade
ice cream and served it to him with his black coffee.
She sat down across from him and watched him eat it
with real enjoyment, her hands propping up her chin,
elbows on the tablecloth.

"You love to cook," he responded.

She nodded. "It isn't an independent woman thing,
I know," she said. "I should be designing buildings or
running a corporation and yelling at subordinates."

"You should be doing what you want to do," he replied.

"In that case, I am."

"Good cooks are thin on the ground." He finished
the pie and leaned back with his coffee cup in his hand,
smiling. "Wonderful food!"

"Thanks."

He sipped coffee. "And the best coffee anywhere."

"Flattery will get you another slice of pie."

He chuckled. "No more tonight. I'm fine."

"Are you ever going to take a vacation?" she asked.

"Sure," he replied. "I've already arranged to have
Christmas Eve off."

She glared at him. "A vacation is longer than one
night long."

He frowned. "It is? Are you sure?"

"There's more to life than just work."

"I'll think about that, when I have time."

"Have you watched the news today?" she asked.

"No. Why?"

"They had a special report about violence on the border. It seems that the remaining Fuentes brother sent an armed party over the border to escort a drug shipment and there was a shootout with some border agents."

He grimaced. "An ongoing problem. Nobody knows how to solve it. Bottom line, if people want drugs, somebody's going to supply them. You stop the demand, you stop the supply."

"Good luck with that" She laughed hollowly. "Never going to happen."

"I totally agree."

"Anyway, they mentioned in passing that one of the captured drug runners said that General Emilio Machado was recruiting men for an armed invasion of his former country."

"The Mexican Government, we hear, is not pleased with that development and they're angry at our government because they think we aren't doing enough to stop it."

"Really?" she exclaimed. "What else do you know?"

"Not much, but you can't repeat anything I tell you," he added.

She grinned. "You know I'm as silent as a clam. Come on. Talk."

"Apparently, the State Department sent people into our office," he replied. "We know they talked to our lieutenant, but we don't know what about."

"State Department!"

"They do have their fingers on the pulse of foreign governments," Rick reminded her. "If anybody knows what's really going on, they do."

"I would have thought one of those other government agencies would have been more involved, especially if the general's trying to recruit Americans for a foreign military action," she pondered.

His eyebrows arched.

"Well, it seems logical, doesn't it?" she asked.

"Actually, it does," he agreed. "I know the FBI and the CIA have counterterrorism units that infiltrate groups like that."

"Yes, and some of them die doing it," Barbara recalled. She grimaced. "They say undercover officers in any organization face the highest risks."

"The military also has counterterrorism units," he replied. He sipped his cooling coffee. "That must be an interesting sort of job."

"Dangerous."

He smiled. "Of course. But patriotic in the extreme, especially when it comes to foreign operatives trying to undermine democratic interests."

"Doesn't the general's former country have great deposits of oil and natural gas?" she wondered aloud.

"So we hear. It's also in a very strategic location, and the general leans toward capitalism rather than socialism or communism. He's friendly toward the United States."

"A point in his favor. Gracie Pendleton says he sings like an angel," she added with a smile.

"I heard."

"Yes, we had that discussion earlier." She was also remembering another discussion over the phone and her face saddened.

He reached across the table and caught her hand in his. "I really am sorry, Mom," he said gently. "I don't know what came over me. I'm not usually like that."

"No, you're not." She hesitated. She wanted to remark that it wasn't until she asked about the lieutenant giving Gwen a rose that he'd gone ballistic. But in the interests of diplomacy, it was probably wiser to say nothing. She smiled. "How about I warm up that coffee?" she asked instead.

Gwen answered the phone absently, her mind still on the previews of next week's episode of her favorite science fiction show.

"Yes?" she murmured, the hated glasses perched on her nose so that she could actually see the screen of her television.

"Cassaway, anything to report?"

She sat up straighter. "Sir!"

"No need to get uptight. I'm just checking in. The wife and I are on our way to a party, but I wanted to make sure things are progressing well."

"They're going very slowly, sir," she said, curling up in her bare feet and jeans and long-sleeved T-shirt on her sofa. "I'm sorry, I haven't found a diplomatic way to get him talking about the subject and find out what he knows. He doesn't like me...."

"I find that hard to believe, Cassaway. You're a good kid."

She winced at the description.

He cleared his throat. "Sorry. Good woman. I try to be PC, you know, but I come from a different generation. Hard for us old-timers to work well in the new world."

She laughed. "You do fine, sir."

"I know this is a tough assignment," he replied. "But I still think you're the best person for the job. You have a way with people."

"Maybe another type of woman would have been a better choice," she began delicately, "maybe someone more open to flirting, and other things..."

"With Marquez? Are you kidding? The guy wrote the book on staunch outlooks! He'd be turned off immediately."

She relaxed a little. "He does seem to be like that."

"Tough, patriotic, a stickler for doing the right thing even when the brass disapproves, and he's got more guts than most men in his position ever develop. Even went right up in the face of a visiting politician to tell him he was putting his foot in his mouth by interfering with a homicide investigation and would regret it when the news media got hold of the story."

She laughed. "I read about that."

"Takes a moral man to be that fearless," her boss continued. "So yes, you're the right choice. You just have to win his confidence. But you're going to have to move a little faster. Things are heating up down in Mexico. We can't be caught lagging when the general makes his move, you know? We have to have intel, we have to be in position to take advantage of any opportunities that present themselves. The general likes us. We want him to continue liking us."

"But we can't help."

He sighed. "No. We can't help. Not obviously. We're in a precarious position these days, and we can't be seen to interfere. But behind the scenes, we can hope to influence people who are in a position to interfere. Marquez is the obvious person to liaison with Machado."

"It's going to be traumatic for him," Gwen said worriedly. "From the little intel I've been able to acquire, he has no idea about his connection to Machado. None at all."

"Pity," he replied. "That's going to make it harder." He put his hand over the receiver and spoke to someone. "Sorry, my wife's ready to leave. I have to go. Keep me in the loop, and watch your back," he added firmly. "We're trying to get the inside track. There are

other people, other operatives, around who would love
nothing better than to see us fall on our faces. Other
countries would do anything to get a foothold in Barrera. I don't need to tell you who they are, or from what
motives they work."

"No, sir, you don't," she agreed. "I'll do the best I
can."

"You always do," he said, and there was faint affection in his tone. "Have a good evening. I'll be in touch."

"Yes, sir."

She hung up the cell phone and sat staring at it in her
hand. She felt a chill. So much was riding on her ability to be diplomatic and quick and discreet. It wasn't
her first difficult assignment; she was not a novice.
But until now, she'd had no personal involvement. Her
growing feelings for Rick Marquez were complicating
things. She shouldn't care so much about how it would
hurt him, but she did. If only there was a way, any way,
that she could give him a heads-up before the fire hit
the fan. Perhaps, she thought, she might be able to work
something out if she spoke to Cash Grier. They shared
a similar background in covert ops and he knew Marquez. It was worth a try.

So Friday morning, her day off, Gwen got in her
small, used foreign car and drove down to Jacobsville,
Texas.

Cash Grier met her at the door of his office, smiling,
and led her inside, motioning to a chair as he closed the
door behind him, locked it and pulled down the shade.

She pursed her lips with a grin. "Unusual precautions," she mused.

He smiled. "I'd put a pillow over the telephone if I thought there might be a wire near it. An ambassador's family habitually did that in Nazi Germany in the 1930s. Even did it in front of the head of the Gestapo once."

Her eyebrows arched as she sat down. "I missed that one."

"New book, about the rise of Hitler, and firsthand American views on the radical changes in society there in the 1930s," he said as he sat down and propped his big booted feet on his desk. "I love World War II history. I could paper my walls with books on the European Theatre and biographies of Patton and Rommel and Montgomery," he added, alluding to three famous World War II generals. "I like to read battle strategies."

"Isn't that a rather strange interest for a guy who worked alone for years, except with an occasional spotter?" she asked, tongue in cheek. It was pretty much an open secret that Grier had been a sniper in his younger days.

He chuckled. "Probably."

"I like history, too," she replied. "But I lean more toward political history."

"Which brings us to the question of why you're here," he replied and smiled.

She drew in a long breath and leaned forward. "I

have a very unpleasant assignment. It involves Rick Marquez."

He nodded and his face sobered. "I know. I still have high-level contacts in your agency."

"He has no idea what's about to go down," she said. "I've argued with my boss until I'm blue in the face, but they won't let me give Marquez even a hint."

"I think his mother knows," he said. "She asked me about it. She overheard some visitors from D.C. talking about connections."

"Do you think she's told him anything?"

"She might know that his mother was romantically involved with Machado at some point. But she wouldn't know the rest. His mother was very close about her private life. Only one or two people even knew what happened." He grimaced. "The problem is that one of the people involved had a cousin who married a high-level agent in D.C., and he spilled his guts. That started this whole chain of events."

"Hard to keep a secret like that, especially one that would have been so obvious." She frowned. "Rick's stepfather must have known. From what little information I've been able to gather about his past, he and his stepfather didn't get along at all."

"The man beat him," Grier said harshly. "A real jewel of a human being. It's one reason Rick had so many problems as a kid. He was in trouble constantly right up until the wreck that killed his mother and stepfather. It was a tragedy that produced golden results.

Barbara took him in, straightened him out and put him on a path that turned him into an exemplary citizen. Without her influence..." He spread his hands expressively.

Gwen stared at her scuffed black loafers. Idly, she noticed that they needed some polish. She dressed casually, but she liked to be as neat as possible. One day her real identity would come out, and she didn't want to give the agency a black eye by being slack in her grooming habits.

"You want me to tell him, don't you?" Grier asked.

She looked up. "You know him a lot better than I do. He's my boss, figuratively speaking. He doesn't like me very much, either."

"He might like you more if you'd wear your damned glasses and stop tripping over evidence in crime scenes," he said, pursing his lips. "Alice Mayfield Jones Fowler, who works in the Crime Scene Unit in San Antonio, was eloquent about the close call."

Gwen flushed. "Yes, I know." She pushed the hated glasses up on her nose, where they'd slipped. "I'm wearing my glasses now."

"I didn't mean to be critical," he said, noting her discomfort. "You're a long way from the homicide detective you started out to be," he added. "I know it's a pain, trying to relearn procedure on the fly."

"It really is," she said. "My credentials did stand up to a background check, thank goodness, but I feel like I'm walking on eggshells. I let slip that my job involved a lot of traveling and Marquez wondered why, since I was apparently working for Atlanta Homicide."

"Ouch," he said.

"I have to remember that I've never been out of the country. It's pretty hard, living two lives."

"I haven't forgotten that aspect of government work," he agreed. "It's why I never had much of a personal life, until Tippy came along."

Everybody local knew that Tippy had been a famous model, and then actress. She and Cash had a rocky trip to the altar, but they had a little girl almost two years old and it was rumored that they wanted another child.

"You got lucky," she said.

He shrugged. "I guess I did. I never could see myself settling down in a small town and becoming a family man. But now, it's second nature. Tris is growing by leaps and bounds. She has red hair, and green eyes, like her mama's."

Gwen noted the color photo on his desk, with himself and Tippy, with Tris and a boy who looked to be in his early teens. "Is that Tippy's brother?" she asked, indicating the photo.

"Rory," he agreed. "He's fourteen." He shook his head. "Time flies."

"It seems to." She leaned back again. "I miss my dad. He's been overseas for a long time, although he's coming back soon for a talk with some very high-level people in D.C. and rumors are flying. Rick Marquez has no idea what sort of background I come from."

"Another shock in store for him," he added. "You should tell him."

"I can't. That would lead to other questions." She sighed. "I'd love to meet my dad at the airport when he flies in. We've had a rough six months since my brother, Larry, died overseas. Dad still mourns my mother, and she's been gone for years. I miss her, too."

"I heard about your brother from a friend in the agency. I'm truly sorry." His dark eyes narrowed. "No other siblings?"

She shook her head.

"My mother's gone, too. But my dad's still alive, and I have three brothers," he replied with a smile. "My older brother, Garon, is SAC at the San Antonio FBI office."

"I've met him. He's very nice." She studied his face. He was a striking man, even with hair that was going silver at the temples. His dark eyes were piercing and steady. He looked intimidating sitting behind a desk. She could only imagine how intimidating he'd look on the job.

"What are you thinking so hard about?" he queried.

"That I never want to break the law in your town." She chuckled.

He grinned. "Thanks. I try to perfect a suitably intimidating demeanor on the job."

"It's quite good."

He sighed. "I'll talk to Marquez's mother and plant

clues. I'll do it discreetly. Nobody will ever know that you mentioned it to me, I promise."

"Least of all my boss, who'd have me on security details for the rest of my professional life," she said with a laugh. "I don't doubt he'd have me transferred as liaison to a police department for real, where he'd make sure I was assigned to duty at school crossings."

"Hey, now, that's a nice job," he protested. "My patrolmen fight over that one." He said it tongue in cheek. "In fact, the last one enjoyed it so much that he transferred to the fire department. It seems that a first-grader kicked him in the leg, repeatedly."

Her fine eyebrows arched. "Why?"

"He told the kid to stay in the crosswalk. Seems the kid had a real attitude problem. The teachers couldn't deal with him, so they finally called us, after the kicking incident. I took the kid home, in the patrol car, and had a long talk with his mother."

"Oh, dear."

His face was grim. "She's a single parent, living alone, no family anywhere, and this kid is one step away from juvy," he added, referencing the juvenile justice system. "He's six years old," he said heavily, "and he already has a record for disobedience and detention at his school."

"They put little kids in detention in grammar school?" she exclaimed.

"Figure of speech. They call it time-out and he sits in the library. Last time he had to go there, he stood on one of the library tables and recited the Bill of Rights to the head librarian."

Her eyes widened in amusement. "Not only a troublemaker, but brilliant to boot."

He nodded. "Everybody's hoping his poor mother will marry a really tough hombre who can control him before he does something unforgivable and gets an arrest record."

She laughed. "The things I miss because I never married," she mused, shaking her head. "It's not an incentive to become a parent."

"On the other end of the spectrum, there's Tippy and me," he replied with a smile. "I love being a dad."

"It suits you," she said.

She got to her feet. "Well, I have to get back to San Antonio. If Sergeant Marquez asks, I had to talk to you about a case, okay?"

"In fact, we really do have a case that might connect," he said surprisingly. "Sit back down and I'll tell you about it."

Chapter Four

Sergeant Marquez came into the office two days later, looking grim. He motioned to Gwen, indicated a chair and closed the door.

She remembered her trip to Cash Grier's office, and wondered if Grier had had time to talk to her superior officer's mother and the information had tricked down.

"The cold case squad has a job for us," he said as he sat down, too.

"What sort of job?"

"They dug up an old murder. It was committed back in 2002 and a man went to prison on evidence largely given by one person. Now it seems the person who gave evidence has been arrested and convicted for a similar crime. They want to know if we can find a connection."

"Well, by chance, that was the case I just spoke to Chief Grier about down in Jacobsville," she told him, happy that she could make a legitimate connection to her impromptu trip out of town. "He has an officer who knew the prisoner's family and could place the man at a party during the murder."

"Did he give evidence?" he asked.

She shook her head. "He was never called to testify," she said. "Nobody knows why."

"Isn't that interesting."

"Very. So the cold case squad wants us to wear out some shoe leather on their behalf?"

He grimaced. "They have plenty of manpower, but they've got two people out sick, one just transferred to the white collar crime unit and their sergeant said they don't want to let this case get buried. Especially not when a similar crime was just committed here. Your case. The college woman who was murdered. It needs investigation, and they don't have enough people." He smiled. "Besides, there's the issue of not stepping on the toes of another unit's investigation."

"I can understand that."

"So, we'll see if we can make a connection, based on available evidence. I'm assigning you as lead detective on this case, as well as on the college freshman murder. Find a connection. Catch the perp. Make me proud."

She grinned at him. "Actually, that might be possible. I just got some new information from running a check on the photo of that odd man in the murder victim's camera. The one I mentioned to you?"

"Yes, I recall that."

She pulled up a file on her phone. "This is him. I used face recognition software to pick him out." She showed him the mug shot on her phone. "The perp. His name is Mickey Dunagan. He has a rap sheet. It's a long one. He's been prosecuted in two aggravated assault cases, never convicted. Here's the clincher. He has a thing for young college girls. He was arrested for attempted assault a few months ago, on a girl who went to the same college as our victim. I have a detective from our unit en route to question her today, and we're interviewing people at the apartment complex about the man in the photograph. If his DNA is on file, and I'm betting it is since he's served time during his trials, and there's enough DNA from the crime scene to type and match…"

"Good work!" he said fervently.

She grinned. "Thanks, sir."

"I wish we could get ironclad evidence that he killed the victim." He grimaced. "Not that ironclad evidence ever got a conviction when some silver-tongued gung-ho public defender got the bit between his teeth."

"Impressive mixing of metaphors, sir," she murmured dryly.

He actually made a face at her. "Correct my grammar, get stakeout duty for the next two months."

"I would never do that!" she protested with wicked, twinkling eyes.

He smiled back. She was very pretty when she smiled. Her mouth was full and lush and sensuous...

He sat back in his chair and forced himself not to notice that. "Get busy."

"I'll get on it right now."

"Just out of curiosity, who was the officer who could place the convicted murderer at a party when the other murder was committed?"

"Officer Dan Travis," she said. "He's at the Jacobsville Police Department. I'm going to drive down and talk to him tomorrow." She checked the notes on her phone. "Dunagan was arrested for assault by a patrolman in South Division named Dave Harris. I'm going to talk to him afterward. He might remember something that would be helpful."

"Good. Keep me in the loop."

"I will." She got up and started for the door.

"Cassaway."

She turned at the door. "Sir?"

His dark eyes narrowed. He seemed deep in thought. He was. He had a strange sense that she knew something important that she was hiding from him. He read body language very well after his long years in law enforcement. He'd once tripped a bank robber up when he noticed the man's behavior and deliberately engaged him in conversation. During the conversation, he'd gotten close enough to see the gun the man was holding under his long coat. Rick had quickly subdued him, cuffed him, and taken him in for questioning. The impromptu encounter had solved a whole string of unsolved bank robberies for the cold case unit, and their sergeant, Dave Murphy, had taken Rick out to lunch in appreciation for the help.

"Sir?" Gwen prompted when he didn't reply.

He sat up straight. His eyes narrowed further as he stared at her. She was almost twitching. "What do you know," he said softly, "that you aren't telling me?"

Her face flushed. "No...nothing. I mean, there's... nothing," she faltered, and could have bitten her tongue for making things worse.

"You need to think about your priorities," he said curtly.

She drew in a long breath. "Believe me, I am."

He grimaced and waved his hand in her direction. "Get to work."

"Yes, sir."

She almost ran out of the office. She was flushed and unsettled. Lieutenant Hollister met her in the hall, and frowned.

"What's up?" he asked gently.

She bit her lip. "Nothing, sir," she said. She drew in a long breath. She wanted, so badly, to tell somebody what was going on.

Hollister's black eyes narrowed. "Come into my office for a minute."

He led her back the way she'd come, past a startled

Marquez, who watched the couple go into the lieutenant's office with an expression that was hard to classify.

"Sit down," Hollister said. He went behind his desk and swung up his long, powerful legs, propping immaculate black boots on the desk. He crossed his arms and leaned back precariously in his chair. "Talk."

She shifted restlessly. "I know something about Sergeant Marquez that I'm not supposed to discuss with anybody."

He lifted a thick blond eyebrow. He even smiled. "I know what it is."

Her green eyes widened.

"The suits who came to see me earlier in the week were feds," he said. "I know who you really are, and what's going on." He sighed. "I want to tell Marquez, too, but my hands are tied."

"I went to see Cash Grier," she said. "He's out of the loop. He can't do anything directly, but he might be able to let something slip at Barbara's Café in Jacobsville. That would at least prepare Sergeant Marquez for what's about to go down."

"Nothing can prepare a man for that sort of revelation, believe me." His eyes narrowed even more. "They want Marquez as a liaison, don't they?"

She nodded. "He'd be the best man for the job. But he's going to be very upset at first and he may refuse to do anything."

"That's a risk they're willing to take. They don't dare

interfere directly, not in the current political climate," he added. "Frankly, I'd just go tell him."

"Would you?" she asked, and smiled.

He laughed deeply and then he shook his head. "Actually, no, I wouldn't. I'm too handsome to spend time in prison. There would be riots. I'd be so much in demand as somebody's significant other."

She laughed, too. She hadn't realized he had a sense of humor. Her face flushed. She looked very pretty.

He cocked his head. "You could just ask Marquez to the ballet and tell him yourself."

"My boss would have me hung in Hogan's Alley up at the FBI Academy with a placard around my neck as a warning to other loose-lipped agents," she told him.

He grinned. "I'd come cut you down, Cassaway. I get along well with the feds. But I'm not prejudiced. I also get along with mercenaries."

"There's a rumor that you used to be one," she fished.

His face closed up, although he was still smiling. "How about that?"

She didn't comment.

He swung his long legs off the desk and stood up. "Let me know how it goes," he said. He walked her to the door. "It's not a bad idea, about asking him to the ballet. He loves ballet. He usually goes alone. He can't get girlfriends."

"Why not?" she asked. She cleared her throat. "I mean, he's rather attractive."

"He wears a gun."

"So do you," she pointed out, indicating the holster. "In fact, we all wear them."

"True, but he likes women who don't," he replied. "And they don't like men who wear guns. He doesn't date colleagues, he says. But you might be able to change his mind."

"Fat chance." She sighed. "He doesn't like me."

"Go solve that murder for the cold case unit, and they'll lobby him for you," he teased.

"How do you know about that?" she asked, surprised.

"I'm the lieutenant," he pointed out. "I know everything," he added smugly.

She laughed. She was still laughing when she walked down the corridor.

Rick heard her from inside his office. He threw a scratch pad across the room and knocked the trash can across the floor with it. Then he grimaced, in case anybody heard and asked what was going on. He couldn't have told them. He didn't know himself why he was behaving so out of character.

The man Gwen was tracking in her semiofficial disguise was an unpleasant, slinky individual who had a rap sheet that read like a short story. She'd gone down to Jacobsville and interviewed Officer Dan Travis. He seemed a decent sort of person, and he could swear that the man who was arrested for the murder was at a holiday party with him, and had never even stepped outside. He had told the assistant DA, but the attorney refused to entertain evidence he considered hearsay. Travis gave her the names of two other people she could contact, who would verify the information. She took notes and arranged for a deposition to be taken from him.

Her next stop was Patrol South Division, in San Antonio, to talk to the arresting officer who'd taken Dunagan in for the attempted assault on a college woman a few months ago, Dave Harris. He was working that day, but was working a wreck when she phoned him. So she arranged to meet him for lunch at a nearby fast food joint.

They sat together over hamburgers and fries and soft drinks, attracting attention with his uniform and her pistol and badge, conspicuously displayed.

"We're being watched," she said in a dramatic tone, indicating two young women at a nearby booth.

"Oh, that's just Joan and Shirley," he said. He looked toward the women, waved and grinned. One of them flushed and almost knocked over her drink. He was blond and blue-eyed, nicely built, and quite handsome. He was also single. "Joan's sweet on me," he added in a whisper. "They know I always eat here, so they come by for lunch. They work at the print shop downtown. Joan's a graphic artist. Very talented."

"Nice," she murmured, biting into the burger.

"Why are you doing a cold case?" he asked as he finished his salad and sipped black coffee.

"It ties in with a current one we're working on," she said, and related what Cash Grier had told her.

His dark eyebrows arched. "They never called a prime witness in the case?"

"Strange, isn't it?" she agreed. "That would be grounds for a mistrial, I'd think, but I'll need to talk to the city attorney's office first. The man who was convicted has been in prison for almost a year."

"Shame, if he's innocent," the patrolman replied.

"I know. Fortunately, such things don't happen often."

"What about the suspect in your current case?"

"A nasty bit of work," she replied. "I can place him at the scene of the crime, and if there's enough trace evidence to do a DNA profile, I think I can connect him with it. Her neighbors reported seeing him around her apartment the morning before the murder. If he's guilty, I don't want him to slip through the cracks on my watch, especially since Sergeant Marquez assigned me to the case as chief investigator."

"Really? How many other people are helping you with the case?"

"Let's see, right now, there's me and one other detective that I borrowed to help question witnesses."

He sighed. "Budget issues again?"

"Afraid so. I can manage. If I need help, the cold case unit will lend me somebody."

"Nice group, that cold case unit."

She smiled. "I think so, too."

"Now about the perp," he added, leaning forward. "This is how it went down."

He described the scene of the assault where he'd arrested Dunagan, the persons involved, the witnesses and his own part in the arrest. Gwen made notes on her phone and saved the file.

"That's a big help," she told him. "Thanks."

He smiled. "You're very welcome." He checked his watch. "I have to get back on patrol. Was there any other information you needed?"

"Nothing I can't find in the file. I appreciate the summary of the case, and your thoughts on it. That really helps."

"You're welcome. Any time."

"Shame about the latest victim," she added as they got up and headed to the trash bin with their trays. "She was very pretty. Her neighbors said she went out of her way to help people in need." She glanced at him. "We had one of your fellow officers on stakeout with us the other night. Sims."

He paused as he dumped the paper waste and placed the tray in its stack on the refuse container top. "He's not our usual sort of patrol officer."

"What do you mean?" she asked, frowning.

"I really can't say anything. It's just that he has an interesting background. There are people in high positions with influence," he added. He smiled. "But he's not my problem. I think you'll do well in the homicide unit. You've got a knack for sorting things out, and you're thorough. Good luck on the case."

"Thanks. Thanks a lot."

He smiled. "You're welcome."

She drove back to the office with her brain spinning. What she'd learned was very helpful. She might crack the case, which would certainly give her points with Rick Marquez. But there was still the problem of what she knew and couldn't tell him. She only hoped that Cash Grier would be able to break some ground with her sergeant.

Cash Grier had a thick ham sandwich with homemade fries and black coffee and then asked for a slice of Barbara's famous apple pie and homemade ice cream.

She served it with a grin. "Don't eat too much of this," she cautioned. "It's very fattening." She was teasing, because he was still as trim as men ten years his junior, and nicely muscled.

He pursed his lips and his black eyes twinkled. "As you can see, I'm running to fat."

She laughed. "That'll be the day."

He studied her quietly. "Can you sit down for a minute?"

She looked around. The lunchtime rush was over and there were only a couple of cowboys and an elderly couple in the café. "Sure." She sat down across from him. "What can I do for you?"

He sipped coffee. "I've been enlisted to get some information to your son without telling him anything."

She blinked. "That's a conundrum."

"Isn't it?" He put down the coffee cup and smiled. "You're a very intelligent woman. You must have some suspicions about his family history."

"Thanks for the compliment. And yes, I have a lot." She studied his hard face. "I overheard some feds who ate here talking about Dolores Ortíz and her connection to General Machado. Dolores worked for me just briefly. She was Rick's birth mother."

"Rick's stepfather was a piece of work," he said coldly. "I've heard plenty about him. He mistreated livestock and was fired for it on the Ballenger feedlot. Gossip is that he did the same to his stepson."

Her face tautened. "When I first adopted him, I lifted my hand to smooth back his hair—you know, that thing mothers do when they feel affectionate. He stiffened and cringed." Her eyes were sad. "That's when I first knew that there was a reason for his bad behavior. I've never hit him. But someone did."

"His stepfather," Grier asserted. "With assorted objects, including, once, a leather whip."

"So that's where he got those scars on his back," she faltered. "I asked, but he would never talk about it."

"It's a blow to a man's pride to have something like that done to him," he said coldly. "Jackson should have been sent to prison on a charge of child abuse."

"I do agree." She hesitated. "Rick's last name is Marquez. But Dolores said that was a name she had legally drawn up when Rick was seven. I never understood."

"She didn't dare put his real father's name on a birth certificate," he replied. "Even at the time, his dad was in trouble with the law in Mexico. She didn't want him to know about Rick. And, later, she had good reason to keep the secret. She married Craig Jackson to give Rick a settled home. She didn't know what sort of man he was until it was too late," he added coldly. "He knew who Rick's real father was and threatened to make it public if Dolores left him. So she stayed and Rick paid for her silence."

Barbara was feeling uncomfortable. "Would his real father happen to be an exiled South American dictator, by any chance?"

Grier nodded.

"Oh, boy."

"And nobody can tell him, because a certain federal agency is hoping to talk him into being a go-between for them, to help coax Machado into a comfortable trade agreement with our country when he gets back into power. Which he certainly will," he added quietly. "The thug who took over his government has human rights advocates bristling all over the world. He's tortured people, murdered dissenters, closed down public media outlets… In general, he's done everything possible to outrage anyone who believes in democracy. At the same time, he's pocketing money from sources of revenue and buying himself every rich man's perk that he can dream up. He's got several Rolls-Royce cars, assorted beautiful women, houses in most affluent European cities and his own private jet to take him to them. He doesn't govern so much as he flaunts his position. Workers are starving and farmers are being forced to grow drug crops to support his extravagant lifestyle." He shook his head. "I've seen dictators come and go, but that man needs a little lead in his diet."

She knew what he was alluding to. "Any plans going to take care of that?" she mused.

"Don't look at me," he warned. "I'm retired. I have a family to think about."

"Eb Scott might have a few people who would be interested in the work."

"Yes, he might, but the general isn't lacking for good help." He glanced up as one of Barbara's workers came, smiling, to refill his coffee cup. "Thanks."

She grinned. "You're welcome. Boss lady, you want some?"

Barbara shook her head. "Thanks, Bess, I'm already flying on a caffeine high."

"Okay."

"So who has to do the dirty work and tell Rick the truth?" Barbara asked.

Grier didn't speak. He just smiled at her.

"Oh, darn it, I won't do it!"

"There's nobody else. The feds have forbidden their agents to tip him off. His lieutenant knows, but he's been gagged, too."

"Then how in the world do they expect him to find out? Why won't they just tell him?"

"Because he might get mad at them for being the source of the revelation and refuse to cooperate. And there isn't anybody else they can find to do the job of contacting Machado."

"They could ask Grange," Barbara said stubbornly. "He's already working for the general, isn't he?"

"Grange doesn't know."

"Why me?" she groaned. "He'll be furious!"

"Yes, but you're his mother and he loves you," he replied. "If you tell him, he'll get over it. He might even be receptive to helping the feds. If they tell him, he'll hold a grudge and they'll never find anyone halfway suitable to do the job."

She was silent. She stared at the festive tablecloth worriedly.

"It will be all right," he assured her gently.

She looked up. "We've already had a disagreement recently."

"You have? Why?" he asked, surprised, because Rick's devotion to his adopted mother was quite well-known locally.

She grimaced. "His lieutenant gave the new detective, Gwen Cassaway, a rose, and I mentioned it in a teasing way. He went ballistic and I hung up on him. He won't admit it, but I think he's got a case on Gwen."

"Well!" he mused.

That was a new and interesting proposition. "Couldn't she tell him?" she asked hopefully.

"She's been cautioned not to."

She sighed. "Darn. Does everybody know?"

"Rick doesn't."

"I noticed."

"So you have to tell him. And soon."

"Or what?"

He leaned forward. "Or six government agencies will send operatives down here to disparage your apple pie and accuse you of subverting government policy by using organic products in your kitchen."

She burst out laughing. "Yes, I did hear that a SWAT team of federal agents raided a farm that was selling unpasteurized milk. Can you believe that? In our country, in this day and time, with all the real problems going on, we have to send armed operatives against people living in a natural harmony with the earth?"

"You're kidding!" he exclaimed.

"I wish I was," she replied. "I guess we're all going to be force-fed Genetically Modified Organisms from now on."

He burst out laughing. "You need to stop hanging out on those covert websites."

"I can't. I'd never know what was really going on in the world, like us having bases on the moon."

He rolled his eyes. "I have to get back to work." He stood up. "You'll tell him, then."

She stood up, too. "Do I have a choice?"

"You could move to Greenland and change your name."

She made a face at him. "That's no choice. Although I would love to visit Greenland. They have snow."

"So do we, occasionally."

"They have lots of snow. Enough to make many snowmen. South Texas isn't famous for that."

"The pie was great, by the way."

She smiled. "Thanks. I do my best."

"I'd have to leave town if you ever closed up," he told her. "I can't live in a town that doesn't have the best food in Texas."

"That will get you extra ice cream on your next slice of apple pie!" she promised him with a grin.

But she wasn't grinning when she went home. It disturbed her that she was going to have to tell her son something that would devastate him. He wasn't going to be pleased. Other than that, she didn't know what the outcome would be. But Grier was right about one thing; it was better that the information came from his mother rather than from some bureaucrat or federal agent who had no personal involvement with Rick and didn't care how the news affected him. It did make her feel good that so far, they hadn't blurted it out. By hesitating, they did show some compassion.

Rick went to his mother's home tired. It had been a long day of meetings and more meetings, with a workshop on gun safety occasioned by the accidental discharge of a pistol by one of the patrol officers. The bullet went into the asphalt but fortunately didn't ricochet and hit anything, or anyone. The officer was disciplined but the chain of command saw an opportunity to emphasize gun safety and they took it. The moral of the story was that even experienced officers could mishandle a gun.

Privately, Marquez wondered how Officer Sims ever got through the police academy, because he was the officer involved. The same guy who'd gone on stakeout with him and Cassaway. He didn't think a lot of the young man's ethics and he'd heard that Sims had an uncle high up in the chain of command who made sure he kept his job. It was disturbing.

"You look worn-out," Barbara said gently. "Come sit down and I'll put supper on the table."

"It's late," he commented, noting his watch.

"We can have supper at midnight," she teased. "Nobody's watching. I'll even pull down the shades if it makes you happy."

He laughed and hugged her. "You're a treasure, Mom. I'll never marry unless I can find a girl like you."

"That's sweet. Thanks."

She started heating up roast beef and buttered rolls, topping off his plate with homemade potato salad. She put the plate in front of him. "Thank goodness for microwave ovens." She laughed. "The cook's best friend."

"This is delicious." He closed his eyes, savoring every bite. "I had a sandwich for lunch and I only had time to eat half of it between meetings."

"I didn't even eat lunch," she said, dipping into her own roast beef.

"Why not?"

"I had a talk with Cash Grier and afterward I lost my appetite."

He stopped eating and stared at her with narrowed eyes. "What did he tell you?"

"Something everybody knows and nobody has the guts to tell you, my darling," she said, stiffening herself mentally. "I have some very unpleasant news."

He put down his fork. "You've got cancer." His face paled. "That's it, isn't it? You should have told me…!"

He got up and hugged her. "We'll get through it together. I'll never leave your side…"

She pulled back, flattered. "I'm fine," she said. "I don't have anything fatal. That isn't what I meant. It's about you. And your real father."

He blinked. "My real father died not long after I was born…"

She took a deep breath. "Rick, your real father is across the border in Mexico amassing a private army in preparation for invading a South American country."

He sat down, hard. His light olive complexion was suddenly very pale. All the gossip and secrecy suddenly made sense. The feds were all over his office, not because they were working on shared cases, but because of Rick.

"My father is General Emilio Machado," he said with sudden realization.

Chapter Five

"My father is a South American dictator," Rick repeated, almost in shock.

"I'm afraid so." Barbara pulled up a chair facing him and held his hand that was resting on the table. "They made me tell you. Nobody else wanted to. I'm so sorry."

"But my mother said my father was dead," he repeated blankly.

"She only wanted to protect you. Machado was in trouble with the Mexican authorities when he lived in the country because he was opposed to foreign interests trying to take over key industries where he lived. He organized protests even when he was in his teens. He was a natural leader. Later, Dolores didn't dare tell you because Machado was the head of a fairly well-known international paramilitary group and that would have made you a target for any extremist with a grudge. He was in the news a lot when you were a child."

"Does he know?" Rick persisted. "Does he know about me?"

Barbara bit her lower lip. "No. She never told him." She sighed. "After Cash told me who your father was, I remembered something that Dolores told me. She said your father was only fourteen when he fathered you. She was older, seventeen, and there was no chance that her family would have let her marry him. She wanted you very much. So she had you, and never even told her parents who the father was. She kept her secret. At least, until she married your stepfather. Cash said that your stepfather got the truth out of her and used it to keep her with him. She didn't dare protest or he'd have made your real identity known. A true charmer," she added sarcastically.

"My stepfather was a sadist," he said quietly. "I've never spoken of him to you. But he made my life hell, and my mother's as well. I got in trouble with the law on purpose. I thought maybe somebody would check out my home life and see the truth and help us. But nobody ever did. Not until you came along and offered my mother work."

"I tried to help," she agreed. "Dolores liked cooking for me, but your stepfather didn't like her having friends or any interest outside of him. He was insanely jealous."

"He also couldn't keep a job. Money was tight. You used to sneak me food," he recalled with a warm smile. "You even came to visit me in the detention center. My mother appreciated that. My stepfather wouldn't let her come."

"I knew that. I did what I could. I tried to get our police chief at the time to investigate, but he was the sort of man who didn't want to rock the boat." She laughed. "Can you imagine Cash Grier turning a blind eye to something like that?"

"He'd have had my stepfather pilloried in the square." Rick smiled, then sobered. "My father is a dictator," he repeated again. It was hard to believe. He'd spent his whole life certain that his biological father was long dead.

"A deposed dictator," Barbara corrected. "His country is going to the dogs under its new administration. People are dying. He wants to accomplish a military coup, but he needs all the help he can get. Which brings us to our present situation," she added. "A paramilitary group is going down to Barrera with him, including some of Eb Scott's guys, some Europeans, one African merc and with ex-army Major Winslow Grange, Jason Pendleton's foreman on his Comanche Wells ranch, to lead them."

"All that firepower and the government hasn't noticed?"

"It wouldn't do them a lot of good. Machado's in Mexico, just over the border," Barbara said. "They can't mount an invasion to stop him. But they can try to find a way to be friendly without overt aid."

"Ah. I see. I'm the goat."

She blinked. "Excuse me?"

"They're going to tether me out to attract the puma."

"Puma." She laughed. "Funny, but one of my customers said that's what the local population calls 'El General.' They say he's cunning and dangerous like a cat, but that he can purr when he wants to." Her face softened. "For a dictator, he's held in high esteem by most democracies. He's intelligent, kind, he reveres women and he isn't afraid to fight for justice."

"Does he wear a red cape?" Rick murmured.

She shook her head. "Sorry."

"Who's in on this?" he asked narrowly. "Does my lieutenant know?"

"Yes," she said. "And there's a covert operative somewhere in your organization," she added. "I got that tidbit from a patrol officer who has a friend on the force in San Antonio. A guy named Sims."

"Sims." His face closed up. "He's got connections. And he's a total ethical wipeout. I hate having a guy like that on the force. He got careless with a pistol and almost shot himself in the foot. He's the reason we just had a gun safety workshop."

"Learning gun safety is not a bad thing."

He sighed. "I know." He was trying to adjust to the shock of his parentage. "Why didn't my mother tell me?" he burst out.

"She was trying to protect you. I'm certain that she would have told you eventually," she added. "She just didn't have time before she died."

He grimaced. "What am I supposed to do now, walk over the border, find the general and say, hey, guess what, I'm your kid?"

"I don't really think that would be wise," she replied. "I'm not sure he'd believe it in the first place. Would you?"

"Now there's a question." He leaned back in the chair, his dark eyes focused on the tablecloth. "I suppose I could have a DNA profile done. There's a private company that can at least rule out paternity by blood type. If mine is compatible with the general's, it might help convince him... Wait a minute," he added coldly. "Why the hell should I care?"

"Because he's your father, Rick," she said gently. "Even though he doesn't know."

"And the government's only purpose in telling me is to help reunite us," he returned angrily.

"Well, no, they want someone to convince the general to make a trade agreement with us once he's back in power. They're certain that he will be, which is why they want you to make friends with him."

"I'm sure he'll be overjoyed to know he has a grown son who's a cop," he said coldly. "Especially since he's wanted by our government for kidnapping."

She leaned forward with her chin resting in her hands, propped by her elbows. "You could arrest him," she pointed out. "And then befriend him in jail. Like the mouse that took the thorn out of the lion's paw and became its friend."

He made a face at her. "I can't walk across the border and arrest anyone. I might have been born in Mexico, but I'm an American citizen. And I did it the hard way," he added firmly. "Legally."

She grimaced.

"Sorry," he said after a minute. "I know you sympathize with all the people hiding out here who couldn't afford to wait for permission. In some of their countries, they could be killed just for paying too much attention to the wrong people."

"It's very bad in some Central American states," she pointed out.

"It's very bad anywhere on our border."

"And getting worse."

He got up and poured himself another cup of coffee. His big hand rested on the coffeemaker as he switched it off. "Who's the mole in my office?"

"I honestly don't know," she replied. "I only know that Sims told his friend, Cash Grier's patrolman, about it. He said it was someone from a federal agency, working undercover."

"I wonder how Sims knew."

"Maybe he's the mole," she teased.

"Unlikely. Most feds have too much respect for the law to abuse it. Sims actually suggested that we confiscate a six-pack of beer from a convenience store as evidence in some pretended case and threaten the clerk with jail if he told on us."

"Good grief! And he works for the police?" she exclaimed, horrified.

"Apparently," he replied. "I didn't like what he said, and I told him so. He seemed repentant, but I'm not sure he really was. Cocky kid. Real attitude problem."

"Doesn't that sound familiar?" she asked the room at large.

"I never suggested breaking the law after I went through the academy and swore under oath to uphold it," he replied.

"Are you sure you didn't overreact, my darling?" she asked gently.

"If I did, so did Cassaway. She was hotter under the collar than I was." He laughed shortly. "And then she beat the lieutenant on the firing range and he let out a bad word. She marched right up to him and said she was offended and he shouldn't talk that way around her." He glanced at her ruefully. "Hence, the rose."

"Oh. An apology." She looked disappointed. "Your lieutenant is very attractive," she mused. "And eligible. I thought he might find Miss Cassaway interesting. Or something."

"Maybe he does," he said vaguely. "God knows why. She's good with a gun, I'll give her that, but she's a walking disaster in other ways. How she ever got a job with the police, I'll never know." He didn't like talking about Cassaway and the lieutenant. It got under his skin, for reasons he couldn't understand.

"She sounds very nice to me."

"Everybody sounds nice to you," he replied. He smiled at her. "You could find one good thing to say about the devil, Mom. You look for the best in people."

"You look for the worst," she pointed out.

He shrugged. "That's my job."

He was thoughtful, and morose. She felt even more guilty when she saw how disturbed he really was.

"I wish there had been some other way to handle this," she muttered angrily. "I hate being made the fall guy."

"Hey, I'm not mad at you," he said, and bent to kiss her hair. "I just...don't know what to do." He sighed.

"'When in doubt, don't,'" she quoted. She frowned. "Who said that?"

"Beats me, but it's probably good advice." He put down his cooling coffee and stretched, yawning. "I'm beat. Too many late nights finishing paperwork and going on stakeouts. I'm going to bed. I'll decide what to do in the morning. Maybe it will come to me in a dream or something," he added.

"Maybe it will. I'm just sorry I had to be the one to tell you."

"I'll get used to the idea," he assured her. "I just need a little time."

She nodded.

* * *

But time was in short supply. Two days later, a tall, elegant man with dark hair and eyes, wearing a visitor's tag but no indication of his identity, walked into Rick's office and closed the door.

"I need to talk to you," he said.

Rick stared at him. "Do I know you?" he asked after a minute, because the man seemed vaguely familiar.

"You should," he replied with a grin. "But it's been a while since we caught Fuentes and his boys in the drug sting in Jacobsville. I'm Rodrigo Ramirez. DEA."

"I knew you looked familiar!" Rick got up and shook the other man's hand. "Yes, it has been a while. You and your wife bought a house here last year."

He nodded. "I work out of San Antonio DEA now instead of Houston, and she works for the local prosecutor, Blake Kemp, in Jacobsville. With her high blood pressure, I'd rather she stayed at home, but she said she'd do it when I did it." He shrugged. "Neither of us was willing to try to change professions at this late date. So we deal with the occasional problem."

"Are you mixed up in the Barrera thing as well?" Rick asked curiously.

"In a way. I'm related, distantly, to a high official in Mexico," he said. "It gives me access to some privileged information." He hesitated. "I don't know how much they've told you."

Rick motioned Ramirez into a chair and sat down behind his desk. "I know that El General has a son

who's a sergeant with San Antonio P.D.," he said sarcastically.

"So you know."

"My mother told me. They wanted me to know, but
nobody had the guts to just say it," he bit off.

"Yes, well, that could have been a big problem. De-
pending on how you were told, and by whom. They
were afraid of alienating you."

"I don't see what help I'm going to be," Rick said
irritably. "I didn't know my biological father was still
alive, much less who he was. The general, I'm told, has
no clue that I even exist. I doubt he'd take my word for
it."

"So do I. Sometimes government agencies are a little
thin on common sense," he added. He crossed his elegant long legs. "I've been elected, you might say, to
do the introductions, by my cousin."

"Your cousin...?"

"He's the president of Mexico."

"Well, damn!"

Ramirez smiled. "That's what I said when he told
me to do it."

"Sorry."

"No problem. It seems we're both stuck with doing
something that goes against the grain. I think the general is going to react very badly. I wish there was someone who could talk to him for us."

"Like my mother talked to me for the feds?" he
mused.

"Exactly."

Rick frowned. "You know, Gracie Pendleton got along quite well with him. She refused to even think of pressing charges. She was asked, in case we could talk about extradition of Machado with the Mexican government. She said no."

"I heard. She's my sister-in-law, although she's not related to my wife. Don't even ask," he added, waving his hand. "It's far too complicated to explain."

"I won't. But I remember Glory very well," he reminded Ramirez. "Cash Grier and I taught her how to shoot a pistol without destroying cars in the parking lot," he added with a grin.

Ramirez laughed. "So you did." He sobered. "Gracie might be willing to speak to the general, if we could get word to him," Ramirez said.

"We had a guy in jail here who was one of the higher-ups in the Fuentes organization. He's going on probation tomorrow."

"An opportunity." Ramirez chuckled.

"Apparently, a timely one. I'll ask him if he'd have the general call Gracie. Now, how do you get Gracie to do that dirty work for you?"

"I'll have my wife bribe her with flowers and chocolate and Christmas decorations."

"Excuse me?" Rick asked.

"Gracie loves to decorate for Christmas. My wife has access to a catalog of rare antique decorations. Gracie can be bribed, if you know how," he added.

Rick smiled. "An assistant district attorney working a bribe. What if somebody tells her boss?"

"He'll laugh," Ramirez assured him. "It's for a just cause, after all."

Rick started down to the jail in time to waylay the departing felon. He spoke to the probation officer on the way and arranged the conversation.

The man was willing to take a message to the general, for a price. That put them on the hot seat, because neither man could be seen offering illegal payment to a felon.

Then Rick had a brainstorm. "Wait a second." He'd spotted the janitor emptying trash baskets nearby. He took the man to one side, handed him two fifties and told him what to do.

The janitor, confused but willing to help, walked over to the prisoner and handed him the money. It was from him, he added, since the prisoner had been pleasant to him during his occupation in the jail. He wanted to help him get started again on the outside.

The prisoner, smiling, understood immediately what was going on. He took the money graciously, with a bow, and proceeded to sing the janitor's praises for his act of generosity. So the message was sent.

Gwen Cassaway was sitting at Rick's desk when he went back to his office, in the chair reserved for visitors. He hated the way his heart jumped at the sight of her. He fought down that unwanted feeling.

"Do they have to issue us these chairs?" she complained when he came in, closing the door behind him. "Honestly, only hospital waiting rooms have chairs that are more uncomfortable."

"The idea is to make you want to leave," he assured her. "What's up?" he added absently as he removed his holstered pistol from his belt and slid it into a desk drawer, then locked the drawer before he sat down. "Something about the case I assigned you to?"

She hesitated. This was going to be difficult. "Something else. Something personal."

He stared at her coolly. "I don't discuss personal issues with colleagues. We have a staff psychologist if you need counseling."

She let out an exasperated sigh. "Honestly, do you have a steel rod glued to your spine?" she burst out. Then she realized what she'd said, clapped her hand over her mouth and looked horrified at the slip.

He didn't react. He just stared.

"I'm sorry!" she said, flustered. "I'm so sorry! I didn't mean to say that…!"

"Cassaway," he began.

"It's about the general," she blurted out.

His dark eyes narrowed. "Lately, everything is. Don't tell me. You're having an affair with him and you have to confess for the sake of your job."

She drew in a long breath. "Actually, the general *is* my job." She got up, opened her wallet and handed it to Rick.

He did an almost comical double take. He looked at her as if she'd grown leaves. "You're a fed?"

She nodded and grimaced. She took back the wallet after he'd looked at it again, just to make sure it didn't come from the toy department in some big store.

She put it back in her fanny pack. "Sorry I couldn't say something before, but they wouldn't let me," she said heavily as she sat down again, with her hands folded on her jeans.

"What the hell are you doing pretending to be a detective?" he asked with some exasperation.

"It was my boss's idea. I did start out with Atlanta P.D., but I've worked in counterterrorism for the agency for about four years now," she confessed. "I'm sorry," she repeated. "This wasn't my idea. They wanted me to find out how much you knew about your family history before they accidentally said or did something that would upset you."

He raised an eyebrow. "I've just been presented with a father who's an exiled South American dictator, whose existence I was unaware of. They didn't think that would upset me?"

"I asked Cash Grier to talk to your mother," she said. "You can't tell anybody. I was ordered not to talk to you about it. But they didn't say I couldn't ask somebody else to do it."

He was touched by her concern. Not that he liked her any better. "I wondered about your shooting skills," he said after a minute. "Not exactly something I expect in a run-of-the-mill detective."

She smiled. "I spend a lot of time on the gun range," she replied. "I've been champion of my unit for two years running."

"Our lieutenant was certainly surprised when he found himself outdone," he remarked.

"He's very nice."

He glared at her.

She wondered what he had against his superior officer, but she didn't comment. "I was told that a DEA officer is going to try to get someone to speak to General Machado about you."

"Yes. Gracie Pendleton will talk with him. Machado likes her."

"He kidnapped her!" she exclaimed. "And the man she's now married to!"

He nodded. "I know. He also saved her from being assaulted by one of Fuentes's men," he added.

"Oh. I didn't know that."

"She's fond of him, too," he replied. "Apparently, he makes friends even of his enemies. A couple of feds I know think he's one of the better insurgents," he added dryly.

"He did install democratic government in Barrera," she pointed out. "He instituted reforms that did away with unlawful detention and surveillance, he invited the foreign media in to oversee elections and he ousted half a dozen petty politicians who were robbing the poor and making themselves into feudal lords. From what we understand, one of those petty politicians helped Machado's second-in-command plan the coup that ousted him."

"While he was out of the country negotiating trade agreements," Rick agreed. "Stabbed in the back."

"Exactly. We'd love to have him back in power, but we can't actually do anything about it," she said quietly. "That's where you come in."

"The general doesn't even know me, let alone that I'm his biological son," he repeated. "Even if he did, I don't think he's going to jump up and invite me to baseball games."

"Soccer," she corrected. "He hates baseball."

His eyebrows lifted. "How do you know that?"

"I have a file on him," she said. "He likes strawberry ice cream, his favorite musical star is Marco Antonio Solís, he wears size 12 shoes and he plays classical guitar. Oh, he was an entertainer on a cruise ship in his youth."

"I did know about that. Not his shoe size," he added with twinkling dark eyes.

"He's never been romantically linked with any particular woman," she continued. "Although he was good friends with an American anthropologist who went to live in his country. She'd found an ancient site that was revolutionary and she was involved in a dig there. Apparently, there are some interesting ruins in Barrera."

"What happened to her?"

"Nobody knows. We couldn't even ascertain her name. What I was able to ferret out was only gossip."

He folded his hands on his desk. "So, you're a fed, I'm one detective short and you're supposed to be heading a murder investigation for me," he said curtly. "What do I do about that?"

"I've been working on it," she protested. "I'm making progress, too. As soon as we get the DNA profile back, I may be able to make an arrest in the college freshman's murder, and solve a cold case involving another dead coed. I have lots of information to go on, now, including eyewitness testimony that can place the suspect at the murdered woman's apartment just before she was killed."

He sat up. "Nice!"

"Thank you. I have an appointment to talk to her best friend, also, the one who took the photo that the suspect showed up in. She gave a statement to the crime scene detective that the victim had complained about visits from a man who made her uneasy."

"They'll let you continue to work on my case, even though you're a fed?"

"Until something happens in the general's case," she said. "I'm keeping up appearances."

"You slipped through the cracks," he translated.

She laughed. "Thanksgiving is just over the horizon and my boss gets a lot of business done in D.C. going from one party to another with his wife."

"I see."

"When is Mrs. Pendleton going to talk to the general, did the DEA agent say?"

He shook his head. "It's only a work in progress right now." He leaned back in his chair. "I thought my father was dead. My mother told me he was killed when I was just a baby. I didn't realize I had a father who never even knew I was on the way."

"He loves children," she pointed out.

"Yes, but I'm not a child."

"I noticed."

He glared at her.

She flushed and averted her eyes.

He felt guilty. "Sorry. I'm not dealing with this well."

"I can understand that," she replied. "I know it must be hard for you."

She had a nice voice, he thought. Soft and medium in pitch, and she colored it in pastels with emotion. He liked her voice. Her choice of T-shirts, however, left a lot to be desired. She had on one today that read Save a Turkey, Eat a Horse for Thanksgiving. He burst out laughing.

"Do you have an open line to a T-shirt manufacturer?" he asked.

"What? Oh!" She glanced down at her shirt. "Well, sort of. There's this online place that lets you make your own T-shirts. I do a lot of business with them, designing my own."

Now he understood her quirky wardrobe.

"Drives my boss nuts," she added with a grin. "He thinks I'm not dignified enough on the job."

"I'm sure you have casual days, even in D.C."

"I don't work in D.C.," she said. "I get sent wherever I'm needed. I live out of a suitcase mostly." She smiled wanly. "It's not much of a life. I loved it when I was younger, but I'd really love to have someplace permanent."

"You could get a job in a local office."

"I guess." She shrugged. "Meanwhile, I've got one right here. I'm sorry I didn't tell you who I was at first," she added. "I would have liked to be honest."

He sensed that. He grimaced. "It's hard for me, too, trying to understand the past. My mother, my adopted mother," he said, just to clarify the point, "said that the general was only fourteen when he fathered me. I'll be thirty-one this year, in late December. That would make him—" he stopped and thought "—forty-five." His eyebrows arched. "That's not a great age for a dictator."

She laughed. "He was forty-one when he became president of Barrera," she said. "In those four years, he did a world of good for his country. His adopted country."

"Yes, well, he's wanted in this country for kidnapping," he reminded her.

"Good luck trying to get him extradited," she cautioned. "First the Mexican authorities would have to actually apprehend him, and he's got a huge complex in northern Sonora. One report is that he even has a howitzer."

"True story," he said, leaning back in his chair. "Pancho Villa, who fought in the Mexican Revolution, was a folk hero in Mexico at the turn of the twentieth century. John Reed, a Harvard graduate and journalist, actually lived with him for several months."

"And wrote articles about his adventures there. They made them into a book," she said, shocking him. "I had to buy it from a rare book shop. It's one of my treasures."

Chapter Six

"I've read that book," Rick said with a slow smile. "*Insurgent Mexico*. I couldn't afford to buy it, unfortunately, so I got it on loan from the library. It was published in 1914. A rare book, indeed."

She shifted uncomfortably. She hadn't meant to let that bit slip. She was still keeping secrets from him. She shouldn't have been able to afford the book on her government salary. Her father had given it to her last Christmas. That was another secret she was keeping, too; her father's identity.

"And would you know Pancho Villa's real name?" he asked suddenly.

She grinned. "He was born Doroteo Arango," she said. The smile faded a little. "He changed his name to

Pancho Villa, according to one source, because he was hunted by the authorities for killing a man who raped his younger sister. It put him on a path of lawlessness, but he fought all his life for a Mexico that was free of foreign oppression and a government that worked for the poor."

He smiled with pure delight. "You read Mexican history," he mused, still surprised.

"Well, yes, but the best of it is in Spanish, so I studied very hard to learn to read it," she confessed. She flushed. "I like the colonial histories, written by priests in the sixteenth century who sailed with the *conquistadores*."

"Spanish colonial history," he said.

She smiled. "I also like to read about Juan Belmonte and Manolete."

His eyebrows arched. "Bullfighters?" he exclaimed.

"Well, yes," she said. "Not the modern ones. I don't know anything about those. I found this book on Juan Belmonte, his biography. I was so fascinated by it that I started reading about Joselito and the others who fought bulls in Spain at the beginning of the twentieth century. They were so brave. Nothing but a cape and courage, facing a bull that was twice their size, all muscle and with horns so sharp…" She cleared her throat. "It's not PC to talk about it, I know."

"Yes, we mustn't mention blood sports," he joked. "The old bullfighters were like soldiers who fought in the world wars—tough and courageous. I like World

War II history, particularly the North African theater of war."

Her eyes opened wide behind the lenses of her glasses. "Rommel. Patton. Montgomery. Alexander…"

His lips fell open. "Yes."

She laughed with some embarrassment. "I'm a history major," she said. "I took my degree in it." She didn't add that she came by her interest in military history quite naturally, nor that her grandfather had known General George S. Patton, Jr., personally.

"Well!"

"You have an associate's degree in criminal justice and you're going to night school working on your B.A.," she blurted out.

He laughed. "What's my shoe size?"

"Eleven." She cleared her throat. "Sorry. I have a file on you, too."

He leaned forward, his large dark eyes narrow. "I'll have to compile one on you. Just to be fair."

She didn't want him to do that, but she just nodded. Maybe he couldn't dig up too much, even if he tried. She kept her private life very private.

She stood up. "I need to get back to work. I just wanted to be honest with you, about my job," she said. "I didn't want you to think I was being deliberately deceitful."

He stood up, too. "I never thought that."

He walked with her to the door. "Uh, is the lieutenant still bringing you roses?" he asked, and could have slapped himself for even asking the question.

"Oh, certainly not," she said primly. "That was just an apology, for using bad language in front of me."

"He's a widower," he said as they reached the door.

She paused and looked up at him. He was very close all of a sudden and she felt the heat from his body as her nostrils caught the faint, exotic scent of the cologne he used. He smelled very masculine and her heart went wild at the proximity. Her head barely topped his shoulder. He was tall and powerfully built, and she had an almost overwhelming hunger to lay her head on that shoulder and press close and bury her lips in that smooth, tanned throat.

She caught her breath and stepped back quickly. She looked up into his searching eyes and stood very still, like a cat in the sights of a hunter. She couldn't even think of anything to say.

Rick was feeling something similar. She smelled of wildflowers today. Her skin was almost translucent and he noticed that she wore little makeup. Her hair was caught up in a high ponytail, but he was certain that if she let it down, it would make a thick platinum curtain all the way to her waist. He wanted, badly, to loosen it and bury his mouth in it.

He stepped back, too. The feelings were uncomfortable. "Better get back to work," he said curtly. He was breathing heavily. His voice didn't sound natural.

"Yes. Uh, m-me, too," she stammered, and flushed, making her skin look even prettier.

He started to open the door for her. But he paused. "Someone told me that you like *The Firebird*."

She laughed nervously. "Yes. Very much."

"The orchestra is doing a tribute to Stravinsky Friday night." He moved one shoulder. He shouldn't do this. But he couldn't help himself. "I have two tickets. I was going to take Mom, but she's going to have to cater some cattlemen's meeting in Jacobsville and she can't go." He took a breath. "So I was wondering..."

"Yes." She cleared her throat. "I mean, if you were going to ask me...?" she blurted, embarrassed.

Her nervousness lessened his. He smiled at her in a way he never had, his chiseled mouth sensuous, his eyes very dark and soft. "Yes. I was going to ask you."

"Oh." She laughed, self-consciously.

He tipped her chin up with his bent forefinger and looked into her soft, pale green eyes. "Six o'clock? We'll have dinner first."

Her breath caught. Her heartbeat shook her T-shirt. "Yes," she whispered breathlessly.

His dark eyes were on her pretty bow of a mouth. It was slightly parted, showing her white teeth. He actually started bending toward it when his phone suddenly rang.

He jerked back, laughing deeply at his own helpless response to her. "Go to work," he said, but he grinned.

"Yes, sir." She started out the door. She looked back

at him. "I live in the Oak Street apartments," she said.
"Number 92."

He smiled back. "I'll remember."

She left, with obvious reluctance.

It took him a minute to realize that his phone was
still ringing. He was going to date a colleague and the
whole department would know. Well, what the hell,
he muttered to himself. He was really tired of going
to concerts and the ballet alone. She was a fed and she
wouldn't be here long. Why shouldn't he have companionship?

Gwen got back to her own office and leaned back
against the door with a long sigh. She was trembling
from the encounter with Rick and so shocked at his invitation that she could barely get her breath back. He
was going to date her. He wanted to take her out. She
could barely believe it!

While she was savoring the invitation, her cell phone
rang. She noted the number and opened it.

"Hi, Dad," she said, smiling. "How's it going?"

"Rough, or don't you watch the news, pudding?"
he asked with a laugh in his deep voice as he used his
nickname for her.

"I do," she said. "I'm really sorry. Politicians should
let the military handle military matters."

"Come up to D.C. and tell the POTUS that," he murmured.

"Why can't you just say President of the United
States?" she teased.

"I'm in the military. We use abbreviations."

"I noticed."

"How's it going with you?"

"I'm working on a sensitive matter."

"I've been talking to your boss about it," he replied. "And I told him that I don't like having you put on the firing line like this."

She winced. She could imagine that encounter. Her boss, while very nice, was also as bullheaded as her father. It would have been interesting to see how it ended.

"And he told you...?"

He sighed. "That I could mind my own damned business, basically," he explained. "We're a lot alike."

"I noticed."

"Anyway, I hope you're packing, and that the detective you're working with is, also."

"We both are, but the general isn't a bad man."

"He's wanted for kidnapping!"

"Yes, well, he's desperate for money, but he didn't really hurt anybody."

"A man was killed in his camp," he returned curtly.

"Yes, the general shot him for trying to assault Gracie Pendleton," she replied. "He caught him in the act. Gracie was bruised and shaken, but he got to her just in time. The guy was one of the Fuentes organization."

There was a long silence. "I didn't hear that part."

"Not many people have."

He sighed. "Well, maybe he's not as bad a man as I thought he was."

"We want him on our side. He has a son that he didn't know about. We're trying to get an entrée into his camp, to make a contact with him. It isn't easy."

"I know about that, too." He paused. "How's your love life?" he teased.

She cleared her throat. "Actually, Sergeant Marquez just invited me to a symphony concert."

There was a longer pause. "He likes classical music?"

"Yes, and the ballet." Her eyes narrowed. "And no smart remarks, if you please."

"I like classical music."

"But you hate ballet," she pointed out. "And you think anybody who does is nuts."

"So I have a few interesting flaws," he conceded.

"He's also a military history buff," she added quickly. "World War II and North Africa."

"How ironic," he chuckled.

She smiled to herself. "Yes, isn't it?"

He drew in a long sigh. "You coming home for Christmas?"

"Of course," she agreed. She smiled sadly. "Especially this year."

"I'm glad." He bit off the words. "It hasn't been easy. Larry's wife calls me every other night, crying."

"Lindy will adjust," she said softly. "It's just going to take time. She and Larry were married for ten years and they didn't have children. That will make it harder for her. But she's strong. She'll manage."

"I hope so." There was a scraping sound, as if he was getting up out of a chair. "His commanding officer got drunk and wrecked a bar up in Maryland, while he was on R&R," he said.

"Larry's death wasn't his fault," she replied tersely. "Any officer who goes into a covert situation knows the risks and has to be willing to take them."

"I told him that," her father replied. "Damn it, he cried...!" He cleared his throat, choking back the emotion. "I called up Brigadier Langston and told him to get that man some help before he becomes a statistic. He promised he would."

"General Langston was fond of Larry, too," she said quietly. "I remember him at the funeral..."

There was a pause. "Let's talk about something else."

"Okay. How do you feel about giving chickens the vote?"

He burst out laughing.

"Or we could decide where we're going to eat on Christmas Eve, because I'm not spending my days off in the kitchen," she said.

"Good thing. We'd starve or die of carbon monoxide poisoning," he replied.

"I can cook! I just don't like to."

"If you'd use timers, we'd have food that didn't turn black before we got to eat it," he said. "I can cook anything," he added smugly.

"I remember." She sighed. "Rick's mom is a great cook," she replied. "She owns a restaurant."

"She does? You should marry him. You'd never have to worry about cooking again." He chuckled.

She blushed. "It's just a date, Dad."

"Your first one in how many years…?"

"Stop that," she muttered. "I date."

"You went to the Laundromat with a guy who lived in your apartment building," he burst out. "That's not a date!"

"It was fun. We ate potato chips and discussed movies while our clothes got done," she replied.

He shook his head. "Pudding, you're hopeless."

"Thanks!"

"I give up. I have to go. I've got a meeting with the Joint Chiefs in ten minutes."

"More war talk?"

"More withdrawal talk," he said. "There's a rumor that the POTUS is going to offer me Hart's job."

"You're kidding!"

"That's what they're saying."

"Will you take it?" she asked, excited.

"Watch the news and we'll find out."

"That would be great!"

"I might be in a position to do something more useful," he said. "But, we'll see. I guess I'd do it, if they ask me."

"Good for you!"

"Say, do you ever see Grange?"

"Grange? You mean, the Pendletons' foreman?" she asked, disconcerted.

"Yes. Winslow Grange. He was in my last overseas command." He smiled. "Had a real pig of an officer, who sent him into harm's way understrength and with a battle plan that some kindergarten kid could have come up with. Grange tied him up, put him in the trunk of his own car and led the assault himself. He was invited to leave the army with an honorable discharge or be court-martialed. He left. But he came back to testify against his commanding officer, who was dishonorably discharged after a nasty trial."

"Good enough for him," she said curtly.

"I do agree. Anyway, Winslow is a friend of mine. I'd love to see him sometime. You might pass that along. We could always use someone like him in D.C. if he gets tired of horse poop."

She wondered if she should tell her father what his buddy Grange was rumored to be doing right now, but that was probably a secret she should keep. "If I see him, I'll tell him," she promised.

"Take care of yourself, okay? You're the only family I've got left." His deep voice was thick with emotion.

"Same here," she replied. "Love you, Dad."

"Mmm-hmm." He wasn't going to say it out loud. He never did. But he loved her, so she didn't make a smart remark.

"I'll call you in a few days, just to check in. Okay?"

"That's a deal." His hand went over the receiver.

"Yes, I'm on my way," he told someone else. "Gotta go. See you, kid."

"Bye, Dad."

He hung up. She put the phone back in her pocket. It seemed to be a day for revelations.

She had a beautiful little couture black dress, with expensive black slingbacks and a frilly black shawl that she'd gotten in Madrid. She wore those for her date with Rick, and she let her hair down, brushing it until it was shiny, like a pale satin curtain down her back. She left her glasses off for once. If she wasn't driving, she didn't need them, and a symphony concert didn't really require perfect vision.

Rick wore a dinner jacket and a black tie. His own hair was still in its elegant ponytail, but tied with a neat black ribbon. He looked very sharp.

He stared at her with disconcerting interest when she opened the door, taking in the nice fit of her dress with its modest rounded neckline and lacy hem that hit just at mid-calf. Her pretty little feet were in strappy high heels that left just a hint of the space between her toes visible. It was oddly sexy.

"You look…very nice," he said, his eyes taking in her flushed, lovely complexion and her perfect mouth, just dabbed with pale lipstick.

"Thanks! So do you," she replied, laughing nervously.

He produced a box from behind his back and handed it to her. It was a beautiful cymbidium orchid, much like the ones she had back at her father's home that the housekeeper faithfully misted each day.

"It's lovely!" she exclaimed.

He raised one shoulder and smiled self-consciously. "They wanted to give me one you wore around the wrist, but I explained that we weren't going to a dance and I wanted one that pinned."

"I like this kind best." She took it out of the box and pinned it to the dress, smiling at the way it complemented the dark background. "Thanks."

"My pleasure. Shall we go?"

"Yes!"

She grabbed her evening bag, closed the door and locked it and let him help her into his pickup truck.

"I should have something more elegant to drive than this," he muttered as he climbed in beside her.

"But I love trucks!" she exclaimed. "My dad has one that he drives around our place when he's home."

He grinned. "Well, maybe I'll get a nice car one day."

"It doesn't matter what you go in, as long as it gets you to your destination," she pointed out. "I even like Humvees."

His eyebrows arched. "And where do you get to ride in those?"

She bit her tongue. "Uh…"

"I forgot. Your brother was in the military, you said," he interrupted. "Sorry. I didn't mean to bring back sad memories for you."

She drew in a long breath. "He died doing what he felt was important for his country," she replied. "He was very patriotic and spec ops was his life."

His eyebrows arched.

"He died in a classified operation," she added. "His commanding officer just went on a huge bender. He feels responsible. He ordered the incursion."

His eyes softened. "That's the sort of man I wouldn't mind serving under," he said quietly. "A man with a conscience, who cares about his men."

She smiled. "My dad's like that, too. I mean, he's a man with a conscience," she said quickly.

He didn't notice the slip. He reached out and touched her soft cheek. "I'm sorry for your loss," he said. "I don't have siblings. But I wish I did."

She managed a smile. "Larry was a wonderful brother and a terrific husband. His wife is taking it hard. They didn't have any kids."

"Tough."

She nodded. "It's going to be hard to get through Christmas," she said. "Larry was a nut about it. He came home to Lindy every year and he brought all sorts of foreign decorations with him. We've got plenty that he sent us…"

He moved closer. His big hands framed her face and lifted it. Her pale green eyes were swimming in tears. He bent, helpless, and softly kissed away the tears.

"Life is often painful," he whispered. "But there are compensations."

While he spoke, his chiseled lips were moving against her eyelids, her nose, her cheeks. Finally, as she held her breath in wild anticipation, his lips hovered just over her perfect bow of a mouth. She could feel his breath, taste its minty freshness, see the hard curve of his lips that filled her vision to the extent of anything else.

She hung there, at his mouth, her eyes half closed, her skin tingling from the warm strength of his hands framing her face, waiting, waiting, waiting…!

He drew in an unsteady breath and bent closer, logic flying out the window as the wildflower scent of her made him weak. Her mouth was perfect. He wanted to feel its softness under his lips, taste her. He was sure that she was going to be delicious…

The sudden sound of a horn blowing raucously on the street behind them shocked them apart. He blinked, as if he was under the influence of alcohol. She didn't seem much calmer. She fumbled with her purse.

"I guess we should go," he said with a forced laugh. "We want to have enough time to eat before the concert."

"Y…yes," she agreed.

"Seat belt," he added, nodding toward it.

"Oh. Yes! I usually put it on at once," she added as she fumbled it into place.

He laughed, securing his own.

Her shy smile made him feel taller. Involuntarily, his fingers linked with hers as he started the truck and pulled out into traffic. He wouldn't even let himself think about how he'd gone in headfirst with a colleague, against all his best instincts. He was too happy.

They ate at a nice restaurant in San Antonio, one with a flamenco theme and a live guitarist with a Spanish dancer in a beautiful red dress with puffy sleeves and the ruffled, long-trained dress that was familiar to followers of the dance style. The performance was short, but the applause went on for a long time. The duet was impressive.

"What a treat," she said enthusiastically. "They're so good!"

"Yes, they are." He grinned. "I love flamenco."

"So do I. I bought this old movie, *Around the World in 80 Days,* and it had a guy named Jose Greco and his flamenco dance troupe in it. That's when I fell in love with flamenco. He was so talented," she said.

"I've seen tapes of Jose Greco dancing," he replied. "He truly was phenomenal."

"My mother used to love Latin dances," she said dreamily, smiling. "She could do them all."

"Is she still alive?" he asked carefully.

She hesitated. She shook her head. "We lost her when I was in my final year of high school. Dad was overseas and couldn't even come back for the funeral, so Larry and I had to do everything. Dad never got over it. He was just starting to, when Larry died."

"Why couldn't your father come home?" he asked, curious.

She swallowed. "He was involved in a classified mission," she said. She held up a hand when he started to follow up with another question, smiling to lessen the sting. "Sorry, but he couldn't even tell me what he was doing. National security stuff."

His eyebrows arched. "Your dad's in the military?"

She hesitated. But it wouldn't hurt to agree. He was. But Rick would be thinking of a regular soldier, and her dad was far from regular. "Yes," she replied.

"I see."

"You don't, but I can't say any more," she told him.

"I guess not. Wouldn't want to tick off the brass by saying something out of turn, right?" he teased.

"Right." She had to fight a laugh. Her father was the brass; one of the highest ranking officers in the U.S. Army, in fact.

The waiter who took their order was back quickly with cups of hot coffee and the appetizers, buffalo wings and French fries with cheese and chili dip.

Rick tasted the wings and laughed as he put it quickly back down. "Hot!" he exclaimed.

"I'm glad I'm wearing black," she sighed. "If I had on a white dress, it would be red-and-white polka dotted when I finished eating. I wear most of my food."

His dark eyebrows arched and he grinned. "Me, too."

She laughed. "I'm glad it's not just me."

He tried again with the French fries. "These are really good. Here. Taste."

She let him place it at her lips. She bit off the end and sighed. "Delicious!"

"They have wonderful food, including a really special barbecue sauce for the wings. Want to know where they got it?" he asked mischievously.

"From your mother?" she guessed.

He shook his head. "It seems that FBI senior agent Jon Blackhawk came here to eat with his brother, Kilraven, one night. Jon tasted their barbecue sauce, made a face, got up, walked into the kitchen and proceeded to have words with the chef."

"You're kidding!"

"I'm not. It didn't come to blows, but only because Jon put on an apron and showed the chef how to make a proper barbecue sauce. When the chef tasted it, so the story goes, he asked which cordon bleu academy in Paris Mr. Blackhawk had attended. He got the shock of his life when Jon named it." He grinned. "You see, he actually went to Paris and took courses. His new wife is one lucky woman. She'll never have to go in the kitchen unless she really wants to."

"I heard about them," she replied. "That's one interesting family."

He munched a French fry thoughtfully. "I'd love to have kids," he said solemnly. "A big family to make up for what I never had." His expression was bitter. "Barbara is the best mother on the planet, but I wish I'd had brothers and sisters."

"You do at least still have a father living," she pointed out.

"A father who's going to get the shock of his life when he's introduced to his grown-up son," he said. "And I wonder if Ramirez has had any luck getting his sister-in-law to approach the general."

As if in answer to the question, his cell phone began vibrating. He checked the number, gave her a stunned glance and got to his feet. "I'll be right back. I have to take this."

She nodded. She liked his consideration for the other diners. He took the call outside on the street, so that he wouldn't disturb other people with his conversation.

He was back in less than five minutes. He sat back down. "Imagine that," he said on a hollow laugh. "Gracie talked to the general. He wants us to come to the border Monday morning for a little chat, as he put it."

Her eyebrows arched. "Progress," she said, approving.

He sighed. "Yes. Progress." He didn't add that he had misgivings and he was nervous as hell. He just finished eating.

Chapter Seven

Rick was preoccupied through the rest of the meal. Gwen didn't talk much, either. She knew he had to be unsettled about the trip to the border, for a lot of reasons.

He held her hand on the way to the car, his strong fingers tangling in hers.

"It will be all right," she blurted out.

They reached the passenger door and he paused, looking down at her. "Will it?"

"You're a good man," she said. "He'll be very proud of you."

He was uncertain. "You think?"

She loved the smell of his body, the warm strength of it near her. She loved everything about him. "Yes."

He smiled tenderly. She made him feel tall, power-ful, important. Women had made him feel undervalued for years, mostly by thinking of him as nothing more than a friend. Gwen was different. She was a working girl, from his own middle-class strata. She was pretty, in her way, and smart. And she knew her way around a handgun, he thought amusedly. But she also stirred his senses in a new and exciting way.

"You're nice," he said suddenly.

She grimaced. "Rub it in."

"No. Nice, in a very positive way," he replied. His expression was somber. "I don't like sophisticated women. I like brains in a woman, and even athletic outlooks. But I do mind women who think of them-selves as party favors. You get me?"

She smiled. "I feel the same way about men like that."

He smiled. "You and I, we don't belong in a modern setting."

"We'd look very nice in a Victorian village," she agreed. "Like Edward in the *Twilight* vampire series of books and movies. I love those. I guess I've seen the movies ten times each and read the books on my iPod every night."

"I don't watch vampire movies. I like werewolves."

"Oh, but there are werewolves in them, too. Nice werewolves."

"You're kidding."

She hesitated. "I've got all the DVDs. I was wondering…"

He moved a step closer, so that she was backed into the car door. "You were wondering?"

"Uh, yes, if you'd like to maybe watch the movies with me?" she asked him. "I could make a pizza. Or we could…order…one…?"

She was whispering now, and her voice was breaking because his mouth had moved closer with every whispered word until it was right against her soft lips.

"Gwen?"

"Hmm?"

"Shut up," he whispered against her lips, and his crushed down on them with warm, sensual, insistent hunger.

A muffled sob broke from her throat as she lifted her arms and pressed her body as close as she could get it to his tall, powerful form. He groaned, too, as the insane delight pulsed through him like fire.

He moved, shifting her, so that one long leg was between her skirt, and his mouth was suddenly invasive, starving.

"Detective!"

He heard a voice. It sounded close. And shocked. And angry. He lifted his head, still reeling from Gwen's soft mouth.

"Hmm?" he murmured, turning his head.

"Detective Sergeant Marquez," a deep, angry voice repeated.

"Sir!" He jumped back, almost saluted, and tried to look normal. He hoped his jacket was covering a blatant reminder of his body's interest in Gwen's.

"What the hell are you doing?" Lieutenant Hollister asked gruffly.

"It's okay, sir," Gwen faltered. "He was, uh, helping me get my earring unstuck from my dress."

He blinked and scowled. "What?"

"My earring, sir." She dangled it in her hand. "It caught on my dress. Detective Marquez was helping me get it loose. I guess it did look odd, the position we were in." She laughed with remarkable acting ability.

"Oh. I see." Hollister cleared his throat. He shoved his hands in his pockets. "I'm very sorry. It looked, well, I mean..." He cleared his throat again. He scowled. "I thought you didn't date colleagues," he shot at Marquez, who had by reciting multiplication tables made a remarkably quick recovery.

"I don't, sir," Marquez agreed. "We both like flamenco, and there's a dancer here..."

Hollister held up his hand and declared, "Say no more. That's why I came. Alone, sadly," he added with a speculative and rather sad look at Gwen.

"She's a great dancer," Gwen said. "And that guitarist!"

He nodded. "Her husband."

"Really!" Gwen exclaimed.

"Oh, yes. They've appeared all over Europe. I understand they're being considered for a bit part in a movie that's filming near here next year."

"That would be so lovely for them," Gwen enthused.

Rick checked his watch. "We'd better go. I've got an appointment early Monday morning. I thought I'd brush up on my Spanish over the weekend," he added dryly.

"Yes, I heard about that," Hollister said quietly. "It will go all right," he told Rick. "You'll see."

Rick was touched. "Thanks."

Hollister shrugged. "You're a credit to my department. Don't let him talk you into going to South America, okay?"

Rick smiled. "I'm not much good with rocket launchers."

"Me, neither," the lieutenant agreed. He glanced at Gwen and smiled. "Well, sorry about the mistake. Have a good evening."

"You, too, sir," Gwen said, and Rick nodded assent.

Hollister nodded back and walked, distracted, toward the restaurant.

Rick helped Gwen into the truck and burst out laughing. So did she.

"Did I ever tell you that I minored in theater in college?" she asked. "They said I had promise."

"You could make movies," he said flatly. He shook his head as he started the truck. "Quick thinking."

"Thanks." She flushed a little.

Neither of them mentioned that they'd been so far gone that anything could have happened, right there in the parking lot, if the lieutenant hadn't shown up. But it was true. Also true was the look the lieutenant had been giving them. He seemed to have more than the usual interest in Gwen. He wasn't really the sort of man to put a rose on a woman's desk unless he meant it. Rick was thinking that he had some major competition there, if he didn't watch his step. Hollister's tone hadn't been one of outraged decorum so much as jealous anger.

Rick left Gwen at her door. He was more cautious this time, but he did pull her close and kiss her goodnight with barely restrained passion.

She held him, kissing him back, loving the warm, soft press of his mouth on hers.

"I'm out of practice," he murmured as he stepped back.

"Me, too," she said breathlessly, her eyes full of stars as they met his in the light from the security lamps.

"I guess we could practice with each other," he murmured dryly.

She flushed and laughed nervously. "I'd like that."

"Yes. So would I." He bent again, brushing his mouth lightly over hers and forcing himself not to go in headfirst. "Are you coming along, in the morning?"

She nodded. "I have to."

He smiled. "Good. I could use the moral support."

She smiled back. "Thanks."

"Well. I'll see you at the office Monday."

"Yes."

He turned and took a step. He stopped. He turned. She was still standing there, her expression confused, waiting, still...

He walked back to her. "Unlock the door," he said quietly.

She fumbled the key into the lock and opened it. He closed it behind him, his arms enveloping her in the dark hallway, illuminated by a single small lamp in the living room. His mouth searched for hers, found it, claimed it, possessed it hungrily.

His arms were insistent, locking her against the length of his powerful body. She moaned, a sound almost like a sob of pleasure.

He was feeling something very similar.

"What the hell," he whispered into her lips as he bent and lifted her, still kissing her, and carried her to the long, soft sofa.

They slid down onto it together, his body covering hers, one long leg insinuating itself between her skirt, between her soft thighs. His lean hands went to the back of the dress, finding the hook and the zipper.

She didn't even have the presence of mind to protest. She was drowning in pleasure. She'd never felt anything remotely similar to the sensations that were washing over her like ripples of unbelievable delight.

He slid the dress off her arms, along with the tiny straps of the black slip she wore under it, exposing a small, black-lace bra that revealed more than it covered. She had pretty little breasts, firm and very soft.

His hand slid under the bra, savoring the warm softness of the flesh, exciting the hard little tip, making her shiver with new sensations.

She hadn't done this before. He knew it without being told. He smiled against her mouth. It was exciting, and new, to be the first man. He never had been. Not that there had even been that many women that he'd been almost intimate with. And, in recent years, nobody. Like Gwen, he'd never indulged in casual sex. He was as innocent, in his way, as she was. Well, he knew a little more than she did. When he touched his mouth to her breast, she lifted toward his lips with a shocked little gasp. He smiled as his mouth opened, taking the hard tip inside and pulling at it gently with his tongue.

Her nails bit into the muscles of his arms as he removed his jacket and tie and shirt, wanting so badly to be closer, closer...

She felt air on her skin and then the hard, warm press of hair and muscle as they locked together, both bare from the waist up.

His mouth was insistent now, hungry, demanding. She felt his hand sliding up her bare thigh and she knew that very soon they would reach a point from which there was no return.

"N...no," she whispered, pushing at his chest. "Rick? Rick!"

He heard her voice through a bloodred haze of desire that locked his muscles so tightly that he could barely move for the tension. She was saying something. What? It sounded like...no?

He lifted his head. He looked into wide, uneasy green eyes. He felt her body tensed, shivering.

"I'm sorry..." she began.

He blinked once, twice. He drew in a breath that sounded as ragged as he felt. "Good Lord," he exhaled.

She swallowed. They were very intimate. Neither of them had anything on above the waist. His hand was still on her thigh. He removed it quickly and lifted up just a little, his high cheekbones flushing when he got a sudden, stark, uninterrupted view of her pretty pink breasts with tight little dusky pink tips very urgently stating the desire of the owner for much more than looking.

Embarrassed, she drew her hands up over them as he levered himself away and sat up.

"I'm sorry," he said, averting his eyes while she fumbled her dress back on. "I didn't mean to..."

"Of c-course not," she stammered. "Neither did I. It's all right."

He laughed. His body felt as if it had been hit with a bat several times in strategic places and he ached from head to toe. "Sure it is."

"Oh, I'm sorry!" she groaned. She wasn't experienced, but she had friends who were, and she knew what was wrong with him. "Here, just a sec."

She went to the kitchen and came back with a cold beer from the fridge. "Detective Rogers comes over from time to time and she likes this brand of light beer," she explained. "I don't drink, but I think people need to sometimes. You need to, a little…?"

He gave her an exasperated sigh. "Gwen, I'm a police detective sergeant!"

"Yes, I know…"

"I can't take a drink and drive!"

She stared at him, looked at the beer. "Oh."

He burst out laughing. It broke the ice and slowly he began to feel normal again.

She looked around them. His jacket and shirt and tie, and her shoes and his holster and pistol were lying in a heap beside the sofa.

His gaze followed hers. He laughed again. "Well."

"Yes. Uh. Well." She looked at the can of beer, laughed, and set it down. Her glasses were where she'd tossed them on the end table but she didn't put them on. She didn't want to see his expression. She was already embarrassed.

He put his shirt and tie back on and slipped into his jacket before he replaced the holstered pistol on his belt. "At least you don't object to the gun," he mused.

She shrugged. "I usually have a concealed carry in my purse," she confessed.

His eyebrows arched. "No ankle holster?" he asked.

She made a face. "Weighs down my leg too much."

He nodded. He looked at her in a different way now. Possessively. Hungrily. He moved forward, but he only took her oval face in his hands and searched her eyes, very close up. He was somber.

"From now on," he said gently, "we say good-night at the door. Right?"

He was hinting at a relationship. "From now on?" she said hesitantly.

He nodded. He searched her eyes. "There aren't that many women running around loose who belong to the Victorian era, don't mind firearms and like to watch flamenco dancing."

She smiled with pure delight. "I was going to say the same about you—well, you're not a woman, of course."

"Of course."

He bent and kissed her very softly. He lifted his head and his large brown eyes narrowed. "If Hollister puts another rose on your desk, I'm going to deck him, and I don't care if he fires me."

Her face became radiant. "Really?"

"Really." His jaw tautened. "You're mine."

She flushed. She lowered her eyes to his strong neck, where a pulse beat very strongly. She nodded.

He hugged her close, rocked her in his arms. He drew in a long breath, finally, and let her go. He smiled ruefully. "After we get through talking with the general, Monday, I'm going to take you to meet my mother."

"You are?"

"You'll love her. She'll love you, too," he promised. He glanced at his watch and grimaced. "I have to get going. I'll pick you up here at 6:00 a.m. sharp, okay?"

"I could drive to the office..."

"I'll pick you up here."

She smiled. Her eyes were bright with pleasure. "Okay."

He chuckled. "Lock the door after me."

"I will. I really enjoyed the flamenco."

"So did I. I know another Latin dance club over on the west side of town. We'll go there next time. Do you like Mexican food?"

"Love it."

He smiled. "Theirs is pretty hot."

"No worries, I don't have any taste buds left. I eat jalapenos raw," she added with a grin.

"Whew! My kind of girl."

She grinned. "I noticed."

He laughed, kissed her hair and walked out the door.

After he climbed back into the pickup truck, he paused and waited until she was safely in her apartment before he drove off.

She didn't sleep that night. Not a wink. She was too excited, exhilarated and hungrily, passionately really in love for the first time in her life.

Rick was somber and nervous Monday morning when he picked Gwen up for the drive to the border. It had turned cold again and she was wearing a sweater and thick jeans with a jacket and boots.

"Summer yesterday, winter today," she remarked, readjusting her seat belt.

"That's Texas," he said fondly.

"Is Ramirez going to meet us at the border station?"

"Yes," he said. "He and Gracie."

Her eyebrows arched. "Mrs. Pendleton is coming, too? Isn't that dangerous?"

"We're not going over the border," he reminded her. "Just up to it."

"Oh. Okay."

He glanced at her, warm memories of the night before still in his dark eyes. She was lovely, he thought. Pretty and smart and good with a gun.

She felt his eyes but she didn't meet them. She was nervous, too. She worried about how he might feel when he learned the truth about her own background. She was still keeping secrets. She hoped he wouldn't feel differently when he learned them.

But right now, the biggest secret of all was about to be revealed to a man who had no apparent family and seemed to be content with his situation. Gwen wondered how the general would feel when he was introduced to a son he didn't even know existed.

They pulled up to the small border station, which wasn't much more than an adobe building beside the road, next to a cross arm that was denoted as the Mexican-American border, with appropriate warning signs.

A tall, sandy-haired man came out to meet them. He introduced himself as the border patrol agent in charge, Don Billings, and indicated a Lincoln town car sitting just a little distance way. He motioned.

The car pulled up, stopped and Rodrigo Ramirez got out, going around to open the door for his sister-in-law, Gracie Pendleton. They came forward and introductions were made.

Gracie was blonde and pretty and very pregnant. She laughed. "The general is going to be surprised when he sees me," she said with a grin. "I didn't mention my interesting condition. Jason and I are just over the moon!"

"Is it a boy or a girl?" Gwen wanted to know.

"We didn't let them tell us," she said. "We want it to be a surprise, so I bought everything yellow instead of pink or blue."

Gwen laughed. "I'd like it to be a surprise, too, if I ever had a baby." Her eyes were dreamy. "I'd love to have a big family."

Rick was watching her and his heart was pounding. He'd like a big family, too. Her family. He cleared his throat. Memories of last night were causing him some difficulty in intimate places. He thought of sports until he calmed down a little.

"He should be here very soon," Ramirez said.

Even as he spoke, a pickup truck came along the dusty road from across the border, stopped and was waved through by the border agent.

The truck stopped. Two doors opened. Winslow Grange, wearing one of the very new high-tech camouflage patterned suits with an automatic pistol strapped to his hip, came forward. Right beside him was a tall, elegant-looking Hispanic man with thick, wavy black hair and large black eyes in a square face with chiseled lips and a big grin for Gracie.

"A baby?" he enthused. "How wonderful!"

She laughed, taking his outstretched hands. "Jason and I think so, too. How have you been?"

"Very busy," he said, indicating Grange. "We're planning a surprise party." He wiggled his eyebrows at the border agent. "I'm sorry that I can't say more."

"So am I." The border patrolman chuckled.

Gwen came forward, her eyes curious and welcoming at the same time. "You and I haven't met, but I think you've heard of me," she said gently. She held out her hand. "I'm Gwendolyn Cassaway. CIA."

He shook her hand warmly, and then raised it to his lips. He glanced at the man with her, a tall young man with long black hair in a ponytail and an oddly familiar face. "Your boyfriend?" he asked, lifting an eyebrow at the reaction the young man gave when he kissed Gwen's hand.

"Uh, well, uh, I mean..." She cleared her throat. "This is Detective Sergeant Ricardo Marquez, San Antonio Police Department."

General Emilio Machado looked at the younger man with narrowed, intent eyes. "Marquez."

"Yes."

Machado was curious. "You look familiar, somehow. Do I know you?"

He studied the general quietly. "No. But my birth

mother was Dolores Ortíz. She was from Sonora. I look like her."

Machado stared at him intently. "She lived in Sonora, in a little village called Dolito. I knew her once," he said. "She married a man named Jackson," he added coldly.

"My stepfather," Rick said curtly.

"I have heard about your late stepfather. He was a brutal man."

Rick liked Machado already. "Yes. I have the scars to prove it," he added quietly.

Machado drew in a long breath. He looked around him. "This is a very unusual place to meet with federal agents, and I feel that I am being set up."

"Not at all," Gwen replied. "But we do have something to tell you. Something that might be upsetting."

Nobody spoke. There were somber, grim faces all around.

"You brought a firing squad?" Machado mused, looking from one to the other. "Or you lured me here to arrest me for kidnapping Gracie?"

"None of the above," Gwen said quietly. She took a deep breath. This was a very unpleasant chore she'd been given. "We were doing a routine background check on you for our files and we came across your relationship with Dolores Ortíz. She gave birth to a child out of wedlock down in Sonora. Thirty-one years ago."

Machado was doing quick math in his head. He looked at Rick pointedly, with slowly growing comprehension. The man had looked familiar. Was it possible...? He moved a step closer and cocked his head as he studied the somber-faced young man.

Then he laughed coldly. "Ah. Now I see. You know that I have spies in my country who are even now planting the seeds of revolution. You know that I have an army and that I am almost certain to retake the government of Barrera. So you are searching for ways to ingratiate yourself with me...excuse me, with my oil and natural gas reserves as well as my very strategic location in South America." He gave Rick a hard glance. "You produce a candidate for my son, and think that I will accept your word that he is who he says he is."

"I haven't said a damned thing," Rick snapped back icily.

Machado's eyebrows shot up. "You deny their conclusion?"

Rick glared at him. "You think I'm thrilled to be lined up as the illegitimate son of some exiled South American dictator?"

Machado just stared at him for a minute. Then he burst out laughing.

"Rick," Gwen groaned from beside him.

"I was perfectly content to think my real father was in a grave somewhere in Mexico," Rick continued. "And then she showed up with this story..." He pointed at Gwen.

She raised her hand. "Cash Grier told your mother,"

she reminded him quickly. "I had nothing to do with telling you."

"All right, my mother told me," he continued.

"Your mother is dead," Machado said, frowning.

"Barbara Ferguson, in Jacobsville, adopted me when my mother and stepfather were killed in an auto accident," Rick continued. "She runs the café there."

Machado didn't speak. He'd never considered the possibility that Dolores would become pregnant. They'd been very close until her parents discovered them one night in an outbuilding and her father threatened to kill Machado if he ever saw him again. He'd gone to work for a big landowner soon afterward and moved to another village. He hadn't seen Dolores again.

Could she have been pregnant? They'd done nothing to prevent a child. But he'd only been fourteen. He couldn't have fathered a son at that age, surely? In fact, he'd never fathered another child in the years since, and he had been coaxed into trying, at least once. The attempt had ended in total failure. It had hurt his pride, hurt his ego, made him uncertain about his manhood. He had thought, since then, that he must be sterile.

But here was, if he could believe the statement, proof of his virility. Could this really be his son?

He moved forward a step. Yes, the man had his eyes. He had Dolores's perfect teeth, as well. He was tall and powerfully built, as Machado was. His hair was long and black and straight, without the natural waves that were in Machado's. But, then, Dolores had long black hair that was smooth as silk and thick and straight.

"You think I would take your word for something this important, even with Gracie's help?" he asked Rick.

"Hey, I didn't come here to convince you of anything," Rick said defensively. "She—" he indicated Gwen "—got him—" he nodded at Ramirez "—to call her—" he pointed toward Gracie "—to have you meet us here. I got pulled into it because some feds think you'll listen to me even if you won't listen to them." He shrugged. "Of course, they haven't decided what to have me tell you just yet. I presume that's in the works and they'll let me know when they can agree on what day it is."

Machado listened to him, pursed his lips and laughed. "Sounds exactly like government policy to me. And I should know. I was head of a government once." His eyes narrowed and glittered. "And I will be, once again."

"I believe you," Gwen agreed.

"But for now," Machado continued, studying Rick. "What evidence exists that you really are my son? And it had better be good."

Chapter Eight

"Don't look at me," Rick said quietly. "I didn't come here to prove anything."

Gwen moved forward, removing a paper from her purse. "We were sure that you wouldn't accept anyone's word, General," she said gently. "So we took the liberty of having a DNA profile made from Sergeant Marquez's last physical when blood was drawn." She gave Rick an apologetic glance. "Sorry."

Rick sighed. "Accepted."

The general read the papers, frowned, read some more and finally handed them back. "That's pretty convincing."

Gwen nodded.

He glanced at Rick, who was standing apart from the

others, hard-faced, with his hands deep in the pockets of his slacks.

The general studied him from under thick black eyelashes, with some consternation. His whole life had just been turned upside-down. He had a son. The man was a law enforcement officer. He was not bad-looking, seemed intelligent, too. Of course, there was that severe attitude problem...

"I don't like baseball," Rick said curtly when he noticed how the general was eyeing him.

Machado's thick eyebrows levered up. "You don't like baseball...?"

"In case you were thinking of father-son activities," Rick remarked drolly. "I don't like baseball. I like soccer."

Machado's dark eyes twinkled. "So do I."

"See?" Gwen said, grasping at straws, because this was becoming awkward. "Already, something in common..."

"Get down!"

While she was trying to understand the quick command from the general, Rick responded by tackling her. Rodrigo had Gracie in the limo, which had bulletproof glass, and Machado hit the ground with his pistol drawn at the same time Grange opened up with an army-issue repeating rifle.

"What the hell...!" Rick exclaimed as he leveled his own automatic, along with Gwen, at an unseen adversary, tracking his direction from the bullets hitting the dust a few yards away.

"Carver, IED, now!" Grange called into a walkie-talkie.

Seconds later, there was a huge explosion, a muffled cry, and a minute later, the sound of an engine starting and roaring, a dust cloud becoming visible as a person or persons unknown took off in the distance.

Grange grinned. "I always have a backup plan," he remarked.

"Good thing," Gwen exclaimed. "I didn't even consider an ambush!"

"Your father would have," Grange began.

She held up her hand and gave a curt shake of her head.

"You know her father?" Rick asked curiously.

"We were poker buddies, a few years back," Grange said. "Good man."

"Thanks," Gwen said, and she wasn't referring totally to the compliment. Grange would keep her secret; she saw it in his eyes.

Rick was brushing thick dust off his jacket and slacks. "Damn. They just came back from the dry cleaner."

"You should wear cotton. It cleans better," Machado suggested, indicating his own jeans and cotton shirt.

"Who was that, do you think?" Gwen asked somberly.

"Fuentes." Machado spat. "He and I have parted

company. He amuses himself by sniping at me and my men."

"The drug lord? I thought his family was dead!" Gwen exclaimed.

"Most of it is. This is the last one of the Fuentes brothers, the stupid one, and he's clinging to power by his fingernails," the general told her. "He spies on me for a federal agency. Not yours," he told Gwen with a smile.

Ramirez left Gracie in the car and came back. "I don't think she should risk coming out here in the open," he said.

"I agree. She is all right?" Machado asked with some concern.

"Yes. Gracie really has guts," he replied. He frowned. "Which agency is Fuentes spying for?"

"Yours, I think, my friend," Machado told the DEA agent.

Ramirez let out a sigh. "We know there's a mole in our agency, someone very high level. We've never found out who it is."

"You should set Kilraven on him," Gwen mused dryly.

"I probably should," Ramirez agreed. "But we have our hands full right now with Mexican military coming over the border to protect drug shipments." He glanced toward the border patrol agent, who was talking to Gracie through a cracked window. "Our men on the border are in peril, always. We almost lost one some months ago, an agent named Kirk. He was very nearly killed. He left the agency and went back to his brothers on their Wyoming ranch. A great loss. He was good at his job, and he had contacts that we now lack."

"I can get you all the contacts you need," Machado promised. He glanced toward the distant hill where the sniper had been emplaced. "First I must deal with Fuentes."

"I didn't hear you say that," Gwen said firmly.

"Nor I," Ramirez echoed.

"Well, I did," Rick replied coldly. "And you're still wanted on kidnapping charges in my country, even though Mrs. Pendleton refuses to press them."

Machado's large eyes widened. "You would turn your own father in to the authorities?"

Rick's eyes narrowed. "The law is the law."

"You keep a book of statutes on your person?" the general asked.

Rick glared at him. "I've been a cop for a long time."

"Amazing. I have spent my life breaking most of the laws that exist, and here I find a son, a stranger, who goes by the book." His eyes narrowed. "I think perhaps they rigged the DNA evidence." He gave the detective a disparaging look. "I would never wear a suit like that, or grow my hair long. You look like a—what is the expression?—a hippie!"

Rick glared at him.

The general glared back.

"Uh, the sniper?" Ramirez reminded them. "He may have gone for reinforcements."

"True." Machado turned to Grange. "Perhaps you should order a sweep on the surrounding hills."

Grange smiled. "I already have."

"Good man. We will soon have a proper government in my country and you will be the commander of the forces in my country."

Ramirez choked. Gwen colored. Rick looked at them, trying to figure out why the hell they were so disturbed.

"We should go," Ramirez said, indicating the car. "I promised her husband that I would have her home very quickly. He might send a search party for us. Not a man to make an enemy of."

"Absolutely," Grange agreed.

"Thank you for making this meeting possible," Machado said, extending his hand to Ramirez.

Ramirez shook it, and then grinned. "It wasn't my idea. I'm related to the president of Mexico. He thought it would be a good idea."

Machado was impressed. "When I retake my country, perhaps you can speak to him for me about a trade agreement."

Ramirez admired the confidence in the other man's voice. "Yes, perhaps I can. Keep well."

"And you."

Gwen and Marquez waved them off before turning back to Machado.

"We should be going, too," Marquez said stiffly. "I have to get back to work."

Machado nodded. He studied his son with curious, strange eyes. "Perhaps, later, we can meet again."

"Perhaps," Rick replied.

"In a place where we do not have to fear an attack from my enemies," Machado said, shaking his head.

"I don't think we can get to Mars yet," Rick quipped.

Machado laughed. "Grange, we should go."

"Yes, sir."

Machado took Gwen's hand and kissed the back of it tenderly. "It has been a pleasure to meet you, *señorita*," he said with pure velvet in his deep voice.

Rick stepped in, took Gwen's hand and pulled her back. He glared at Machado, which made Gwen almost giddy with delight.

Machado's dark eyes twinkled. "So it is like that, huh?"

"Like what?" Rick asked innocently. He dropped Gwen's hand and looked uncomfortable.

"Never mind. I will be in touch."

"Thank you for coming," Gwen told the general.

"It was truly a pleasure." He winked at her, gave Rick a droll look and climbed back into the truck with Grange. They disappeared over the border. Rick stood staring after the truck with mixed feelings. Then he turned, said goodbye to the border agent and walked back to his truck with Gwen.

* * *

Rick kept to himself for the next couple of days. Gwen didn't intrude. She knew that he was dealing with some emotional issues that he had to resolve in his own mind.

Meanwhile, she went on interviews with neighbors of the murdered college freshman, the case she'd been assigned to as lead detective.

"Did she have any close friends that you know of?" she asked the third neighbor, an elderly woman who seemed to have a whole roomful of cats. They were clean, brushed, well fed and there was no odor, so she must be taking excellent care of them.

"Oh, you've noticed the cats?" the woman asked her with a grin that made her seem years younger. "I'm babysitting."

Gwen blinked. "Excuse me?"

"Babysitting. I have four neighbors with cats, and we've had a problem with animals disappearing around here. So they leave their cats with me while they're at work, and I feed them. It's a nice little windfall for me, since I'm disabled, and the owners have emotional security since they don't have to worry about their furry 'families' going missing."

Gwen laughed. "Impressive."

"Thanks. I love animals. I wish I could afford to keep a cat, but I can't. This is the next best thing."

Gwen noted several pill bottles on the end table by the elderly lady's recliner.

"By the time I pay for all those out of my social security check," she told Gwen, "there's not much left over for bills and food."

Gwen winced. "That's not right."

The woman sighed. "The economy is terrible. I expect something awful will have to happen to finally set things right." She looked at Gwen over her glasses. "I don't expect to still be around then. But if aliens exist, and they want somebody to experiment on..." She raised her hand. "I'm ready to go. To some nice, green planet with lots of meadows and trees and no greedy humans destroying it all for a quick profit."

"You and I would get along," Gwen said with a smile.

The woman nodded. "Now, back to my neighbor. I do keep a watch on the apartment complex, mostly to try to protect myself. I can't fight off an intruder and I don't own a gun. So I make sure I know who belongs here and who doesn't." Her eyes narrowed. "There was a grimy young man with greasy hair who kept coming to see the college girl. She was trying to be nice, you could tell from her expression, but she never let him inside. Once, the last time he came, the police went to her apartment and stayed for several minutes."

Gwen's heart jumped. If there had been police presence, there would be a report, with details of the conversation. She jotted that down on her phone app, making virtual notes.

"That thing is neat," the elderly lady said. "One of

my cat-owning friends has one. He can surf the net on it, buy groceries, books, all sorts of things. I never realized we had such things in the modern world. I suppose I live in the past."

Gwen made a mental note to make sure this nice lady got a phone and several phone cards for Christmas, from an anonymous source. It would revolutionize her life.

"Yes, they are quite nice," Gwen said. She smiled. "Thanks for talking to me. You've been a very big help."

"It was my pleasure. I know you young folks don't have much free time, but if you're ever at a loose end, you can come and see me and I'll tell you about the FBI in the seventies."

Gwen stared at her.

"I was a federal agent," the woman told her. "One of the first women in the bureau."

"I would love to hear some stories about those days," Gwen told her. "And I'll make time."

The wrinkled face lit up. "Thank you!"

"No, thank you. I'm fond of pioneers," she replied. She told Rick about the elderly woman.

"Yes, Evelyn Dorsey." He nodded, smiling. "She's something of a legend over at the FBI field office. Garon Grier goes to see her from time to time." He was the SAC, the special agent in charge, at the San Antonio Field Office now. "She shot it out with a gang of would-be kidnappers right over on the 410 Loop. Hit two of them before they shot her, almost fatally, and escaped. But she had a description of the car, right down to the license plate number, and she managed to get it out on the radio before she passed out. They nabbed the perps ten miles away. Back in those days, the radio was in the car, not on a belt. It was harder to be in law enforcement."

"I expect so. Ms. Dorsey was very helpful on our college freshman case, by the way. We did have a patrol unit respond to the freshman's call. I'm tracking down the officer who filed the report now."

"I hope we can catch the guy," he replied.

"The cold case unit wants him very badly. They think he's connected to the old case they're working on," she said. "One of those detectives was related to the victim in it."

"Sad."

"Yes." She moved closer to the desk. "You doing okay?"

He grimaced. "No," he said, with a faint smile.

"Why don't you come over and watch the Twilight movies with me tonight? We can order a pizza."

He cocked his head and the smile grew. "You know, that sounds like a very good idea."

She grinned. "Glad you think so. I like mushrooms and cheese and pepperoni."

His eyebrows lifted. "Have you been checking out my profile?"

"No. Why?"

"That's my favorite."

She beamed. "Another thing in common."

"We'll find more, I think."

"Yes."

Rick wasn't comfortable with so-called chick flicks, but he was drawn into the movie almost at once. He barely noticed when the pizza delivery girl showed up, and only lifted his hand for the plate and coffee cup without taking his eyes off the screen.

Gwen was delighted. It was her favorite film. She kicked off her shoes and curled up beside him on the sofa to watch it again, sipping coffee and munching pizza in a contented silence. It was amazing, she thought, how comfortable they were with each other, even at this early stage of their relationship.

He glanced at her while the vampire was showing off his skills to the heroine on the screen. "You're right. This is very good."

"So are the books. I love all of them."

"I guess I'll have to buy them. It isn't often you find so many likable people in a story chain."

She sipped coffee. "You know, I hadn't thought of it that way, but you're right. Even the vampires are likable."

"Odd, isn't it? Likable monsters."

"But they aren't really monsters. They're just misunderstood living-challenged people."

He burst out laughing.

"More pizza?" she asked.

"I think I could hold one more slice."

"Me, too." She jumped up and went to get it.

After they finished eating, she curled up against him through the heroine's introduction to her boyfriend's family, the baseball game in the rain, the arrival of the more dangerous vampires, the heroine's brush with death and, finally, her appearance at the prom in a cast with her boyfriend.

"That was a roller coaster ride," he remarked. "Are there more?"

"Two more. Want to watch the next one?"

He turned toward her, his dark eyes on her radiant face. He pursed his lips. "Yes, I would. But not right now." He pulled her across his lap. "I'm suffering from affection deprivation. Do you think you could assist me?"

"Could I!" she whispered as his mouth came down on hers.

Each kiss became harder, more urgent. As they grew accustomed to the feel and taste of each other, the pleasure grew and it became more difficult to pull back.

He actually groaned when he found himself lying over her with half their clothes out of the way, just like before. He buried his face in her warm, frantically pulsing throat.

"I'm dying," he ground out.

"Me, too," she whispered back, shivering.

He lifted his head. His eyes were tormented. "How do you feel about marriage?"

She blinked.

He realized that he, the most non-impulsive man on earth, was doing something totally out of character. But he was already crazy about Gwen and the lieutenant was lurking. Even Machado had been giving her long looks. He didn't want her to end up with some other man while he was waiting for the right moment to do something. And besides, he was traditional, so was she, and there was this incredible, almost unbelievable physical compatibility.

He sighed. "Look, we get along very well. We're incredibly suited physically. We have similar jobs, outlooks on life, philosophies, and we're on the same social level. Why don't we drive over the border and get married? Right now. Afterward," he added with a speaking glance, "we can do what we're both dying to do without lingering feelings of guilt."

Her lips parted. She should have challenged that social level comparison immediately, but her body was on fire and all she could think of was relief. She loved him. He was at least fond of her. They both wanted kids. It would work. She would make it work.

"Yes," she blurted out.

He forced himself to get up and he pulled out his cell phone, scrolled down a list of names and punched in a button. "Yes. Ramirez? Sorry to call so late. Can you get me a direct line to the general? I need his help on a—" he glanced at Gwen "—personal matter."

Ramirez sighed. "All right. But you owe me one."

"Yes, I do."

There was a pause, another pause. Rick motioned Gwen for a pencil and paper. He wrote down a number. "Thanks!" he told Ramirez, and hung up. He dialed the number.

"Yes, it's your—" he hesitated "—your son. How do you feel about giving away the bride at a Mexican wedding? Oh, in about thirty minutes."

There was a burst of Spanish from the other end of the line. Rick replied in the same language, protesting that he wasn't up to anything immoral, he was trying to make sure everything was done properly and that meant a proper wedding. The general seemed to calm down. Another hesitation. Rick grinned.

"Thanks," he said, and hung up. He turned to Gwen and pursed his lips. "Do you have a white dress?"

"Do I have a white dress!" she exclaimed, and ran into the next room to put it on.

She left her hair long. The dress was close-fitting, with puffy sleeves and a draped beaded shawl. She looked young and very innocent. And most incredibly sexy.

Rick's body reacted to her visibly. He cleared his throat. "Don't notice that," he said curtly.

"Oh. Okay." She giggled as she joined him and looked up into his dark eyes. "Are you sure?" she asked hesitantly.

He framed her face in his hands and kissed her with

breathless tenderness. "I don't know why, but I've never been so sure of anything. No cold feet?"

She shook her head. Her eyes were full of dreams. "Oh, no. Not at all."

He smiled. "Same here. We can share ammunition, too, so it will be cost effective to get married."

She burst out laughing. "I'll be sure to tell my father that when I explain why I didn't invite him to the ceremony."

He grimaced. "I'll have to do the same for my mother. But we don't have time to get them all together. We're eloping."

"Your father will have to be the audience," she said.

"My father." He smiled. "Let's go."

The general was waiting for them at the border. They followed him down a long dusty road to a small village and stopped in front of a mission church with a shiny new bell.

"I donated the bell," the general informed them proudly. "They are good people here, and the priest is a nice young man, from the United States." He hesitated, glancing from one to the other. "I did not think to ask which religious denomination...?"

"Catholic." They both spoke at once, stared at each other, and then burst out laughing.

"We hadn't discussed it before," Rick said.

"Well, it will be good," the general said with a big smile. "Come, the priest is waiting. You two, you're sure about this?"

Gwen looked at Rick with her heart in her eyes. "Very."

"Very, very," Rick added, his dark eyes shining.

"Then we shall proceed."

The general took Gwen down the aisle of the church on his arm. The whole village came to watch, including a number of small children who seemed to find the blonde lady's hair fascinating.

The priest smiled benevolently, read the marriage service. Then they came to the part about a ring.

Rick turned white. "Oh, no."

The general punched him. "Here. I remember everything." He handed him a small circle of gold that looked just right for Gwen's hand. "Something old. It belonged to my *abuela*," he added, "my grandmother." He smiled. "She would want it to stay in the family."

"It's beautiful," Gwen whispered. "Thank you."

The general nodded. Rick took the small circle of gold and slid it gently onto Gwen's finger, where it was a perfect fit. The priest pronounced them man and wife, and Rick bent to kiss her. And they were married.

Neither of them remembered much about the rest of the evening. Back at Gwen's apartment, there was a feverish removal of cotton and lace, followed by an incredibly long session in bed that left them both covered in sweat, boneless with pleasure and totally exhausted.

Not that exhaustion stopped them. As soon as they were breathing normally again, they reached for each other, and started all over.

"You know, it never occurred to me that marriage would be so much fun," Rick commented when they were finally sleepy.

Gwen, curled up against him, warm and satisfied, laughed softly. "Me, either. I always thought of it as something a little more dignified. You know, for children and..." She stopped.

He turned and looked down at her guilty face. "Hey. You want kids. I want kids. What's the problem?"

She relaxed. "You make it seem so simple."

"It is simple. Two people fall in love, get married and have a family." His eyes were on fire with his feelings. "We'll grow old together. But not right away. Maybe not at all," he added worriedly, "when my mother realizes that I got married without even telling her."

"My dad is going to go ballistic, too," she replied. "But he couldn't have come even if I'd had time to ask him. He's tied up with military stuff right now."

"Is he on active duty?"

"Oh, yes," she said, and there was another worry. She still had to tell Rick who her dad was, and all about the family he'd married into. That might be a source of discord. So she wasn't about to face it tonight.

She curled up close and wound her arms around him. "For a guy who never indulged, you're very good."

He laughed. "Compliment returned." He hugged her close. "They said it comes naturally. I guess it does. Of course, there were all these books I read. For educational purposes only."

She grinned. "I read a few of those, too."

He bent and brushed his mouth gently over hers. "I'm glad we waited," he said seriously, searching her eyes. "I know we're out of step with the world. But I don't care. This was right for us."

"Yes, it was. Thank you for having enough restraint," she added. "We couldn't have counted on me for it. I was on fire!"

"So was I. But I was thinking about later, generations later, when we tell our grandchildren and great-grandchildren about how it was when we fell in love and got married." He closed his eyes. "It's a golden memory. Not a legalization of something that had gone on before."

She pressed her mouth into his warm, muscular shoulder with a smile. "And the nicest thing is that you're already my best friend."

"You're mine, too." He kissed her hair. "Go to sleep. We'll get up tomorrow and face the music."

"What?"

"I was just thinking," he mused, "that the lieutenant is going to foam at the mouth when we tell him."

"What?" she exclaimed.

"Just a hunch." He thought the lieutenant had a case on Gwen. Maybe, maybe not. But he was expecting fireworks the next day.

Chapter Nine

"Fireworks" was, if anything, an understatement.

"You're married?" Lieutenant Hollister exclaimed.

Gwen moved a little closer to Rick. "Yes. Sorry, we would have invited you, but we didn't want the expense of a big wedding, so we eloped," she told him, stretching the truth.

"Eloped." Hollister leaned back in his chair with a grumpy sigh. He glared at Marquez. "Well, it was certainly quick."

"We knew how we felt at once," Rick replied with a smile at his wife. "No sense having a long engagement."

She smiled back. "Absolutely."

"Well, congratulations," Hollister said after a minute.

He got up, smiled and shook hands with both of them. "How did your mother take it?" he asked Rick.

Rick grimaced. "Haven't told her."

"Why don't you two take the day off and call it a honeymoon," Hollister suggested. "Gail Rogers can sub for you," he told Rick. "I don't want Barbara coming after me with a bazooka because she heard the news from somebody else."

"Good idea," Rick said. "Thanks!"

"My pleasure. A wedding present. A short one," he added. "You have to be back on the job tomorrow. And when are we losing you?" he asked Gwen.

She wasn't sure what he meant, and then she realized that she belonged to a federal agency. "I'm not sure. I'll have to talk to my boss and he'll have to discuss it with the captain here."

Hollister nodded. "You've done very well. I'll be sorry to lose you."

She smiled. "I'll be sorry to go. I may have to make some minor adjustments in my career path, as well," she added with a worried glance at Rick. "I don't really want to keep a job that sends me around the world every other week. Not now."

Hollister pursed his lips. "We can always use another detective," he pointed out. "You'd pick it back up in no time, and we have all sorts of workshops and training courses."

She beamed. "You mean it?"

"Of course," he assured her.

"Wait a minute, you'd give up working for the feds, for me?" Rick asked, as if he couldn't quite believe it.

"I would," she said solemnly. "I'm tired of living out of a suitcase. And I really like San Antonio." She didn't add that she was also very tired of the D.C. social scene and being required to hostess parties for her dad. It was never enjoyable. She didn't like crowds or parties. To give him his due, neither did her father. But he was certainly going to be in the center of the Washington social whirl very soon. She dreaded having to tell Rick about it.

"Well," Rick said, and couldn't resist a charming smile.

She laughed. "And now for the really hard part. We have to break the news to your mother."

"She'll kill me," he groaned.

"No. We'll take her a pot of flowers," Gwen said firmly. "She's a gardener. I know she wouldn't mind a bribe that she could plant."

They all laughed.

And actually, Barbara wasn't mad. She burst into tears, hugged them both and rambled on for several minutes about how depressed she'd been that women never seemed to see Rick as a potential mate as much as a shoulder to cry on.

"I'm just so happy!"

"I'm so glad," Gwen enthused. "But we still brought you a bribe."

"A bribe?" Barbara asked, wiping away tears.

Gwen went onto the porch and came back inside carrying a huge potted plant.

"It's an umbrella plant!" Barbara exclaimed. "I've wanted one for years, but I could never find one the right size. It's perfect!"

"I thought you could plant it," Gwen said.

"Oh, no, I'll let it live inside. I'll put grow lights around it and fertilize it and..." She hesitated. "You two didn't have to get married?"

They howled.

"She's as Victorian as we are," Rick told his mother with a warm smile.

"That's wonderful! Welcome to the stone age, my dear!" she told Gwen and hugged her, hard.

"Where are you going to live? In San Antonio?" Barbara asked, resigned.

Gwen and Rick had discussed this. "The old Andrews place is up for sale, right in downtown Jacobsville," Rick said, "next door to the Griers. In fact, I put in an offer for it this morning."

"Oh!" Barbara started crying again. "I thought you'd want to live where your jobs are."

Explanation about Gwen's job could come later, Rick decided. "We want to live near you," Rick replied.

"Because when the kids come along," Gwen added with a grin, "you'll want to be able to see them."

Barbara felt her forehead. "Maybe I'm feverish. You want to have kids?"

"Oh, yes," Gwen replied, smiling.

"Lots of kids," Rick added.

"I can buy a toy store," Barbara murmured to herself. "But first I need to stock up on organic seeds, so that I can make healthy stuff for the baby."

"We just got married yesterday," Rick pointed out.

"That's right, and this is November." She went looking for a calendar. "And nine months from now is harvest season!" she called back.

Rick and Gwen shook their heads.

They stayed for supper, a delicious affair, and then settled down to watch the news. Gwen, sitting contentedly beside her husband, had no warning of what was about to happen.

A newscaster smiled as a picture of a four-star general, very well-known to the public, was splashed across the screen. "And this just in. Amid rumors that he was retiring or resigning from the service, we have just learned that General David Cassaway, former U.S. Commander in Iraq, has been named director of the Central Intelligence Agency. General Cassaway, a former covert ops commander, has commanded American troops in Iraq for the past two years. He was rumored to be retiring from the military, but it seems that he was only considering a new job."

Barbara glanced at Gwen. "Why, what a coincidence. That's your last name."

The newscaster was adding, "General Cassaway's only son, Larry, died in a classified operation in the Middle East just a few months ago. We wish General

Cassaway the best of luck in his new position. Now for other news…"

Rick was staring at Gwen as if she'd grown horns. "Your brother's name was Larry, wasn't it?" he asked. "The one who was killed in action?"

Barbara was staring. So was Rick.

Gwen took a deep breath. "He's my father," she confessed.

Rick wasn't handling this well. "Your father is the new head of the CIA?"

"Well, sort of," she said, nodding worriedly.

Rick knew about Washington society from people in his department who had to deal with the socialites in D.C. He was certain that there were no poor generals in the military, and the head of the CIA would certainly not be in line for food stamps.

"What sort of place do you live in, when you go home?" Rick asked very quietly.

Gwen sighed. "We have a big house in Maryland, on several acres of land. My dad likes horses. He raises, well, thoroughbreds." She was almost cringing by now.

"And drives a…?"

She swallowed. "Jaguar."

Rick got up and turned away with an exasperated sigh. "Why didn't you tell me?"

"Because I was afraid you'd do just what you're doing now," Gwen moaned. "Judging me by the company I keep. I hate parties. I hate receptions. I hate hostessing! I'm perfectly happy working a federal job, or a police job, any sort of job that doesn't require me to put on an evening gown and look rich!"

"Rich." Rick ran his fingers through his hair.

"I'm not rich," she pointed out.

"But your father is."

She grimaced. "He was born into one of the founding families. He went to Harvard, and then to West Point," she said. "But he's just a regular person. He doesn't put on airs."

"Sure."

"Rick—" she got up and went to him "—I'm not my family. I don't have money. I work for my living. For heaven's sake, this suit is a year old!"

He turned around. His face was hard. "My suit is three years old," he said stiffly. "I drive a pickup truck. I can barely afford tickets to the theater."

She gave him a strained look. "You'll get used to this," she promised him. "It will just take a little time. You've had one too many upsets in the past few weeks."

He sighed heavily. "We should have waited to get married," he ground out.

"No," she returned. "If we'd waited and you'd found out, you'd never have married me at all."

Before Rick could open his mouth and destroy his future, Barbara got up and stood between them. "She's right," she told her son. "You need to stop before you say something you'll regret. Let Gwen go home for tonight, and you sleep on it. Things will look better in the morning." She went to get her cell phone and dialed a number. She waited until the call was answered. "Cash? Gwen Cassaway's going back to San Antonio for the night and I don't want her driving up there alone, do you have someone who can take her?"

"No…!" Gwen protested.

Barbara held up a hand. She grinned. "I thought you might. Thanks! I owe you a nice apple pie." She hung up. "One of Cash's men lives in San Antonio and he's on his way home. He'll swing by and give you a lift. He won't mind, and he's very nice. His name is Carlton Ames. He'll take good care of you."

Rick was cursing himself for not letting Gwen drive her car down instead of insisting that she come with him. He didn't like the idea of her riding with another man. They were married. At least, temporarily.

"Go home and don't worry," Barbara said, hugging her. "It will be all right."

Gwen managed a smile. She looked at Rick, but he wouldn't meet her eyes. She drew in a long breath and put on her coat and picked up her purse. She walked out to the front porch with Barbara, who closed the door behind them.

"He's still upset about meeting his father," Barbara said gently. "He'll get over this. You just get a good night's sleep and don't worry. It will work out. I'm so happy he married you!" She hugged the younger woman again. "You're going to be very happy together once he gets over the shock."

"I hope you're right. I should have told him. I was afraid to."

"Have you talked to your father?"

She shook her head. "I have to do that tonight." She grimaced. "He's not going to be happy, either."

"Does he have prejudices…?" Barbara worried at once.

Gwen laughed. "Heavens, no! Dad doesn't see color or race or religion. He's very liberal. No, he'll be hurt that I didn't tell him first."

"That's all right then. You'll make it up with him. And with Rick. Oh, there's Carlton!"

She waved as an off-duty police car pulled up at the porch. A nice young man got out and smiled. "I'm going to have company for the ride, I hear?" he asked.

"Yes, this is my new daughter-in-law, Gwen." Barbara introduced them. "That's Carlton," she added with a grin. "She didn't drive her own car and she has to get back to San Antonio to pick it up. Thanks for giving her a ride."

"Should I follow you back down here, then?" he offered.

Gwen shook her head. "I have things to get together in my apartment. But thanks."

"No problem. Shall we go?"

Gwen looked toward the porch, but the door was still closed. She saw Barbara wince. She managed a smile. "I'll see you later, then," she said. "Have a good night."

"You, too, dear," Barbara said. She forced a smile. "Good night."

She watched them leave. Then she went back in the house and closed the door. "Rick?"

He was on the phone. She wondered who he could be calling at this hour of the night. Perhaps it was work.

He hung up and came into the living room, looking more unapproachable than she'd ever seen him. "I'm going for a drive. I won't be long."

"She was very upset," she said gently. "She can't help who her father is, any more than you can."

He looked torn. "I know that. But she should have told me."

"I think she was afraid to. She's very much in love, you know."

He flushed and looked away. "I won't be long."

She watched him go, feeling a new and bitter distance between them, something she'd never felt before. She hoped they could work things out. She liked Gwen a lot.

Rick pulled up to the country bar, locked the truck and walked inside. It was late and there were only a couple of cowboys sitting in booths. A man in the back motioned to Rick, who walked down the aisle to sit across from him.

The older man gave him an amused smile. "Should I be flattered that you called me when you needed sympathy? Why not talk to your mother?"

Rick sighed. "It's not really something a woman would understand," he muttered.

General Machado pursed his lips. "No? Perhaps not." He motioned to the waiter, who came over at once, grinning. "Coffee for my young friend, please."

"At once!"

Rick's eyebrows arched at the man's quick manner.

"He wants to go and help liberate my country," Machado told Rick with a grin. "I have the ability to inspire revolutions."

"I noticed," Rick said dryly.

General Emilio Machado leaned back against the booth, studying the young man who looked so much like himself. "You know, we do favor each other."

"A bit."

The waiter came back with the coffee, placing a mug in front of Rick, along with small containers of cream and sugar, and a spoon. "Anything else for you, sir?" he asked the general with respect.

"No, that will do for now, thank you."

"A pleasure! If you need anything, just call."

"I will."

The waiter scampered away. Machado watched Rick sip hot coffee. "Just married, and already you quarrel?"

"She lied to me. Well, she lied by omission," he corrected coolly.

"About what?"

"It turns out that her father is the new head of the CIA."

"Ah, yes, General Cassaway. He and Grange are friends."

Rick recalled an odd conversation that Gwen and Grange had shared at the first meeting with Machado at the border. It had puzzled him at the time. Now he knew that she had been cautioning Grange not to give away her identity. It made him even sadder.

"He's rich," Rick said curtly.

"And you are not." Machado understood the problem. "Does it matter so much, if you care for the woman? What if it was your mother who was wealthy, and her father who was poor?"

He shifted restlessly. "I don't know."

"But of course you do. You would not care."

Rick sipped more coffee. He was losing the argument.

Machado toyed with his own cup. "I was a millionaire, in my country," he confided. "I had everything a man could possibly want, right down to a Rolls-Royce and a private helicopter. Perhaps I had too much, and God resented the fact that I spent more money on me than I did on the poor villagers who were being displaced and murdered by my underling's minions as he worked to bring in foreign oil corporations. The oil and natural gas are quite valuable, and the villagers considered them a nuisance that interfered with the fishing." He smiled. "They have no interest in great wealth. They live from day to day, quietly, with no clocks, no supermarkets, no strip malls. Perhaps they have the right idea, and the rest of the world has gone insane from this disease called civilization."

Rick smiled back. "It would be a less hectic life."

"Yes, indeed." His dark eyes were thoughtful. "I was careless. I will never be careless again. And the man who usurped my place and made my people suffer will pay a very high price for his arrogance and greed, I promise you." The look on his face gave Rick cold chills.

"We've heard what he did to private citizens," Rick agreed.

"That is my fault. I should have listened. A…friend of mine, an archaeologist, tried to warn me about what his people were doing to the native tribes. I thought she was overstating, trying to get me to clamp down on foreign interests in the name of preserving archaeological treasures."

"A female archaeologist?"

He chuckled. "There are many these days. Yes, she taught at a small college in the United States. She was visiting my country when she stumbled onto a find so amazing that she hesitated to even announce it before she had time to substantiate her claim with evidence." His face hardened. "There was gossip that they put her in prison. I shudder to think what might have been done to her. That will be on my soul forever, if she was harmed."

"Maybe she escaped," Rick said, trying to find

something comforting to say. "Rumors and gossip are usually pretty far off the mark."

"You think so?" Machado's dark eyes were sad but hopeful.

"Anything is possible."

Machado sighed. "I suppose."

The waiter came scurrying up looking worried. "El General, there is a police car coming this way," he said excitedly.

Machado looked at Rick.

"I'm not involved in any attempts to kidnap or arrest you," he said dryly.

"Is the car local?" Machado asked.

"Yes. It is a Jacobsville police car."

Machado weighed his options. While he was trying to decide whether to make a break out the back door, a tall, imposing man in a police uniform with large dark eyes and his long hair in a ponytail came in the door, looked around and spotted Rick with the general.

Rick relaxed. "It's all right," he said. "That's Cash Grier."

"You know him?"

"Yes. He's our police chief. He's a good man. Used to be a government assassin, or that's the rumor," Rick mused.

Machado laughed under his breath.

Cash walked over to their table. He wasn't smiling. "I'm afraid I have some bad news."

"You're here to arrest me?" Machado asked dryly.

Cash glanced at him. "Have you broken the law?" he asked curiously. It was obvious that he didn't recognize the bar's famous patron.

"Not lately," Machado lied.

Cash looked back at Rick, who was going tense.

"Gwen," he burst out.

Cash grimaced. "I'm afraid so. There's been a wreck…"

Rick was out of the booth in a flash. "How badly is she hurt?" he asked at once, white-faced. "Is she all right?"

"They've transported her and Ames to Jacobsville General," he said quietly. "Ames is pretty bad. Ms. Cassaway has at the very least a broken rib…!" Rick was already out of the bar, running for his truck.

"Wait! I'm coming with you!" Machado called after him, and stopped just long enough to pay the waiter, who bowed respectfully.

Cash, confused by the two men, got back in his patrol car and followed the pickup truck down the long road to the hospital. To his credit, he didn't pull out his ticket book when he pulled in behind Rick at the emergency entrance.

"My wife, Gwen Cassaway," Rick told the clerk at the desk. "They just brought her in."

The clerk studied him. "Oh, that's you, Detective Marquez," she said, smiling. "Yes, and she's your wife? Congratulations! Yes, she's in X-ray right now. Dr. Coltrain is treating her…"

"Copper or Lou?" Rick asked, because the married Coltrains were both doctors.

"Lou," came the reply.

"Thanks."

"You can have a seat right over there," the clerk said gently, "and I'll have someone ask Dr. Coltrain to come see you, okay?"

Rick wanted to rush behind the counter, but he knew better. He ground his teeth together. "Okay."

"Be just a sec." The clerk picked up the phone.

"She will be all right," Machado told his son with a warm smile. "She has great courage for one so young."

Rick felt rocked to the soles of his feet. He never should have reacted as he had. He'd upset her. But... she hadn't been driving, and Ames was one of Cash's better drivers...

He turned to the police chief. "Ames wrecked the car? How?"

"That's what I'd like to know," Cash said curtly. "There was another set of tracks in the dirt nearby, as if a car had sideswiped them. I've got men tracking right now."

"If you need help, I can provide a tracker who might even excel your own," Machado offered quietly.

Cash had been sizing the other man up. He pursed his lips. "You look familiar."

"There are very few photographs of me," Machado replied.

"Yes, but we've met. I can't remember where. Maybe it will come back to me."

Machado raised an eyebrow. "It would be just as well if your memory lapses for the next few hours. My son can use the company."

"Your son?" Cash's dark eyes narrowed on the older man. "Machado."

The older man nodded and smiled.

"Gwen had a photo of you. I had to break the news to Rick's mother, about your connection to him."

"Ah, yes, that was how he was told. Ingenious." The general's expression sombered. "I hope she and the officer will be all right."

"So do I," Cash said. "I can't help being concerned about that other car."

Machado came a step closer. "The Fuentes bunch have much reason to interfere with my plans. They are being paid by my successor to spy on me. There is also a very high level mole in the DEA. I do not know who it is," he added. "But even I am aware of him."

"Damn," Cash muttered.

"Yes, things are quite complicated. I did not mean to involve the children in my war," he added, with a rueful glance at Rick, who was pacing the floor.

"No parent would. Sometimes fate intervenes. Her father should be told."

"Yes," Machado replied. "He should." He excused himself and spoke to Rick.

"Her father." Rick groaned. "How am I going to find him?"

Machado grinned. "I think I can solve that problem." He pulled out his disposable cell phone, one of many, and dialed a number. "Grange? Yes. Gwen has been injured in an automobile accident. I need you to call her father and tell him. We don't know details yet. She has at least a broken rib. The rest we don't know...but he should come."

There was a pause. "Yes. Thank you. She is at the Jacobsville hospital. Yes. All right." He hung up. "Grange and her father are friends. He will make the call."

Rick averted his eyes. "Hell of a way to meet in-laws," he muttered.

"I do agree," Machado said. He put an affectionate arm around his son's neck. "But you will get through it. Come. Sit down and stop pacing, before you wear a hole in the floor."

Rick allowed himself to be led to a chair. It was kind of nice, having a father.

Dr. Louise Coltrain came into the room in her white lab coat, smiling. She was introduced to Gwen's husband and father-in-law with some surprise, because no one locally knew about the wedding.

"Congratulations," she told Rick. "She'll be all right," she added quickly. "She does have a broken rib, but the other injuries are mostly bruises. Patrolman Ames has a head injury," she told Cash. "His prognosis is going to be trickier. I'm having him airlifted to

San Antonio, to the Marshall Center. He's holding his own so far, though. Do you have a way to notify his family?"

Cash shook his head. "He doesn't have any family that I'm aware of. Just me," he added with a grim smile. "So I'm the one to notify."

She nodded. "I'll keep you in the loop. Detective Marquez, you can see your wife now. I'll take you back..."

"Where the hell is my daughter?"

Rick felt a shiver go down his spine. That voice, deep and cold with authority, froze everyone in the waiting room. Rick turned to find the face that went with it, and understood at once how this man had risen to become a four-star general. He was in full uniform, every button polished, his hat at the perfect angle, his hard face almost bristling with antagonism, his black eyes glittering with it.

"And who's responsible for putting her in the hospital?" he added in a tone that was only a little less intimidating.

While Rick was working on an answer, Barbara came in the door, worried and unsettled by his call. She paused beside the military man who was raising Cain in the waiting room.

"My goodness, someone had his razor blade soup this morning, I see!" she exclaimed with pure hostility. "Now you calm down and stop shouting at people. This is a hospital, not a military installation!"

Chapter Ten

General Cassaway turned and looked down at the willowy blonde woman who was glaring up at him.

"Who the hell are you?" he demanded.

"The woman who's going to have you arrested if you don't calm down," she replied. "Rick, how is she?" she asked, holding out her arms.

Rick came and held her close. "Broken rib," he said. "And some bruising. She'll be all right."

"Who are you?" General Cassaway demanded.

Rick turned. "I'm Gwen's husband. Detective Sergeant Rick Marquez," he said coldly, not backing down an inch.

"Her husband?"

"Yes. And he's my son," Barbara added.

"And also my son," General Machado said, joining them. He smiled at Barbara, who smiled back.

"You two are married?" Cassaway asked.

Barbara laughed. "No. He's much too young for me," she said.

Machado gave her an amused look. "I do like older women," he admitted.

She just shook her head.

"I want to see my daughter," Cassaway told Lou Coltrain.

"Of course. Come this way. You, too, Rick."

Cassaway was surprised at the first name basis.

"We all know each other here," Lou told him. "I'm a newcomer, so to speak, but my husband is from here. He's known Rick since Barbara adopted him."

"I see."

Gwen was heavily sedated, but her eyes opened and she brightened when she saw her husband and her father walk into the recovery room.

"Dad! Rick!"

Rick went on one side to take a hand, her father on the other.

"I'm so sorry," she began.

"Don't be absurd." Rick kissed her forehead. "I was an idiot. I'm sorry! I never should have let you go with Ames."

"Ames! How is he?" she asked. "The other car came out of nowhere! We didn't even see it until it hit us. There were three men in it…"

"Did you recognize any of them?"

"No," she replied. "But it could have been Fuentes. The last of the living brothers, the drug lords."

"By God, I'll have them hunted down like rats," Cassaway said icily.

"My father will beat you to it," Rick replied coolly.

"Just who is your father?" Cassaway asked suddenly. "He looks very familiar."

"General Emilio Machado," Rick said, and with a hint of pride that reflected in the tilt of his chin.

Cassaway pursed his lips. "Grange's boss. Yes, we know about that upcoming operation. We can't be involved, of course."

"Of course," Rick replied with twinkling eyes.

"But we are rooting for the good guys," came the amused comment.

Rick chuckled.

"So you're married," Cassaway said. He shook his head. "Your mother would have loved seeing you married." He winced. "I would have, too."

"I'm so sorry," she said. "But I hadn't told Rick who you were." She bit her lip.

"What did that have to do with anything?" the older man asked, puzzled.

"I'm a city detective," Rick said sardonically. "I wear three-year-old suits and I drive a pickup truck."

"Hell, I drive a pickup truck, too," the general said, shrugging. "So what?"

Rick liked the man already. He grinned.

"See?" Gwen asked her husband. "I told you he wasn't what you thought."

"Snob," the general said, glaring at Rick. "I don't pick my friends for their bank accounts."

"Sorry," Rick said. "I didn't know you."

"You'll get there, son."

"Congratulations on the appointment," Rick said.

The general shrugged. "I don't know how long I'll last. I don't kiss butt, if you know what I mean, and I say what I think. Not very popular to speak your mind sometimes."

"I think honesty never goes out of style, and has value," Rick replied.

The general's eyes twinkled. "You did good," he told his daughter.

She just smiled.

Out in the waiting room, Cash Grier was talking on the phone to someone in San Antonio while the general thumbed through a magazine. Barbara paced, worried. Gwen's father was a hard case. She hoped he and Rick would learn to get along.

Cash closed his flip phone grimly. "They found a car, abandoned, a few miles outside of Comanche Wells," he said. "We can't say for sure that it's the one that hit Ames, but it has black paint on the fender, and Ames's car is black. We ran wants and warrants on it— it was stolen."

"Fuentes," Machado said quietly. His dark eyes narrowed. "I have had just about enough of him. I think he will have to meet with a similar accident soon."

"I didn't hear you say that," Cash told him.

"Did I say something?" Machado asked. "Why, I was simply voicing a prediction."

"Terroristic threats and acts," he said, waving a finger at Machado. "And I'm conveniently forgetting your connection with the Pendleton kidnapping for the next hour or so. After that," he added with pursed lips, "things could get interesting here."

Machado grinned. "I will be long gone by then. My son needed me."

Cash smiled. "I have a daughter," he said. "She's going on three years old. Red hair and green eyes and a temper worse than mine."

"I would like to have known my son when he was small," Machado said sadly. "I did not know about him. Dolores kept her secret all the way to the grave. A pity."

"It was nice for me, that you didn't know," Barbara said gently. "When I adopted him, he gave me a reason to live." She stood up. "Do you think things happen for a reason?" she asked philosophically.

"Yes, I do," Machado replied with a smile. "Perhaps fate had a hand in all this."

"Well, I suppose…" she began.

"I have to get back home," General Cassaway was saying as he walked out with Rick. "But it's been a pleasure meeting you, son." He shook hands with Rick.

"Same here," Rick told him. "I'll take better care of

your daughter from now on. And I won't be so inflex-
ible next time she springs a surprise on me," he added
with a laugh.

"See that you aren't. Remember what I do for a
living now," he told the younger man with a grin. "I
can find you anywhere, anytime."

"Yes, sir," Rick replied.

The general turned to Machado. "And you'd better
hightail it out of Mexico pretty soon," he said in a con-
fidential tone. "Things are going to heat up in Sonora.
A storm's coming. You don't want to be in its way."

Machado nodded. "Thank you."

"Oh, I have ulterior motives," Cassaway assured
him. "I want that rat out of Barrera before he turns
your country into the world's largest cocaine distribution center."

"So do I," Machado replied quietly. "I promise you,
his days of power will soon come to an end."

"Wish I could help," Cassaway told him. "But I think
you have enough intel and mercs to do the job."

"Including a friend of yours," Machado replied,
smiling.

"A very good one. He'll get the job done." He shook
hands with Machado. Then he turned to Barbara.
"You've got a smart mouth on you."

She glared at him. "And you've got a sharp tongue
on you."

He smiled. "I like pepper."

She shifted. "Me, too."

"She's a great cook," Rick said, sliding his arm around her shoulders. "She owns the local café here, and does most of the cooking for it."

"Really! I'm something of a chef myself," Cassaway replied. "I grow my own vegetables and I get a local grandmother to come over and help me can every summer."

Barbara moved closer. "I can, too. I like to dry herbs as well."

"Now I've got a herb garden of my own," the general said. "But it isn't doing as well as I'd like."

"Do you have a composter?" Barbara asked.

His eyebrows lifted. "A what?"

"A composter, for organic waste from the kitchen." She went on to explain to him how it worked and what you did with it.

"A fellow gardener," Cassaway said with a beaming smile. "What a surprise! So few women garden these days."

"Oh, we have plenty around Jacobsville who plant gardens," Barbara said. "You'll have to come and visit us next summer. I can show you how to grow corn ten feet high, even in a drought," she added.

Cassaway moved a step closer. He was huge, Barbara thought, tall and good-looking and built like a tank. He had thick black hair and black eyes and a tan complexion. Nice mouth.

Cassaway was thinking the same thing about Barbara. She was tall and willowy and very pretty.

"I might visit sooner than that," he said in a low, deep tone. "Is there a hotel?"

"Yes, but I have a big Victorian house. Rick and Gwen can stay there, too. We'll have a family reunion." She flushed a little, and laughed, and then looked at Machado. "That invitation includes you, also," she added. "If you're through with your revolution by then," she said ruefully.

"I think that is a good possibility, and I will accept the invitation," Machado said. He kissed her hand and bowed. "Thank you for taking such good care of my son."

She smiled. "He's been the joy of my life. I had nobody until Rick needed a home."

"I only have a daughter," General Cassaway said sadly. "I lost my son earlier this year to an IED, and my wife died some years ago."

"I'm so sorry," Barbara said with genuine sympathy. "I miscarried the only child I ever had. It must be terrible to lose one who's grown."

"Worse than death," Cassaway agreed. He cleared his throat and looked away. He drew in a long breath. "Well, my adjutant is doing the ants' dance, so I guess we'd better go," he said, nodding toward a young officer standing in the doorway.

"The ants' dance?" Barbara asked.

"He moves around like that when he's in a hurry to do something, like he's got ants climbing his legs. Good man, but a little testy." He shrugged. "Like me.

He suits me." He shook hands with Rick. "I've heard good things about you from Grange. Your police chief over there—" he nodded toward Cash, who was talking on the phone again "—speaks highly of you."

Rick smiled. "Nice to know. I love my job. I like to think I'm good at it."

"Take care of my little girl."

"You know I will."

He paused at Barbara and looked down at her with quiet admiration. "And I'll see you later."

She grinned. "Okay!"

He nodded at the others, and walked toward the young man, who was now motioning frantically.

Cash joined them a minute later. "Sorry, I wasn't trying to be rude. I've got a man working on the hit-and-run, and I've been checking in. There was an incident at the border crossing over near Del Rio," he added. "Three men jumped a border agent, knocked him out and took off over the crossing into Mexico. We think it was the same men who ran Ames off the road."

"Great," Rick muttered. "Just great. Now we work on trying to get them extradited back to the States. That will be good for a year, even if we can get a positive identification of who they are."

Machado pursed his lips. "I would not worry about that. Such men are easy to find, for a good tracker, and equally easy to deal with."

"I didn't hear that," Cash said.

Machado chuckled. "Of course not. I was, again, making a prediction."

"Thanks for coming with me," Rick told Machado. "And for the shoulder earlier."

Machado embraced his son in a bear hug. "I will always be around, whenever you need me." He searched the younger man's face. "I am very proud to have such a man for my son."

Rick swallowed hard. "I'm proud to have such a man for my father."

Machado's eyes were suspiciously bright. He laughed suddenly. "We will both be wailing in another minute. I must go. Grange is waiting for me in the parking lot."

"I can't say anything officially," Cash told the general. "But privately, I wish you good luck."

Machado shook his hand. "Thank you, my friend. I hope your patrolman will be all right."

"So do I," Cash said.

Rick walked Machado to the door. Outside, Winslow Grange was sitting behind the wheel of Machado's pickup truck, waiting.

Machado turned to his son. "When the time comes, I will be happy to let you become my liaison with the American authorities. And it will come," he added solemnly. "My country has many resources that will appeal to outside interests. I would prefer to deal with republics or democracies rather than totalitarian states."

"A wise decision," Rick said. "And when the time comes, I'll be here."

Machado smiled. *"Que vayas con Dios, mi hijo,"* he said, using the familiar tense that was only applied to family and close friends.

It made Rick feel warm inside, that his father already felt affection for him. He waved as the two men in the truck departed. He hoped his father wouldn't get killed in the attempt to retake Barrera. But, then, Machado was a general, and he'd won the title fairly, in many battles. He would be all right. Rick was certain of it.

Gwen came home two days later. She wore a rib belt and winced every time she moved. The lieutenant had granted her sick leave, but she was impatient to get back on the job. Rick had to make threats to keep her in bed at all, at Barbara's house.

"And I'm a burden on your poor mother," Gwen protested. "She has a business to run, and here she is bringing me food on trays...!"

"She doesn't mind," Rick assured her.

"Of course she doesn't mind," Barbara said as she brought in soup and crackers. "She's working on planning a fantastic Thanksgiving dinner in a couple of weeks. I'm going to invite your father," she told Gwen and then flushed a little. "I guess that would be all right. I don't know," she hesitated, looking around her. "He's head of the CIA and used to crystal and fine china..."

"He doesn't use the good place settings at home," Gwen said dryly. "He likes plain white ceramic plates and thick Starbucks coffee mugs and just plain fare to eat. He isn't a fancy mannered person, although he can blend into high society when he has to. He'll think of it as a welcome relief from the D.C. whirl. Which I'm happy to be out of," she added heavily. "I never liked having to hostess parties. I like working in law enforcement."

"Me, too," Rick said, smiling warmly at his wife. "I'm just sorry about what happened to you and Ames."

"Yes. Have we heard anything about Ames?"

"Cash Grier said that he regained consciousness this morning," Barbara said with a smile. "It's all coming back to him. He remembered what the men looked like. He got a better view of them than you did," she told the younger woman. "He recognized Fuentes."

"Fuentes himself?" Gwen was shocked. "Why would he do his own dirty work?"

"Fuentes knows that you're married to me, and that I'm General Machado's son," Rick said somberly. "I think he was trying to get back at the general, in a roundabout way. He may have thought it was me driving. He wouldn't have known that you were with Ames."

"Yes," Barbara said worriedly. "And he may try again. You can't go anywhere alone from now on, at least until Fuentes is arrested."

"He won't be," Rick said coldly. "Dozens of policemen have tried to pin him down, nobody has succeeded. He has a hideout in the mountains and guards at every checkpoint. An undercover agent died trying to infiltrate his camp a few weeks ago. I'd love to see him behind bars. It's trying to get him there that's the problem."

"Well, your father's not too happy with him right now," Barbara remarked.

"And the general has ways and means that we don't have access to," Gwen agreed.

"True," Rick said.

"I think we may hear some good news soon about Fuentes and his bunch," Barbara said. "But for now, my main focus is getting your wife back on her feet," she told her son. "Good food and a little spoiling always does the trick."

"You're a nice mother," Rick said.

"A very nice mother and I'm so happy that you're going to be mine, too," Gwen told her with a warm smile. She shifted in the bed and groaned.

"Time for meds," Barbara said, and went out to get them.

Rick bent and kissed Gwen gently between her eyes. "You get better," he whispered. "I have erotic plans for you at some future time very soon."

She laughed, wincing, and lifted her mouth to touch his. "You aren't the only one with plans. Darn this rib!"

"Bad timing, and Fuentes's fault," Rick murmured as he brushed her mouth tenderly with his. "But we have forever."

"Yes," she whispered, beaming. "Forever."

Thanksgiving came suddenly and with, of all things, snow! Rick and Gwen walked out into the yard at Barbara's house and laughed as it piled down on the bare limbs of the trees around the fence line.

"Snow!" she exclaimed. "I didn't know it snowed in Texas!"

"Hey, it snowed in South Africa twice in August," he pointed out. "The weather is loopy."

She smiled and hugged him, still wincing a little, because her rib was tender. She was healing quickly, though. Soon, she would be whole again and ready for more amorous adventures with her new husband.

"Is your father coming down?" he asked Gwen.

"Oh, yes. He said he wouldn't miss a homemade Thanksgiving dinner for the world. He can cook, but he hates doing it on holidays, and he mostly eats out. He's very excited. And not only about the meal," she added with an impish grin. "I think he likes your mother."

"Wouldn't that be a match?" he mused.

"Yes, it would. They're both alone and about the same age. Dad's quite a guy."

"But he's head of a federal agency. He lives in D.C. and she owns a restaurant here," Rick pointed out.

"If they really want to, they'll find a way."

"I guess so." He turned to her, in the white flaky curtain, and drew her gently to his chest. "The best thing I ever did in life was marry you," he said somberly. "I may not say it a lot but I love you very much."

She caught her breath at the tenderness in his deep voice. "I love you, too," she whispered back.

He bent and drew her mouth under his, teasing the

upper lip with his tongue, parting her lips so that his could cover them hungrily. He forgot everything in the flashpoint heat of desire. His arms closed around her, enveloping her so tightly that she moaned.

He heard that, and drew back at once. "Sorry," he said quickly. "I forgot!"

She laughed breathily. "It's okay. I forgot, too. Just another week or two, and I'll be in fine shape."

He lifted an eyebrow and looked down at her trim, curvy body in jeans and a tight sweater. "I'll say you're in fine shape," he murmured dryly.

"Oh, you!" She punched him lightly in the chest.

"Shapely, sexy and sweet. I'm a lucky man."

She reached up and kissed him back. "We're both lucky."

He sighed. "I suppose we should go back inside and offer to peel potatoes."

"I suppose so."

He kissed her again, smiling. "In a minute."

She sighed. "Yes. In a minute…or two…or three…"

Ten minutes later, they went back inside. Barbara gave them an amused look and handed Rick a huge pan full of potatoes and a paring knife. He sighed and got to work.

The general came with an entourage, but they were housed in the local hotel in Jacobsville. General Cassaway did allow his adjutant and a clerk to move into Barbara's house with him, with her permission of course, and he had a case full of electronic equipment that had to find living space as well.

"I have to keep in touch with everyone in my department, monitor the web, answer queries, inform the proper people at Homeland Security about my activities," the general said, rattling off his duties. "It's a great job, but it takes most of my time. That's why I've been remiss in the email department," he added with a smile at Gwen.

"I think you do very well, considering how little free time you have, Dad," she told him.

"Thanks." He dug into the dressing, closing his eyes as he savored it and the giblet gravy. "This is wonderful, Barbara."

"Thank you," she replied, with a big smile. "I love to cook."

"Me, too," Gwen added. "Barbara's teaching me how to do things properly."

"She's a quick study, too," Barbara replied, smiling at her daughter-in-law. "Her corn bread is wonderful, and I didn't teach her that…it's her own recipe. She's very talented."

"Thanks."

"What about this Fuentes character who sideswiped that car you were in?" he asked Gwen suddenly.

"Strange thing," she replied, tongue in cheek. "Fuentes seems to have gone missing. Nobody's seen him since the wreck."

"How very odd," the general remarked.

"Isn't it?"

"How about the young man who was driving you?" he added as he dipped his fork into potato salad.

"He's out of the hospital and back at work," Gwen said warmly. "He's going to be fine, thank goodness."

"I'm glad about that." He glanced across the table at Rick. "I understand that your father has left Mexico."

Rick smiled. "Yes, I did hear about that."

"So things are going to heat up in Barrera very soon, I would expect," the general added.

Rick nodded. "Very soon."

"No more talk of revolution," Barbara said firmly. She got to her feet with a big grin. "I have a surprise."

She went into the kitchen and came back in with a huge coconut cream pie. She put it on the table.

"Is that...?"

"Coconut cream." Barbara nodded. "I heard that it's someone's favorite."

"Mine!" General Cassaway said. "Thanks!"

"My pleasure." She cut it into slices and put one on a saucer for him. "If you still have room after all that turkey and dressing..."

"I'll make room," he said with such fervor that everyone laughed.

The general stayed for two days. Rick and Gwen and Barbara drove him around Jacobsville and introduced him to people. He fit in as if he'd been born there. He was coming back for Christmas, he assured them. He had to do a vanishing act to get out of all those holiday parties in Washington, D.C.

Rick heard from his father, too. The mercenaries had landed in a country friendly to Machado, near the border of Barrera, and they were massing for an attack. Machado told Rick not to worry, he was certain of victory. But just in case, he wanted Rick to know that the high point of his life so far had been meeting his own son. Rick had been overwhelmed with that statement. He told Gwen later that it had meant more to him than anything. Well, anything except marrying her, of course.

They moved back into her apartment, because it was closer to their jobs, leaving Rick's vacant for the moment.

She went home early one Friday night and when Rick walked in the door, he found her standing by the sofa wearing a negligee set that sent his heart racing like a bass drum.

"Here I was trying on my new outfit and there you are, home early. What perfect timing!" she purred, and moved toward him with her hair long and soft around her shoulders, her arms lifting to envelope him hungrily.

He barely got the door closed in time, before they wound up in a feverish tangle on the carpet....

Chapter Eleven

"Your ribs," Rick gasped.

"Are fine," Gwen whispered, lifting to the slow, hard rhythm. Her eyes rolled back in her head at the over-whelming wave of pleasure that accompanied the move-ments. "Oh, my gosh!" she groaned, shivering.

"It just gets better...and better," he bit off.

"Yes...!" A high-pitched little cry escaped her tight throat. She opened her eyes wide as he began to shud-der and she watched him. His body rippled in the throes of ecstasy. He closed his eyes and groaned helplessly as he arched up and gave himself to the pleasure.

Watching him set her own body on fire. She moved involuntarily, lifting, lifting, tightening as she felt the pleasure grow and grow and grow, like a volcano throwing out rocks and flame before it suddenly exploded and sent fiery rain into the sky. She was like the volcano, echoing its explosions, feeling her body burn and flame and consume itself in the endless fires of passion.

She couldn't stop moving, even when the pinnacle was reached and she was falling from the hot peak, down into the warm ashes.

"No," she choked. "No...it's too soon...!"

"Shhhhh," he whispered at her ear. "I won't stop until you ask me to." He brushed her mouth with his and moved back into a slow, deep rhythm that very quickly brought her from one peak to an even higher one.

He lifted his head and looked down at her pretty pink breasts, hard-tipped and thrusting as she lifted to him, her flat belly reaching up to tempt his to lie on it, press it into the soft carpet as the rhythm grew suddenly quick and hard and urgent.

"Now, now, now," she moaned helplessly, shivering as the pleasure began to grow beyond anything she'd experienced before in his arms. "Oh, please, now!"

He pushed down, hard, and felt her ripple around him, a flutter of motion that sent him careening off the edge into space. He cried out, his body contracting as he tried to get even closer.

They shuddered and shuddered together, until the pleasure finally began to seep into manageable levels. He collapsed on her, his body heavy and hard and hot, and she held him while they started to breathe normally again.

"That was incredible," she whispered into his throat.

"I thought we'd already found the limit," he whispered back. "But apparently, we hadn't." He laughed weakly. He lifted his head. "Your rib," he said suddenly.

"It's fine," she assured him. "I wouldn't have felt it if it wasn't fine," she added with a becoming flush. She searched his dark eyes. "You're just awesome."

He grinned. "So are you." He lifted an eyebrow. "I hope you plan to make a habit of meeting me at the door in a see-through pink negligee. Because I have to tell you, I really like it."

She laughed softly. "It was impromptu. I was trying it on and I heard your key in the door. The rest is history."

He kissed her softly. "History indeed."

He started to lift away and she grimaced.

"Sorry," he said, and moved more gently. "We went at it a little too hard."

"No, we didn't," she denied, smiling even through the discomfort.

He led her into the bedroom and tucked them both into bed, leaving the clothes where they'd been strewn.

"We haven't had supper," she protested.

"We had dessert. Supper can wait." He pulled her into his arms and turned out the light. And they slept until morning.

* * *

Christmas Day brought a huge meal, the whole family except for General Machado, and holiday music around the Christmas tree in the living room of Barbara's house. Rick and Gwen had bid on the nearby house and the family selling it accepted. They were signing the papers the following month. It was an exciting time.

Barbara and General Gene Cassaway were getting along from time to time, but with minor and unexpected explosions every few hours. The general was very opinionated, it seemed, and he had very definite ideas on certain methods of cooking. Considering that he'd only started being a chef five years before, and Barbara had been doing it for years, they were bound to clash. And they did. The more they discussed recipes, the louder the arguments became.

Gwen had resigned her federal job, with her father's blessing, and was now working full-time as a detective on Rick's squad at San Antonio P.D.

Her fledgling efforts had resulted in murder charges against Mickey Dunagan, the man arrested but not convicted on assault charges concerning a college coed. He was also the subject of another investigation on a similar cold case, in which charges were pending. He'd been seen at the most recent victim's apartment before her death in San Antonio.

Faced with ironclad evidence of his guilt, a partial fingerprint and conclusive DNA matching fluids found on the victim's body, he'd confessed. A public defender had tried to argue that the Miranda rights hadn't been read, but the prisoner himself had assured his legal counsel that he'd been read them, and that he stood on his confession. He'd started crying. He hadn't meant to hurt any of them, but they were so pretty and he could never even get a girl to go out with him. He'd killed that other girl, too, because she'd made fun of him and laughed.

This girl he'd just killed, she'd been kind. He didn't care if he went to prison, he told Gwen. He didn't want to hurt anybody else.

She'd handed him over to the prosecutor's office with a sad smile. A murderer with a conscience. How unusual. But it didn't bring the dead women back. On the other hand, the cold case squad was feeling a sense of satisfaction. They owed Gwen a nice dinner, they told her, and would deliver any time she asked. She also spoke with the parents of the dead women, and gave them some consolation, in the fact that the killer would be brought to justice and, most likely, without a long and painful trial that would only bring back horrible memories of the tragedies.

The San Antonio patrolman, Sims, who'd gone on stakeout with Rick and Gwen, had been resigned from the force suddenly, with no reason given. Nobody in the department knew what had happened.

Patrolman Ames in Jacobsville was happily back on the job and with no apparent ill effects.

Down in Barrera, there were rumors of an invasion.

It was all over the news. General Cassaway, when asked about the truth of those rumors, just smiled.

Gwen handed Rick a wrapped gift and waited patiently for him to open it.

He looked inside and then back at her with wonder. "How did you know...?"

She grinned and nodded toward Barbara, who laughed.

"Thanks!" he said, pulling out a DVD of an important United States vs. Mexico soccer match that he'd had to miss because of work. "I'll really enjoy it."

"I know you saw the results, but it was a great game," Gwen said.

"Here. Open yours," he said, and handed her a small present.

She pulled it open. It was a jeweler's box. She pulled the lid up and there was a small, beautiful diamond ring.

He pulled it out and slid it onto her finger. "I thought you should have one. It isn't the biggest around, but it's given with my whole heart."

He kissed it. She burst into tears and hugged him close. "I wouldn't care if it was a cigar band," she said.

"I know. That's why I wanted you to have it."

"Sweet man," she murmured.

He sighed. "Happy man," he added, kissing her hair.

She looked up at him with eyes full of love. "You know," she said, glancing toward her mother and General Cassaway, who were looking at recipe books they'd given each other, "I think this is the best Christmas of my life."

"I know it's the best of mine," he replied. "And only the first of many."

"Yes," she said, smiling from ear to ear as she touched his cheek with her fingertips. "The first of many. Merry Christmas."

He kissed her. "Merry Christmas."

The sudden buzz of his cell phone interrupted them. He reached into his pocket with a grimace. It was probably a case and he'd have to go to San Antonio on Christmas Day....

He looked at the number. It was an odd sort of number....

"Hello?" he said.

"Feliz Navidad," a deep voice sang, "Feliz Navidad, Feliz Navidad, something-somethingy felicidad!"

"You forgot the words?" Rick laughed, delighted. "Shame! It's '*Feliz Navidad, próspero año y felicidad,*'" he added smugly.

"Yes, shame, but I am very busy and my mind is on other things. Happy Christmas, my son."

"Happy Christmas to you, Dad," he said, glowing because his father had taken time out of a revolution to wish him well.

"Things are going fine here. Perhaps soon you and your lovely wife will come to visit me, and I will send a plane for you."

"That would be nice," Rick said. He mouthed "Dad" to Gwen, who grinned.

"Meanwhile, be a good boy and Santa Claus will send you something very nice in the near future."

"I didn't get you anything," Rick said with sadness.

There was a deep chuckle. "You did. The hope of grandchildren. That is a gift beyond measure."

"I'll do my best," Rick replied, tongue in cheek.

There was an interruption. "Yes, I will be right there. Sorry. I have to go. Wish me luck."

"You know I do."

"And Happy Christmas, my son."

"Happy Christmas."

He hung up.

"That was a very nice surprise," Rick said.

She smiled. "Yes."

"It's not a simple recipe," the general was growling. "Nobody can make that right! It's a stupid recipe, it curdles every time!"

"It's not stupid, and yes, you can," Barbara growled back.

"I'm telling you, it's impossible! I know, I've tried!"

"Oh, for heaven's sake! Come on in here and I'll show you. It's not hard!"

"That's what you think!"

"Stop growling. It's Christmas."

The general made a face. "All right, damn it."

"Gene!"

He sighed. "Darn it."

"Much better," she said with a grin.

"I won't be reformed by a cook," he informed her. "And just in case you didn't notice, I'm head of the CIA!"

"In this house, you're an apprentice chef. Now stop muttering and come on. This is one of the easiest sauces in the world, and you won't curdle it if you'll just pay attention."

The general was still muttering as he followed Barbara into the kitchen. There was a loud rattle of pots and pans and the opening of the fridge. Voices murmured.

Rick pulled Gwen into his arms and kissed her hungrily. "I love you."

"I love you, too."

"See? I told you! That's curdling!"

"It's not curdling, it's reducing!"

"Damn it, you put the butter in too soon!" the general was raging.

"I did not!"

Rick rolled his eyes. "Do you think you could do something about your father?"

"If you'll do something about your mother," she returned with a grin.

"I'm not raising the heat. That book is wrong!" the general snapped.

Rick looked at Gwen. Gwen looked at Rick. In the kitchen, the voices were growing louder. Without a word, they went to the front door, opened it and ran for their car.

Rick was laughing. "They won't even miss us," he said as he started the vehicle. "And maybe if they're left alone, they'll make peace."

"You think?" she teased.

He drove off to the house they were buying, cut off the engine and stared at it.

"We're going to be very happy here," Gwen said, sighing. "I'll make a garden and your mother can teach me how to can."

"Yes." He pulled her close. "If she and your father don't kill each other," he added.

"They'll have to learn to get along."

"Ha!"

The phone rang. Rick opened it. "Hello?"

"Could you come home for a minute?" Barbara asked.

"Sure. If it's safe," he teased. "What do you need?"

"Well, we could use a little help in the kitchen."

"Making the sauce?"

"Getting hollandaise sauce out of hair. And curtains. And cabinets. And on walls…"

"Mom!" he exclaimed. "What happened?"

"He thought I was making it wrong and I thought he was making it wrong, and, well, we sort of, uh, tossed the pan up."

"Are you okay?"

"Actually, you know, I think he was right. It tastes pretty good with less salt."

"I see."

"He's looking for another frying pan, so could you hurry?" she whispered, and then hung up.

"What's going on?" Gwen asked.

He grinned as he started the car. "War of the Worlds Part I. We get to help clean up the carnage in the kitchen."

"Excuse me?"

"They trashed the hollandaise sauce all over the kitchen."

"At least they're speaking," she pointed out.

He just shook his head. The general and his mother might eventually agree to a truce, but Rick had a feeling that it was going to be a long winter.

He pulled Gwen close and kissed the top of her head. He could manage anything, he thought, as long as he had her.

She sighed and closed her eyes. "Too many cooks spoil the broth?" she wondered aloud.

"I was thinking the same thing," he agreed. "Let's go referee."

"Done!"

They drove home through the colorful streets, with strings of red and blue and yellow and green lights and garlands of holly and fir. In the middle of the town square was a huge Christmas tree full of decorations, under which were wooden painted presents.

"One day," Rick said, "we'll bring our kids here when they light the tree."

She beamed. "Yes," she said, and it was a promise. "One day."

The tree grew smaller and smaller in the rearview mirror as they turned down the long road that led to Barbara's house. It was, Rick thought, truly the best Christmas of his life. He looked down at Gwen, and he saw in her eyes that she was thinking the very same thing.

Two lonely people, who found in each other the answer to a dream.

* * * * *

A Lawman's Christmas:

A McKettricks of Texas Novel

LINDA LAEL MILLER

In memory of Kathy Bannon.
We sure do miss you, Teach.

Chapter 1

Early December, 1914

If the spark-throwing screech of iron-on-iron hadn't wrenched Clay McKettrick out of his uneasy sleep, the train's lurching stop—which nearly pitched him onto the facing seat—would surely have done the trick.

Grumbling, Clay sat up straight and glowered out the window, shoving splayed fingers through his dark hair.

Blue River, Texas. His new home. And more, for as the new marshal, he'd be responsible for protecting the town and its residents.

Not that he could see much of it just then, with all that steam from the smokestack billowing between the train and the depot.

The view didn't particularly matter to him, anyhow,

since he'd paid a brief visit to the town a few months back and seen what there was to see—which hadn't been much, even in the sun-spangled, blue-sky days of summer. Now that winter was coming on—Clay's grand-dad, Angus, claimed it snowed dust and chiggers in that part of Texas—the rutted roads and weathered facades of the ramshackle buildings would no doubt be of bleak appearance.

With an inward sigh, Clay stood to retrieve his black, round-brimmed hat and worn duster from the wooden rack overhead. In the process, he allowed himself to ponder, yet again, all he'd left behind to come to this place at the hind end of beyond and carve out a life of his own making.

He'd left plenty.

A woman, to start with. And then there was his family, the sprawling McKettrick clan, including his ma and pa, Chloe and Jeb, his two older sisters and the thriving Triple M Ranch, with its plentitude of space and water and good grass.

A fragment of a Bible verse strayed across his brain. *The cattle on a thousand hills...*

There were considerably fewer than a thousand hills on the Triple M, big as it was, but the cattle were legion.

To his granddad's way of thinking, those hills and the land they anchored might have been on loan from the

Almighty, but everything else—cows, cousins, mineral deposits and timber included—belonged to Angus Mc-Kettrick, his four sons and his daughter, Katie.

Clay shrugged into the long coat and put on his hat. His holster and pistol were stowed in his trunk in the baggage compartment, and his paint gelding, Outlaw, rode all alone in the car reserved for livestock.

The only other passenger on board, an angular woman with severe features and no noticeable inclination toward small talk, remained seated, with the biggest Bible Clay had ever seen resting open on her lap. She seemed poised to leap right into the pages at the first hint of sin and disappear into all those apocalyptic threats and grand promises. According to the conductor, a fitful little fellow bearing the pitted scars of a long-ago case of small-pox, the lady had come all the way from Cincinnati with the express purpose of saving the heathen.

Clay—bone-tired, homesick for the ranch and for his kinfolks, and wryly amused, all of a piece—nodded a respectful farewell to the woman as he passed her seat, resisting the temptation to stop and inquire about the apparent shortage of heathens in Cincinnati.

Most likely, he decided, reaching the door, she'd already converted the bunch of them, and now she was out to wrestle the devil for the whole state of Texas. He wouldn't have given two cents for old Scratch's chances.

A chill wind, laced with tiny flakes of snow, buffeted Clay as he stepped down onto the small platform, where all three members of the town council, each one stuffed into his Sunday best and half-strangled by a celluloid collar, waited to greet the new marshal.

Mayor Wilson Ponder spoke for the group. "Welcome to Blue River, Mr. McKettrick," the fat man boomed, a blustery old cuss with white muttonchop whiskers and piano-key teeth that seemed to operate independently of his gums.

Clay, still in his late twenties and among the youngest of the McKettrick cousins, wasn't accustomed to being addressed as "mister"—around home, he answered to "hey, you"—and he sort of liked the novelty of it. "Call me Clay," he said.

There were handshakes all around.

The conductor lugged Clay's trunk out of the baggage car and plunked it down on the platform, then busily consulted his pocket watch.

"Better unload that horse of yours," he told Clay, in the officious tone so often adopted by short men who didn't weigh a hundred pounds sopping wet, "if you don't want him going right on to Fort Worth. This train pulls out in five minutes."

Clay nodded, figuring Outlaw would be ready by

now for fresh air and a chance to stretch his legs, since he'd been cooped up in a rolling box ever since Flagstaff.

Taking his leave from the welcoming committee with a touch to the brim of his hat and a promise to meet them later at the marshal's office, he crossed the small platform, descended the rough-hewn steps and walked through cinders and lingering wisps of steam to the open door of the livestock car. He lowered the heavy ramp himself and climbed into the dim, horse-scented enclosure.

Outlaw nickered a greeting, and Clay smiled and patted the horse's long neck before picking up his saddle and other gear and tossing the lot of it to the ground beside the tracks.

That done, he loosed the knot in Outlaw's halter rope and led the animal toward the ramp.

Some horses balked at the unfamiliar, but not Outlaw. He and Clay had been sidekicks for more than a decade, and they trusted each other in all circumstances.

Outside, in the brisk, snow-dappled wind, having traversed the slanted iron plate with no difficulty, Outlaw blinked, adjusting his unusual blue eyes to the light of midafternoon. Clay meant to let the gelding stand untethered while he put the ramp back in place, but before he could turn around, a little girl hurried around the corner of the brick depot and took a competent hold on the lead rope.

She couldn't have been older than seven, and she was small even for that tender age. She wore a threadbare calico dress, a brown bonnet and a coat that, although clean, had seen many a better day. A blond sausage curl tumbled from inside the bonnet to gleam against her forehead, and she smiled with the confidence of a seasoned wrangler.

"My name is Miss Edrina Nolan," she announced importantly. "Are you the new marshal?"

Amused, Clay tugged at his hat brim to acknowledge her properly and replied, "I am. Name's Clay McKettrick."

Edrina put out her free hand. "How do you do, Mr. McKettrick?" she asked.

"I do just fine," he said, with a little smile. Growing up on the Triple M, he and all his cousins had been around horses all their lives, so the child's remarkable ease with a critter many times her size did not surprise him.

It was impressive, though.

"I'll hold your horse," she said. "You'd better help the railroad man with that ramp. He's liable to hurt himself if you don't."

Clay looked back over one shoulder and, sure enough, there was the banty rooster of a conductor, struggling to hoist that heavy slab of rust-speckled iron off the ground so the train could get under way again. He lent his assistance, figuring he'd just spared the man a hernia, if not a heart attack, and got a glare for his trouble, rather than thanks.

Since the fellow's opinion made no real never-mind to Clay either way, he simply turned back to the little girl, ready to reclaim his horse.

She was up on the horse's back, her faded skirts billowing around her, and with the snow-strained sunlight framing her, she looked like one of those cherub-children gracing the pages of calendars, Valentines and boxes of ready-made cookies.

"Whoa, now," he said, automatically taking hold of the lead rope. Given that he hadn't saddled Outlaw yet, he was somewhat mystified as to how she'd managed to mount up the way she had. Maybe she really was a cherub, with little stubby wings hidden under that thin black coat.

Up ahead, the engineer blew the whistle to signal imminent departure, and Outlaw started at the sound, though he didn't buck, thank the good Lord.

"Whoa," Clay repeated, very calmly but with a note of sternness. It was then that he spotted the stump on the other side of the horse and realized that Edrina must have scrambled up on that to reach Outlaw's back.

They all waited—man, horse and cherub—until the train pulled out and the racket subsided somewhat.

Edrina smiled serenely down at him. "Mama says we'll all have to go to the poorhouse, now that you're here," she announced.

"Is that so?" Clay asked mildly, as he reached up, took the child by the waist and lifted her off the horse, setting her gently on her feet. Then he commenced to collecting Outlaw's blanket, saddle and bridle from where they'd landed when he tossed them out of the railroad car, and tacking up. Out of the corner of his eye, he saw the town-council contingent straggling off the platform.

Edrina nodded in reply to his rhetorical question, still smiling, and the curl resting on her forehead bobbed with the motion of her head. "My papa was the marshal a while back," she informed Clay matter-of-factly, "but then he died in the arms of a misguided woman in a room above the Bitter Gulch Saloon and left us high and dry."

Clay blinked, wondering if he'd mistaken Edrina Nolan for a child when she was actually a lot older. Say, forty.

"I see," he said, after clearing his throat. "That's unfortunate. That your papa passed on, I mean." Clay had known the details of his predecessor's death, having been regaled with the story the first time he set foot in Blue River, but it took him aback that Edrina knew it, too.

She folded her arms and watched critically as he threw on Outlaw's beat-up saddle and put the cinch through the buckle. "Can you shoot a gun and everything?" she wanted to know.

Clay spared her a sidelong glance and a nod. Why wasn't this child in school? Did her mother know she was running loose like a wild Indian and leaping onto the backs of other people's horses when they weren't looking?

And where the heck had a kid her age learned to ride like that?

"Good," Edrina said, with a relieved sigh, her little arms still folded. "Because Papa couldn't be trusted with a firearm. Once, when he was cleaning a pistol, meaning to go out and hunt rabbits for stew, it went off by accident and made a big hole in the floor. Mama put a chair over it—she said it was so my sister, Harriet, and I wouldn't fall in and wind up under the house, with all the cobwebs and the mice, but I know it was really because she was embarrassed for anybody to see what Papa had done. Even Harriet has more sense than to fall in a hole, for heaven's sake, and she's only five."

Clay suppressed a smile, tugged at the saddle to make sure it would hold his weight, put a foot into the stirrup

and swung up. Adjusted his hat in a gesture of farewell.
"I'll be seeing you, chatterbox," he said kindly.

"What about your trunk?" Edrina wanted to know.
"Are you just going to leave it behind, on the platform?"

"I mean to come back for it later in the day," Clay explained, wondering why he felt compelled to clarify the
matter at all. "This horse and I, we've been on that train
for a goodly while, and right now, we need to stretch
our muscles a bit."

"I could show you where our house is," Edrina persisted, scampering along beside Outlaw when Clay urged
the horse into a walk. "Well, I guess it's *your* house now."

"Maybe you ought to run along home," Clay said.
"Your mama's probably worried about you."

"No," Edrina said. "Mama has no call to worry. She
thinks I'm in school."

Clay bit back another grin.

They'd climbed the grassy embankment leading to the
street curving past the depot and on into Blue River by
then. The members of the town's governing body wad-
dled just ahead, single file, along a plank sidewalk like
a trio of black ducks wearing top hats.

"And why *aren't* you in school?" Clay inquired affably, adjusting his hat again, and squaring his shoulders
against the nippy breeze and the swirling specks of snow,
each one sharp-edged as a razor.

She shivered slightly, but that was the only sign that she'd paid any notice at all to the state of the weather. While Miss Edrina Nolan pondered her reply, Clay maneuvered the horse to her other side, hoping to block the bitter wind at least a little.

"I already know everything they have to teach at that school," Edrina said at last, in a tone of unshakable conviction. "And then some."

Clay chuckled under his breath, though he refrained from comment. It wasn't as if anybody were asking his opinion.

The first ragtag shreds of Blue River were no more impressive than he recalled them to be—a livery on one side of the road, and an abandoned saloon on the other. Waist-high grass, most of it dead, surrounded the latter; craggy shards of filthy glass edged its one narrow window, and the sign above the door dangled by a lone, rusty nail.

Last Hope: Saloon and Games of Chance, it read in painted letters nearly worn away by time and weather.

"You shouldn't be out in this weather," Clay told Edrina, who was still hiking along beside him and Outlaw, eschewing the broken plank sidewalk for the road. "Too cold."

"I like it," she said. "The cold is very bracing, don't you think? Makes a body feel wide-awake."

The town's buildings, though unpainted, began to look a little better as they progressed. Smoke curled from twisted chimneys and doors were closed up tight.

There were few people on the streets, Clay noticed, though he glimpsed curious faces at various windows as they went by.

He raised his collar against the rising wind, figuring he'd had all the "bracing" he needed, thank you very much, and he was sure enough "wide-awake" now that he was off the train and back in the saddle.

He was hungry, too, and he wanted a bath and barbering.

And ten to twelve hours of sleep, lying prone instead of sitting upright in a hard seat.

"I reckon maybe you ought to show me where you live, after all," he said, at some length. At least that way, he could steer the child homeward, where she belonged, make sure she got there, and rest easy thereafter, where her welfare was concerned.

Edrina pointed past a general store, a telegraph and telephone office, the humble jailhouse where he would soon be officiating and a tiny white church surrounded by a rickety picket fence, much in need of whitewash. "It's one street over," she said, already veering off a little, as though she meant to duck between buildings and take off. "Our place, that is. It's the one with an apple tree in the yard and a chicken house out back."

Clay drew up his horse with a nearly imperceptible tug of the reins. "Hold it right there," he said, with quiet authority, when Edrina started to turn away.

She froze. Turned slowly to look at him with huge china-blue eyes. "You're going to tell Mama I haven't been at school, aren't you?" she asked, sounding sadly resigned to whatever fate awaited her.

"I reckon it's *your* place to tell her that, not mine."

Edrina blinked, and a series of emotions flashed across her face—confusion, hope and, finally, despair. "She'll be sorely vexed when she finds out," the girl said. "Mama places great store in learning."

"Most sensible people do," Clay observed, biting the inside of his lower lip so he wouldn't laugh out loud. Edrina might have been little more than a baby, but she sat a horse like a Comanche brave—he'd seen that for himself back at the depot—and carried herself with a dignity out of all proportion to her size, situation and hand-me-down clothes. "Maybe from now on, you ought to pay better heed to what your mama says. She has your best interests at heart, you know."

Edrina gave a great, theatrical sigh, one that seemed to involve her entire small personage. "I suppose Miss

Krenshaw will tell Mama I've been absent since recess, anyway," she said. "Even if *you* don't."

Miss Krenshaw, Clay figured, was probably the schoolmarm.

Outlaw's well-shod hooves made a lonely, *clompety-clip* kind of sound on the hard dirt of the road. The horse turned a little, to go around a trough with a lacy green scum floating atop the water.

"Word's sure to get out," Clay agreed reasonably, thinking of all those faces, at all those windows, "one way or another."

"Thunderation and spit!" Edrina exclaimed, with the vigor of total sincerity. "I don't know why folks can't just tend to their own affairs and leave me to do as I please."

Clay made a choking sound, disguised it as a cough, as best he could, anyway. "How old are you?" he asked, genuinely interested in the answer.

"Six," Edrina replied.

He'd have bet she was a short ten, maybe even eleven. "So you're in the first grade at school?"

"I'm in the second," Edrina said, trudging along beside his horse. "I already knew how to read when I started in September, and I can cipher, too, so Miss Krenshaw let me skip a grade. Actually, she suggested I enter *third* grade, but Mama said no, that wouldn't do at all, because I needed time to be a child. As if I could *help* being a child."

She sounded wholly exasperated.

Clay hid yet another grin by tilting his head, in hopes that his hat brim would cast a shadow over his face. "You'll be all grown up sooner than you think," he allowed. "I reckon if asked, I'd be inclined to take your mama's part in the matter."

"You weren't asked, though," Edrina pointed out thoughtfully, and with an utter lack of guile or rancor.

"True enough," Clay agreed moderately.

They were quiet, passing by the little white church, then the adjoining graveyard, where, Clay speculated, the last marshal, Parnell Nolan, must be buried. Edrina hurried ahead when they reached the corner, and Clay and Outlaw followed at an easy pace.

Clay hadn't bothered to visit the house that came with the marshal's job on his previous stopover in Blue River. At the time, he'd just signed the deed for two thousand acres of raw ranch land, and his thoughts had been on the house and barn he meant to build there, the cattle and horses he would buy, the wells he would dig and the fences he would put up. He could have waited, of course, bided on the Triple M until spring, living the life he'd always lived, but he'd been too impatient and too proud to do that.

Besides, it was his nature to be restless, and so, in order to keep himself occupied until spring, he'd accepted the town's offer of a laughable salary and a star-shaped badge to pin on his coat until they could rustle up some damn fool to take up the occupation for good.

"There it is," Edrina said, with a note of sadness in her voice that caught and pulled at Clay's heart like a fish-hook snagging on something underwater.

Clay barely had time to take in the ramshackle place—the council referred to it as a "cottage," though he would have called it a shack—before one of the prettiest women he'd ever laid eyes on shot out through the front door like a bullet and stormed down the path toward them.

Chickens scattered, clucking and squawking, as she passed.

Her hair was the color of pale cider, pinned up in back and fluffing out around her flushed face, as was the fashion among his sisters and female cousins back home in Arizona. Her eyes might have been blue, but they might have been green, too, and right now, they were shooting fire hot enough to brand the toughest hide.

Reaching the rusty-hinged gate in the falling-down fence, she stopped suddenly, fixed those changeable eyes on him and glared.

Clay felt a jolt inside, as though Zeus had flung a light-ning bolt his way and he'd caught it with both hands instead of sidestepping it, like a wiser man would have done.

The woman's gaze sliced to the little girl.

"Edrina Louise Nolan," she said, through a fine set of straight white teeth, "what am I going to do with you?" Her skin was good, too, Clay observed, with that part of his brain that usually stood back and assessed things. Smooth, with a peachy glow underneath.

"Let me go to third grade?" Edrina ventured bravely.

Clay gave an appreciative chuckle, quickly quelled by a glare from the lady. He didn't wither easily, though he knew that was the result she'd intended, and he did take some pleasure in thwarting her.

At that, the woman gave a huffy little sigh and turned her attention back to her daughter. She threw out one arm—like Edrina, she wore calico—and pointed toward the gaping door of the shack. "That will be quite enough of your nonsense, young lady," she said, with a reassuring combination of affection and anger, thrusting open the creaky gate. "Get yourself into the house *now* and prepare to contemplate the error of your ways!"

Before obeying her mother's command, Edrina paused just long enough to look up at Clay, who was still in the saddle, as though hoping he'd intercede.

That was a thing he had no right to do, of course, but he felt a pang on the little girl's behalf just the same.

And against his own better judgment he dismounted, took off his hat, holding it in one hand and shoving the other through his hair, fingers splayed.

"You go on and do what your mama tells you," he said to Edrina, though his words had the tone of a suggestion, rather than a command.

Edrina's very fetching mother looked him over again, this time with something that might have been chagrin. Then she bristled again, like a little bird ruffling up faded feathers. "You're *him,* aren't you?" she accused. "The new marshal?"

"Yes, ma'am," Clay said, confounded by the strange mixture of terror and jubilation rising up within him. "I am the new marshal. And you are…?"

"Dara Rose Nolan. You may address me as *Mrs.* Nolan, if you have any further *reason* to address me, which I do not anticipate."

With that, she turned on one shabby-heeled shoe and pointed herself toward the "cottage," with its sagging roof, leaking rain barrel and sparkling-clean windows.

Edrina and another little girl—the aforementioned Harriet, no doubt—darted out of the doorway as their mother approached, vanishing into the interior of the house.

Clay watched appreciatively as the widow Nolan retreated hurriedly up the walk, with nary a backward glance.

Chickens, pecking peacefully at the ground, squawked and flapped their wings as they fled.

The door slammed behind her.

Clay smiled, resettled his hat and got back on his horse.

Before, he'd dreaded the long and probably idle months ahead, expecting the season to be a lonesome one, and boring, to boot, since he knew nothing much ever happened in Blue River, when it came to crime. That was the main reason the town fathers hadn't been in any big rush to replace Parnell Nolan.

Now, reining Outlaw away toward the edge of town, and the open country beyond, meaning to ride up onto a ridge he knew of, where the view extended for miles in every direction, Clay figured the coming winter might not be so dull, after all.

INSIDE THE HOUSE, Dara Rose drew a deep breath and sighed it out hard.

Heaven knew, she hadn't been looking forward to the new marshal's arrival, given the problems that were sure to result, but she hadn't planned on losing her composure and behaving rudely, either. Poor as she was, Dara Rose still had high standards, and she believed in setting a good example for her children, prided herself on her good manners and even temperament.

Imagining how she must have looked to Clay Mc-Kettrick, rushing out of the house, scaring the chickens half to death in the process, she closed her eyes for a moment, then sighed again.

Edrina and Harriet watched her from the big rocking chair over by the wood-burning stove, Edrina wisely holding her tongue, Harriet perched close beside her, her rag doll, Molly, resting in the curve of one small arm.

The regulator clock ticked ponderously on the wall, lending a solemn rhythm to the silence, and snow swirled past the windows, as if trying to find a way in.

Dara Rose shivered.

"What are we going to do, Mama?" Edrina asked reasonably, and at some length. She was a good child, normally, helpful and even tempered, but her restlessness and curiosity often led her straight into mischief.

Dara Rose looked up at the oval-framed image of her late husband, Parnell Nolan, and her throat thickened as fresh despair swept over her. Despite the scandalous way he died, she missed him, missed the steadiness of his presence, missed his quiet ways and his wit.

"I don't rightly know," Dara Rose admitted, after swallowing hard and blinking back the scalding tears that were always so close to the surface these days. "But never you mind—I'll think of something."

Edrina slipped a reassuring arm around Harriet, who was sucking her thumb.

Dara Rose didn't comment on the thumb-sucking, though it was worrisome to her. Harriet had left that habit behind when she was three, but after Parnell's death, nearly a year ago now, she'd taken it up again. It wasn't hard to figure out why—the poor little thing was frightened and confused.

So was Dara Rose, for that matter, though of course she didn't let on. With heavy-handed generosity, Mayor Ponder and the town council had allowed her and the children to remain in the cottage on the stipulation that they'd have to vacate when a marshal was hired to take Parnell's place.

"Don't worry," Edrina told her sister, tightening her little arm around the child, just briefly. "Mama *always* thinks of something."

It was true that Dara Rose had managed to put food on the table by raising vegetables in her garden patch, taking in sewing and the occasional bundle of laundry and sometimes sweeping floors in the shops and businesses along Main Street. As industrious as she was, however, the pickings were already slim; without the house, the situation would go from worrisome to destitute.

Oh, she had choices—there were always choices, weren't there?—but they were wretched ones.

She could become a lady of the evening over at the Bitter Gulch Saloon and maybe—*maybe*—earn enough to board her children somewhere nearby, where she could see them now and then. How long would it be before they realized how she was earning their living and came to despise her? A year, two years? Three?

Her second option was only slightly more palatable; Ezra Maddox had offered her a job as his cook and housekeeper, on his remote ranch, but he'd plainly stipulated that she couldn't bring her little girls along. In fact, he'd come right out and said she ought to just put Edrina and Harriet in an orphan's home or farm them out to work for their keep. It would be good for their character, he'd claimed.

In fact, the last time he'd come to call, the previous Sunday after church, he'd stood in this very room, beaming at his own generosity, and announced that if Dara Rose measured up, he might even marry her.

The mere thought made her shudder.

And the *audacity* of the man. He expected her to turn her daughters over to strangers and spend the rest of her days darning his socks and cooking his food, and in return, he offered room, board and a pittance in wages. If she "measured up," as he put it, she'd be required to share his bed and give up the salary he'd been paying her, too.

Dara Rose's final prospect was to take her paltry savings—she kept them in a fruit jar, hidden behind the cookstove in the tiny kitchen—purchase train tickets for herself and her children and travel to San Antonio or Dallas or Houston, where she might find honest work and decent lodgings.

But suppose she *didn't* find work? Times were hard. The little bit of money she had would soon be eaten up by living expenses, and *then* what?

Dara Rose knew she'd be paralyzed by these various scenarios if she didn't put them out of her head and get busy doing something constructive, so she headed for the kitchen, meaning to start supper.

Last fall, someone had given her the hindquarter of a deer, and she'd cut the meat into strips and carefully preserved it in jars. There were green beans and corn and stubby orange carrots from the garden, too, along with apples and pears from the fruit trees growing behind the church, and berries she and the girls had gathered during the summer and brought home in lard tins and baskets. Thanks to the chickens, there were plenty of eggs, some of which she sold, and some she traded over at the mercantile for small amounts of sugar and flour

and other staples. Once in a great while, she bought tea,
but that was a luxury.

She straightened her spine when she realized Edrina
had followed her into the little lean-to of a kitchen.

"I like Mr. McKettrick," the child said conversation-
ally. "Don't you?"

Keeping her back to the child, Dara Rose donned
her apron and tied it in back with brisk motions of her
hands. "My opinion of the new marshal is neither here
nor there," she replied. "And don't think for one moment, Edrina Louise Nolan, that I've forgotten that you
ran away from school again. You are in serious trouble."

Edrina gave a philosophical little sigh. "How serious?"
she wanted to know.

"*Very* serious," Dara Rose answered, adding wood to
the fire in the cookstove and jabbing at it with a poker.

"I think we're *all* in serious trouble," Edrina observed
sagely.

Out of the mouths of babes, Dara Rose thought.

"Do we have to be orphans now, Mama?" Harriet
asked. As usual, she'd followed Edrina.

Dara Rose put the poker back in its stand beside the
stove and turned to look at her daughters. Harriet clung
to her big sister's hand, looking up at her mother with
enormous, worried eyes.

"We are a family," she said, kneeling and wrapping

an arm around each of them, pulling them close, drawing in the sweet scent of their hair and skin, "and we are going to stay together. I promise."

Now to find a way to *keep* that promise.

Chapter 2

⟨⟩⧫⟨⟩

The snow was coming down harder and faster when Clay returned to Blue River from the high ridge, where he'd breathed in the sight of his land, the wide expanse of it and the sheer potential, Outlaw strong and steady beneath him.

Dusk was fast approaching now, and lamps glowed in some of the windows on Main Street, along with the occasional stark dazzle of a lightbulb. Clay had yet to decide whether or not he'd have his place wired for electricity when the time came; like the telephone, it was still a newfangled invention as far as he was concerned, and he wasn't entirely sure it would last.

At the livery stable, Clay made arrangements for Outlaw and then headed in the direction of the Bitter Gulch Saloon, where he figured the mayor and the town council were most likely to be waiting for him.

Most of the businesses were sealed up tight against the weather, but the saloon's swinging doors were all that stood between the crowded interior and the sidewalk. A piano tinkled a merry if discordant tune somewhere in all that roiling blue cigar smoke, and bottles rattled against the rims of glasses.

The floor was covered in sawdust; the bar was long and ornately carved with various bare-breasted women pouring water into urns decorated with all sorts of flowers and mythical animals and assorted other decorations.

Clay removed his hat, thumped the underside of the brim with one forefinger to knock off the light coating of snow and caught a glimpse of his own reflection in the chipped and murky glass of the mirror in back of the bar.

He didn't commonly frequent saloons, not being much of a drinker, but he knew he'd be dropping in at the Bitter Gulch on a regular basis, once he'd been sworn in as marshal and taken up his duties. Douse the seeds of trouble with enough whiskey and they were bound to take root, break ground and sprout foliage faster than the green beans his ma liked to plant in her garden every spring.

One glance told him he'd been right to look for Mayor Ponder and his cronies here—they'd gathered around a table over in the corner, near the potbellied stove, each with his own glass and his own bottle.

Inwardly, Clay sighed, but he managed a smile as he approached the table, snow melting on the shoulders of his duster.

"Good to see you, Clay," Mayor Ponder said cordially, as one of the others in the party dragged a chair over from a nearby table. "Sent a boy to fetch your trunk from the depot," the older man went on, as Clay joined them, taking the offered seat without removing his coat. He didn't plan on staying long. "You didn't say where you wanted your gear sent, so I told Billy to haul it over to the jailhouse for the time being."

"Thanks," Clay said mildly, setting his hat on the table. At home, the McKettrick women enforced their own private ordinance against such liberties, on the grounds that it was not only unmannerly, but bad luck and a mite on the slovenly side, too.

"Have a drink with us?" Ponder asked, studying Clay thoughtfully through the shifting haze of smoke. The smell of unwashed bodies and poor dental hygiene was so thick it was nearly visible, and he felt a strong and sudden yearning to be outside again, in the fresh air.

Clay shook his head. "Not now," he said. "It's been a long day, and I'm ready for a meal, a hot bath and a bed."

Ponder cleared his throat. "Speaking of, well, beds, I'm afraid the house we offered you is still occupied. We've been telling Dara Rose that she'd have to move when we found a replacement for Parnell, but so far, she's stayed put."

Dara Rose. Clay smiled slightly at the reminder of the fiery little woman who'd burst through the door of that shack a couple of hours before when he showed up with Edrina, stormed through a flock of cacophonous chickens and let him know, in no uncertain terms, that she wasn't at all glad to see him.

There had been no shortage of women in Clay Mc-Kettrick's life—he'd even fallen in love with one, to his eventual sorrow—but none of them had affected him quite the way the widow Nolan did.

"No hurry," Clay said easily, resting his hands on his thighs. "I can get a room at the hotel, or bunk in at the jailhouse."

"The town of Blue River cannot stand good for the cost of lodgings," Ponder said, looking worried. "Having that power line strung all the way out here from Austin depleted our treasury."

One of the other men huffed at that, and poured himself another shot of whiskey. "Hell," he said, with a hiccup, "we're flat busted and up to our hind ends in debt."

Ponder flushed, and his big whiskers quivered along with those heavy jowls of his. "We *can* pay the agreed-upon salary," he stated, after glaring over at his colleague for a long moment. "Seventy-five dollars a month and living quarters, as agreed." He paused, flushed. "I'll speak to Mrs. Nolan in the morning," he clarified. "Tell her she needs to make other arrangements immediately."

"Don't do that," Clay said, quietly but quickly, too. He took a breath, slowed himself down on the inside. "I don't mind paying for a hotel room or sleeping at the jail, for the time being."

The little group exchanged looks.

Snow spun at the few high windows the Bitter Gulch Saloon boasted, like millions of tiny ghosts in search of someplace to haunt.

"A deal," Ponder finally blustered, "is a deal. We offered you a place to live as part of your salary, and we intend to keep our word."

Clay rubbed his chin thoughtfully. His beard was coming in again, even though he'd shaved that morning, on board the train. Nearly cut his own throat in the process, as it happened, because of the way the car jostled along the tracks. "Where are Mrs. Nolan and her little girls likely to wind up?" he asked, hoping he didn't sound too concerned. "Once they've moved out of that house, I mean."

"Ezra Maddox offered for her," said another member of the council. "He's a hard man, old Ezra, but he's got a farm and a herd of dairy cows and money in the bank, and she could do a lot worse when it comes to husbands."

Clay felt a strange stab at the news, deep inside, but he was careful not to let his reaction show. He felt *something* for Dara Rose Nolan, but what that something was exactly was a matter that would require some sorting out.

"Ezra ain't willing to take the girls along with their mama, though," imparted the first man, pouring himself yet another dose of whiskey and throwing it back without so much as a shudder or a wince. The stuff might have been creek water, for all the effect it seemed to have going down the fellow's gullet. "And he didn't actually offer to marry up with Dara Rose right there at the beginning, either. He means to try her out as a housekeeper before he makes her his wife. Ezra likes to know what he's getting."

Someplace in the middle of Clay's chest, one emotion broke away from the tangle and filled all the space he occupied.

It was pure anger, cold and urgent and prickly around the edges.

What kind of man expects a woman to part with her own children? he wondered, silently furious. His neck turned hot, and he had to release his jaw muscles by force of will.

"Dara Rose is a bit shy on choices at the moment, if you ask me," Ponder put in, taking a defensive tone suggesting he was a friend of Ezra Maddox's and meant to take the man's part if a controversy arose. With a wave of one hand, he indicated their surroundings, including the half dozen saloon girls, waiting tables in their moth-eaten finery. "If she turns Ezra down, she'll wind up right here." He paused to indulge in a slight smile, and Clay underwent another internal struggle just to keep from backhanding the mayor of Blue Creek hard enough to send him sprawling in the dirty sawdust. "Can't say as I'd mind that, really."

Clay seethed, but his expression was schooled to quiet amusement. He'd grown up playing poker with his granddad, his pa and uncles, his many rambunctious cousins, male and female. He knew how to keep his emotions to himself.

Mostly.

"And you a married man," scolded one of the other council members, but his tone was indulgent. "For shame."

Clay pushed his chair back, slowly, and stood. Stretched before retrieving his hat from its place on the table. "I will leave you gentlemen to your discussion," he said, with a slight but ironic emphasis on the word *gentlemen*.

"But we meant to swear you in," Ponder protested. "Make it official."

"Morning will be here soon enough," Clay said, putting his hat on. "I'll meet you at the jailhouse at eight o'clock. Bring a badge and a Bible."

Ponder did not look pleased; he was used to piping the tune, it was obvious, and most folks probably danced to it.

Most folks weren't McKettricks, though.

Clay smiled an idle smile, tugged at the brim of his hat in a gesture of farewell and turned to leave the saloon. Just beyond the swinging doors, he paused on the sidewalk to draw in some fresh air and look up at the sky.

It was snow-shrouded and dark, that sky, and Clay wished for a glimpse, however brief, of the stars.

He'd come to Blue River to start a ranch of his own, marry some good woman and raise a bunch of kids with her, build a legacy comparable to the one his granddad had established on the Triple M. Figuring he'd never love anybody but Annabel Carson, who had made up her mind to wed his cousin Sawyer, come hell or high water, he hadn't been especially stringent with his requirements for a bride.

He wanted a wife and a partner, somebody loyal who'd stand shoulder to shoulder with him in good times and bad. She had to be smart and have a sense of humor—ranching was too hard a life for folks lacking in those characteristics, in his opinion—but she didn't necessarily have to be pretty.

Annabel was mighty easy on the eyes, after all, and look where *that* got him. Up shit creek without a paddle, that was where. She'd claimed to love Clay with her whole heart, but at the first disagreement, she'd thrown his promise ring in his face and gone chasing after Sawyer.

Even now, all these months later, the recollection carried a powerful sting, racing through Clay's veins like snake venom.

Crossing the street to the town's only hotel, its electric lights glowing a dull gold at the downstairs windows, Clay rode out the sensation, the way he'd trained himself to do, but a remarkable thing happened at the point when Annabel's face usually loomed up in his mind's eye.

He saw Dara Rose Nolan there instead.

BY THE TIME DARA ROSE got up the next morning, washed and dressed and built up the fires, then headed out to feed and water the chickens and gather the eggs, the snow had stopped, the ground was bare and the sky was a soft blue.

She hadn't slept well, but the crisp bite of approaching winter cleared some of the cobwebs from her beleaguered brain, and she smiled as she worked. Her situation was as dire as ever, of course, but daylight invariably raised her hopes and quieted her fears.

When the sun was up, she could believe things would work out in the long run if she did her best and maintained her faith.

She *would* find a way to earn an honest living and keep her family together. She had to believe that to keep putting one foot in front of the other.

This very day, as soon as the children had had their breakfast and Edrina had gone off to school, Dara Rose decided, flinging out ground corn for the chickens, now clucking and flapping around her skirts and pecking at the ground, she and her youngest daughter would set out to knock on every respectable door in town if they had to.

Someone in Blue River surely needed a cook, a housekeeper, a nurse or some combination thereof. She'd work for room and board, for herself and the girls, and they wouldn't take up much space, the three of them. What little cash they needed, she could earn by taking in sewing.

The idea wasn't new, and it wasn't likely to come to fruition, either, given that most people in town were only a little better off than she was and therefore not in the market for household help, but it heartened Dara Rose a little, just the same, as she finished feeding the chickens, dusted her hands together and went to retrieve the egg basket, hanging by its handle from a nail near the back door.

Holding her skirts up with one hand, Dara Rose ducked into the tumbledown chicken coop and began gathering eggs from the straw where the hens roosted.

That morning, there were more than a dozen—fifteen, by her count—which meant she and Edrina and Harriet could each have one for breakfast. The remainder could be traded at the mercantile for salt—she was running a little low on that—and perhaps some lard and a small scoop of white sugar.

Thinking these thoughts, Dara Rose was humming under her breath as she left the chicken coop, carrying the egg basket.

She nearly dropped the whole bunch of them right to the ground when she caught sight of the new marshal, riding his fancy spotted horse, reining in just the other side of the fence, a shiny nickel star gleaming on his worn coat.

It made him look like a gunslinger, that long coat, and the round-brimmed hat only added to the rakish impression.

Already bristling, Dara Rose drew a deep breath and rustled up a smile. It wasn't as if the man existed merely to irritate and inconvenience *her,* after all.

The marshal, swinging down out of the saddle and

approaching the rickety side gate to stroll, bold as any-thing, into her yard, did not smile back.

Dara Rose's high hopes shriveled instantly as the ob-vious finally struck her: Clay McKettrick had come to send her and the children packing. He'd want to move himself—and possibly a family—in, and soon. The fact that he had a fair claim to the house did nothing what-soever to make her feel better.

"Mornin'," he said, standing directly in front of her now, and pulling politely at the brim of his hat before taking it off.

"Good morning," Dara Rose replied cautiously, still mindful of her rudeness the day before and the regret it had caused her. Her gaze moved to the polished star pinned to his coat, and she felt an achy twinge of loss, remembering Parnell.

Poor, well-meaning, chivalrous Parnell.

Greetings exchanged, both of them just stood there looking at each other, for what seemed like a long time.

Finally, Marshal McKettrick cleared his throat, hold-ing his hat in both hands now, and the wintry sun caught in his dark hair. He looked as clean as could be, stand-ing there, his clothes fresh, except for the coat, and his boots brushed to a shine.

Dara Rose felt a small, peculiar shift in a place be-hind her heart.

"I just wanted to say," the man began awkwardly, in-clining his head toward the house, "that there's no need for you and the kids to clear out right away. I spent last night at the hotel, but there's a cot and a stove at the jail-house, and that will suit me fine for now."

Dara Rose's throat tightened, and the backs of her eyes burned. She didn't quite dare to believe her own ears. "But you're entitled to live here," she reminded him, and then could have nipped off her tongue. "And surely your wife wouldn't want to set up housekeeping in a—"

In that instant, the awkwardness was gone. The mar-shal's mouth slanted in a grin, and mischief sparkled in his eyes. They were the color of new denim, those eyes.

"I don't have a wife," he said simply. "Not yet, any-how."

That grin. It did something unnerving to Dara Rose's insides.

Her heartbeat quickened inexplicably, nearly racing, then fairly lurched to a stop. Did Clay McKettrick expect something in return for his kindness? If he was looking for favors, he was going to be disappointed, because she wasn't that kind of woman.

Not anymore.

"It's almost Christmas," Clay said, assessing the sky briefly before meeting her gaze again.

Confused, Dara Rose squinted up at him. Christmas

was important to Edrina and Harriet, as it was to most children, but it was the least of her own concerns.

"Do you need spectacles?" Clay asked.

Taken aback by the question, Dara Rose opened her mouth to speak, found herself at a complete loss for words and pressed her lips together. Then she shook her head.

Clay McKettrick chuckled and reached for the egg basket.

It wasn't heavy, and the contents were precious, but Dara Rose offered no resistance. She let him take it.

"Where did Edrina learn to ride a horse?" he asked.

They were moving now, heading slowly toward the house, as though it were the least bit proper for the two of them to be behind closed doors together.

Dara Rose blinked, feeling as muddled as if he'd spoken to her in a foreign language instead of plain English. "I beg your pardon?"

They stepped into the small kitchen, with its slanted wall and iron cookstove, Dara Rose in the lead, and the marshal set the basket of eggs on the table, which was comprised of two barrels with a board nailed across their tops.

"Edrina was there to meet Outlaw and me when we got off the train yesterday," Clay explained quietly, keeping his distance and folding his arms loosely across his chest. "The child has a way with horses."

Dara Rose heard the girls stirring in the tiny room the three of them shared, just off the kitchen, and such a rush of love for her babies came over her that she almost teared up. "Yes," she said. "Parnell—my husband—kept a strawberry roan named Gawain. Edrina's been quite at home in the saddle since she was a tiny thing."

"What happened to him?" Clay asked.

"Parnell?" Dara Rose asked stupidly, feeling her cheeks go crimson.

"I know what happened to your husband, ma'am," Clay said quietly. "I was asking about the horse."

Dara Rose felt dazed, but she straightened her spine and looked Clay McKettrick in the eye. "We had to sell Gawain after my husband died," she said. It was the simple truth, and almost as much of a sore spot as Parnell's death. They'd all loved the gelding, but Ezra Maddox had offered a good price for him, and Dara Rose had needed the money for food and firewood and kerosene for the lamps.

Edrina, already mourning the man she'd believed to be her father, had cried for days.

"I see," Clay said gravely, a bright smile breaking over his handsome face like a sunrise as Edrina and Harriet hopped into the room and hurried to stand by the stove, wearing their calico dresses but no shoes or stockings.

"Do we have to go live in the poorhouse now?" Harriet asked, groping for Edrina's hand, finding it and evidently forgetting that the floor was cold enough to sting her bare feet. In the dead of winter, the planks sometimes frosted over.

To Dara Rose's surprise, Clay crouched, putting himself nearly at eye level with both children. He kept his balance easily, still holding his hat, and when his coat opened a ways, she caught an ominous glimpse of the gun belt buckled around his lean hips.

"You don't have to go anywhere," he said, very solemnly.

Edrina's eyes widened. Her unbrushed curls rioted around her face, like gold in motion, and her bow-shaped lips formed a smile. "Really and truly?" she asked. "We can stay here?"

Clay nodded.

"But where will *you* live?" Harriet wanted to know. Like her sister, she was astute and well-spoken. Dara Rose had never used baby talk with her girls, and she'd been reading aloud to them since before they were born.

"I'll be fine over at the jailhouse, at least until spring," Clay replied, rising once again to his full height. He was tall, this man from Arizona, broad through the shoulders and thick in the chest, but the impression he gave was of leanness and agility. He was probably fast with that pistol he carried, Dara Rose thought, and was disturbed by the knowledge.

It was the twentieth century, after all, and the West was no longer wild. Hardly anyone, save sheriffs and marshals, carried a firearm.

"I'm going to school today," Edrina announced happily, "and I plan on staying until Miss Krenshaw rings the bell at three o'clock, too."

Clay crooked a smile, but his gaze, Dara Rose discovered, had found its way back to her. "That's good," he said.

"Why don't you stay for breakfast?" Edrina asked the man wearing her father's badge pinned to his coat.

"Edrina," Dara Rose almost whispered, embarrassed.

"I've already eaten," Clay replied. "Had the ham and egg special in the hotel dining room before Mayor Ponder swore me in."

"Oh," Edrina said, clearly disappointed.

"That's a fine horse, mister," Harriet chimed in, her head tipped way back so she could look up into Clay's recently shaven face.

Dara Rose was still trying to bring the newest blush in her cheeks under control, and she could only manage that by avoiding Clay McKettrick's eyes.

"Yes, indeed," Clay answered the child. "His name's

Outlaw, but you can't go by that. He's a good old cay-use."

"I got to ride him yesterday, down by the railroad tracks," Edrina boasted. Then her face fell a little. "Sort of."

"If it's all right with your mother," Clay offered, "and you go to school like you ought to, you can ride Out-law again."

"Me, too?" Harriet asked, breathless with excitement at the prospect.

Clay caught Dara Rose's gaze again. "That's your mother's decision to make, not mine," he said, so at home in his own skin that she wondered what kind of life he'd led, before his arrival in Blue River. An easy one, most likely.

But something in his eyes refuted that.

"We'll see," Dara Rose said.

Both girls groaned, wanting a "yes" instead of a "maybe."

"I'd best be getting on with my day," Clay said, with another slow, crooked grin.

And then he was at the door, ducking his head so he wouldn't bump it, putting on his hat and walking away.

Dara Rose watched through the little window over the sink until he'd gone through the side gate and mounted his horse.

50

LINDA LAEL MILLER

"We don't have to go to the orphanage!" Harriet crowed, clapping her plump little hands in celebration.

"There will be no more talk of orphanages," Dara Rose decreed briskly, pumping water at the rusty sink to wash her hands.

"Does Mr. McKettrick have a wife?" Edrina piped up. "Because if he doesn't, you could marry him. I don't think he'd send Harriet and me away, like Mr. Maddox wants to do."

Dara Rose kept her back to her daughters as she began breakfast preparations, using all her considerable will-power to keep her voice calm and even. "That's none of your business," she said firmly. "Nor mine, either. And don't you *dare* pry into Mr. McKettrick's private affairs by asking, either one of you."

Both girls sighed at this.

"Go get your shoes and stockings on," Dara Rose ordered, setting the cast-iron skillet on the stove, plopping in the last smidgeon of bacon grease to keep the eggs from sticking.

"I need to go to the outhouse," Harriet said.

"Put your shoes on first," Dara Rose countered. "It's a nice day out, but the ground is cold."

The children obeyed readily, which threw her a little. She was raising her daughters to have minds of their own, but that meant they were often obstinate and sometimes even defiant.

Parnell had accused her of spoiling them, though he'd indulged the girls plenty himself, buying them hair ribbons and peppermint sticks and letting them ride his horse. Edrina, rough and tumble as any boy but at the same time all girl, was virtually fearless as well as outspoken, and trying as the child sometimes was, Dara Rose wouldn't have changed anything about her. Except, of course, for her tendency to play hooky from school.

Harriet, just a year younger than her sister, was more tentative, less likely to take risks than Edrina was. Too small to really understand death, Harriet very probably expected her papa to come home one day, riding Gawain, his saddlebags bulging with presents.

Dara Rose's eyes smarted again and, inwardly, she brought herself up short.

She and the girls had been given a reprieve, that was all. They could go on living in the marshal's house for a while, but other arrangements would have to be made eventually, just the same.

Which was why, when she and the girls had eaten, and the dishes had been washed and the fires banked, Dara Rose followed through with her original plan.

She and Harriet walked Edrina to the one-room

schoolhouse at the edge of town, and then took the eggs to the mercantile, to be traded for staples.

It was warm inside the general store, and Harriet became so captivated by the lovely doll on display in the tinsel-draped front window that Dara Rose feared the child would refuse to leave the place at all.

"Look, Mama," she breathed, without taking her eyes from the beautiful toy when Dara Rose approached and took her hand. "Isn't she pretty? She's almost as tall as *I am*."

"She's pretty," Dara Rose conceded, trying to keep the sadness out of her voice. "But not nearly as pretty as you are."

Harriet looked up at her, enchanted. "Edrina says there's no such person as St. Nicholas," she said. "She says it was you and Papa who filled our stockings last Christmas Eve."

Dara Rose's throat ached. She had to swallow before she replied, "Edrina is right, sweetheart," she said hoarsely. Other people could afford to pretend that magical things happened, at least while their children were young, but she did not have that luxury.

"I guess the doll probably costs a lot," Harriet said, her voice small and wistful.

Dara Rose checked the price tag dangling from the

doll's delicate wrist, though she already knew it would be far out of her reach.

Two dollars and fifty cents.

What was the world coming to?

"She comes with a trunk full of clothes," the store-keeper put in helpfully. Philo Bickham meant well, to be sure, but he wasn't the most thoughtful man on earth. "That's real human hair on her head, too, and she came all the way from Germany."

Harriet's eyes widened with something that might have been alarm. "But didn't the hair *belong* to someone?" she asked, no doubt picturing a bald child wandering sadly through the Black Forest.

"People sometimes sell their hair," Dara Rose explained, giving Mr. Bickham a less than friendly glance as she drew her daughter toward the door. "And then it grows back."

Harriet immediately brightened. "Could we sell *my* hair? For two dollars and fifty cents?"

"No," Dara Rose said, and instantly regretted speaking so abruptly. She dropped to her haunches, tucked stray golden curls into Harriet's tattered bonnet. "Your hair is much too beautiful to sell, sweetheart."

"But I could grow more," Harriet reasoned. "You said so yourself, Mama."

Dara Rose smiled, mainly to keep from crying, and

stood very straight, juggling the egg basket, now containing a small tin of lard, roughly three-quarters of a cup of sugar scooped into a paper sack and a box of table salt, from one wrist to the other.

"We'll be on our way now, Harriet," she said. "We have things to do."

Chapter 3

As he rode slowly along every street in Blue River that morning, touching his hat brim to all he encountered so the town folks would know they had a marshal again, one who meant to live up to the accompanying responsibilities, Clay found himself thinking about Parnell Nolan. Blessed with a beautiful wife and two fine daughters, and well-liked from what little Clay had learned about him, Nolan had still managed to be in a whorehouse when he drew his last breath.

Yes, plenty of men indulged themselves in brothels—bachelors and husbands, sons and fathers alike—but they usually exercised some degree of discretion, in Clay's experience.

Always inclined to give somebody the benefit of the doubt, at least until they'd proven themselves unworthy of the courtesy, Clay figured Parnell might have done his sinning in secret, with the notion that he was therefore protecting his wife and children from scandal. But Blue River was a small place, like Clay's hometown of Indian Rock, and stories that were too good not to tell had a way of getting around. Fast.

Of course, Nolan surely hadn't planned on dying that particular night, in the midst of awkward circumstances.

Reaching the end of the last street in town, near the schoolhouse, Clay stopped to watch, leaning on the pommel of his saddle and letting Outlaw nibble at the patchy grass, as children spilled out the door of the little red building, shouting to one another, eager to make the most of recess.

He spotted Edrina right away—her bonnet hung down her back by its laces, revealing that unmistakable head of spun-gold hair, and her cheeks glowed with exuberance and good health and the nippy coolness of the weather.

As Clay watched, she found a stick, etched the squares for a game of hopscotch in the bare dirt and jumped right in. Within moments, the other little girls were clamoring to join her, while the boys played kick-the-can at an artfully disdainful distance, making as much racket as they could muster up.

The schoolmarm—a plain woman, spare and tall, and probably younger than she looked—surveyed the melee from the steps of the building, but she was quick to notice the horse and rider looking on from the road.

Clay tugged at his hat brim and nodded a silent greeting. His ma, Chloe, had been a schoolteacher when she was younger, and he had an ingrained respect for the profession. It was invariably a hard row to hoe.

The teacher nodded back, descended the schoolhouse steps with care, lest she trip over the hem of her brown woolen dress. Instead of a coat or a cloak, she wore a dark blue shawl to keep warm.

Clay waited as she approached, then dismounted to meet her at the gate, though he kept to his own side and she kept to hers, as was proper.

The lady introduced herself. "Miss Alvira Krenshaw," she said, putting out a bony hand. She hadn't missed the star pinned to his coat, of course; her eyes had gone right to it. "You must be our new town marshal."

Clay shook her hand and acknowledged her supposition with another nod and, "Clay McKettrick."

"How do you do?" she said, not expecting an answer.

Clay gave her one, anyway. "So far, so good," he replied, with a slight grin. Miss Alvira Krenshaw looked like a sturdy, no-nonsense soul, and although she wasn't pretty, she wasn't homely, either. She'd probably make some man a good wife, given half a chance, and though thin, she looked capable of carrying healthy babies to

full-term, delivering them without a lot of fuss and raising them to competent adulthood.

Wanting a wife to carry over the threshold of his new
house, come spring, and impregnate as soon as possible,
Clay might have set right to courting Miss Alvira, provided she was receptive to such attentions, if not for one
problem. He'd gone and met Dara Rose Nolan.

Stepping off the train the day before, he'd been sure of
almost everything that concerned him. What he wanted,
what sort of man he was, all of it. Now, after just two
brief encounters with his predecessor's widow, he wasn't
sure of much of *anything*.

Considerable figuring out would be called for before
he undertook to win himself a bride, and that was for
certain.

Over Alvira's shoulder, he saw a boy run over to where
the girls were playing hopscotch, grab at Edrina's dangling bonnet and yank on it hard enough to knock her
down.

The bonnet laces held, though, and the boy ran,
laughing, his friends shouting a mingling of mockery
and encouragement, while a disgruntled, flaming-faced
Edrina got back to her feet, dusting off her coat as she
glared at the transgressor.

"Looks like trouble," Clay observed dryly, causing

Miss Alvira to flare out her long, narrow nostrils and then spin around to see for herself.

Edrina, still flushed with fury, marched right into the middle of that cluster of small but earnest rascals, stood face-to-face with the primary mischief-maker and landed a solid punch to his middle. Knocked the wind right out of him.

Miss Alvira was on the run by then, blowing shrill toots through the whistle every schoolmarm seemed to come equipped with, but the damage, such as it was, was done.

The thwarted bonnet thief was on his knees now, clutching his belly and gasping for breath, and though his dignity had certainly suffered, he didn't look seriously hurt.

Clay suppressed a smile and lingered there by the gate, watching.

Edrina looked a mite calmer by then, but she was still pink in the face and her fists remained clenched. She stood her ground, spotted Clay when she turned her head toward Miss Alvira and that earsplitting whistle of hers.

"What is going on here?" Alvira demanded, her voice carrying, almost as shrill as the whistle. She reached down, caught the gasping boy from behind, where his suspenders crossed, and wrenched him unceremoniously to his feet.

Clay felt a flash of sympathy for the little fellow. Like as not, he'd taken a shine to Edrina and, boys being what boys have always been, hoped to gain her notice by snatching her bonnet and running off with it—the equivalent of tugging at a girl's pigtail or surprising her with a close-up look at a bullfrog or a squirmy garter snake, and glory be and hallelujah if she squealed.

Miss Alvira, still gripping the boy's suspenders, turned to frown at Edrina.

"Edrina Nolan," she said, "young ladies do not strike others with their fists."

Edrina, who had been looking in Clay's direction until that moment, faced her accuser, folded her arms and staunchly replied, "He had it coming."

"Go inside this instant," Alvira ordered both children, indicating the open door of the schoolhouse with a pointing of her index finger. "Thomas, you will stand in the corner behind my desk, by the bookcase. Edrina, you will occupy the one next to the cloakroom."

"For how long?" Edrina wanted to know.

Clay had to admire the child's spirit.

"Until I tell you that you may take your seats," Miss Alvira answered firmly, shooing the rest of her brood toward the hallowed halls of learning with a waving motion of her free arm. "Inside," she called. "All of you. Recess is over."

The command elicited groans of protest, but the children obeyed.

Thomas, clearly humiliated because he'd been publicly bested by a girl, slunk, head down, toward the schoolhouse, and Edrina followed in her own time, literally dragging her feet by scuffing the toe of first one shoe and then the other in the dirt as she walked. Finally, she looked back over one shoulder, caught Clay's eye and gave an eloquent little shrug of resignation.

He hoped the distance and the shadow cast by the brim of his hat would hide his smile.

That kid should have been born a McKettrick.

DARA ROSE MADE THE ROUNDS that morning just as she'd planned, swallowing her pride and knocking on each door to ask for work, with little Harriet trudging along, uncomplaining, at her side.

There were only half a dozen real *houses* in Blue River; the rest were mostly hovels and shanties, shacks like the one she lived in. The folks there were no better off than she was and, in many cases, things were worse for them. Thin smoke wafted from crooked chimneys and scrawny chickens pecked at the small expanses of bare dirt that passed for yards.

Mrs. O'Reilly, whose husband had run off with a dance hall girl six months ago and left her with three children to look after, all of them under five years old, was outside. The woman was probably in her early twenties, but she looked a generation older; there were already streaks of gray at her temples and she'd lost one of her eye teeth.

She had a bonfire going, with a big tin washtub teetering atop the works, full of other people's laundry. Steam boiled up into the crisp air as she stirred the soapy soup, and Peg O'Reilly managed a semblance of a smile when she caught sight of Dara Rose and Harriet.

Two of the O'Reilly children, both boys, ran whooping around their mother like Sioux braves on the warpath, both of them barefoot and coatless. Their older sister, Addie, must have been inside, where it was, Dara Rose devoutly hoped, comparatively warm.

"Mornin', Miz Nolan," Peg called, though she didn't smile. She was probably self-conscious about that missing tooth, Dara Rose figured, with a stab of well-hidden pity.

Dara Rose smiled, offered a wave and paused at the edge of the road, even though she'd meant to keep going. Lord knew, she had reason enough to be discouraged herself, after being turned away from all those doors, but she just couldn't bring herself to pass on by.

Harriet, no doubt weary from keeping up with Dara

Rose all morning, tugged reluctantly at her mother's hand, wanting to go on.

"How's Addie?" Dara Rose asked.

"She's poorly," Peg replied. "Been abed since yesterday, so she's not much help with these little yahoos." Still tending to the wash, which was just coming to a simmer, she indicated the boys with a nod of her head.

They had both stopped their chasing game to stare at Harriet in abject wonder. Even in her poor clothes and the shoes she would outgrow all too soon, she probably looked as pretty to them as that doll over at the mercantile did to her.

"Mama," Harriet whispered, looking up at Dara Rose from beneath the drooping brim of her bonnet, "what's that smell?"

"Hush," Dara Rose whispered back, hoping Peg hadn't heard the little girl's voice over the crackling of the fire and the barking of a neighbor's dog.

Peg let go of the old broomstick she used to stir the shirts and trousers and small clothes as they soaked, and wiped a forearm across her brow. The sleeves of her calico dress were rolled up to her elbows, and her apron was little more than a rag.

"Could you use some eggs?" Dara Rose asked, in the manner of one asking a favor. "I've got plenty put by."

A flicker of yearning showed in Peg O'Reilly's care-worn face before she squared her shoulders and raised her chin a notch. "I'd say no, on grounds that I've got my pride and I know you're having a hard time of it, too, but for the young'uns," she replied. "The last of the oatmeal is used up, and we're almost out of pinto beans, but a nice fried egg might put some color in Addie's cheeks and that's for sure."

"I'll send Edrina over with a basket right after she gets home from school," Dara Rose said.

"You understand that I can't pay you nothin'," Peg warned, stiffening her backbone.

"I understand," Dara Rose confirmed lightly, though every egg her hens laid was precious, since it could be sold for cash money or traded for things she couldn't raise, like flour. "I've got too many, and I don't want them to go to waste."

"Mama," Harriet interjected, "we don't—"

This time, Dara Rose didn't hush her daughter out loud, but simply squeezed the child's hand a little more tightly than she might otherwise have done.

"Obliged, then," Peg said, and went back to her stirring.

Dara Rose nodded and started off toward home again, poor Harriet scrambling to keep up.

"Mama," the child insisted, half-breathless, "you already traded away all the eggs, remember? Over at the mercantile? And the hens probably haven't laid any new ones yet."

"There are nearly two dozen in the crock on the pantry shelf," Dara Rose reminded her daughter. Like the potatoes, carrots, turnips and onions she'd squirreled away down in the root cellar, along with a few bushels of apples from the tree in her yard, the eggs suspended in water glass were part of her skimpy reserves, something she and the girls could eat if the hens stopped laying or the hawks got them.

"Yes," Harriet reasoned, intrepidly logical, "but what if there's a hard winter and *we* need to eat them?"

"Harriet," Dara Rose replied, walking a little faster because it was almost time for Edrina to come home for the midday meal, "there are times when a person simply has to help somebody who needs a hand and hope the good Lord pays heed and makes recompense." Parting with a few eggs didn't trouble her nearly as much as the realization that her five-year-old daughter had obviously been worrying about whether or not there would be enough food to get them through.

"What's 'recompense'?" Harriet asked.

"Never mind," Dara Rose answered.

They reached the house, removed their bonnets and their wraps—Dara Rose's cloak and Harriet's coat—and

Dara Rose ladled warm water out of the stove reservoir for the washing of hands.

In her mind, she heard Peg O'Reilly's words of brave despair. *The last of the oatmeal is used up, and we're almost out of pinto beans....*

Peg earned a pittance taking in laundry as it was, and what little money she earned probably went to pay for starvation rations and to meet the rent on that converted chicken coop of a house they all lived in.

As she reheated the canned venison leftover from last night's supper, then sliced and thinly buttered the last of the bread she'd made a few days before, Dara Rose silently reminded herself of something Parnell had often told her. "No matter how tough things get," he used to say, "you won't have to look far to find somebody else who'd be glad to trade places with you."

Her children were healthy, unlike Peg's eldest, and the three of them had a roof over their heads. And Parnell, at least, hadn't left them willingly, the way Jack O'Reilly had done.

Harriet, her mother's busy little helper, set three places at the table and then dragged a chair over to the side window so she could stand on the seat and keep a lookout for her sister. Although they had their scuffles and tiffs, like all children, Harriet's admiration for Edrina knew no bounds.

"There she is!" Harriet shouted gleefully, after a few moments of peering through the glass. "There's Edrina!"

Dara Rose smiled and began ladling warm venison and broth into enamel-coated bowls. She'd just set the bread plate in the middle of the improvised table when Edrina dragged in, looking despondent.

"You might as well know straightaway that I'm in trouble again," she immediately confessed. "Thomas Phillips tried to steal my bonnet at recess, and near strangled me with the ties while he was at it, and I socked him in the stomach. Miss Krenshaw made me stand in the corner for a whole hour, and I have to stay after school to wash the blackboard every day this week."

Dara Rose sighed, shook her head in feigned dismay and placed her hands on her hips. "Edrina," she said, on a long breath, and shook her head again.

"Did Thomas have to stand in the corner, too?" Harriet inquired, already a great believer in fair play.

"Yes," Edrina answered, with precious little satisfaction. "He has to carry in the drinking water for the whole school."

"Wash your hands," Dara Rose said mildly, when her elder daughter would have sat down to her meal instead.

Edrina obeyed, with a sigh of her own, and pulled the stool out from under the sink to climb up and plunge

her small hands into the basin of warm water Dara Rose
had set there.

"Mr. McKettrick came by the schoolhouse today," the
child announced. "That sure is a fine horse he rides."

Dara Rose felt an odd little catch at the mention of the
new marshal and, to her shame, caught herself wondering if he'd found Alvira Krenshaw at all fetching. She
was certainly eligible, Miss Krenshaw was, and while she
wouldn't win any prizes for looks, most people agreed
that she was a handsome woman with a good head on
her shoulders.

"Was there some kind of trouble? Besides your disagreement with Thomas?"

Edrina had finished washing up, and she climbed
deftly back down off the stool, drying her hands on her
skirts as she approached the table. "No," she replied, "but
he talked to Miss Krenshaw at the gate for a long time."

Dara Rose, who had long since learned to choose her
battles, decided to let the hand-drying incident pass. She
hoisted Harriet onto the stool, helped her lather to her
elbows and then rinse and lifted her down again.

The three of them gathered at the table.

It was Harriet's turn to say grace. "Thank you for the
venison and the bread," she said, in her direct way, her
bright head bowed and her eyes squeezed shut. "And if
there's any way I could get that pretty doll in the win-

dow of the mercantile for my very own, I would appreciate the kindness. Amen."

Dara Rose suppressed a smile even as she endured another pang to her heart. Much as she'd have loved to give her daughters toys for Christmas, she couldn't afford to do it. And even if she'd had any spare money at all, Edrina and Harriet needed shoes and warm clothes and nourishing food, like milk.

"What do you want St. Nicholas to bring you for Christmas?" Harriet asked Edrina, with companionable interest, as they all began to eat.

Edrina answered without hesitation, a note of gentle tolerance in her voice. "You know there isn't any St. Nicholas, Harriet," she reminded her sister. "He's just a story person, made up by that Mr. Moore."

"Couldn't we just *pretend* he's real?" Harriet wanted to know. "Just 'til lunch is over?" She sounded more like an adult than a little girl and Dara Rose, though proud of her bright daughters, hoped they weren't growing up too fast.

"It wouldn't hurt to pretend," she put in quietly.

Harriet's face lit up. "What do *you* want for Christmas, Mama?" she asked eagerly, forgetting all about her food.

Dara Rose pretended to think very hard for a few moments. "A cow, I think," she finally decided. "Then we'd have milk and butter of our own. Maybe even cheese."

Harriet looked nonplussed. "A cow?" she repeated.

Edrina glanced at Dara Rose, her expression almost conspiratorial, and considered the question under discussion. "I know what *I'd* want," she said presently. "Books. Exciting ones, with bears and outlaws and spooks in them."

Again, Dara Rose's heart pinched. She'd be lucky to afford peppermint sticks to drop into the girls' Christmas stockings this year, never mind dolls and books.

She cleared her throat. "Harriet and I stopped by the O'Reilly place today," she said. "Little Addie's under the weather again, and those boys looked hungry enough to dip spoons into the laundry kettle."

"And something smells bad there," Harriet added.

Dara Rose didn't scold her, but went right on. "I think they'd be grateful to have firewood and enough to eat, like we do," she said, hoping she'd made her point and wouldn't have to follow up with a sermon on Christian charity.

"Mama's giving them some of our eggs," Harriet said matter-of-factly. "She says sometimes a person just has to help somebody else and hope the good Lord pays heed and makes competition."

Edrina didn't say anything, since she had a mouthful of bread.

Dara Rose wondered if Harriet even knew what it

meant to pay heed. "The two of you can take a basket over to the O'Reillys', as soon as school's out for the day," she said. "And furthermore, Harriet Nolan, you will *not* remark on the bad smell."

"It's probably the outhouse that stinks," Edrina said. "Ours might get that way, too, without Papa around to shovel lye into it once in a while."

"Edrina," Dara Rose said, "we are at the table."

A long pause ensued.

"I have to stay after to wash the blackboard," Edrina reminded her mother.

"Fine," Dara Rose answered, pushing back her chair and carrying her bowl and spoon to the sink. "I'll wash the eggs and put them in the basket and you can drop them off at the O'Reilly place on your way back to school."

"There will be hell to pay if I'm late for class," Edrina said frankly. "Don't forget, I'm already in trouble for slugging Thomas Phillips in the stomach."

Dara Rose bit the inside of her lower lip to keep from smiling. "I won't forget," she said, heading for the single shelf that served as a pantry, bowl in hand, and fishing eight perfect brown ovals out of the crock filled to the brim with water glass. "If you hurry, you can deliver the eggs and still get back to school before Miss Krenshaw rings the bell. *And* I will thank you not to swear, Edrina Nolan."

Harriet, who staunchly maintained that she was too old to take naps, was already getting heavy-lidded, chin drooping, and yawning a little.

Dara Rose washed the eggs and put them into the basket, covering them with a flour-sack dish towel. She handed them to Edrina, who was already buttoning her coat. "Wear your bonnet," she instructed. "The sky may be blue as summer, but the wind has a bite to it."

Edrina nodded, resigned, and let herself out, taking the egg basket with her.

"Bring that basket home," Dara Rose called after her. "And the dish towel, too."

Edrina replied, but Dara Rose didn't hear what she said. She was already scooping up her sleepy child and carrying her to bed.

CLAY CHECKED THE BITTER Gulch Saloon and looked in at the bank, but there was no malfeasance afoot in either place.

Figuring it was indeed going to be a long winter, he walked back to the jailhouse, where he had a tiny office, a potbellied stove and a cot, and helped himself to a cup of the passable coffee he'd made earlier.

The stuff was stale and lukewarm, but stout enough to rouse a dead man from his eternal rest.

That, he supposed, was what this coming winter was going to feel like. Eternal rest.

He sighed, crossed to the single cell and peered through the bars, almost wishing he had a prisoner. That way, there would have been somebody to talk to, at least.

Alas, lawbreakers seemed to be pretty thin on the ground around those parts at the moment, a fact he supposed he should have been grateful to note.

Clay sat down in the creaky wooden chair behind the scarred wooden table that served as a desk and reached for the dusty stack of wanted posters and old mail piled on one corner.

If anybody stopped by, he'd like to give the impression that he was working, even if he wasn't. It made him smile to imagine what his granddad would think if he could see him now, collecting seventy-five dollars a month for doing not much of anything except drinking bad coffee and flipping through somebody else's correspondence.

He set aside the older wanted posters and read the few missives that looked even remotely official—none of them were, it turned out—and he was thinking maybe he ought to meander over to the livery stable and brush old Outlaw down, when he came to the last two letters and realized they were addressed to Mrs. Parnell B. Nolan.

The first, from an outfit called the Wildflower Salve Company, was most likely a sales pitch of some kind, but the second looked personal and smelled faintly of lemon verbena. The envelope was fat, made of good vellum, and the handwriting on the front was flowing cursive, with all kinds of loops and swirls.

Clay looked at the postmark, but couldn't make out where the letter had been mailed, or when, and there wasn't any return address.

Not that any of this was his concern in the first place.

Clay frowned, wondering how long the letters had been moldering in that pile, and then he smiled, holding the envelopes in one hand and lightly slapping them against the opposite palm.

Maybe it wasn't his sworn duty to make sure the mail got delivered, but it was as good an excuse as any for calling on Dara Rose Nolan.

Clay rose from his chair, fetched his coat and hat and set out on foot.

THERE HE STOOD, on her front doorstep this time, looking affably handsome.

For the briefest fraction of a moment, Dara Rose feared that Clay McKettrick had changed his mind, decided he wanted the house, after all. Her stomach quivered in a peculiar way that didn't seem to have much to do with the fear of eviction.

"I found these letters over at the office," he said, and produced two envelopes from an inside pocket of his duster. "They're addressed to you."

Dara Rose's eyes rounded. Getting a letter was a rare thing indeed. Getting two at once was virtually unheard of.

She opened the door a little wider, extended a hand for the envelopes and spoke very quietly because Harriet was napping. "Thank you," she said.

He let her take the envelopes, but he held on to them for a second longer than necessary, too.

Although her curiosity was great, Dara Rose wanted to savor the prospect of those letters for a little while. She'd read them later, by lamplight, when the girls were both down for the night and the house was quiet.

She tucked them into the pocket of her apron, blushing a little.

"Come in," she heard her own voice say, much to her surprise.

It simply wasn't proper for a widow to invite a man into her home, even in broad daylight, but she'd done just that and already stepped back so he could pass, and the marshal didn't hesitate to step over the threshold.

He stood in the middle of the front room, seeming to fill it to capacity with the width of his shoulders and the sheer unwieldy substance of his presence. His gaze went straight to the oversize daguerreotype of Parnell on one wall.

He seemed to consider her late husband's visage for a few moments, before turning to meet her eyes.

"He doesn't look like the kind of man who'd die in a brothel," he remarked.

Dara Rose was jangled, but not offended. Everyone knew what had happened to Parnell, and the scandal, though still alive, had long since died down to an occasional whisper, especially since Jack O'Reilly had left his wife and children for a sloe-eyed girl from the Bitter Gulch Saloon.

"He wasn't," she said, very softly, and then colored up again. "That kind of man, I mean. Not really."

Dara Rose had never confided the truth about her marriage to Parnell Nolan to a single living soul west of the Mississippi River, and she was confounded by a sudden urge to tell Marshal McKettrick everything.

Not a chance, she thought, running her hands down the front of her apron as if they'd been wet.

"It must have been hard for you and the children," Clay said quietly. His eyes, blue as cornflowers in high summer, took on a solemn expression. "Not just his dying, but being left on your own and all."

"We manage," Dara Rose said.

"I reckon you do," he agreed, and he looked more puzzled than solemn now.

She knew he was wondering why she hadn't found another husband, but she wasn't about to volunteer an explanation. Maybe she hadn't actually loved Parnell Nolan, but she'd liked him. Depended on him. Even respected him.

Parnell had been kind to her, cherished the girls like they were his daughters instead of his nieces, and married her.

She would have felt disloyal, discussing Parnell with a relative stranger; though, oddly enough, in some ways she felt as if she'd always known Clay McKettrick, and known him well. He stirred vague memories in her, like dreams that left only an echo behind when the sun rose.

The silence was awkward.

Dara Rose didn't ask the marshal to sit down, and she couldn't offer him coffee because she didn't have any.

So the two of them just stood there, each one waiting for the other to speak.

Finally, Clay grinned ever so slightly and turned his hat decisively in his hands. He went to the door and opened it, pausing to look back at Dara Rose, his impressive form rimmed in wintry light.

"Good day to you, Mrs. Nolan," he said.

Dara Rose swallowed. "Good day, Mr. McKettrick," she replied formally. "And, once again, thank you."

"Anytime," he said, and then he left the house, closed the door behind him.

Dara Rose resisted the temptation to rush to the window and watch him heading down the walk.

Harriet appeared in the doorway to the bedroom, hair rumpled, rubbing her eyes with the backs of her hands. "I thought I heard Papa's voice," she said.

Dara Rose's heart cracked and then split down the middle. "Sweetheart," she said, bending her knees so she could look directly into the child's sleep-flushed face, "Papa's gone to heaven, remember?"

Harriet's lower lip wobbled, which further bruised Dara Rose's already injured heart. How could such a small child be expected to understand the permanence of death?

"Is heaven a real place?" Harriet asked. "Or is it just pretend, like St. Nicholas?"

"I believe it's a real place," Dara Rose said.

Harriet frowned, obviously puzzled. "Is it like here? Are there trees and kittens and trains to ride?"

Dara Rose blinked rapidly and rose back to her full

height. "I don't know, sweetheart. One day, a long, long time from now, we'll find out for sure, but right now, we have to live in *this* world, and we might as well make the best of it."

"I think I would like this world better," Harriet told her, "if there was a St. Nicholas in it."

Dara Rose gave a small, strangled chuckle at that, and pulled her daughter close for a hug. "We don't need St. Nicholas, you and Edrina and me," she said. "We have one another."

Chapter 4

⁓✦⁓

After the chickens were fed and had retreated into their coop to roost for the night, Dara Rose made a simple supper of baked potatoes and last summer's string beans, boiled with bits of salt pork and onion, for herself and the girls, and the three of them sat at the table in the kitchen, eating by the light of a kerosene lantern and chatting quietly.

The subject of St. Nicholas did not come up again, thankfully. In Dara Rose's humble opinion, Clement C. Moore had a lot to answer for. By writing that lengthy and admittedly charming poem, "'Twas the Night Before Christmas," he'd created expectations in children that many parents couldn't hope to meet.

Instead, Edrina recounted her visit to the O'Reillys' after lunch, and fretted that it wasn't fair that she had to wash the blackboard every single day for a week when all she'd done was defend herself against that wretched Thomas. Large flakes of snow drifted, like benevolent ghosts, past the darkened window next to the back door, and brought a sigh to hover in the back of Dara Rose's throat.

Winter. As a privileged only child, back in Massachusetts, she'd loved everything about that season, even the cold. It was a time to skate and sled and build castles out of snow and then drink hot chocolate by the fire while Nanny told stories or recited long, exciting poems about shipwrecks and ghosts and Paul Revere's ride.

Had she ever really lived such a life? Dara Rose wondered now, as she did whenever her childhood came to mind.

"Mama?" Edrina said, breaking the sudden spell the sight of snowflakes had cast over Dara Rose. "Did you hear what I said about Addie O'Reilly?"

Dara Rose gave herself an inward shake and sat up a little straighter in her chair. "I'm sorry," she said, because she was always truthful with the children. "I'm afraid I was woolgathering."

Edrina's perfect little face glowed, heart-shaped, in the light of love and a kerosene lantern. "She's really sick," she informed her mother, in a tone of good-natured patience, as though she were the parent and Dara Rose the child. "Mrs. O'Reilly told me she has romantic fever."

Dara Rose did not correct Edrina. She was too stricken by the tragedy of it, the patent unfairness. *Rheumatic fever.* Was there no end to the sorrows and hardships visited on that poor family?

"That's dreadful," she said.

"And Addie gets lonely, staying inside all the time," Edrina went on. "So I said Harriet and I would come to visit on Saturday morning. We can, can't we, Mama? Because I promised."

Dara Rose's heart swelled with affection for her daughter, and then sank a little. It was like her spirited Edrina to make such an offer, and follow through on it, too, whether or not she had her mother's permission. When Edrina made a promise, she kept it, which meant she was really asking if Harriet could go with her.

As far as Dara Rose knew, rheumatic fever wasn't contagious, but heaven only knew what other diseases her children might contract during a visit to the O'Reilly house—diphtheria, the dreaded influenza, perhaps even typhoid or cholera.

"You mustn't promise such things, in the future, without speaking to me first," Dara Rose told Edrina, hedging. "I feel as sorry for the O'Reillys as you do, Edrina, but there are other considerations."

"And it stinks over there," Harriet interjected solemnly, her nose twitching a little at the memory.

Dara Rose had lost her appetite, which was fine, because she'd had enough to eat, anyway. "Harriet," she said. "That will be enough of that sort of talk. It is not suitable for the supper table."

Harriet sighed. "It's *never* suitable," she lamented.

"Hush," Dara Rose told her, her attention focused, for the moment, on her elder daughter. "You may visit the O'Reillys on Saturday morning," she stated, rising to begin clearing the table. "But only because you gave your word and I would not ask you to break it."

"If I hadn't promised, you wouldn't let me go?" Edrina pressed. She'd never been one to quit while the quitting was good, a trait she came by honestly, Dara Rose had to admit. She had the same shortcoming herself.

"That's right," she replied, at some length. "I have to think about your safety, Edrina, and that of your sister."

"My safety? The O'Reillys wouldn't hurt us."

"Not deliberately," Dara Rose allowed, "but it isn't the most sanitary place in the world, and you might catch something."

Although she didn't mention it, she was thinking of the diphtheria outbreak two years before, during which four children had perished, all of them from one family.

"Is that suitable talk for the supper table?" Harriet asked sincerely.

"Never mind," Dara Rose said. "It's time you both got

ready for bed. Shall I walk with you to the outhouse, or are you brave enough to go on your own?"

Edrina scraped back her chair, rose to fetch her coat and Harriet's from the pegs near the back door. Her expression said she was brave enough to do anything, and protect her little sister in the bargain.

"Maybe that's why Addie's so lonesome," Edrina said, opening the door to the chilly night, with its flurries of snow. "Because everybody is afraid of catching something if they visit."

Chagrin swept over Dara Rose—*out of the mouths of babes*—but she assumed a stern countenance. "Don't stand there with the door open," she said.

Later, when the children were in bed, and she'd read them a story from their one dog-eared book of fairy tales and heard their prayers—Harriet put in another request for the doll from the mercantile—kissed them good-night and tucked them in, Dara Rose returned to the kitchen.

There, she took the two letters Mr. McKettrick had delivered earlier from her apron pocket, and sat down.

The kerosene in the lamp was getting low, and the wick was smoking a little, but Dara Rose did not hurry.

She knew the plump missive was from her cousin, Piper, who taught school in a small town in Maine. She meant to save that one for last, and she took the time to weigh it in her hand, run her fingers over the vellum and examine the stamp before setting it carefully aside.

She opened the letter from the Wildflower Salve Company first, even though she knew it was an advertisement and nothing more, and carefully smoothed the single page on the tabletop.

Her eyes widened a little as she read, and her heart fluttered up into her throat as her excitement grew.

Bold print declared that Dara Rose was holding the key to financial security right there in her hand. She could win prizes, it fairly shouted. She could earn money. And all she had to do was introduce her friends and neighbors to the wonders of Wildflower Salve. Each colorfully decorated round tin—an elegant keepsake in its own right, according to the Wildflower Salve people— sold for a mere fifty cents. And she would get to keep a whopping twenty-five cents for her commission.

Dara Rose sat back, thinking.

Twenty-five cents was a lot of money.

And there were prizes. All sorts of prizes—toys, household goods, luxuries of all sorts—could be had in lieu of commissions, if the "independent business person" preferred.

Out of the goodness of their hearts, the folks at the Wildflower Salve Company, of Racine, Wisconsin, would be happy to send her a full twenty tins of this "medicinal miracle" in good faith. If for some incomprehensible reason her "friends and relations" didn't snap up the whole shipment practically as soon as she opened the parcel, she could return the merchandise and owe nothing.

Five dollars, Dara Rose thought. If she sold twenty tins of Wildflower Salve, she would earn *five dollars*—a virtual fortune.

The kerosene lamp flickered, reminding her that she'd soon be sitting in the dark, and Dara Rose set aside "the opportunity of a lifetime" to open the letter from Piper.

A crisp ten-dollar bill fell out, nearly stopping Dara Rose's heart.

She set it carefully aside, and her hands trembled as she unfolded the clump of pages covered in Piper's lovely cursive. The date was nearly eight months in the past.

"Dearest Cousin," the missive began. "News of your tragic misfortune reached me yesterday, via the telegraph…"

Piper's letter, misplaced all this time, went on to say that she hoped Dara Rose could put the money enclosed to good use—that the weather was fine in Maine, with the spring coming, but she already dreaded the winter. How were the girls faring? Did Dara Rose intend to stay on in "that little Texas town," or would she and the children consider coming to live with her? The teacher's quarters were small, she wrote, bringing tears to Dara Rose's eyes, but they could make do, the four of them, couldn't they? There were crocuses and tulips and daffodils shooting up in people's flower beds, Piper went on to relate, and the days were distinctly longer. For all that, alas, she was lonesome when she wasn't teaching. She'd been briefly engaged, but the fellow had turned out to be a rascal and a rounder, and there didn't seem to be any likely prospects on the horizon.

Dara Rose read the whole letter and then immediately read it again. Besides Edrina and Harriet, Piper was the only blood relation she had left in all the world, and Dara Rose missed her sorely. Holding the letter, seeing the familiar handwriting spanning the pages, was the next best thing to having her cousin right there, in the flesh, sitting across the table from her.

But what must Piper think of her? Dara Rose fretted, after a third reading. She'd written this letter so long ago, and sent such a generous gift of money, only to receive silence in return.

The lantern guttered out.

Dara Rose sighed, folded the letter carefully and tucked it back into its envelope. She took the ten-dollar bill with her to the bedroom, where the girls were sound asleep, and placed it carefully between the pages in her Bible for safekeeping.

She undressed quickly, since the little room was cold, and donned her flannel nightgown, returned to the kitchen carrying a lighted candle stuck to a jar lid and dipped water from the stove reservoir to wash her face. When that was done, she brushed her teeth at the sink and steeled herself to make the trek to the outhouse, through the snowy cold.

When she got back, she locked the door, used the candle to light her way back to the bedroom, blew out the flame and climbed into bed with her daughters.

She was tired, but too excited to fall asleep right away.

She had ten precious dollars.

The Wildflower Salve Company had offered her honest work.

She'd as good as—well, *almost* as good as—spent an evening with her cousin and dearest friend, Piper.

And Marshal Clay McKettrick had the bluest eyes she'd ever seen.

THE JAILHOUSE, CLAY SOON discovered, was a lonely place at night.

He'd already had supper over at the hotel dining room—chicken and dumplings almost as good as his ma's—and he'd paid a visit to Outlaw, over at the livery stable, too. He'd even sent a telegram north to Indian

Rock, to let his family know he'd arrived and was settling in nicely.

That done, Clay had filled the water bucket and set up
the coffeepot for morning, then filled the wood box next
to the potbellied stove. There being no place to hang up
his clothes, he left them folded in his travel trunk, there
in the back room, where the bed was. Most of his books
hadn't arrived yet—he had a passel of them and they had
to be shipped down from Indian Rock in crates—and
he couldn't seem to settle down to read the one favorite he'd brought along on the train, Jules Verne's *Around
the World in Eighty Days*. He must have read that book a
dozen times over the years, and he never got tired of it,
but that night, it failed to hold his interest.

He kept thinking about Dara Rose Nolan, the gold of
her hair and the fiery blue spirit in her eyes. He thought
about her shapely breasts and small waist and smooth skin
and that flash of pride that was so easy to arouse in her.

And the same old question plagued him: Why in the
devil would a man with a wife like that squander his
time in a whorehouse, the way her husband had done?

Nobody could help dying, of course, but they had at
least some choice about *where* they died, didn't they? It
was simple common sense—folks didn't turn up their
toes in places they hadn't ventured into in the first place.

Knowing he wouldn't sleep, anyhow, Clay strapped

on his gun belt, shrugged into his duster and reached for his hat.

He was the marshal, after all.

He'd just take a little stroll up and down Main Street and make sure any visiting cowpokes or drifters were minding their manners. If anybody needed arresting, he'd throw them in the hoosegow and start up a conversation.

What he really needed, he supposed, stepping out onto the dark sidewalk, was a woman. Someone like Dara Rose Nolan.

Maybe he'd get himself a dog—that would provide some companionship. He'd have to do all the talking, of course, but he liked critters. He'd grown up with all manner of them on the ranch.

Yes, sir, he needed a dog.

He hadn't even reached the corner when he heard the first yelp.

He frowned, stopped to pinpoint the direction.

"Dutch, you kick that dog again," he heard a male voice say, "and I'll shoot *you*, 'stead of him!"

Clay, having located the disturbance, pushed his coat back to uncover the handle of his .45 and stepped into the alley.

It was dark, and the snow veiled the moon, but light struggled through the filthy windows of the buildings on either side, and he could make out two men, one holding a pistol, standing over a shivering form huddled close to the ground.

"Hold it right there," Clay said, in deadly earnest, when the man with the pistol raised it to shoot. "What's going on here?"

The dog whimpered.

"Nothin', Marshal," one of the men answered, in a drunken whine. "The poor mutt's half-starved, just a bag of bones. We figured on putting it out of its misery, that's all. Meant it as a kindness."

"Get the hell out of here," Clay said. He could not abide a bully.

The two men responded by turning on their heels and running in the other direction.

Clay waited until they were out of sight before he put the .45 back in its holster and approached the dog. "You in a bad way there, fella?" he asked, crouching to offer a hand.

The animal sniffed cautiously at his fingers and whimpered again.

"Where'd you come from?" Clay asked, gently examining the critter for broken bones or open wounds. He seemed to be all right, though his ribs protruded and his belly was concave and he stunk like all get-out.

The dog whined, though this time there was less sorrow in the sound.

"You know," Clay told the animal companionably, "I was just thinking to myself that what I need is a dog to keep me company. Now, here you are. How'd you like to help me keep the peace in this sorry excuse for a town?"

The dog seemed amenable to the idea, and raised himself slowly, teetering a little, to his four fur-covered feet. He had burrs stuck in his coat, that poor cuss, and there was no telling what color he was, or if he leaned toward any particular breed.

"You come on with me, if you can walk," Clay said. "I brought home what was left of my supper, and it seems to me you could use a decent meal."

With that, he turned to head back toward the sidewalk. The dog limped after him, pausing every few moments, as though afraid he'd committed some transgression without knowing about it.

Back at the jailhouse, Clay got a better look at the dog, after lighting a lantern to see by, but seeing didn't help much. The creature was neither big nor little, and he had floppy ears, but that was the extent of what Clay could make out.

Glad to have something to do, not to mention some companionship, Clay poured the remains of his chicken and dumplings onto the one tin plate he possessed and set it on the floor, near the stove.

The dog sniffed at the food, looked up at Clay with the kind of uncertainty that breaks a decent person's heart and waited.

"You go ahead and have supper," Clay said gently. "I imagine you could use some water, too."

Slowly, cautiously, the dog lowered his muzzle and began to eat.

Clay walked softly, approaching the water bucket, and ladled up a dipperful.

The dog lapped thirstily from the well of the dipper, then returned to his supper, clearly ravenous, licking the plate clean as a whistle.

Clay carried in more water from the pump out back, heated it bucket by bucket on the potbellied stove and finally filled the washtub he'd found in one of the cells. He eased the dog into the warm water and sluiced him down before lathering his hide with his own bar of soap.

The animal didn't raise any fuss, he simply stood there, shivering and looking like nothing so much as a half-drowned rat. Gradually, it became clear that his coat was brown and white, speckled like a pinto horse.

Clay dried him off with one of the two towels he'd purchased earlier, over at the mercantile, hefted him out of the tub and set him gently on his feet, near the stove.

The dog looked up at him curiously, head tilted to one side.

Clay chuckled. "Now, then," he said. "You look a lot more presentable than you did before."

The dog gave a single, tentative *woof,* obviously unsure how the remark would be received in present company.

Clay leaned to pat the animal's damp head. "What you are," he said, "is a coincidence. Like I told you, I was thinking about how much I'd like to have a dog, and then you and I made our acquaintance. But since 'coincidence' would be too much trouble for a name, I figure I'll call you Chester."

"Woof," said Chester, with more confidence than before.

Clay laughed. "Chester it is, then," he agreed.

Using a rough blanket from the cot in the jail cell, Clay fashioned a bed for the dog, close to the stove. Chester sniffed the cloth, stepped gingerly onto it, made a circle and settled down with a sigh.

"'Night," Clay said.

Chester closed his eyes, sighed again and slept.

THE HENS HAD ONLY LAID three eggs between the lot of them, Dara Rose discovered the next morning, when she visited the chicken coop, but she wasn't as disappointed by this as she normally would have been.

She had ten dollars tucked between the leaves of her Bible—a fortune.

And she had a future, a bright one, as Blue River, Texas's sole distributor of Wildflower Salve. All she had to do was fill out the coupon and mail it in, and before the New Year, she'd be in business.

Granted, there weren't a lot of people in Blue River, but there were plenty of surrounding farms and ranches, and those isolated women would be thrilled to purchase salve in a pretty tin, especially after she explained the benefits of regular use.

Not that she knew exactly what those benefits *were,* but the Wildflower Salve people had promised to send a training guide along with her first shipment.

As soon as she'd gotten Edrina off to school, she intended to write a long letter to Piper, explaining that *her* letter had been accidentally misplaced all this time, and she'd only received it the day before, and that was why her answer was so late in coming. Of course she'd thank her cousin profusely for the generous gift of ten dollars, and bring Piper up-to-date where she and the girls were concerned.

Her mind bumbled back and forth between the planned letter and her impending career in merchandising like a bee trapped inside a jar while she prepared oatmeal for breakfast, toasted bread in the oven and officiated over a debate between Edrina and Harriet, concerning whose turn it was sleep in the middle of the bed that night.

Neither one wanted to, and Dara Rose finally said *she'd* take the middle, for heaven's sake, and what had she done to deserve two such argumentative daughters?

After breakfast, Dara Rose and Harriet bundled up to walk Edrina to school. Normally, Edrina managed the distance on her own, but today, Dara Rose wanted a word with Miss Krenshaw.

"I'm *already* being punished," Edrina fussed, as the three of them hurried along a road hoary with frost and hardened snow. "I *told you* I have to stay after and wash the blackboard. So why do you need to talk to Miss Krenshaw, when you know all that?"

Dara Rose hid a smile. She was holding Harriet's hand, and trying to pace herself to the child's much shorter strides. "I merely want to inquire about the Christmas pageant," she replied. There was always some sort of program at the schoolhouse, whether it was carol singing, a Nativity play or an evening of recitals, and everyone attended.

"Oh," said Edrina, still sounding not only mystified, but apparently a little nervous, too.

Dara Rose wondered if there was something her daughter should have told her, but hadn't.

"Do you think it will snow again, Mama?" Harriet asked, tilting her head way back to look up at the glowering sky. "Christmas is less than two weeks away, and St. Nicholas will need a lot of snow, since he travels in a sleigh."

"Goose," Edrina said, nudging her sister with one elbow. "There *isn't* any St. Nicholas, remember?"

"Edrina," Dara Rose interceded gently.

"I'm *pretending,* that's all," Harriet said, with a toss of her head. "You can't *stop* me, either."

"Pretending is *stupid,*" Edrina said. "It's for babies."

Dara Rose stopped, and both her children had to stop, too, since she was holding Harriet's hand at the time and it was easy to catch Edrina by the shoulder and halt her progress.

"Enough," Dara Rose said firmly.

They began to walk again.

THE SKY WAS HEAVY and gray that morning when Clay left Chester to digest the leftovers from his hotel dining room breakfast within the warm radius of the jailhouse stove and headed over to the livery stable to fetch Outlaw.

It was cold and getting colder, so Clay raised the collar of his duster as he led the saddled gelding out into the road. There had been snow during the night, leaving a hard crust on the ground, and there would be more, judging by the weighted clouds brooding overhead, but the ride was a short one and he'd be back in Blue River before any serious weather had a chance to set in.

Raised in the high country, where a soft, slow, feathery snowfall could turn into a raging blizzard within a span of ten minutes, he had a sense of what signs he ought to look out for, as well as those he could safely ignore.

Today, all the indications—the direction of wind, the foul promise of the darkening sky, the way the cold bit through the heavy canvas of his duster—inclined a man toward caution.

He let Outlaw have his head once they were out of town, let the horse run for the sheer joy of it, and they soon reached their destination, the flat acres where Clay intended to erect a house and a barn.

There, he dismounted and left Outlaw to catch his breath and graze on the scant remains of last summer's grass, paced off the perimeters of the house and marked the corners with piles of small rocks. He did the same for the barn, then stood a while, the wind slicing clear to his marrow, and imagined the place, finished.

The house, a kit he'd sent away to Sears, Roebuck and Company for, amounted to a sensible rectangle, the kind he could easily add on to as the years went by, with windows on all sides, white clapboard walls and a shingled roof. He'd have to hire some help to put the thing together, of course, but he planned to do a lot of the work with his own hands, and that included everything from laying floorboards to gathering rock for the fireplace and then mortaring the stones together.

With the McKettrick family expanding the way it had been for some years, Clay had helped build several houses, and put up additions, too. The kit wouldn't arrive until late April, but he'd need to have the foundation ready, and the well dug, too.

Of course, a lot depended on what kind of winter they were in for—Blue River was in the Hill Country, and therefore the climate wasn't as temperate as it was in some parts of Texas—but he could already feel the heft of a shovel in his hands, the steady strain in his muscles, and he was heartened.

Next year at this time, he promised himself, he'd be ranching, right here on this land. He'd have a wife and, if possible, a baby on the way. Christmas would be getting close, and he'd go out and cut a tree and bring it into the house to be hung with ornaments and paper garlands, and there would be a fire crackling on the hearth—

But that was next year, and this was now, Clay reminded himself, with a sigh. He assessed the sky again, then whistled, low, for Outlaw.

The horse trotted over, reins dangling, and Clay gathered them and swung up into the saddle.

"We've got our work cut out for us," he told the animal.

The snow began coming down, slowly at first and then in earnest, when they were still about a mile outside of town, and by the time he and Outlaw reached the livery, it was hard to see farther than a dozen feet in any direction.

Zeb Dooley, the old man who ran the stable and adjoining blacksmith's shop, came out to meet him. Taking Outlaw's reins as soon as Clay had stepped down from the saddle, Zeb shouted to be heard over the rising screech of the wind. "Best head on over to the jailhouse or the Bitter Gulch, Marshal, because this blow is bound to get worse before it gets better!"

Clay took the reins back. "I want to look in over at the schoolhouse," he called in reply. "Make sure the children are all right."

Zeb, clad for the cold in dungarees and a heavy coat, shook his balding head. "Miss Krenshaw will keep them there 'til it's safe to leave. The town makes sure there's always a stash of firewood and grub, in case they need it."

Clay's worries were only partially allayed by Zeb's reassurance. A storm like this sure as hell meant trouble for *somebody,* and he didn't feel right about heading for the jailhouse to hunker down with Chester and wait it out, not just yet, anyway.

Clay turned away, mounted up again, bent low over Outlaw's neck to speak to him and started for the far edge of town.

He rode slowly, Outlaw stalwartly shouldering his way through the thickening snow, up one street and down another, until he'd covered all of them. Nobody called out to him as he passed, and lantern light glowed in most of the windows so, after half an hour, he and the horse felt their way back to the livery.

There was no sign of Zeb, and the big double doors of the stables were latched and rattling under the assault of the wind.

Clay opened them, led Outlaw inside and into his stall, gave him hay and made sure his water trough was full. Then he retraced his steps, latched the doors again and walked, wind-battered, toward the jailhouse.

Chapter 5

⁓⁓⁓

Dara Rose rubbed the glass in the door of the mercantile with one gloved hand, clearing a circle to look through and seeing nothing but dizzying flurries of angry white. She'd come here to mail her letter to Piper and send off the coupon to the Wildflower Salve Company, and now she wished she hadn't been in such a hurry to leave home.

Mr. Bickham doubled as Blue River's postmaster. Being in a position to know who wrote to whom, and who received letters from whom, he tended to mind everybody's business but his own.

"You might just as well sit down here by the stove as try to see any farther than the end of your nose in weather like this," Philo counseled, from behind his long counter. "That's about the tenth time you wiped off that window, and it just keeps fogging up again."

Dara Rose bit her lower lip, still fretful. She and Harriet were safe and warm, but what about Edrina? Suppose she tried to walk home from school in this storm? Miss Krenshaw could be depended upon to keep her students inside, of course, but Edrina was, as recent history proved, well able to get past her teacher when she chose.

Harriet, who considered the whole thing a marvelous lark, sat on top of a pickle barrel and gazed raptly at the exquisite doll in the display window. Dara Rose, noting this, felt another pinch to the heart.

She had the ten dollars Piper had sent; she could buy the doll for Harriet and several books for Edrina, set it all out for them after they went to bed on Christmas Eve, to find in the morning and rejoice over. But both children still needed warm coats, and sturdy shoes that fit properly, and for all the vegetables she'd stored in the root cellar and the chickens producing fresh eggs right along—until this morning, that is—there was barely enough food to see them through the winter.

This year, with Parnell gone and even the roof over their heads a precarious blessing, there would be no store-bought presents, no brightly decorated tree, no goose or turkey for Christmas dinner.

"I could let you have that doll for two dollars even," Philo whispered, suddenly standing beside Dara Rose and startling her half out of her skin. Because of the thick layers of sawdust covering the floor, she hadn't heard him approach. "Put a dollar down, and you can pay the rest over time, out of the egg money."

Dara Rose looked at him sharply, momentarily distracted from her worry over Edrina, who might at any moment take it into her head to strike out for home, blizzard or no blizzard, perhaps concerned about her mother and sister and the chickens.

That would be like Edrina.

"No, Mr. Bickham," Dara Rose whispered back, while Harriet paid neither one of them a whit of notice, "I will not be purchasing the doll, and that's final."

"But look at your little girl," the storekeeper cajoled. "She wants that pretty thing in the worst way."

Dara Rose's cheeks throbbed, and her throat thickened. It was only by the sternest exercise of self-control that she did not burst into tears. "I can barely afford to give my children what they *need*," she told him pointedly, though in a very quiet voice. "What they *want* is out of the question just now. Please do not press the matter further."

Philo gave a deep sigh and, at the same moment, the door Dara Rose had been standing next to only moments before burst open on a gust of wind.

Snow blew in, along with a swift and bitter chill, and then Clay McKettrick stepped over the threshold, accompanied by a medium-size dog, coated in white. Even for a strong man like he was, shutting that door again was an effort.

Dara Rose stood looking at the marshal and the dog, feeling oddly stricken, a state this man seemed to inflict upon her at every encounter. *She* might have been the one braving the frigid weather outside, instead of Clay, the way her breath stalled in the back of her throat.

With a smile, Clay took off his hat, dusting off the snow with his other hand, and nodded. "Afternoon, Mrs. Nolan," he said.

His voice was deep and quiet, his manner unhurried.

Dara Rose didn't answer, merely inclined her head briefly in response.

Harriet, meanwhile, forgot the doll she'd been so fascinated by until now, leaped nimbly off the pickle barrel and slowly approached the newcomers.

"Does that dog bite?" she asked forthrightly, studying the animal closely before tilting her head back to look up at Clay.

"I can't rightly say, one way or the other," Clay replied honestly. "He and I just took up with each other last night, so we're not all that well acquainted yet. Offhand, though, I'd say you oughtn't to pet old Chester until we know a little more about his nature."

Harriet smiled, enchanted. "Hullo, Chester," she said.

Chester looked her over, but stayed close to Clay's side.

"I don't normally allow dogs in my store," Philo said. Then, with a smile and a genial spreading of his hands, "But I'll make an exception for you, Marshal."

"I'm obliged," Clay said. "It's a fair hike back to the jailhouse and I'd rather not leave him alone there, anyhow."

Dara Rose opened her mouth, closed it again. When it came to Clay McKettrick, she was as bad as Harriet with the doll, prone to ogle and be struck dumb with awe.

As if to prove himself a gentleman, Chester ambled away from Clay to nestle down in the warm sawdust in front of the stove. With a sigh of grateful contentment, the dog closed his eyes and went to sleep.

Harriet giggled. "He must be tired," she said.

"I reckon he is at that," Clay agreed. "I think old Chester traveled a hard road before he found his way to me."

Dara Rose had never envied a dog before, but she did in that moment. She'd traveled a hard road, too, she and the girls, but it hadn't led to a handsome, steady-minded man who was probably able to handle just about anything.

She cleared her throat, fixing to make another attempt at speaking, but before a word came to her, Harriet had reached out and taken Clay's hand, tugging him in the direction of the display window.

"Look," she said reverently, pointing at the doll.

Dara Rose finally found her voice, but it didn't hold up for long. "Harriet—"

Clay lifted the child easily, holding her in one arm, so she was at eye level with the splendid toy.

"Isn't she pretty?" Harriet murmured, wonderstruck again.

"Not as pretty as you are," Clay told her. His gaze sought Dara Rose, found her, and brought yet another embarrassing blush to her cheeks. His expression was solemn, as if he wanted to ask some question but knew it would be improper to do so.

"If I sold my hair for two dollars and fifty cents," Harriet prattled on, wide-eyed, seemingly as at home in Clay's arms as she would have been in Parnell's, "I could take her home with me for good. Do you know of a place where folks buy hair?"

Dara Rose closed her eyes briefly, mortified.

"Can't say as I do," Clay replied affably. He was still looking at Dara Rose, though; she could feel it.

She opened her eyes, watched, tongue-tied with misery, as he gently set Harriet back on her feet.

"I'd name her Florence," Harriet continued. "Don't you think that's a pretty name? Florence?"

Clay allowed as how it was a very nice name.

Dara Rose realized she was staring and looked quickly away, only to have her gaze collide with Mr. Bickham's. A benevolent smirk wreathed the storekeeper's round face.

"Looks like the snow's letting up a little," Bickham said, with a glance at the window. "Maybe the marshal and his dog here could see you and little Harriet home safe while there's a lull."

Dara Rose needed to get back to her place, in case Edrina was there or on her way, but it wouldn't be wise for her and Harriet to attempt the journey, however short, on their own. So she swallowed her pride and turned back to Clay. "Would you mind?" she asked.

Clay cleared his throat before answering, but his words still came out sounding husky. "No, ma'am," he said, almost shyly. "I wouldn't mind."

So Dara Rose bundled Harriet up as warmly as she could, and then herself, and Clay lifted Harriet up again, simultaneously whistling for the dog.

Chester got up immediately, ready to go.

"You give some thought to what I said, Miz Nolan," Philo shouted after her, as she followed Clay out into the waning snowstorm. "Ain't no shame in buying on credit!"

Dara Rose ignored him.

The snow, having fallen hard and fast all morning, was nearly knee-deep and powdery. Clay and the dog seemed to navigate it with relative ease, Chester moving in a hopping way that might have been comical under more ordinary circumstances, and Dara Rose picked her way along in the tracks of the marshal's boots.

Harriet, snug against Clay's chest, with the front of his coat around her, looked back over his shoulder at Dara Rose, her eyes merry with adventure. The child was clearly reveling in *Mr. McKettrick's* attention—it was imprudent to think of him as "Clay," Dara Rose had decided—and no doubt pretending she had a papa again.

The thought made Dara Rose's throat ache like one big bruise, and her eyes scalded. She was glad Mr. Mc-Kettrick couldn't see her face.

They trooped on, Clay forging a way for all of them when the dog grew tired, and the snow was thickening again by the time they reached the house. The respite, it seemed, was nearly over.

The air was shiver-cold, and Chester needed to rest. Even though Dara Rose was mildly alarmed by the thought of the new marshal filling her house with his purely masculine presence, she had no choice but to ask him in.

There was no sign of Edrina, which was both a re-lief and a worry to Dara Rose. Once she had her elder daughter at home, safe and sound, she'd move on to the other concerns—how the chickens were faring, for a start, and the state of the woodpile stacked against the back of the house. Thanks to the town council, there was a good supply of firewood, but some of it would need drying out before it could be burned.

Clay—*Mr. McKettrick* suddenly seemed too unwieldy even in her thoughts—walked straight through to the kitchen, set Harriet on her feet and went about building up the dwindling fire in the cookstove.

Chester practically collapsed on the rug in front of the sink.

"I'll go on to the schoolhouse," Clay told Dara Rose, when he'd finished at the stove, "and see about bringing Edrina home. It would be a favor to me, Mrs. Nolan, if you'd let my dog stay here while I'm gone, since he's probably too tuckered out to go much farther."

This time, Dara Rose welcomed the heat that surged through her, pulsing in her face. They weren't without their blessings, she and the children. "Of course," she said awkwardly. "Harriet and I will look after Chester. And I don't mind admitting I'm worried that Edrina might try to make her way home on her own."

Clay nodded, grinned a little. "She might, at that," he said.

That grin *did* something to Dara Rose. She told herself

it was simple thankfulness. She needed help, and someone was there to give it and that was that.

"What about the other children?" she asked, as Clay
started for the back door.

"If any of them are stranded at the schoolhouse," he
answered, his hand on the knob, "I'll make sure they
get where they're supposed to go—after I bring your
girl home, that is." He turned toward Harriet, who was
now on her knees next to Chester, all concern for his
temperament evidently past, drying off his coat with a
flour-sack dish towel, and tugged at the brim of his hat.
"Thank you for minding my friend, there," he told the
child. "Looks as though he likes you."

Harriet beamed. "I *knew* he wouldn't bite me," she
said.

Clay smiled briefly then, opened the door, leaned into
the wind that rushed to meet him and stepped outside.
The door closed behind him.

CLAY FOUND HIS WAY to the schoolhouse more from
memory than by use of his eyesight, and Miss Krenshaw
met him at the door, took him firmly by the arm and
pulled him inside, out of the cold and the wind and the
blinding assault of the snow.

Except for Edrina, who was huddled close to the stove
and bundled inside a faded quilt, the schoolmarm was

alone. Evidently, the other kids had already been collected by kinfolks and taken home.

Edrina smiled at him. "I knew you'd come to fetch
me, if Mama didn't," she said, with a certainty that
warmed his heart.

"Sit down, Marshal," Miss Krenshaw all but commanded, indicating her desk chair, which was the only
one in the schoolroom big enough for an adult. "I've got
some coffee brewing in back."

Clay didn't plan to tarry long, since the storm was
more likely to get worse than it was to get better, and he
wanted to get Edrina back to her mother and sister while
the getting was good. But hot coffee sounded mighty
nice to him just then, and he wouldn't mind sitting for
a few minutes, either. He was still a young man, and fit,
but that cold made his bones ache.

"Thank you," he said, and took the offered chair.

Miss Krenshaw disappeared into the back, where she
probably had private quarters, and returned promptly
with the promised coffee.

"Thanks," Clay repeated, taking the steaming mug
from her hand.

Not one to be idle, it would seem, Miss Alvira got
busy erasing the day's lessons off the blackboard.

"You'll be all right here, on your own?" Clay asked
presently, restored by the tasty brew. Miss Alvira had

laced it with whiskey, which raised her a notch in his already high estimation. Too bad he couldn't work up an interest in courting the lady.

"I'll be just fine," Miss Alvira said, still busy. She sounded a mite affronted by the question, in fact. "I have everything I need, right here."

Edrina, still seated by the stove, took in the conversation, but offered no comment. She did look somewhat pensive, though, and Clay wondered briefly what was going through that busy little brain of hers.

He finished the coffee, got to his feet, glanced at one of the windows.

There was no letup to the snow, as far as he could tell.

Miss Alvira marched into the cloakroom, came out with Edrina's coat and bonnet and briskly prepared the child for the journey home. For good measure, she wrapped the quilt around Edrina again, too.

"There," she said, with a slight smile.

Clay put his hat back on—he'd left it on a peg next to the door, coming in—and hoisted Edrina, quilt and all, into his arms. As he'd done with Harriet, leaving the mercantile, he tried to cover her with his coat, as well.

"You're sure there's nowhere you'd like to go?" he asked Miss Alvira, before opening the door. "To the hotel, maybe? There're bound to be some folks around, and I could walk you over—"

The schoolmarm gave a little sniff and hiked up her chin again. "Marshal," she said, putting a point on the word, "as I've already told you, I am quite capable of looking after myself, and besides, I wouldn't think of spending good money on a hotel room."

"All right, then," Clay said, with a slight smile and a nod of farewell.

He followed his own quickly disappearing boot prints back to Dara Rose's front door, shoulders braced against the wind, his arms tight around the little girl tucked in the folds of that old quilt.

A lamp burned in the center of Dara Rose's kitchen table, and the house was not only blessedly warm, but there was something savory simmering on the stove.

Her face lit up at their return, and even though Clay knew most of that joy was for Edrina, he basked in the welcome, anyway. And Chester was just about beside himself, he was so happy to see Clay.

"You'll stay for supper," Dara Rose informed Clay briskly, once he'd set Edrina down, and then she commenced to unwinding that now-damp quilt from around the little girl.

Clay just stood there for a long moment, in his snowy duster and his wet hat, waiting for his bones and sinews to thaw and just enjoying the sight of her. Dara Rose's aquamarine eyes were bright and her cheeks flushed, probably from the heat of the stove and happiness because Edrina was home.

"All right," he said, finally realizing that her statement called for some kind of response, however mundane. "Whatever you're cooking, it smells good."

She smiled at him, briefly, distractedly, and all but set him back on his heels by the doing of it.

"Edrina, you go in and change into dry clothes," she told the child.

Edrina hesitated, then left the room. Harriet, after trying in vain to get Chester to come along on the jaunt, followed her sister, chattering about the walk home from the mercantile.

It was a heady thing, being alone with Dara Rose in that steamy little room.

And Clay, a quiet man but not a shy one, couldn't come up with a single thing to say.

Dara Rose tightened the bands on her apron, a reach-back motion that made her shapely bosom rise and jut out a little. "If the chickens survive this," she said, with an anxious glance toward the room's one opaque window, "it will be a miracle, and I sure hope some of the men in town give a thought to the O'Reillys, like they generally do at times like this...."

Her voice fell away, and she gnawed fretfully at her

lower lip, likely pondering the fate of the poultry, the family she'd just mentioned, or both.

"The O'Reillys?" Clay croaked out, grabbing hold of the rapidly sinking conversational lifeline with the first thing that jumped off his tongue.

Dara Rose sighed again, turned away from him to stir whatever was cooking in that pot. The scent of it made his stomach rumble, and it came to him that, except for Miss Krenshaw's whiskeyed-up coffee, he hadn't had anything since breakfast.

"Peg O'Reilly's no-good excuse for a husband," she said quietly, after a glance in the direction of the doorway the little girls had hurried through earlier, "ran off with some...some...*woman* he met at the Bitter Gulch Saloon, and left a wife and three children behind to fend for themselves!"

For a moment, Clay was taken aback—not by the story, which unfortunately was not an uncommon one, especially with the war in Europe picking up momentum—but by Dara Rose's apparent failure to draw any correlation between Mrs. O'Reilly's situation and her own. Except for one obvious variable—Parnell had had the bad fortune to die, while the long-gone Mr. O'Reilly was presumably still alive—the two women had essentially been dealt the same bad hand of cards.

Dara Rose seemed to sense that he was looking at her,

and she turned to meet his gaze, colored up again and looked quickly away. The girls returned to the kitchen just then, before anything more could be said, Harriet going on about that doll she meant to name Florence, and Edrina replying in lofty, big-sister fashion that Harriet ought to wish in one hand and spit in the other and see which one got full faster.

Clay went to the sink, rolled up his shirtsleeves and commenced to washing his hands with the harsh yellow soap Dara Rose kept in an old saucer wedged behind the pump handle.

He felt a combination of things while he was at it, but mainly, he realized, he was glad. Glad just to be where he was, right there in that kitchen, out of the cold wind, with a lovely woman, two kids and a dog for company.

For the first time since he'd left Arizona, Clay didn't have to fight down a hankering for home, didn't second-guess his decision to strike out on his own instead of making a life on the ever-expanding Triple M with the rest of the family.

Be sure you're leaving because it's what you really want to do, Clay, his pa had counseled him, *and not because Annabel Carson broke your heart.*

It made Clay smile a little to remember that conversation, and others like it, with various members of the home outfit, and he reckoned now that Annabel hadn't broken his heart at all—she'd just sprained it a little.

The stuff in the pot on the stove turned out to be some kind of mixture of canned venison and leftover vegetable preserves, and it was better, in Clay's opinion, than a big steak at Delmonico's.

"Miss Krenshaw keeps a picture of a soldier in her top desk drawer," Edrina chimed, in the middle of the meal, pretty much out of nowhere.

Snow rasped at the windows and the small cookstove seemed to strain to put out more heat.

"And how would you know a thing like that, Edrina Nolan?" Dara Rose asked, arching one eyebrow, her spoon poised halfway between her mouth and the bowl of soup sitting in front of her.

"She takes it out and looks at it, when she thinks nobody's looking," Edrina explained nonchalantly. "Sometimes, she gets tears in her eyes, and her lips move like she's talking to somebody."

Clay's gaze connected with Dara Rose's.

"Are you going to fight in the war, Mr. McKettrick?" Edrina asked, without missing a beat.

"No," Clay answered. The armed forces would need beef, and plenty of it, and like his granddad said, somebody had to raise the critters. "But my cousin Gabriel thinks he might join up, if things don't simmer down some over the next year or two."

A sad expression flickered across Dara Rose's expressive face; he figured the war was a subject she tried not to think about, since there was nothing she could do to change it.

After supper, Edrina and Harriet cleared the table and set the dishes in the sink, without being told.

Dara Rose crossed the room to take her cloak and bonnet down from their peg near the door. She clearly dreaded whatever she was about to do, and Clay found himself beside her before he'd made a conscious decision to move, reaching for his hat and duster.

Dara Rose looked up at him, and he caught the briefest glimpse into the shimmering vastness of her heart and mind and spirit. There was so much more to her than just her flesh-and-blood person, he realized, with a start akin to waking up suddenly after a long, deep sleep.

"The chickens—" she began, and then went silent.

"I'll see to them," Clay said, very quietly. "You stay here, with the girls."

She considered the idea briefly, then shook her head no. She meant to go out to that chicken coop and that was that. He'd be wasting his breath to argue.

"I'll heat water to wash the dishes when I get back,"

she told the children. "Don't get too close to the stove, and no scuffling."

"Oh, Mama," Edrina said, with a roll of her eyes. "You've told us that a *thousand times* already."

A smile quirked at one corner of Dara Rose's mouth. Like the rest of her, visible and invisible, that mouth fascinated Clay out of all good sense and reason. "Well," she said, "now it's a thousand and *one*."

After a glance at Clay's face, she opened the door and stepped right out into that blizzard.

Clay followed, and the wind was so strong that it buffeted her back a step, so they collided, her back to his torso. He put his arms out to steady her, and a powerful jolt of...*something*...shot through him.

Since it was too cold to dally, they recovered quickly and advanced toward the rickety coop.

The chickens had taken refuge inside and, with the exception of the rooster, who squawked indignantly as he paced the floor of that shed, as though fussing over the pure injustice of a snowstorm, the birds huddled close to one another on the length of wood that served as a roost.

There was a visible easing in Dara Rose as she looked around. "At least none of them have frozen to death," she said, and she might have been addressing herself, not him, trundling over to lift the lid off a wooden bend and lean inside to scoop out feed. Judging by how *far* she had to lean—Lordy, she had a shapely backside—the supply was starting to run low.

Like a lot of other things in her life, probably.

Clay watched, offering no comment, as Dara Rose filled a shallow pan with feed and set it out for the hens to peck at. That done, she picked up a second pan, went to the doorway and shoveled up some snow. The stuff was already melting around the edges, cold as that chicken coop was, when Dara Rose waded back into the center of the noisy flock to set the second pan down beside the first.

They fought their way back to the house, side by side, heads down, shoulders braced. Clay wanted to put an arm around Dara Rose's waist, so she wouldn't fall or blow away, but every instinct warned against it.

The woman had a right to her pride, probably needed it just to press on from one day to the next.

By the time they got back inside the house, the girls had left the kitchen for the front room.

Their voices carried, a happy sound, like the chiming of bells somewhere off in the muffled distance.

Dara Rose moved to untie her bonnet laces, but Clay closed his hands over hers. "You've done a fine job raising those girls of yours," he said, though he hadn't actually planned the words ahead of time.

Those wonderful eyes of hers searched his face, almost warily. Then she smiled and went on to take off her bonnet, Clay's hands falling away from hers and back to his sides.

"Thank you, Mr. McKettrick," she said, stepping back to shed her snow-speckled cloak.

"Clay," he said, knowing she wanted him to step aside so she could get on with whatever it was she planned to do next but stubbornly holding his ground. "I don't generally answer to 'Mr. McKettrick,' as it happens. Usually, when folks use that moniker, they're talking to my granddad."

She blushed, but her eyes flashed. "When I say it," she told him, "I'm addressing *you*. We haven't known each other long enough to use first names."

He chuckled at that. Curved his finger sideways under her chin and lifted. "Have it your way…Dara Rose," he said, partly to get under her hide and partly because he just liked saying her name.

Still wearing his coat and hat, he summoned the dog with a soft whistle.

Edrina and Harriet immediately appeared in the inside doorway, squashed together as though there was barely enough room in the gap to contain both of them. Their eyes were wide with curiosity and something else— maybe worry.

"You're going?" Edrina asked.

"And taking Chester?" Harriet added.

Clay touched the brim of his hat, momentarily ignoring Dara Rose, who was probably still prickly over his impertinent use of her Christian name. "Yep," he said. "Chester and I ought to be getting over to the jailhouse, in case somebody comes looking for us."

"But it's getting dark," Edrina protested.

"And it's still snowing *really hard,*" Harriet said. "What if you and Chester get lost?"

"We'll find our way," Clay promised, his voice a little huskier than normal. "Don't you worry about us."

Dara Rose surprised him by laying a hand on his arm. "Take the lantern," she said.

Clay was moved by the offer, but he didn't let it show, of course. He just shook his head and smiled a little. "It wouldn't do much good, hard as the wind's blowing," he said. "But I thank you kindly, just the same. And thanks for supper, too, and a right pleasant evening."

Dara Rose opened her mouth, closed it again and then sighed. "Be careful," she said.

"I will certainly do that, ma'am," he answered.

The winter night bit into him like teeth when he moved out into it, Chester struggling along at his side.

Before they got as far as the gate, the dog was practically sinking out of sight with every cautious step, so

Clay picked him up, carrying him in the curve of his right arm.

With his free hand, Clay pulled his hat brim down low over his eyes and blinked a couple of times, until he could see. If it weren't for thin snatches of lamplight, spilling from various windows along the way, he and Chester might have been in some trouble.

As it was, Clay was half-frozen by the time he fumbled with the latch on his office door, stepped over the threshold and set the dog down to feel along the wall for the metal box that held the matches for the stove and the lanterns.

Chester gave a low growl as Clay struck the match.

There was a shuffling clatter over by the desk, followed by the sound of boot soles striking the plank floor and a grumbled curse.

"Damn it, Clay," growled his cousin Sawyer, "you oughtn't to sneak up on a man like that, especially when he's sleeping."

Chapter 6

"I thought it didn't snow in Texas," Sawyer said, after stretching and letting go with a lusty yawn.

Clay patted the dog, reassured him with a few quiet words and lit one of the two lanterns he had on hand. "What are you doing here, Sawyer?" he countered gruffly.

"I *was* catching up on my shut-eye," Sawyer replied affably, grinning that cocky grin that sometimes made Clay want to backhand his cousin, "until you came banging through the door and disturbed me."

Clay lit the other lantern, the one that stood on the bookcase, and then went to the stove to build up the fire. The last time he'd seen his cousin and one-time best friend, they'd had words, not just about Annabel, but about a few other things, too.

"You're a long way from home, cousin," Clay finally remarked.

"So are you," Sawyer answered, perching on the edge of Clay's desk now, with his arms folded. The youngest son of Clay's uncle Kade, and aunt Mandy, Sawyer had the fair hair and dark blue eyes that ran in intergenerational streaks through the McKettrick bloodline.

Clay shut the stove door with a clang and rustled up some leftovers for Chester, who seemed to have decided that the surprise visitor made acceptable company.

Which just went to show what a dog knew about anything, Clay thought glumly. Most of them liked everybody, and Chester was no exception.

"I'm going to ask you once more," Clay said evenly, "*just once,* what you're doing here, and if I don't get a clear answer, I swear I'll toss you behind bars on a trespassing charge."

Sawyer chuckled. "I'm just passing through," he said. "Since I was in your neck of the woods, I decided to board my horse in San Antonio and take the train to Blue River, see how you're faring and all."

"I'm faring just fine," Clay responded, "so you can get on tomorrow's train, if it makes it through, and go right back to San Antonio."

Sawyer strolled to the window, in no evident hurry to get there. He had the born horseman's rolling, easy stride. "Good thing I didn't bring the horse," he said, as though Clay hadn't as good as told him, straight out, that he wasn't welcome. "We'd probably be out there in the blizzard someplace, freezing to death." A visible shudder moved through his lean, agile form, but he didn't turn around. "Like I said, nothing anybody ever told me about Texas prepared me for ass-deep snow."

Clay ladled water into the coffeepot, a dented metal receptacle coated with blue enamel, and set it on top of the potbellied stove. Then he commenced to spoon ground coffee beans into it, along with a pinch of salt to make the grounds settle after the stuff brewed. "That's the thing about weather," he said, at considerable length. "It's unpredictable."

Sawyer finally turned around, but he lingered at the window, frost-coated and all but opaque behind him. "Annabel Carson got married soon after you left," he said, gruffly and with care.

"Not to you, it appears," Clay said, turning his back to the stove and absorbing the heat.

Sawyer made a sound that might have been a chuckle, though it contained no noticeable amusement. "Not to me," he confirmed. "She got hitched to Whit Taggard, over near Stone Creek. You know, that banker in his fifties, with more money than one man ever ought to have? She swears it's a love match."

"You came all the way to Blue River to tell me that?" Clay asked, strangely unmoved by news that probably would have devastated him not so long ago. Chester had finished his meal of leftovers from the hotel dining room and gone to curl up on his blanket. The wind howled and hissed under the eaves, as if it were fixing to raise the roof right off that old jailhouse and carry it next door, if not farther.

"No," Sawyer said. "I came all the way to Blue River because your mama's been worried about you, and I love my aunt Chloe."

Clay sighed. "I already sent Ma and Pa a wire," he said, mildly exasperated. "They know I'm fine."

"Your saying it and their knowing it for sure are two different things, Clay," Sawyer went on, his tone reasonable and quiet, as if he were calming a jittery horse or a cow mired in deep mud and struggling against the ropes meant to pull it onto dry ground. "It's not every day a man picks up and leaves the place and the people he's known all his life."

Clay had no answer for that, had already done all the explaining he ever intended to do, where the decision to put home behind him for good—at least as far as living there—was concerned, anyhow. Much as he loved his granddad and his pa and his uncles, he didn't want to spend the rest of his life taking orders from them. He wanted to build and run his own outfit, marry and have sons and daughters, grandchildren and great-grandchildren.

"You hungry?" Clay asked, hoping to get the conversation going in another direction.

"I had fried chicken over at the hotel, soon as I'd checked in and stowed my gear," Sawyer answered, with a shake of his head. He looked around at the humble quarters Clay presently called home, sighed. "Nobody can accuse you of living high on the hog, I reckon," he finished, sounding weary now.

Clay shoved a hand through his hair, recalling the difficult trek back from Dara Rose's place. It had taken him and Chester the better part of half an hour to cover the five hundred yards or so between the jail and that snug little house.

Once he'd warmed up, had some coffee and put on long johns and an extra layer of clothes, he meant to venture out again, track down that family Dara Rose had mentioned—the O'Reillys—and see for himself that they were warm and had something to eat. He figured it was his duty, as marshal, to see that folks made it through when there was an emergency like that snowstorm, especially women and children.

"Finding your way back to the hotel in this blizzard

might be tricky," Clay told his cousin, in his own good time. "You can bunk in the cell there if you want."

One side of Sawyer's mouth quirked upward in a grin. "And give you a prime opportunity to lock me up, soon as I shut my eyes, and then drop the key down a deep well? Not likely, cousin."

"You sorely overestimate my ability to tolerate your company," Clay responded dryly. "The sooner you're on your way, the happier I'm going to be."

Sawyer didn't reply right away, which was a telling thing, because he was usually quick to shoot off his mouth. There *was* a whole other side to Sawyer, though—one nobody, including Clay, really knew much about.

"You must know I never laid a hand on your girl, Clay," Sawyer said, as a chunk of wood crackled and splintered to embers inside the stove. "So what exactly is it about me that sticks in your craw? We used to be as close as brothers."

Too warm now that he'd been standing near the stove for a while, Clay moved on to his desk, reclaimed the creaky wooden chair, sat back in it with his hands cupped behind his head. Chester, lying nearby on his blanket pile, gave a single, chortling snore, and another piece of wood collapsed in the fire, with a series of sharp snaps.

"You come here," Clay answered presently, "uninvited, I might add, and let on that I'm a grief to the family, like some prodigal son off squandering his birthright in a far country, and then you have the gall to ask what sticks in my craw? It's the hypocrisy of it. *You're a gunslinger,* Sawyer, a hired gun. Little better than an outlaw, most likely. It might even be that if I went through all these wanted posters on my desk, I'd come across a fair likeness of your face."

"I'm not an outlaw," Sawyer said flatly. "You know that."

"Do I?" Clay asked. "You blow through the Triple M every few years like a breeze—just long enough last time to turn my girl's head—and then, one fine day, a telegram comes in, and you're gone again, without a word to anybody. Like you know somebody's picked up your trail so you'd better be moving on, pronto."

Sawyer sighed again, and it came out raspy. "I don't reckon anything I say is going to get through that inch-thick layer of bone you call a skull," he said. "You made up your mind about me a long time ago, didn't you, cousin?"

There was no denying that. "I reckon I did," Clay replied quietly, feeling wrung out. "You can tell Ma and the rest of the family that you've seen me and I'm fine. Seems to me that your business here is finished."

Even as he spoke those words, Clay wondered what

the *real* reason for Sawyer's visit might be. Blue River was too far out of his cousin's way for this to be about Annabel, or a favor to Clay's ma and pa.

Sawyer crossed to the door, took his hat and canvas duster down from their pegs and put them on. Then he hesitated, one hand on the old-fashioned iron latch. "You're right," he said, with more sadness than Clay had heard in his voice since they were ten years old and Sawyer's dog took sick and died. "I guess there's no getting back on your good side. I'll be on tomorrow's train, if it gets here, and you can get on with whatever the hell it is you think you're doing."

With that, Sawyer opened the door and went out, letting in a blast of snow-speckled cold that reached into the deepest parts of Clay and held on.

He almost relented, almost called Sawyer back—but in the end, he figured it was best to let him go.

THE SNOW LAY LIKE A THICK, glittering mantle over the countryside when Dara Rose went out to feed the chickens, carrying the egg basket and a jug to refill their water pan, but the sky was the purest blue, cloudless and benign. As quickly as it had arisen, the storm was over; water dripped rhythmically from the edges of the roof, and the path to the henhouse was slushy under the soles of her high-button shoes.

Hope stirred, springlike, in Dara Rose's heart, as she crossed the yard. She could hear the chickens clucking away in the coop, wanting their breakfast and their liberty from a long night of confinement.

Using the side of her foot, Dara Rose cleared a patch of ground for the birds and let them out while she ducked inside to fetch the water pan. Pleased to see that every member of her little flock had survived, she scattered their feed and then went on to collect the eggs.

There were six—a better count than the day before, though still less than she'd hoped for—and Dara Rose set each one carefully in the basket and returned to the house.

Edrina and Harriet were up and dressed, Edrina full of glee because she didn't have to go to school that day, and Harriet equally happy to have a playmate.

Dara Rose took off her bonnet and cloak, hung them up, washed her hands at the pump in the sink and put a pot of water on to boil, for oatmeal.

In the middle of the meal, a knock sounded at the front door.

Frowning, wondering who would be out and about so early, with the snow still deep enough to make traveling through it a trial, she pushed back her chair, told the children to finish eating and behave themselves and hurried through the small parlor. On some level, she realized, she'd hoped to find Clay McKettrick standing on her tiny porch, but this only came to her when she saw Mayor Wilson Ponder there instead.

Through the glass oval in the door, the older man's face looked purposeful, and a little grim.

Dara Rose opened the door. "Mayor Ponder," she said, not bothering to hide her surprise. He'd arrived, she saw now, looking past him to the street, in a sleigh drawn by two sturdy mules. "Come in."

"I won't tarry," Ponder said gravely, with a distracted tug at the brim of his bowler hat. He remained where he was, forcing Dara Rose to stand in the bright cold of the doorway and wait to hear what business he had with her. "I know this isn't a convenient time, what with the blizzard and all, but frankly, I'm not comfortable putting the task off any longer." He reddened slightly, though that might have been because of the weather, and not any sense of chagrin, and his muttonchop whiskers wobbled as he prepared to go on. "The town purchased this house for the use of the marshal, Mrs. Nolan, and if Clay McKettrick doesn't mean to use the place, well, we—the town council, that is—would prefer to sell it."

Dara Rose felt the floor shift under her feet, but she kept her shoulders squared and even managed not to shiver at the cold, and the news the mayor had just delivered.

"Oh," she said, hugging herself and wishing for her cloak, wishing for summer and better times. "Do you have a prospective buyer?"

"Ezra Maddox wants the property," Mayor Ponder said, after more whisker-wriggling. "He's offering two hundred and fifty dollars cash money and, what with bringing in electricity, the town could use the funds."

Ezra Maddox owned a farm, Dara Rose thought, dazed and frustrated and quite cornered. What did the man want with a run-down house miles from his crops and his dairy cows?

By now, everyone knew Clay had decided to live over at the jailhouse. Could it be that Mr. Maddox was simply trying to force her hand by buying the house out from under her? Was he hoping she would give in and accept his offer of a so-called housekeeping job, possibly followed by marriage, and send her children away in the bargain?

Dara Rose seethed, even as cold terror overtook her. "How long until we have to move?" she asked, amazed at how calm she sounded.

Mayor Ponder hesitated before he answered, perhaps ashamed of that morning's mission. On the other hand, he'd gone to all the bother of hitching mules to a sleigh to get there bright and early, which did not indicate any real degree of reluctance on his part. "Ezra's mighty anxious to take possession of the place," he finally said. "But since Christmas is just two weeks away, well, he's— *we're*—willing to let you stay until the first of the year."

Dara Rose gripped the door frame with one hand, thinking she might actually swoon. Behind her, in the kitchen, the girls' voices rang like chimes as they conducted some merry disagreement, laced with giggles.

"Well, then," Dara Rose managed, meeting the mayor's gaze, seeing both sympathy and resolve there, "that's that, isn't it? Thank you for letting me know."

With that, she shut the door in his face.

And stood trembling, there in the small parlor, until she heard his footsteps retreating on the porch.

"Mama?" Harriet, light-footed as ever and half again too perceptive for a five-year-old, was standing directly behind her. "Can we get a dog? Edrina says we don't need another mouth to feed, but a puppy wouldn't eat very much, would it?"

All of Dara Rose's considerable strength gave way then, like a dam under the strain of rising water. She uttered a small, choked sob, shook her head and fled to the bedroom.

Dara Rose seldom cried—even at Parnell's funeral service, she'd been dry-eyed—but she was only human, after all.

And she'd come to the end of her resources, at least for the moment.

So she sat on the edge of the bed she shared with her daughters—Parnell had slept on the settee in the parlor—covered her face with both hands and wept softly into her palms.

CLAY WAS HAVING BREAKFAST over at the hotel dining room—bacon and eggs and hotcakes, with plenty of hot, fresh coffee—when Sawyer wandered in, looking well-rested and clean-shaven, his manner at once affable and distant.

"Mind if I join you?" he said, pulling back a chair opposite Clay and sitting down before Clay could answer. He picked up the menu and studied it with the same grave concentration their illustrious granddad reserved for government beef contracts.

Politicians and pencil pushers, Angus had been known to remark, on the occasions he did business with such officials. *A man would have to be simpleminded to trust a one of them.*

"Make yourself at home," Clay said, dryly and long after the fact. He hadn't slept much the night before, thanks to Dara Rose and Sawyer's unexpected presence and the long slog through the snow to the O'Reilly place.

He'd found them huddled around a poor fire like characters in a Dickens novel, wrapped in thin blankets. They'd had fried eggs for supper, Mrs. O'Reilly had told him, and those were all gone, and he was welcome to what was left of yesterday's pinto beans if he was hungry.

Clay had thanked her kindly and said he'd already had supper, which happened to be the truth, though he would have lied without a qualm if it hadn't been, and then he'd carried in most of their dwindling wood supply to dry beside the homemade stove. Before coming to the hotel for breakfast that morning, he'd stopped by the mercantile, pounded at the front door until the storekeeper let him in, and purchased a sackful of dried beans, along with flour, sugar, a pound of coffee and assorted canned goods for the O'Reillys. He'd paid extra to have the food delivered before the store was open for business.

Now, sitting across from his pensive cousin in a warm, clean, well-lighted place where good food could be had in plenty, he felt vaguely ashamed of his own prosperity. While the McKettricks didn't live grandly, they didn't lack for money, either. Clay had never missed a meal in his life, never had to go without shoes or wear clothes that had belonged to somebody else first. Unlike the O'Reilly children, and too many others like them, he'd had a strong, committed father, backed up by three uncles and a granddad.

The cook, a round-bellied man who doubled as a waiter, came over to the table to greet Sawyer and take his order.

Sawyer simply pointed toward Clay's plate and said, "That looks good."

The cook nodded and went away.

Sawyer sat there, easy in his hide, dressed like a prosperous gambler. Instead of his usual plain shirt and even plainer denim trousers, he sported a suit, complete with a white shirt, a string tie and a brocade vest. "You look miserable this morning, cousin," he said cheerfully, "but something tells me it isn't remorse over the uncharitable welcome you offered last night."

Clay gave a raw chuckle, void of mirth. His appetite was gone, all of a sudden, and he set down his knife and fork, pushed his plate away. "It definitely isn't remorse," he said.

Sawyer helped himself to a slice of toasted bread and bit into it, chewed appreciatively. Though his eyes twinkled, his voice was serious when he replied, "You could still go back to the Triple M, you know. They'd welcome you back into the fold with open arms and shouts of 'hurrah.'"

"I'll pay them a visit one of these days," he said. "There aren't any hard feelings on my side."

"Nor theirs, either." Sawyer shoved a hand through

his unruly dark-gold hair, which was always a little too
long. "You're lucky, Clay," he said, his gaze moving to
the window next to their table. "Pa and Granddad can't
seem to make up their minds whether to kill the fat-
ted calf in my honor or take a horsewhip to me." He
frowned, squinted at the foggy glass. "I think somebody's
trying to get your attention," he observed.

Clay looked, and there, on the other side of that
steamed-up window, was Edrina, practically pressing
her nose to the glass. She waved one unmittened hand
and retreated a step.

"I'll be damned," Clay muttered, gesturing for the
child to come inside.

"Who's the kid?" Sawyer wanted to know.

"Friend of mine," Clay answered, as Edrina scampered
toward the entrance to the dining room.

She hurried over to the table, face flushed with cold
and purpose, and stood there like a little soldier.

"Mama's crying," she said. "Mama *never* cries."

Clay scraped back his chair, took Edrina's small hands
into his own, trying to chafe some warmth into them.
"Where's your bonnet?" he fussed, trying to process the
idea of Dara Rose in tears. "You aren't wearing any mittens, and your coat is unbuttoned—"

"I was in a *hurry*," Edrina told him, with a little sigh
of impatience. She spared Sawyer the briefest glance,

then looked back at Clay with a proud plea in her eyes. "You'll come home with me, won't you? Right now? Because Mama is crying and Mama never, *ever* cries."

"Go on," Sawyer said to Clay. "I'll settle up for your breakfast."

Clay got up, retrieved his duster from the back of the chair beside his and his hat from the seat and put them on. "What's the matter with her?" he asked, more worried than he could ever remember being before. "Is she sick?"

Gravely, Edrina took his hand, tugged him in the direction of the door. "I don't know," she said fretfully. "Maybe. But she was fine while we were having our oatmeal. Then Mr. Ponder stopped by, and they talked, and when Harriet asked Mama if we could please get a dog, Mama commenced to blubbering and ran right out of the room."

Outside, the snow was melting under a steadily warming sky, but it was still deep. Clay curved an arm around Edrina's waist, much as he had done with Chester the night before, and set off for Dara Rose's place with long strides.

DARA ROSE MARCHED herself out into the kitchen, pumped cold water into the basin she kept on hand and splashed her face repeatedly while Harriet watched her solemnly from the doorway.

"Are you through crying, Mama?" the child asked, very softly.

Dara Rose felt ashamed. Now she'd upset Edrina and Harriet, and for what? A few moments of self-pity?

"I'm quite through," she said, drying her still-puffy face with a dish towel. "And I haven't the slightest idea what came over me." She hugged Harriet, then frowned, looking around. "Where is Edrina?"

Harriet bit her lower lip, clearly reluctant to answer.

"Harriet?" Dara Rose said, taking her little girl gently but firmly by the shoulders. *"Where is your sister?"*

Harriet's eyes were huge and luminous. "She went to fetch Mr. McKettrick," she finally replied.

Alarm rushed through Dara Rose, and not just because a glance at the row of hooks beside the back door revealed that Edrina had gone off through the deep snow without her bonnet or her mittens. She was just reaching for her own cloak when she heard footsteps on the front porch—boots, stomping off snow.

Clay knocked, but then he came right in, carrying Edrina. His gaze locked with Dara Rose's as he set the little girl down and pulled the door closed behind him.

She'd never seen a man look so worried before, not even when Parnell came to that settlement house in Bangor, Maine, to claim her and the children. They'd been mere babies then, Edrina and Harriet, and memories of their real father, Parnell's younger brother, Luke, soon faded.

"Are you sick?" Clay demanded, in the same tone he might have employed to confront a drunk with disorderly conduct.

Dara Rose wasn't sick, except with mortification. "I'm quite all right," she said, but she didn't sound very convincing, even to herself. She shifted her attention to her elder daughter, letting her know with a look that she was in big trouble. "I apologize for any inconvenience—"

Clay's neck reddened, and his eyes narrowed. "I'd be obliged if you girls would wait in the kitchen," he said, though he never looked away from Dara Rose's face.

Edrina and Harriet, always ready with a protest when *she* made such a request, fled the room like rabbits with a fox on their trail.

"That little girl," Clay said, in a furious whisper, one index finger jabbing in the general direction of the kitchen a few times, "was so worried about you that she braved all that snow to find me and bring me here. So don't think for one minute that you're going to put me off with an apology for any *inconvenience*."

Dara Rose stared at him. "Why are you so angry?" she finally asked. *And why does it thrill me to see you like this?*

"I'm not angry," Clay rasped out, wrenching off his Wyatt Earp–style hat and flinging it so that it landed on the settee, teetered there and dropped to the floor. "Damn it, Dara Rose, whatever went on here this morning scared your daughter half to death, and since Edrina is the most courageous kid I've ever come across, *I* got scared, too."

The thrill didn't subside, and Dara Rose prayed her feelings didn't show. "I lost my composure for a moment," she confessed, as stiffly proud as a Puritan even as her heart raced and her breath threatened to catch in the back of her throat and never come loose. "Believe me, I regret it. I certainly didn't mean to frighten the children—"

"Well," Clay said, in earnest, "you *did.* And I'm not leaving here until you tell me what Ponder said to you that made you go to pieces the way you did."

Dara Rose swallowed, looked down at the floor. Right or wrong, Clay meant what he said—that much was obvious from his tone and his countenance. He wouldn't be going anywhere until she answered him.

"Dara Rose?" He was standing close to her now, his hands resting lightly on her shoulders. He smelled of fresh air, snow and something woodsy. "Tell me."

She knew she ought to pull away from him, ought to look anywhere but up into his face, but she couldn't manage either response. "Mayor Ponder stopped by to tell me that, since you don't want this house, the town council plans to sell it to Ezra Maddox for two hundred and fifty dollars," she said. It was remarkable how calm she sounded, she thought, when her insides were buzzing like a swarm of bees smoked out of their hive. "We have to be out by the first of the year."

"That son of a—" Clay ground out, before catching himself.

Dara Rose felt tears burning behind her eyes again, and she was determined not to disgrace herself by shedding them. "I have ten dollars," she said, like someone talking in their sleep. "And I've saved some of the egg money. It won't take us far, but it's enough to leave town."

"Where would you go?" Clay immediately asked.

"I don't know," Dara Rose replied honestly. "Somewhere."

"The town isn't going to sell this house," Clay said.

"Of course they are," Dara Rose argued, though not with any spirit.

"I'm the marshal," Clay told her, "and under the terms of our agreement, I'm entitled to living quarters. It just so happens that I've decided I'd rather live here than in the jailhouse."

Dara Rose's jaw dropped, and it took her a moment to recover. A *long* moment. "But, we couldn't... Where would the children and I—?"

Clay hooked a finger under her chin. "Right here," he said. "You and Edrina and Harriet could live right here, with me—if you and I were married."

Dara Rose nearly choked. *"Married?"*

"It wouldn't do for us to live under the same roof otherwise," Clay said reasonably.

"But, we're nearly total strangers—"

"For now," Clay went on, when her words fell away, "it would be a private arrangement. All business. I won't press you to bed down with me, Dara Rose. This place is too small for such shenanigans, anyhow, with the girls around."

Dara Rose couldn't believe what she was hearing. It was Parnell, all over again. Clay was offering a marriage that *wasn't* a marriage, offering shelter and safety and respectability. But unless she wanted to send her children away and move in with Ezra Maddox, she couldn't afford to refuse.

"Why?" she asked, barely breathing the word. "Why would you want to do this, Clay McKettrick?"

He smiled at her. Tucked a tendril of hair behind her right ear, where it had escaped its pins. "I want a wife," he said, as though that explained everything, instead of raising dozens, if not hundreds, of new questions.

"But you said the marriage wouldn't be real."

"It won't be, at first," Clay told her. Where did he get

all that certainty, all that confidence? All that *audacity?*
"But maybe, with time..."

"What if nothing changes?" Dara Rose broke in, feeling almost as though she needed to shout to be heard
over the thrumming of her heartbeat, though of course
she *didn't* shout, because the children would have heard.

"Then there'll be no harm done," Clay said. "We'll
have the marriage annulled, I'll set you and the girls up
in decent circumstances somewhere far from Blue River,
and we'll go our separate ways."

No harm done? He spoke so blithely.

Was the man insane?

Possibly, Dara Rose decided. But he was also an in-
finitely better bet than Ezra Maddox.

Chapter 7

By the following morning, Sawyer was long gone and the snow had turned to mud so deep that folks had had to lay weathered boards and old doors in the street, just to get from one side to the other without sinking to their knees in the muck. Hardly anybody rode a horse or drove a wagon through town or along the side roads, either, but the sun shone like the herald of an early spring, and the breezes were almost balmy.

Clay considered all this as he stood in his small room at the jailhouse, stooping a little to peer at himself in the cracked shaving mirror fixed to the wall. He'd washed up and shaved, and then shaken out and put on the only suit he'd brought to Blue River—the getup consisted of a black woolen coat fitted at the waist, matching trousers, his best white shirt, starched and pressed for him at the

Chinese laundry before he left Indian Rock, a brown brocade vest and a string tie.

He hated ties.

Hated starched shirts, too, for that matter.

He'd worn this suit exactly three times since he bought it—to one wedding and two funerals. Today, it was a wedding—his own—and even though it was his choice to get married, the occasion had its somber aspects, as well.

Up home, the ceremony would have been a community event, like a circus or a tent revival or the Independence Day fireworks, drawing crowds from miles around and working the womenfolk up into a frenzy of sewing and cooking and marking their calendars so they'd know how long the first baby took to show up. The men would complain about having to wear their Sunday duds, sip moonshine from a shared fruit jar out in the orchard behind the church after the "I do's" had been said and lament that another unwitting member of their sex had been roped in and hog-tied.

Clay smiled to think of all that nuptial chaos and was glad he'd managed to escape it, though he felt a twinge of nostalgia, too. He and Dara Rose would be married quietly and sensibly, in a civil ceremony performed by Mayor Ponder at her place, with Edrina and Harriet the only guests. There would be no cake, no photographs, no rings and no wedding night, let alone a honeymoon, because this was an arrangement, a transaction—not a love match.

Which wasn't to say that Clay didn't fully expect to bed Dara Rose when the time came, and if they got a baby started right away, too, so much the better. He figured the actual consummation of their union would probably have to wait until spring, though, when the ranch house was finished and he and Dara Rose had a room to themselves.

Fine as the weather was, spring seemed a long way off when he thought of it in terms of making love to his wife.

Resigned, and leaving his hat behind because it didn't look right with the suit, Clay bid his dog a temporary farewell—Chester had taken to curling up on the cot inside the jail's one cell whenever he wanted to sleep, which was often—and set out for Dara Rose's little house, following the sidewalk as far as he could and then crossing the street by way of the peculiar system of planks and discarded doors and the beds of old wagons.

Mayor Ponder arrived by the same means, followed single file by a thin woman in very prim garb and one of the town council members—they'd come along to serve as witnesses, Clay supposed. Clutching a copy of the Good Book and a rolled sheet of paper as he minced his way over the swamplike road, Ponder looked none too pleased at the prospect of joining the new marshal and the pretty widow in holy matrimony.

Clay disliked the mayor, mainly because of the remark Ponder had made about not minding if Dara Rose wound up working upstairs at the Bitter Gulch Saloon, but he could tolerate the man long enough to get hitched. The rest of the time, Wilson Ponder was fairly easy to ignore.

"There's still time to change your mind," Ponder boomed out, as if he wanted the whole town to hear, when he and Clay met at Dara Rose's front gate. "Charity is charity, but I think you might be taking it a little too far in this instance."

Charity is charity.

The front door of the house was open, probably to admit as much fresh air as possible before the winter weather returned, and Clay had to unlock his jawbones by an act of will. What if Dara Rose had heard what Ponder said? Or the children?

He didn't respond, but simply glowered at Ponder until the other man cleared his throat and muttered, "Well, let's get on with it, then."

Edrina and Harriet appeared in the doorway, beaming. They had ribbons in their hair, and they were wearing summer dresses, very nearly outgrown and obviously their best.

"Mama looks so pretty in her wedding dress!" Edrina enthused, as Clay moved ahead of the others, stepped onto the porch and immediately swept both children off their feet, one in the curve of each arm.

They giggled at that, and the sound heartened Clay. Reminded him that he'd put on that itchy suit because he was going to a *wedding,* not a funeral.

Behind him, the female witness made a sighlike sound, long-suffering and full of righteous indignation.

Once again, Clay tamped down his temper. He wanted to pin that old biddy's ears back, verbally, any-how—he'd never struck a woman, a child or an animal, and never intended to, though he'd landed plenty of punches in the faces of his boy cousins growing up—but today was neither the time nor the place to hold forth on what he thought of nasty-natured gossips.

For one thing, he didn't want to spoil the day for Edrina and Harriet. They were clearly overjoyed at the prospect of a wedding, though with Edrina, it was partly about being allowed to miss a few hours of school.

"I'll bet your mama *does* look pretty," Clay agreed, in belated reply to Edrina's statement. "Almost as pretty as the pair of you, maybe."

That got them both giggling again, and Clay smiled as he set them on their feet.

And then nearly tripped over them when Dara Rose

appeared, wearing an ivory silk gown with puffed-out sleeves and lace trim at the cuffs. Her cheeks were pink, her eyes bright with a combination of nervousness and hope, her hair done up in a soft knot at her nape and billowing cloudlike around her face.

The sight of her knocked the wind out of Clay as surely as if he'd been thrown from a horse and landed spread-eagle on hard ground.

Ponder cleared his throat again, and the wedding party assembled itself, with surprising grace, in the middle of that cramped front room.

Dara Rose's trim shoulder bumped Clay's arm as she took her place beside him, and he felt a jolt of sweet fire at her touch.

Ponder opened the book, and then his mouth, but before he could get a word said, a ruckus erupted out in the road.

Looking down at Dara Rose, Clay saw her shut her eyes, felt her stiffen next to him.

Outside, a mule brayed, and a drunken voice bellowed.

Clay took Dara Rose's hand and squeezed it lightly before turning to head for the doorway.

Edrina and Harriet were already there, staring out.

"Mama's not going to marry you, Ezra Maddox!" Edrina shouted to the stumbling man trying to free his feet from the deep mud. "She's taken, so you'd better just get your sorry self out of here before there's trouble!"

Clay had to choke back a laugh. He rested one hand on the top of Edrina's head and one on Harriet's, and said quietly, "Go stand with your mama. I'll handle this."

Maddox was a big man, broad-shouldered and clad in work clothes, and his hair and beard were grizzled, wiry. Once he'd gotten loose from the mud, he practically tore the gate off its rusty hinges, getting it open, and stormed in Clay's direction like a locomotive.

Clay stepped out onto the porch, waited.

Behind him, Ponder said, "Now, Ezra, don't be a sore loser. You're out of the running where Dara Rose is concerned, and making a damn fool of yourself won't change that."

Ezra came to a shambling stop in the middle of the path, not because he'd taken Mayor Ponder's sage advice to heart, Clay reckoned, but because he was used to folks clearing the way between him and whatever it was he aimed to have.

Clay didn't move.

The two men studied each other, at a distance of a dozen yards or so, and Maddox swayed slightly, ran the back of one arm across his mouth. His gaze narrowed.

"Did you get to the part where the justice of the peace inquires as to whether or not anybody has reason to object to this marriage?" Maddox ranted. "Because that's when I mean to say my piece."

"Let's hear it," Clay said, in an affable drawl. He hoped the situation wouldn't disintegrate into a howling brawl in the mud, with him and Maddox rolling back and forth with their hands on each other's throats, because he didn't want that to be what Dara Rose, Edrina and Harriet remembered when they looked back on this day.

Another part of him relished the idea of a knock-down-drag-out fisticuff.

Maddox straightened, swayed again and spoke with alacrity. "I have already offered for you, Dara Rose Nolan, and you belong to me," he said, as she stepped up beside Clay and put her hand on his arm.

A thrill of something rushed through Clay, though he'd hoped Dara Rose would stay inside, out of harm's way, until he and Maddox had settled their differences.

"You belong to me," Maddox reiterated.

"I belong to myself," Dara Rose informed him. "And no one else, except for my children. I want nothing to do with you, Mr. Maddox, and I'll count it as a favor if you leave, right now."

"All right," Maddox erupted, flinging his beefy arms out from his sides with such force that he nearly fell over sideways, "you can bring the girls along, and I'll marry you straight off—today, if that's what you want."

"You are too late, Mr. Maddox," Dara Rose said, in a clear and steady voice. "Please be on your way so we can get on with the wedding."

Clay wondered distractedly if Dara Rose had ever seriously considered taking up with a lug like Maddox. He couldn't imagine her parting with her children.

Maddox just stood there, evidently weighing his options, which were few, and broke the ensuing silence by spitting violently and barking out, "This feller might have a badge, Dara Rose, but he ain't Parnell come back to life."

He turned partially, as if to walk away, but he jabbed a finger in Dara Rose's direction and went right on running off at the mouth. "I'll tell you what he is, this man you're so dead set on marryin'—he's a *stranger,* a lying drifter, for all you know—and when he moves on, leavin' you with another babe in your belly and no way to feed your brood, don't you come cryin' to me!"

Clay's restraint snapped then, but before he could take more than a single step in Maddox's direction, Dara Rose tightened her grip on his arm and stopped him.

Maddox spat again, but then he whirled around and headed for the gate and the waiting mule, every step he took making a sucking sound because of the mud.

Dara Rose let go of Clay's arm and walked, with highchinned dignity, back into the house, leaving Clay and Mayor Ponder standing on the porch.

Ponder's gaze followed Maddox as he mounted the mule to ride away. "I'd watch my back if I were you, Marshal," he said thoughtfully. "Ezra's the kind to hold a grudge, and he's got a sneaky side to him."

INSIDE, DARA ROSE was shaken, but she made sure it didn't show.

Mayor Ponder's wife, Heliotrope, was a scandalmonger with nothing better to do than spread gossip, heavily laced with her own interpretation of any given person or situation, of course, and thanks to Ezra Maddox's unexpected visit, she'd have plenty of fodder as it was.

Dara Rose wasn't about to give her more to work with.

Besides, the children were watching her, and they'd follow whatever example she set. She wanted them to see strength in their mother, and courage, and dignity.

So she straightened her spine, lifted her chin and once again took her place at Clay McKettrick's side.

Mayor Ponder opened his book again and began to read out the words that would bind her to this tall man standing next to her.

The mayor's voice turned to a drone, and the very atmosphere seemed to pulse and buzz around Dara Rose, making her light-headed.

She spoke when spoken to, answered by rote.

After three weddings, she could have gotten married in her sleep.

Questions plagued her, swooped down on her like raucous birds. *What if Ezra had been right? Suppose Clay was a liar and a drifter—or worse? Was she marrying him because some deluded part of her had him confused with Parnell?*

"I now pronounce you man and wife," Mayor Ponder said, slamming the book closed between his pawlike hands. "Mr. McKettrick, you may kiss the bride."

Clay looked down at her, one eyebrow slightly raised, and a grin crooked at a corner of his mouth.

On impulse, and to get it over with, Dara Rose stood on tiptoe and kissed that mouth, very lightly, very quickly and very briefly.

"There," she said. "It's done."

Clay merely chuckled.

She could still back out, Dara Rose reminded herself fitfully. She could refuse to sign the marriage certificate, ask Mayor Ponder to reverse the declaration that they were now man and wife.

Was that legal?

For a moment, Dara Rose thought she might swoon, just faint dead away right there in her own front parlor.

But Clay slipped a strong arm around her waist, effectively holding her up until she signaled, with a furtive glance his way, that she could stand without help.

Thoughts still clamored through her mind, though, and her hand shook slightly when she signed "Dara Rose McKettrick" on the line reserved for the bride.

What had she *done?*

Suppose Clay was really a rascal and a drunk, instead of the solid man he seemed to be? Suppose he already *had* a wife tucked away somewhere, and he'd just made them both bigamists? And what if this stranger had spoken falsely when he promised not to exercise his rights as a husband unless and until she declared herself ready and willing?

The room felt hot, even with a chinook breeze sweeping in through the open door.

Edrina tugged at Dara Rose's hand, bringing her back into the present moment. "Now you're Mrs. Mc-Kettrick," the little girl crowed. "Can Harriet and I be McKettricks, too?"

Dara Rose had no idea how to answer.

Clay, who had clearly overheard, judging by that little smile resting on his mouth as he bent to scrawl his name on the marriage certificate, said nothing. He waited while Mayor Ponder and both witnesses added their signatures where appropriate. Then money changed hands, and the ordeal was over.

The official part of it, at least.

Mayor Ponder and his companions took their leave, and Dara Rose was alone with her new husband and her delighted children.

"We want to be McKettricks, too," Edrina insisted.

"You're Nolans," Dara Rose reasoned. "What would your papa think if you changed your names?"

"*You* changed *yours*," Edrina pointed out. "And, anyhow, Papa's dead."

Harriet's eyes rounded. "Papa's dead?"

"Of course he is, dolt," Edrina snapped. "Why do you suppose we put flowers on a grave with his name on it?"

"Edrina," Dara Rose reprimanded. "Stop it."

"I can't read," Harriet lamented, looking up at Dara Rose now, with tears welling in her eyes. "You said Papa was *gone*—"

Dara Rose exchanged glances with a somber-faced Clay and then bent her knees so she was crouching before her daughter, in the dress she'd worn to marry Luke, and then Parnell, and now Clay.

"Sweetheart," she said softly, "that's what 'gone' means sometimes. I know it's hard for you to understand, but you have to try."

Harriet turned, much to Dara Rose's surprise, and

buried her face in one side of Clay's fancy suit coat, wailing in despair. This was unusual behavior, especially for even-tempered Harriet, but Dara Rose put it down to all the excitement of a front-room wedding.

"There, now," Clay said gruffly, as Dara Rose straightened, hoisting Harriet up into his arms. "You go right ahead and cry 'til you feel like stopping."

Dara Rose sank onto the settee, close to tears herself.

She was *married,* and there was so much she didn't know about Clay.

So much he didn't know about her.

Harriet bawled like a banshee—Dara Rose realized the child was going for effect now—her face hidden in Clay's shoulder.

"Here's what I think we ought to do," Clay said, to all of them. "We ought to go out to my ranch—I'll rent a buckboard and a couple of stout mules—and find ourselves a Christmas tree."

Harriet immediately stopped wailing.

Edrina lit up like a lightbulb wired to a power pole.

"A Christmas tree?" Dara Rose repeated, confounded.

"The roads are pretty muddy," Edrina speculated, but she was obviously warming to the idea, and so was Harriet, who had reared back to look at Clay in wet-eyed wonder.

"That's why we need mules," Clay replied.

"Do you believe in St. Nicholas?" Harriet asked him, in a hushed voice.

Clay looked directly at Dara Rose, silently dared her to say otherwise and replied, "I do indeed. One Christmas Eve, when my cousin Sawyer and I were about your age, we caught a glimpse of him flying over the roof of our granddad's barn in that sleigh of his, with eight reindeer harnessed to the rig."

Edrina blinked, swallowed. *"Really?"* she breathed, wanting so much to believe, even at the advanced age of six, that she'd been wrong to think there was no magic in the world.

Dara Rose's heart ached.

"Can't think what else it could have been," Clay answered, as serious in tone and expression as a man bearing witness in a court of law, under oath. "A sleigh pulled by eight reindeer is a fairly distinctive sight."

"Thunderation," Edrina exclaimed softly, while Harriet favored her older sister with a smug I-told-you-so look.

Dara Rose glared up at her bridegroom. "Mr. McKettrick," she began, but he cut her off before she could go on.

"Call me Clay," he said mildly. "I'm your husband now, remember?"

Dara Rose got to her feet. "*Clay*, then," she said dangerously. "I will have you know—"

Again he interrupted, setting Harriet on her feet and saying, "You two go on and change your clothes. Get your bonnets and your coats, too."

Edrina and Harriet rushed to obey.

Dara Rose stood there in her sorry-luck wedding dress, trembling with frustration. "How dare you get their hopes up like that?" she whispered furiously, flushed and near tears again. "How *dare* you encourage them to believe in things that aren't even real?"

"Whoa," Clay said, cupping her chin gently in one hand. "Are you saying that St. Nicholas *isn't real?*"

"Of *course* that's what I'm saying," Dara Rose retorted, under her breath but with plenty of bluster. "He *isn't*."

Clay gave a long, low whistle of surprise, though his too-blue eyes danced with delighted mischief. "I got here just in time," he said.

Dara Rose was brought up short. *"What?"* she managed, with more effort than a single word should have required.

Clay shook his head, as though he couldn't believe another human being could be so deluded as Dara Rose clearly was. "They're only going to be little girls once," he said, "and for a very short time. If I hadn't shown up when I did, you might have ruined one of the best things about being a kid—believing."

Dara Rose's mouth fell open. Clay closed it for her by levering up on her chin with that work-roughened and yet extraordinarily gentle hand of his.

"Now," he went on decisively, "Edrina and Harriet and I are going out to find a Christmas tree. You can either come with us, Mrs. McKettrick, or you can stay right here with the chickens. Which is it going to be?"

Dara Rose wasn't about to send her children out into the countryside in a mule-drawn buckboard with a stranger, but neither did she have the heart to insist that they forget the whole crazy plan.

"Edrina and Harriet are *my* children," she said, hearing the girls laugh and scuffle in the small bedroom as they went about exchanging their wedding garb for warmer things, "and I will not have them misled."

"Fair enough," Clay said, letting his eyes drop. "Shouldn't you get out of that fancy dress before we head out?"

THE MUD WAS DEEP, but the mules that came with the hired buckboard were strong and sure-footed. Once Clay had arranged the transaction, changed his clothes and collected Chester from the jailhouse, they made the short journey to the ranch with no trouble at all—

in fact, it seemed to Clay that those mules knew how to avoid the worst of the muck and plant their hooves on solid ground.

He pulled back on the brake lever and simultaneously reined in the mules right where the kit-house would go up, come spring.

He jumped down, smiling as Edrina and Harriet piled eagerly out of the back of the buckboard, Chester leaping after them and barking fit to split a man's eardrums, and went around to reach up a hand to Dara Rose.

She hadn't said two words to him since they'd left town, and her color was high, but she let Clay lift her down.

Gasped when he made sure their bodies collided in the process.

He laughed, though she'd roused an ache inside him.

She blushed and straightened her bonnet with both hands, which made her bosom rise in that tantalizing way he so enjoyed.

"You gave your word," she whispered, narrow-eyed.

"And I'll keep it," Clay assured her. This was what he got for putting his mouth in motion before his head was in gear, he figured. A wife to contradict everything he said and no wedding night to make up for the inevitable difficulties of an intimate alliance.

If Sawyer had been there, he'd surely have called Clay

crazy, denying himself the pleasures of matrimony, especially when he was married to a woman like Dara Rose.

And Clay would have had to admit his cousin was right.

He *was* crazy.

But a promise was a promise.

"Let's go," he said, reaching into the wagon-bed for the short-handled ax he'd borrowed when he rented the team and buckboard over at the livery stable. "It'll be dark in a few hours, and there's no telling when the snow will start up again, so we'd better get started."

Edrina and Harriet were practically beside themselves with excitement, and Chester trotted around them all in big, swoopy circles, livelier than Clay had yet seen him.

The "tree" they finally settled upon looked more like a tumbleweed to Clay, who was used to the lush, fragrant firs that grew in northern Arizona, but Edrina and Harriet were enchanted. So Clay chopped down that waist-high scrub pine and carried it in one hand back to the wagon.

Dara Rose bore silent witness to all this, cautiously enjoying her daughters' delight.

Edrina had noticed the stone markers Clay had set in place the last time he was there, and she squatted on her haunches to peer at one of them. Harriet and Chester stood nearby.

"What *is* this?" Edrina asked.

Clay smiled, tossed the tree into the bed of the wagon and walked back to stand over the little girl. He was aware of Dara Rose on the periphery of things, but he didn't look in her direction.

"This is where I plan to put up my—*our*—house, once it arrives, that is."

Edrina looked up at him, brow crinkling a little. "Houses don't *arrive*," she said.

"This one will," Clay replied, enjoying the exchange. "It's coming by rail, from Sears, Roebuck and Company, all the way out in Chicago, Illinois."

"A *house* can't ride on a train!" Harriet proclaimed gleefully. "Houses are too *big* to fit!"

Clay laughed, crouched between the two girls, to put himself at eye level with them. Chester nuzzled his arm and then, quick as can be, licked Clay's face.

"I guess you'd say this house is kind of like a jigsaw puzzle," Clay told the children. "It's broken down into parts and packed in crates. When it gets here, I'll have to put it together."

Edrina frowned, absorbing his words. Then she whistled, through her teeth, and said, *"Thunderation and spit."*

"Speak in a ladylike fashion, Edrina Nolan," Dara Rose interceded coolly, "or do not speak at all."

Clay tossed a look in his wife's direction and stood

tall again, resting one hand on each bonneted head. "I reckon we'll head back to town now," he said. "I don't like the looks of that cloud bank over there on the horizon."

The wind was beginning to pick up a little, too.

Dara Rose shooed the girls toward the hired buckboard, but they didn't need anybody's help to climb inside. They shinnied up the rear wheels, agile as a pair of monkeys, and planted themselves on either side of the scrub pine.

Clay hoisted Chester aboard and fastened the tailgate, but before he could get to Dara Rose and offer her a hand up, she was already in the front of the wagon, perched on the seat and looking straight ahead.

"Will there be room for us in your new house?" Harriet asked, just as Clay settled in to take the reins.

Clay looked down at Dara Rose, who didn't acknowledge him in any visible way. "Yes," he said. "You and Edrina will have to share a room at first, most likely, but after a year or two, I'll be building on, and you'll each have one of your own."

"Then where will Mama be?" Harriet wanted to know. "In my room, or in Edrina's?"

"Neither," Clay said.

A flush bloomed into Dara Rose's cheeks and, even though she hastened to adjust her bonnet, Clay had already seen. "Harriet," Dara Rose said, "please sit down immediately."

Harriet sat.

Clay bit the inside of his lip, so he wouldn't smile, turned the team and wagon in a wide semicircle and headed toward town.

The girls chattered behind him and Dara Rose, in the bed of the buckboard, Chester no doubt hanging on every word. The wagon wheels, in need of greasing, squealed as the mules pulled the rig overland, puffing clouds of white fog from their nostrils, and the harnesses creaked.

For all that, Clay would remember that trip home as a silent one, because, once again, Dara Rose didn't say a word.

When they drove on along Main Street, passing the road that fronted the house without turning in, Dara Rose nudged him lightly with one elbow but still didn't speak.

"Where are we going?" Edrina called, from the back.

"We're having supper at the hotel tonight," Clay said, with a sidelong glance at Dara Rose. "Call it a celebration," he added dryly.

"Don't be silly," Dara Rose muttered in protest, but the girls were cheering by then, causing Chester to bark, and all of those noises combined to drown her out.

What with all the planks and doors in the road, Clay had to weave the team and wagon in and out half the length of Main Street, but he finally reined in, in front of the Texas Arms Hotel and Dining Room, and set the brake.

"This is extravagant," Dara Rose whispered to Clay, when everybody except Chester was standing on the board sidewalk. "We have food at home...."

"Tonight is special," Clay replied, before shifting his attention to Chester. "You stay put, dog, and I'll bring you out some supper."

Chester seemed to understand; he settled down next to the Christmas tree, resting his muzzle on his outstretched front legs, sighed once and closed his eyes.

Edrina and Harriet raced, giggling, toward the main entrance to the hotel.

Dara Rose hesitated, though, and took a light but firm hold on Clay's arm. "You mustn't spoil my children," she said. "I don't want Edrina and Harriet getting used to luxuries I cannot hope to provide for them myself."

Clay suppressed a sigh. "Food," he said reasonably, "is not a luxury."

"It is when it's paid for, and someone else cooked and served it," Dara Rose insisted.

Clay smiled down at his bride. "Try to enjoy it just the same," he advised, taking her elbow and gently steering her across the sidewalk.

Chapter 8

The small rustic dining establishment serving the Texas Arms Hotel was full of savory smells, causing Dara Rose's stomach to rumble.

Someone had hung a wreath made of holly sprigs behind the cash register, and limp tinsel garlands drooped from the edges of a long counter lined with stools.

Only one of the six tables was in use. A man, a woman and a little girl, probably a year or two older than Edrina, dined in companionable silence, their clothes exceedingly fine, their manners impeccable. Since Dara Rose had never laid eyes on them before, she knew they must have arrived on the afternoon train.

She wondered if they were just passing through, or if they'd come to Blue River to spend Christmas with friends or family.

Clay nodded a taciturn greeting to the man and the man nodded back.

Edrina and Harriet, stealing glances at the little girl, scrambled onto chairs at a table in front of the window, sitting side by side and swinging their feet. It had been an exciting day for them—first, the wedding, then the expedition to find a Christmas tree, and now a restaurant meal.

By the time they tumbled into bed that night, Dara Rose thought fondly, her daughters would be so deliciously exhausted, so saturated with fresh air, that they'd sleep like stones settling deep into the silt of a quiet pond.

Clay was just pulling back a chair for Dara Rose when the cook-waiter appeared, smiling a welcome. "I hear this is a wedding supper!" the man thundered. "Congratulations, Marshal."

It wouldn't have been proper to congratulate Dara Rose, since there would inevitably be an implication that she'd somehow *captured* her new husband, rounded him up like a rogue steer, and not by pure feminine allure. While she appreciated the courtesy, she did wish the man hadn't spoken so loudly, because the woman at the other table turned in their direction, her expression impassive, her gaze flickering briefly over Dara Rose's faded cloak, with its frayed, mud-splattered hem.

"Thanks, Roy," Clay responded, addressing the cook,

with whom he was obviously acquainted, and the two men shook hands.

Dara Rose was not a person to compare herself to others, but as Clay pulled back a chair for her and she sat down, she couldn't help thinking how shabby she and the children must seem, in the eyes of that elegantly dressed woman and her little girl.

"What's it going to be, ladies?" Clay asked the children, while Dara Rose perused the menu, nearly overwhelmed by all the choices. "I can definitely recommend the fried chicken dinner, and the meat loaf is good, too."

"What's meat loaf?" Harriet wanted to know.

"You'll have the chicken dinner," Dara Rose said, without looking away from the menu. "One will be plenty for both of you."

She thought she might have felt Clay stiffen beside her, but then, as though she hadn't spoken at all, he simply answered Harriet's inquiry about the nature of meat loaf.

"I want that," Harriet said, when he'd finished. "Please."

"And I'll have stew with dumplings," Edrina added, sounding like a small adult, "if I may, please."

"You may," Clay said, without looking at Dara Rose, though she *did* see his mouth quirk briefly at one corner. "This is a very special occasion," he added, after clearing his throat quietly. "And, anyhow, Chester will be pleased to accept any leftovers. He's still building up his strength, you know."

Dara Rose's cheeks flamed. She loved animals. Her rooster and hens all had names, and she went out of her way to take good care of them. But she'd been so poor for so long—since she'd "married" Luke Nolan, a few months before Edrina was born—that the idea of giving a dog restaurant food just wouldn't fit into any of the compartments in her mind.

"There are *people* in this town who could put anything extra to good use," she said, sounding way more prim than she'd intended.

"Like the O'Reillys," Edrina said, with a sigh.

"Among others," Dara Rose agreed.

Clay was watching her so directly, and with such intensity, that she was forced to meet his gaze. "Shall we just scrape it all into a pan," he began, "and set it on the floor of their shanty, the way we'd do with Chester?"

Dara Rose blushed even harder. If they hadn't been in a public place, and if she'd been given to violence, she'd have slapped him across the face.

Before she could speak, Clay summoned Roy, the cook, back to their table with a polite gesture of one hand.

The man hurried over, eager to please.

Clay placed everyone's order—except for Dara

Rose's—and then asked the cook to pack up enough fried chicken, meat loaf and trimmings to feed four people. He'd pay for and collect the extra food at the end of the meal, he said, and then looked pointedly at Dara Rose.

Confounded, and a little stung, she asked for chicken.

Edrina and Harriet were watching Clay raptly—they might have expected a laurel wreath or a winged helmet to appear on his head, from their expressions—and, not surprisingly, it was Edrina who broke the pulsing silence.

"Are we taking supper to the O'Reillys?" she asked.

"Yes," Clay said.

"Harriet and I are planning to visit Addie tomorrow," Edrina said. She turned a vaguely challenging glance in Dara Rose's direction. "Mama said we could."

Dara Rose, still feeling as though she'd been put smartly in her place and none too happy about it, thank you very much, returned Edrina's look in spades. "I said *you* could visit," she reminded her child, "since you'd already promised. I did *not* give permission for Harriet to accompany you."

"What's the harm?" Clay asked mildly, though his eyes contained a challenge, just as Edrina's had before. "That little girl looked to me as though she could use some company. Especially somebody close to her own age."

"She has romantic fever," Edrina said solemnly.

"That's not catching," Clay replied, and though his tone was serious, there was a twinkle in his eyes now. "In fact, I'd say your mother is immune to it."

"Other things *are* catching," Dara Rose felt compelled to say, though she knew there was some kind of battle being waged here, and she was losing ground. Fast.

"It's probably too cold for lice and fleas at this time of year," Clay said.

Dara Rose didn't get a chance to respond. The food arrived, heaped on steaming plates, the children's first, and then Clay's and Dara Rose's.

The family of strangers, meanwhile, had finished their meal, and the man was settling the bill. The mother and the child rose from their chairs, and then the little girl walked right over to Edrina and Harriet and put out one tiny, porcelain-white hand.

"My name is Madeline Howard," she said. With her long, shining brown hair, deep green eyes and fitted emerald velvet dress, she bore a striking resemblance to the doll in the mercantile window. "What's yours?"

"I'm Edrina," answered Dara Rose's elder daughter, barely able to see over the mountain of food before her. "And this is my sister, Harriet."

"We're going to live in Blue River from now on," Madeline said. "Mama and Papa and me, I mean. Papa's going to build an office, and we'll have rooms upstairs."

The woman approached, laid a hand on Madeline's shoulder, offered a pained smile to everyone in general and no one in particular. "You mustn't bother people when they're eating, darling," she said.

Clay stood, put out his hand, and the woman shook it, after the briefest hesitation. "Clay McKettrick," he said. "This is my wife, Dara Rose."

This is my wife, Dara Rose.

No words could have sounded stranger to Dara Rose, and she had to swallow a ridiculous urge to explain, all in a rush, that theirs was a marriage of convenience, not a real one.

She merely nodded, though, and the woman nodded back. Like her daughter, she wore velvet, though her gown and short cape were a rich shade of brown instead of green. Not only that, but the pile on that fabric was plush, not worn away in places like most of the velvet one saw in Blue River, Texas.

The man had reached the table by then, and smiled as he and Clay shook hands. "Glad to meet you, Marshal," he said. "I'm Jim Howard, and my wife is Eloise."

Another stiff smile from Eloise. "My husband is a dentist," she said. "Most people address him as 'Dr. Howard,' of course."

Dara Rose, who had been trying to decide whether

or not good manners required that she stand, like Clay, decided to stay seated.

"We could use a dentist around here," Clay said, with a grin dancing in his eyes but not quite reaching his mouth.

Madeline smiled broadly at Edrina and Harriet. "You both have very good teeth," she said admiringly. Her own were like small, square pearls, perfectly strung.

Jim Howard—*Dr.* Howard—chuckled at that. "We'll let you finish your meal in peace," he said, steering his womenfolk gently away, toward the hotel's modest lobby and then the stairs beyond.

Clay sat down. "Nice people," he said.

Madeline, Dara Rose noticed, kept looking back, her expression one of friendly longing, as though she would have liked to stay and chat with Edrina and Harriet.

"The lady is snooty," Edrina announced, holding a dinner roll daintily between a thumb and index finger. "But I like Madeline, and her papa, too."

Dara Rose was keenly aware, in that moment, that Edrina was following her lead. Hadn't she disliked Mrs. Howard almost immediately, and returned coolness for coolness instead of making an effort to be neighborly, offer a welcome to the newcomers?

It was tremendously difficult sometimes, she thought glumly, to be the sort of person she wanted her *daughters* to be, when they grew up. And she'd fallen far short of that standard tonight.

Unexpectedly, Clay reached over and gently squeezed her hand, just once and very briefly, but the gesture raised Dara Rose's flagging spirits.

It also sent something sharp and hot racing through her, a fiery ache she had to work very hard to ignore.

"Perhaps when we get to know Mrs. Howard better," she told Edrina, somehow managing a normal tone of voice, "we'll discover that she's a very nice person."

"Perhaps," Edrina agreed doubtfully.

The girls were practically nodding off in their chairs by the time the meal ended.

Clay took the leftovers out to Chester on a borrowed plate, while Roy packed the O'Reillys' supper into a large wooden crate, carefully covered with a dish towel. The bill was paid—the cost of it would have kept Dara Rose and the girls in groceries for the better part of a month—and Clay carried the crate out to the wagon, stowed it under the seat, where Chester couldn't get at it, and returned with the empty plate.

By then, Dara Rose had put on her cloak, Edrina was wearing her outdoor garb and, together, they maneuvered a sleepy Harriet into her coat and bonnet. Clay whisked the child up into his arms and carried her to the wagon.

A light snowfall was just beginning, and the wind was picking up, so Clay took Dara Rose, the children and Chester back to the house first, saw them inside, and announced quietly that he'd return as soon as he'd dropped off the food at the O'Reilly place and turned in the mules and wagon at the livery.

Dara Rose moved by rote, helping the girls prepare for bed, tucking them in, hearing their prayers.

Harriet asked for the doll again.

Edrina said she was glad to have a new papa, then promised not to forget the old one.

Dara Rose was glad she'd turned down the wick in the kerosene lantern, leaving the room mostly in shadow, because there were tears in her eyes as she told her children good-night and kissed their foreheads.

THE SETTEE IN DARA ROSE'S parlor was about a foot shorter than he was, by Clay's estimation, but he'd slept in less comfortable places in his time, just the same. And Dara Rose *had* been considerate enough to set out a blanket and a pillow for him.

He smiled just imagining the joshing he'd get if Sawyer and the rest of his McKettrick cousins knew he was spending his wedding night alone, with his feet hanging over one end of a short sofa. He'd be lucky if he didn't wake up with his spine in the shape of a horseshoe and his toes numb from lack of circulation.

Chester, who'd settled himself nearby on the blanket Clay had brought over from the jailhouse, watched as he sat down on the settee to kick off his boots.

"Believe it or not," he told the dog, low-voiced, "I got married today."

Chester offered no comment.

The tumbleweed Christmas tree stood undecorated in a corner of the room, stuck in a bucket of water and looking about as festive as Clay felt, but it had a nice pine scent that reminded him of home.

Because the house was small and he was mindful of the children, Clay decided to sleep in his clothes. He was about to extinguish the lantern and stretch out, as best he could, on that blasted settee, when Dara Rose stepped out of the bedroom.

Her hair was down, tumbling well past her waist, and she wore a long nightgown, covered with a plain flannel wrapper, cinched tight at her middle.

Clay's heart skipped a couple of beats, though he knew full well she wasn't there to render an annulment legally and morally impossible.

She stopped, glanced over at the hopeful tumbleweed and then stood a little straighter. This raised her to her full and unremarkable height, but whatever her errand, she sure enough looked like she meant business.

"Either you are an irresponsible man," Dara Rose said, making it clear how Edrina came by her bold certainty about everything, "or you have more money than you let on. Which is it?"

Clay stood, though he suddenly felt bone-tired, because there was a lady in the room. "I never said I was broke, Mrs. McKettrick," he replied dryly.

"Don't call me 'Mrs. McKettrick'!" Dara Rose immediately responded. "We made an agreement. This is a marriage in name only."

"Oh, I'm well aware of that," Clay responded, thinking he'd wait forever for this woman, if that was what he had to do. "But you are legally my wife, and that makes you Mrs. McKettrick."

She pulled so tight on the cinches of her wrapper then that it was a wonder she didn't split right in two, like one of those showgirls in a magician's act. "Why do you keep pointing out that we are married in the eyes of the law?"

Clay was enjoying her discomfort a lot more than was gentlemanly. "Aren't we?" he asked, raising one eyebrow.

"Yes," she retorted, setting her hands down hard on her hips now and jutting out her elbows, "but it was a matter of expediency on my part, and nothing more."

"Gosh," Clay said, playing the rube. "Thanks."

"I would do anything for my daughters!" she blurted out. "Including marry a virtual stranger. I agreed to this arrangement *because* of them, not out of any desire to be your...your wife...." She stammered to a halt and turned a glorious shade of primrose-pink.

Clay waited a few moments before he spoke again. "That was quite a scene Maddox made today."

Dara Rose hesitated, trembled once and hugged herself as if she thought she might suddenly scatter in every direction, and it was all Clay could do not to cross the room and take her into his arms. "I suppose he believed he had call to object to—to our getting married," she continued, after a few moments of miserable struggle, "and it's true enough that he proposed—sort of."

"Sort of?" He'd known about the situation between Dara Rose and Maddox from Ponder and the others, but he wanted to hear it directly from her.

It was a long time before she answered. "I was supposed to work as his housekeeper for a year, so he could be sure I'd make a suitable wife. Then, if I passed muster, he'd put a ring on my finger."

Clay felt a fresh surge of rage rise up within him, and he waited for it to subside before he said anything. "Where did Edrina and Harriet fit into all this?"

He knew the answer to that question, too, at least indirectly but, again, he wanted the first-hand truth from Dara Rose herself.

Her eyes welled, but she looked so proud and so vulnerable that Clay continued to keep his distance. He figured she *might* actually shatter into bits if he touched her.

"They didn't," she said, at long last. Then, speaking so softly that Clay barely heard her, she went on. "He wanted me to put my children in an orphanage, or send them out to work for their board and room."

That was when Clay took a chance. He held his arms out to her.

Dara Rose paused briefly, considering, and then moved slowly into his embrace.

Clay rested his chin on top of her head. "No matter how things turn out between you and me, Dara Rose," he told her, "you will never have to send your girls away, I promise you that."

She looked up at him, her eyes moist, though she still wouldn't allow tears to fall. "How can you make a promise like that, Clay?" she whispered brokenly. "How?"

At least she hadn't called him "Mr. McKettrick." Wasn't that progress?

"I just *did* make a promise like that," he replied, wanting to kiss her more than he'd ever wanted to kiss a woman before, and still unwilling to take the chance, "and you'll find that I'm a man of my word."

She blinked. "There's so much you don't know about me," she said.

He grinned, holding her loosely, with his hands clasped behind the small of her back. "There are, as it happens, a few things you don't know about me," he replied. "I didn't come to Blue River to work as the town marshal for the rest of my life, for one. I mean to be a rancher, Dara Rose—I come from a family of them. That's why I bought two thousand acres of good grazing land, and that's why I plan to build a house on the site we visited today."

"And that's why you wanted a wife," she said, almost forlornly.

"Not just any wife," he pointed out.

"Parnell and I—" She looked at the large likeness on the wall. And suddenly, she choked up again. Couldn't seem to go on.

"It's all right, Dara Rose," Clay said, kissing her lightly on her crown, where her silken hair parted. She smelled sweetly of rainwater and flowery soap. "We've both got stories to tell, but it doesn't have to happen tonight."

She sniffled, smiled bravely, but otherwise she gave no response.

"Exactly why did you come out here in the first place?" Clay asked.

Dara Rose looked flustered. "I forgot to feed the

chickens," she said. "And I was hoping you'd be asleep so I could sneak past."

Clay chuckled. "Well, I have to admit, that's something of a disappointment."

"I *never* forget to feed the chickens," Dara Rose fretted, chagrined. "The poor things—"

"I fed them, Dara Rose," Clay said.

"When?"

"Before we went to find the Christmas tree," he said, with a nod toward the tumbleweed.

She seemed to realize then that he was still holding her, and she stepped back suddenly, as though startled. "About Christmas," she began.

"What about Christmas?"

"I'd really rather you didn't encourage Edrina and Harriet to entertain fanciful notions."

"Such as?" Clay asked, feigning innocence.

Dara Rose bristled up again.

He loved it when she did that.

"Well," she huffed, "there *was* that tall tale about seeing St. Nicholas flying past your grandfather's barn roof in a sleigh drawn by reindeer—"

He smiled. "Why, Mrs. McKettrick—are you calling me a liar?"

"You and your cousin must have been inebriated."

"We were eight," Clay said.

"Then you were dreaming."

"The same dream, at the same time? Sawyer and I are blood kin, but we don't share a brain."

Dara Rose sighed again. It was plain that she didn't know what to say next, or what to do, either.

Both were encouraging signs, Clay figured.

"Get some sleep," he told her. "You've had a long day."

She glanced at the settee, then took his measure with her eyes. Drew the obvious conclusion. "You are in for an uncomfortable night," she said, without any discernible concern.

For more reasons than one, Clay thought. But what he said was, "I'll be just fine. See you in the morning."

Dara Rose nodded, turned around and went back into the bedroom.

Clay watched her go, rubbing his chin with one hand, calculating the number of settee nights he'd have to put in between now and spring, when the house would be ready.

In the end, he slept on the floor, next to Chester.

At least that way, he could stretch out.

WHEN HE OPENED HIS EYES again, it was morning, and Edrina and Harriet were standing over him, looking worried.

"We thought you might be dead," Edrina said, with a relieved and somewhat wobbly smile.

"But you're not," Harriet added emphatically.

"No," Clay said, with a laugh, as he sat up. "I do believe I'm still among the living."

Both children were dressed for daytime, with their curly hair brushed and held back at the sides of their heads by small combs. Their faces were rosy from a recent scrubbing and their eyes shone.

"Mama is taking us over to the O'Reillys' place to visit Addie," Edrina said, "as soon as she's finished feeding the chickens and gathering the eggs and making breakfast."

Clay yawned expansively and got to his feet. "Where's Chester?"

"He's outside with Mama," Harriet replied. "She said he needed to do his business."

"What time is it?" Clay wondered aloud. He owned a pocket watch but seldom carried it; there had been no real need for that, back on the Triple M. There, where there was always a full day's work to do, you started at sunrise and finished when you finished, whatever time it was.

Before either child replied, he caught sight of the time-piece hanging prominently on the wall. Eight o'clock.

"When we get back from the O'Reillys'," Harriet piped up, "can we decorate the Christmas tree?"

Clay hesitated to answer, realizing that he didn't even know if Dara Rose *owned* any decorations, or whether she'd take kindly to his buying some for her, over at the mercantile.

Reckon you should have thought about that before you cut down that sorry sprig of sagebrush you're calling a Christmas tree, he told himself silently.

"That's up to your mama," he finally said.

Both children looked deflated.

"She'll just say it's a whole week 'til Christmas and St. Nicholas isn't coming, anyhow, so what do we need with a silly tree," Edrina said, in a rush of words.

Inwardly, Clay sighed. These were Dara Rose's children, and she had a perfect right to raise them as she saw fit, but he hoped she'd ease up on that rigid personal code of hers a little, and let them be kids while they could.

In the near distance, the back door opened, and Clay felt the rush of cool air where he stood. Dara Rose called out, "Girls? You're not bothering Mr. McKettrick, are you?"

Chester trotted through the inside doorway, came over to greet him.

Clay smiled and ruffled the dog's ears.

"We don't want to call you 'Mr. McKettrick,'" Edrina told Clay.

"We want to call you 'Papa,'" Harriet said.

The backs of Clay's eyes stung a little. "I'd like that,"

he said quietly, "but that's another thing that's got to be left up to your mama."

"What's to be left up to me?" Dara Rose asked, standing in the doorway. Her hair was pinned up, unlike last night, and like the girls', her cheeks were pink with well-being.

"Whether or not we can call Mr. McKettrick 'Papa,'" Harriet answered.

"And if we can put baubles on the Christmas tree," Edrina added.

Both of them stared expectantly at their mother.

"Oh," she finally said, shifting the handle of the egg basket from one wrist to the other. Her gaze flicked to Clay's face and then back to the girls. "It's too soon to address Mr. McKettrick in such a familiar fashion," she said. "But I don't see why we couldn't get out the Christmas things."

So she *had* Christmas things, Clay thought. That was something, anyway.

Edrina and Harriet swapped glances and made what would seem to be a tacit agreement to take what they could get.

"Breakfast will be ready in a few minutes," Dara Rose said. "And there are plenty of eggs this morning. We can each have one—Mr. McKettrick may have two, if he wishes—and there will still be enough left to sell over at the mercantile."

"One egg will suit me fine," Clay said, gruff-voiced. Soon as he'd put in a few hours over at the jailhouse and walked through the town once or twice to make sure there wasn't any trouble brewing, he'd head over to the mercantile and stock up on foodstuffs. See if old Philo would agree to deliver what he bought.

Dara Rose wouldn't like it, he supposed, when the storekeeper turned up with sugar and coffee beans and a wagonload of other goods, but he already had an argument ready. He didn't expect her to feed him and Chester; therefore, he wanted to contribute to the grubstake.

Plus, he had to have coffee of a morning, to get himself going.

So they ate their simple breakfast, the girls so excited, between the promised outing and the tree waiting to be festooned with geegaws, that they could barely sit still.

Dara Rose cleared the table while Clay donned his duster and his hat and summoned the dog. He'd left his gun belt and pistol over at the jailhouse, because of Edrina and Harriet, but he'd strap on the long-barreled .45 before he set out on his rounds. It wasn't that he expected to need a firearm, but he wanted any potential troublemakers to know the new marshal was serious about upholding his duties.

"Thanks for breakfast," Clay said, with a tug at his hat brim.

Dara Rose nodded, then looked away.

THE VISIT TO LITTLE Addie O'Reilly was necessarily brief since the child was bedridden. Last night's snow hadn't stuck, thank heaven, but there was still a bitter chill in the air, and Addie's two younger brothers sat on the bare floor near the odd, cobbled-together stove, playing with half a dozen marbles.

Peg tried to put a good face on things, but Dara Rose could tell she was embarrassed. There was no place to sit, except on one of the two beds or an upended crate— undoubtedly the same one that had contained last night's donated supper.

The girls, meanwhile, chatted with Addie.

"Somebody left a box of hot food at my doorstep," Peg said, following Dara Rose's gaze to the crate. Four clean plates, plus utensils, were stacked beside it. "We sure did have ourselves a fine feast, and there's enough left to get us through today, too."

"That's...wonderful," Dara Rose said.

"I figure it had to come from the dining room over to the hotel," Peg went on, wiping her hands down the skirt of her calico dress. "I mean to take the plates and silverware back later."

Dara Rose merely nodded. Clay must have wanted to keep his part in the enterprise a secret, so she didn't say anything.

Fortunately, neither did Edrina or Harriet. They were busy telling Addie all about the little girl, Madeline, whose papa was a dentist.

"You'll never guess who stopped by here yesterday," Peg said, taking Dara Rose by surprise.

"Who?" Dara Rose asked, simply to make conversation.

"Ezra Maddox," Peg said. "He's offered me housekeeping work, Mrs. Nolan. The job doesn't pay much, but at least there'll be plenty of good farm food for these kids, and if things work out, Mr. Maddox and me will be married come the spring." She paused. "You don't mind, do you? Now that you've married the marshal and all?"

Dara Rose smiled. "I don't mind," she was quick to say. Then, cautiously, afraid Peg O'Reilly might have misunderstood Maddox's offer, she asked, "He didn't object to your bringing the children along?"

"He did," Peg confided, in a whisper, "but I told him I wouldn't be parted from my little ones for anything or anybody, and he finally agreed to take them in."

The boys were still busy with their game of marbles, and Edrina was telling Addie that there wasn't going to be a Christmas program over at the schoolhouse this year because that last snowstorm threw everything out of whack.

"What about—?"

"My husband?" Peg asked. "Ezra knows about him, of course. Says we'll look into getting me a divorce if it comes to that."

Dara Rose's heart ached for Peg O'Reilly. "This is what you want to do?" she asked, very quietly.

"It's the answer to a prayer," Peg replied, looking a little surprised by Dara Rose's question.

Ezra Maddox, the answer to a prayer?

It just went to show, Dara Rose thought, that one woman's idea of hell was *another* woman's idea of heaven.

Chapter 9

❦

Full of consternation, Dara Rose studied the Closed sign on the door at the mercantile, the handle of the egg basket looped over one wrist, and wondered what on earth could have prompted Mr. Bickham to close his establishment at midmorning. Edrina and Harriet, meanwhile, climbed onto the bench in front of the store and peered in through the display window.

"Mama!" Harriet suddenly cried, so startling Dara Rose that she almost dropped the egg basket. "She's gone! *Florence is gone!*"

Dara Rose caught her breath, the fingers of her free hand splayed across her breastbone to keep her heart from jumping right out of her chest.

Florence?

Harriet let out a despairing wail.

"Hush!" Edrina told her sister, speaking sternly but

slipping an arm around the child's shoulders just the same. The two of them looked so small, standing there on the seat of that bench, like a pair of beautiful urchins.

The doll, Dara Rose realized belatedly.

Of course. Florence was the doll Harriet had been admiring—yearning after—ever since it first appeared in the mercantile window, the day after Thanksgiving. And now the doll was gone.

It would be set out for some other child to find on Christmas morning.

Although Dara Rose had never for one moment believed she could buy that doll for her little girl, Harriet's disappointment grieved her sorely. Like any mother, she longed to give her children nice things, but that was a pleasure she couldn't afford; they needed practical things, and some small measure of security, be it the egg money she squirreled away a penny at a time, or the ten dollars resting between the pages of her Bible.

Hurting as much as her child was—maybe more—and doing her best to hide it, Dara Rose set the egg basket down carefully and gathered Harriet into her arms, lifting her off the bench and holding her tightly. "There, now," she whispered, her throat so thick she could barely speak. Not that there was a great deal to say at a moment like that, anyway. "There, now."

"I should have sold my hair!" Harriet sobbed. "Then I would have had the money to buy Florence!"

Once again, Dara Rose thought of Piper's gift, safe at home, and ached.

Edrina jumped down from the bench, tomboylike, and tugged at Harriet's dangling foot. "Stop carrying on, goose," she commanded, but there was a slight quaver in her voice. "You'll have the whole town staring at us."

Harriet shuddered and buried her wet face in Dara Rose's neck. "I—really—thought—I—could—have—Florence—for—my—very—own," she said, punctuating her words with small but violent hiccups.

"Shh," Dara Rose said gently, still holding the child. "Everything will be all right, sweetheart. We'll go home now. Edrina, bring the egg basket."

By the time the three of them reached the end of Main Street and turned toward the house, Harriet had settled down to the occasional quivering sniffle.

A buckboard stood near Dara Rose's front gate, with two mules hitched to it.

Philo Bickham sat in the wagon box, reins in hand, beaming at Dara Rose as she approached with the children.

"I was just about to unload all this merchandise and leave it on the porch," he said. "The marshal said he'd be here to accept delivery, but there's been no sign of him so far."

Dara Rose frowned, at once wary and intrigued.

Edrina bolted forward and scrambled right up the side of that buckboard, skillful as a monkey, using the wheel spokes as footholds. "Thunderation!" she whooped.

Mr. Bickham jumped to the ground, nimble for a man of his age and bulk. He strode around to the back of the wagon and lowered the tailgate. "He darned near bought the place out, your new husband," the storekeeper crowed, no doubt pleased to make such a sale. Blue River was not a wealthy community, which meant the owner of the mercantile scraped by like most everyone else.

"Mama," Edrina spouted, "there's a tin of tea...and a big ham...and *peaches*...and all sorts of things wrapped in brown paper—"

"Edrina Nolan," Dara Rose said, setting Harriet on her feet, "get down from there this instant."

"Don't go poking around in those packages," Mr. Bickham said good-naturedly, shaking a finger at Edrina and then Harriet. "The marshal made himself mighty clear on that score. After all, it's almost Christmas, and there's a secret or two afoot."

Dara Rose was still trying to think what to say when

Clay rode around the corner on Outlaw, Chester trotting in their wake.

Mr. Bickham hailed him, and Dara Rose sent the girls inside, over their protests.

"Sorry if I held you up any, Philo," Clay told Mr. Bickham, barely glancing at Dara Rose as he swung down from the saddle. "A telegram came in from Sears, Roebuck and Company. They've shipped the makings of my house out by rail, and the whole works will be arriving here in about ten days."

"You'd better get that foundation dug and that well put in, then," Mr. Bickham said, giving Clay a congratulatory slap on one shoulder. "Reckon you can round up some hired help down at the Bitter Gulch, and if this weather holds, since you've got a put-together house coming, you'll be out there on your own place in no time."

Clay nodded and, once again, his gaze touched on Dara Rose's face.

"What is all this?" she asked evenly, as soon as Mr. Bickham had hoisted the first box from the back of the wagon and started toward the house with it.

Clay gave her a wry look and lifted out a second box. "Chester and I," he said, with a twinkle, "don't believe in freeloading. We always pay our own way."

Dara Rose opened her mouth, closed it again. "But all those packages, and the tea, and that enormous ham—"

"You like tea, don't you?" Clay teased, starting toward the house.

Dara Rose scurried to keep up with his long strides. "Of course I like tea," she said, flustered, "but it's a luxury, and we don't need it—"

"Sure you do," Clay replied, climbing the porch steps now. "What do you plan on serving all the ladies of Blue River when they start dropping by to see for themselves just what kind of mischief we're up to over here?"

Harriet and Edrina, huddled in the doorway, scattered to let them through.

Mr. Bickham was coming from the other direction, and Clay sidestepped him.

"Mr. McKettrick," Dara Rose persisted, when the two of them were alone in the kitchen, "I do have my pride."

"Yes, Mrs. McKettrick," Clay agreed. "I have taken note of that fact." He took a large tin from the box he'd carried in. "Would you mind putting some coffee on to brew while Bickham and I finish unloading that wagon? I've got a hankering for the stuff, and I like it strong and black."

Dara Rose couldn't seem to untangle her tongue.

"You do own a coffeepot, don't you?" Clay asked offhandedly.

"Yes," she managed, blushing. "Parnell drank coffee every morning."

Clay merely nodded, as though she'd confirmed something he already knew, and went out again.

Dara Rose got out Parnell's coffeepot, rinsed it at the sink and pumped fresh water into it. Then she had to ferret out the grinder, with its black wrought-iron handle.

She was wiping the dust out of the contraption with one corner of a flour-sack dish towel when Clay and Mr. Bickham came in again, both of them carrying boxes.

Edrina and Harriet were, of course, consumed with curiosity.

Harriet, though puffy-eyed, had long since stopped crying.

"Sugar," Edrina cataloged, joyfully examining each item. "And flour. And lard. And *raisins*. Mama, you could bake a pie."

"Perhaps," Dara Rose agreed, afraid to say too much because she wasn't sure she could control all the contradictory emotions welling up inside her. Her pride stung like a snakebite, but in some ways, she was as jubilant as the children.

Tea. Sugar. Flour.

A whole ham, big enough to feed half the town of Blue River.

They'd been doing without such things for so long that it was impossible not to rejoice, at least inwardly.

Firmly, Dara Rose brought herself up short. She squared her shoulders and poured coffee beans into the grinder and began turning the handle, enjoying the rich aroma. "Mr. McKettrick has been very generous," she said, not looking at Edrina and Harriet. "But we mustn't come to expect such things—"

"Why not?" The voice was Clay's.

Dara Rose kept her back to him, spooning freshly ground coffee beans into the well of her dented pot, setting it on to boil. "Because we mustn't, that's all," she said. She bent and opened the stove door and pitched in more wood. Jabbed at the embers with the poker.

"There's some stuff for the Christmas tree in the box I left on the settee," Clay said quietly, sending the girls scampering with chimelike hurrahs into the front room.

Dara Rose, thinking Mr. Bickham must be within earshot, taking it all in, turned to look for him. He was as big a gossip as Heliotrope Ponder and, running the only general store in town, he got plenty of chances to tell everything he knew and then some.

But there was only Clay, filling the doorway, watching her. Philo Bickham must have been outside, fetching another box from the buckboard.

"It's almost Christmas," Clay said gruffly. "Just this once, Dara Rose, let yourself be happy. Let your *daughters* be happy."

Her face burned, and she couldn't help remembering all the times Parnell had splurged on some little treat for the girls, running up an account at the mercantile that had taken her months to pay off.

"Did you go into debt for all this?" she asked, keeping her voice down so the girls and Mr. Bickham wouldn't hear. Nobody knew better than she did how little the marshal of Blue River actually earned.

Clay smiled, though his eyes remained solemn, and then he shook his head, not in reply, but in disbelief. "I paid cash money," he said, turning to walk away.

By the time the coffee was ready, the kitchen and part of the front room were jammed with boxes and crates and brown parcels, tied shut with twine.

"Where's Mr. Bickham?" Dara Rose asked, when Clay returned to the kitchen, squeezed past her to wash his hands at the sink pump. "I thought he'd stay for coffee."

"He has a store to run," Clay said quietly.

In the next room, the girls giggled and Chester barked and the noise was pleasant to hear, even though Dara Rose was uncommon jittery.

She put away the cup she'd set out for Mr. Bickham and filled the remaining one, returned the pot to the stove.

"Mr. McKettrick?"

"What, Mrs. McKettrick?" Clay countered wearily,

as he drew back a chair, sat down and reached for the steaming cup of coffee.

Dara Rose brought out the sugar bowl, long unused, filled it from the newly purchased bag and set it on the table, along with a teaspoon.

"Thank you," she said meekly, not looking at him. "For all these groceries, I mean—"

That was when he pulled her onto his lap. His thighs felt hard as a wagon seat under her backside, and *that* realization started all sorts of untoward things rioting inside her.

"You're welcome," he said, in a throaty drawl.

Dara Rose's heart pounded, and she felt dizzy. "Clay— the *children*—"

He sighed. "They're busy squeezing parcels," he said.

Dara Rose sat very still, afraid to move.

Clay watched her mouth for a few moments, and managed to leave Dara Rose as breathless as if he'd actually kissed her, and soundly. Then he said, very quietly, "Just so we understand each other, Mrs. McKettrick, I do mean to bed you, right and proper, one day soon."

Dara Rose gulped, knowing she ought to pull free and get back on her own two feet but strangely unable to do so. "But you said—"

He rested an index finger on her mouth, and a hot shiver went through her. "I know what I said, Dara

Rose, and I'll keep my word. But it's only fair to tell you that I'm fixing to do everything I can to bring you around to my way of thinking."

Dara Rose absolutely could not speak. She was full of indignation and longing and searing heat.

That was when he kissed her—softly at first, and then in a deep way that made everything inside her melt, including her very bones.

When their mouths finally parted, it was Clay's doing, not Dara Rose's.

She'd have been content to let that kiss go on forever, it felt so good.

"I believe I'm making progress," he said, with a certain satisfaction.

He was indeed, Dara Rose thought. If Edrina and Harriet hadn't been in the house, never mind the very next room, she might have taken Marshal Clay McKettrick by the hand and led him straight to her bed. She sighed wistfully.

It had been so long since she'd been held in a strong man's arms, reveled in the sweet responses lovemaking roused in her.

She glanced at the doorway, but her children were still in the front room, playing some game with the dog, filling that little house with barks and giggles. "Parnell and I—we weren't...we didn't..."

Clay simply listened, looking thoughtful.

"What I mean is, we were never...*intimate*," Dara Rose confessed. Even saying that much—telling such a small part of her story—was a tremendous relief. "He married me to give my children a name."

"Go on," Clay said.

Dara Rose checked the doorway again. "I was married—or I *thought* I was married—to Parnell's younger brother, Luke." She swallowed hard. "Edrina was born, and then Harriet, and then—"

Clay didn't prompt her. He was a patient man.

"And then Luke was thrown from a horse and killed, and I learned—I learned that he'd had another wife all along. A *real* wife, and several children. I'd been a—a kept woman from the first, without even knowing it, and our—*my*—children had been born out of wedlock."

Something moved in Clay's handsome face.

Pain? Fury? Pity, perhaps? She couldn't tell.

Afraid she'd lose her courage if she didn't finish the story right now, Dara Rose went on. "I had no money, and no place to go, and after his brother's funeral, Parnell came to me and offered marriage. He was such a good man, Clay." She realized she was crying. When had the tears begun? "When he died upstairs at the Bitter Gulch, everyone felt so sorry for the children and me, and there was this huge scandal, and I couldn't—

I couldn't explain that I wasn't a true wife to him. He must have been so lonely...."

When she didn't go on, Clay set her on her feet, and try though she did, Dara Rose couldn't read his expression.

He got up from his chair, his coffee forgotten on the table, and whistled for his dog.

Chester came to him eagerly, without hesitation, as Clay was putting on his duster and his distinctive round-brimmed hat.

"This calls for some thinking about, Dara Rose," he said. "And I need to get Outlaw back to the livery stable, see that he's put up proper for the night."

With that, Clay opened the back door, and he and Chester went out.

Edrina and Harriet appeared in the inside doorway the instant he'd closed the door behind him.

"Aren't we going to decorate the Christmas tree?" Edrina asked plaintively.

Dara Rose didn't answer. She hurried across the kitchen and through the front room to watch through the window as Clay rounded a corner of the house, passed through the gate, gathered his horse's reins and mounted up.

"What about the Christmas tree?" Harriet trilled, from somewhere behind Dara Rose.

"After supper," she heard herself say, as her heart climbed into her throat. "We'll tend to it after supper."

And Clay McKettrick rode away, Chester following, leaving Dara Rose to wonder if he meant to come back.

WHEN HE REACHED the jailhouse, Clay let himself in, started a fire in the potbellied stove and nearly fell over the large crate waiting by his desk.

He approached the box, apparently delivered while he was away, peering down at the return address: *The Triple M. Indian Rock, Arizona.*

He felt a twinge of homesickness, but it passed quickly.

Much as he loved the ranch, and his family, the Triple M wasn't home anymore. Home, for better or for worse, was wherever Dara Rose happened to be.

When had he fallen in love with her?

He wasn't sure. It might have been today, when she sat on his lap in her tiny kitchen and poured out her heart to him.

Or it might have been when he first laid eyes on her, just a few days before.

All he could say for sure was that it felt a lot like being kicked in the belly by a mule, this falling in love.

He was exultant.

He was crushed.

Dara Rose had loved another man, and that man had

betrayed her, and if Luke Nolan hadn't already been dead, Clay would have cheerfully killed him.

His deepest regret? That he hadn't been there to step in and make things right for her and for the kids, as illogical as that was. Parnell had been the one to rescue her, give his two-timing brother's family a legal right to the Nolan name.

Clay McKettrick was jealous of a dead man and, at the same time, he knew he could never have settled for the kind of empty marriage Dara Rose and Parnell had had together. He was a young man, and red-blooded, and he needed more.

He wanted everything—wanted Dara Rose's heart, as well as her body. Wanted to adopt Edrina and Harriet, change their last name for good, raise them as McKettricks.

And he surely wanted to make more babies with Dara Rose.

Oh, yes, he wanted it all.

He drew in a deep breath. *Slow down, cowboy,* he thought. *Get a grip.*

There was no telling what Dara Rose thought when he'd walked out on her that way, but he needed to sort things through, needed to *think*.

That was the kind of man he was.

He fetched a knife, pried up the lid on the crate his

mother had sent from the Triple M. She must have paid a hefty freight charge to get it there before Christmas, even by train.

Inside, carefully nestled in straw, he found a dozen succulent oranges, a tin full of exotic nuts and a number of his favorite books, some of which he'd owned since he first learned to read. There was more, but Clay's eyes were so blurred by then that he was lucky to be able to read his mother's letter and, even then, he only got this word and that.

"Sawyer wired that you're married...two stepdaughters...bring them home when you can...we're all so anxious to welcome your wife and your children to the family—"

Clay closed his eyes, drew a deep breath. That was Chloe McKettrick for you. If he loved a woman, and that woman's children, then his mother was ready to enfold them in the warmth of her heart, receive them as her own.

It was the McKettrick way. Babies were born into the family, or they arrived by marriage, and it made no difference either way. Once a McKettrick, always a McKettrick.

No matter what happened between him and Dara Rose, Edrina and Harriet were part of the fold, now and forever. If he died tomorrow, or Dara Rose did, his pa and ma, his aunts and uncles and sisters and brothers and cousins—even old Angus and his wife, Concepcion—would take them in and love them like their own flesh and blood.

The knowledge made Clay's throat tighten and his eyes scald.

He wanted to go back to Dara Rose right then, wanted that more than anything, but he didn't give in to the desire.

Yes, she was his wife.

And yes, it was a safe bet that she wanted him as much as he wanted her, after that episode in her kitchen.

But what mattered now was the children.

And that was why Clay McKettrick decided to spend his second night as a married man in the spare room behind the jailhouse. If he'd gone back to Dara Rose's place, he wasn't at all sure he could have resisted her.

He needed her.

He *loved* her.

And that was precisely why he couldn't go home to that little house, with its tiny rooms and its thin walls.

Clay McKettrick knew his limits.

And, where Dara Rose was concerned, he'd reached them.

DARA ROSE LISTENED for Clay's footstep on the back

porch as she peeled potatoes to fry up for supper with some of the salt pork he'd bought at the store. When the meal was over and the dishes had been washed and put away and he still wasn't back, she declared that it was time to decorate the Christmas tree.

"We'd rather wait for Mr. McKettrick," Edrina said, looking glum.

"Where did he go?" Harriet asked.

Dara Rose sighed. She'd been a fool to go against her own better judgment and marry Clay McKettrick. Men couldn't be depended upon to stick around. They lied and cheated and got themselves thrown from horses and killed, they died in the arms of prostitutes above some saloon or, like Mr. O'Reilly, they simply decided they'd rather be elsewhere and took to their heels.

Devil take the hindmost.

"To the livery stable, I think," Dara Rose finally replied.

"He left a long time ago," Edrina reasoned. "It's getting dark outside."

Harriet's lower lip wobbled. "Maybe he's not coming back," she said.

Dara Rose pretended not to hear. "I'll fetch the Christmas box from the cedar chest," she told the children, marching into the front room. "And then we'll see what we can do with this tree."

The girls didn't speak, so she turned her head to look at them.

They stood side by side, arms folded, expressions recalcitrant.

"That wouldn't be right," Edrina said staunchly. "Mr. McKettrick cut that tree down himself. We wouldn't even have it if it weren't for him."

Harriet nodded in grim agreement.

Dara Rose thought fast. "Wouldn't it be a nice surprise, though, if he came home to find it all sparkling and merry?"

Edrina, self-appointed spokeswoman for her little sister as well as for herself, stood her ground. "We'd rather wait," she reiterated.

Dara Rose shook her head, proceeded into the bedroom to give the children a chance to change their minds and lifted the lid of the cedar chest at the foot of the bed. She kept the few simple ornaments they owned, most of them homemade, tucked away there, inside an old boot box of Parnell's.

There was a shining paper chain, made of salvaged foils of all sorts.

There were stars, cut from tin, with the sharp edges hammered down to a child-safe smoothness, and ribbons, and Parnell's broken pocket watch.

And there were two tiny angels, sewn up from scraps

of calico and embroidered with Edrina's and Harriet's
names, their wings improvised out of layers of old newspapers, cut out and pasted together.

Dara Rose had always treasured these humble decorations, as had the girls, but now, in the dim light of the
rising moon, falling softly through the window, they
looked humble indeed. Nearly pitiful, in fact.

She swallowed, straightened her spine, and returned
to the front room with the dog-eared carton, only to
find Edrina and Harriet busy with the one Clay had
spoken of earlier.

*There's some stuff for the Christmas tree in the box I left on
the settee,* he'd said.

The children looked wonder-struck as they lifted one
glistening item after another out of the box—a porcelain
angel, with feathers for wings and a golden halo fashioned of thin wire; shimmering baubles of blown glass,
in bright shades of red and blue and gold and silver; a
package of glittering tinsel that flashed in the lamplight
like a tiny waterfall.

Dara Rose spoke in a normal tone, but it was a struggle. "Shall we decorate the tree after all, then?" she
asked.

But Edrina and Harriet shook their heads.

Slowly, carefully, they put all the exquisite ornaments

Clay had purchased back into the box from the mercantile.

"We'll wait," Edrina said.

And that was that.

The girls went off to get ready for bed, without being told.

Dara Rose, not quite sure *what* she was feeling exactly, put on her cloak and went outside to make sure the chickens were safe in their coop, with their feed and water pans full.

When that was done, she tarried, looking up at the silvery stars popping out all over the black-velvet sky, hoping Clay would step through the backyard gate.

He didn't, of course.

So Dara Rose went back into the house, to her children, to oversee the washing of faces and the brushing of teeth and the saying of prayers.

Edrina, hands clenched together and one eye slightly open, asked God to make sure Mr. McKettrick and Chester found their way back home, please, and soon.

Harriet said she hoped whatever little girl had Florence would take good care of her and not lose the doll's shoes or break her head.

Dara Rose offered no comment on either prayer.

She simply kissed her precocious children good-night, tucked them in and left the room.

In the kitchen, she brewed tea, and sat savoring it at the table, with the kerosene lantern burning low on the narrow counter.

After Luke, and again after Parnell, Dara Rose had solemnly promised herself she would never wait up for another man as long as she lived.

And here she was, waiting for Clay McKettrick.

HAVING MADE HIS DECISION, Clay locked up the street door and banked the dwindling fire, and he collapsed onto the bed in the back room of the jailhouse, not expecting to sleep.

He must have been more tired than he thought, because he awakened with sunlight streaming into his face through the one grimy window, and Chester snoring away in the nearby cell.

Clay got up, made his way into the office, made a fire in the stove and put on a pot of coffee. He let Chester out the rear door and stood on what passed for a porch, studying the sky.

It was bluer than blue, that sky, and the day promised to be unseasonably warm.

Even with half his mind down the road, following Dara Rose around that little house of hers, there was room in Clay's brain for all the things that needed to be done before the kit-house arrived.

He heated water on the stove top, once the coffee had come to a good boil, and washed up as best he could, but his shaving gear and his spare clothes were stashed behind the settee at Dara Rose's.

In the near distance, church bells rang, and Clay realized it was Sunday.

The good folks of the town would be settling themselves in pews right about now, waiting for the sermon to start—and then waiting for it to end.

The ones who wouldn't mind working on the Sabbath Day, on the other hand, were probably gathered down at the Bitter Gulch Saloon, defiant in their state of sin.

Since he needed a well dug, and a foundation, too, Clay figured he'd better get to the latter bunch before they got a real good start on the day's drinking.

An hour later, Chester stuck to his heels the whole time, he'd hired seven men, roused a blinking and grimacing Philo Bickham to open the mercantile and sell him picks and shovels, a pair of trousers and a plain shirt, and rented two mules and a wagon from the livery to haul the workers and the tools out to the ranch.

For a pack of habitual drunks, those men got a lot of digging done.

Clay worked right alongside them, while Chester roamed the range, probably hunting for rabbits. He'd make a fine cattle-dog when there was a herd to tend.

At noon, Clay drove the team and wagon back to town, Chester along for the ride, bought food enough for an army at the hotel dining room and returned to the work site and his hungry crew.

He'd felt a pang passing the turn to Dara Rose's place, having finally remembered that he'd promised Edrina and Harriet that they'd decorate the Christmas tree the night before, but he'd make that up to them later.

Somehow.

Just about supper time, Clay called a halt to the work, satisfied that the foundation was dug and they'd made good progress on the well. The crew climbed into the back of the wagon, as did Chester, and the marshal of Blue River, Texas, turned the mules townward.

He paid the men generously, turned the team and wagon in at the livery and took his time tending to Outlaw, lest the horse feel neglected after being left to stand idle in his stall all day.

Too tired to bother with supper, and too dirty to stand himself for much longer, Clay returned to the lonely jailhouse, lit a lantern, fed Chester some leftovers from the midday meal and commenced carrying and heating water to fill the round washtub he'd found hanging from a nail just outside the back door.

The new clothes he'd bought that morning were stiff with newness and smelled of starch.

Once there was enough hot water in the washtub to suit him, Clay stripped off his filthy clothes, climbed in and sat down, cross-legged like an Apache at a campfire, sighing as the strain eased out of his muscles. He was no stranger to hard physical work, coming from a family of ranchers, but it had been a while since he'd swung a pick or wielded a shovel.

He was sore.

As the water cooled, Clay scoured off a couple of layers of grime and sweat and planned what he'd say to Dara Rose, later tonight, when he intended to knock at her kitchen door and ask if he and Chester could bunk in her front room again. In the morning, they could talk things through.

Only it didn't happen that way.

Clay was just coming to grips with the fact that he didn't have a towel handy when the jailhouse door flew open and Dara Rose stormed in, wearing her cloak but no bonnet and, temper-wise, loaded for bear.

Seeing Clay sitting there in the washtub in the altogether, she stopped in her tracks and gasped.

"You're just in time, Mrs. McKettrick," he said. "It seems I'm in something of a predicament here."

Dara Rose blinked and looked quickly away, keeping her head turned and not asking what the predicament might happen to be.

"My children," she said, "refuse to decorate the Christmas tree unless you're there."

"If you'll fetch me a towel, Mrs. McKettrick," Clay drawled, enjoying her discomfort more than he'd enjoyed much of anything since yesterday's kiss at her kitchen table, "I'll make myself decent, and we'll attend to that Christmas tree."

Dara Rose kept her face averted. "Where...?"

"The towel? It's hanging from a hook next to my shaving mirror, in the back room."

"I meant to say," Dara Rose sputtered, still not looking in his direction, "*where have you been* since last night?" She gave him a wide berth as she went in search of the towel.

"I'm glad you asked," Clay said, smiling to himself as he waited for her to come back, so he could dry off and get dressed in his new duds. "It shows you care."

She returned, flung the towel at him and turned her back. "Nonsense," she said. "Edrina and Harriet were very disappointed when you left—that's the only reason I'm here."

Clay rose out of the tub, the towel around his middle, and sloshed his way into the spare room, where he hastily wiped himself dry and put on the other set of clothes.

Dara Rose had her eyes covered with both hands when he came back. "Are you dressed?" she asked pettishly.

"Yes, Mrs. McKettrick," he said easily. "I am properly attired."

She lowered her hands, looked at him with enough female fury to sear off some of his hide and repeated her original question, dead set on an answer.

"Where *were* you, Clay McKettrick?"

Chapter 10

~~~❦~~~

Where were you, Clay McKettrick?
Clay crossed to Dara Rose, laid his hands gently on her shoulders and felt a tremor go through her slight but sumptuous body. "First," he began, his voice low, "I'll tell you where I *wasn't,* Mrs. McKettrick. I wasn't with a secret wife, and I wasn't upstairs at the Bitter Gulch Saloon, enjoying the favors of a dance-hall girl. I'm not Luke, and I'm not Parnell. I'm *Clay McKettrick,* and it would behoove you to get that straight in your mind. As for where I was, I slept right here last night, and this morning I hired a crew and went out to the ranch to start digging a foundation and a well. The makings of our house will be here right after the first of the year, as I told Philo Bickham yesterday, in your presence and hearing. And as long as the weather cooperates, I plan to spend as much time as I can out there, making the

necessary preparations, because the sooner we can move into a place of our own, the better."

She looked up at him, confused and probably startled by the uncommon length of the speech he'd just given. He could see that she was still afraid to hope, afraid to trust, when it came to any personal dealings with a man. She bit down on her lower lip but didn't speak.

Clay smiled, kissed the top of her head. She wasn't wearing her bonnet, and her hair was coming loose from the knot at her nape, tendrils falling around her cheeks and across her forehead.

I love you, he thought. He was ready to say it right out loud, but he wasn't sure Dara Rose was ready to *hear* it, so he put the declaration by for later.

"I think we'd better get over to the house and decorate the Christmas tree," Clay drawled, enjoying the soft, pliant warmth of her, standing there in his arms, innately uncertain and, at the same time, one of the strongest women he'd ever encountered. "You see, Mrs. McKettrick, if we stay here much longer, I'm liable to seduce you, and I surely do not want our first time together to happen in a jailhouse."

She pinkened in that delightful way that only made him ache to see the rest of her, bare of all that calico, and mischief danced in her upturned eyes. Every signal she was sending out, however subtle, said she was a woman who enjoyed the intimate attentions of a man, who wasn't afraid or ashamed to uncover herself, body, mind and spirit, and then lose herself in the pleasures of making love.

Glory be.

"You seem to have a great deal of confidence in your powers of seduction, *Mr.* McKettrick," she remarked, after twinkling up at him for a few spicy moments. "What makes you think you could persuade me to give in?"

He cupped her chin in his hand, bent to nibble briefly at her mouth. Another shiver went through her at his touch. "Trust me," he said gruffly, after drawing back. "I am a persuasive man."

She sighed. "Yes," she admitted. "I believe you are."

He steered her in the direction of the door, whistled for Chester, took his hat and coat from their pegs. "For instance," he teased, as they stepped out onto the blustery sidewalk, the dog following, "I talked you into marrying me, when we'd only known each other for a few days. And I didn't even ask you to work as my housekeeper for a year before I decided whether to keep you or throw you back."

Dara Rose elbowed him, walked a little faster. "I agreed to your proposal," she whispered, though there was no one on the street to overhear, "*only* because I was desperate to keep my family together, with a roof over our heads."

"Speaking of your children," Clay drawled, "did you leave them home alone to come over here to the jail and hector me?"

She stopped, right there on the sidewalk, with Clay between her and the empty street. "Of *course* not," she said, as indignant as a little hen with her feathers ruffled. "Alvira Krenshaw is with them."

"The schoolmarm?"

Dara Rose nodded pertly. "The woman you probably considered courting before you turned your charms on me," she said.

Clay slipped an arm around Dara Rose's small waist and got her moving again, in the direction of the house where he'd be spending another night on the front room floor, with his dog. "Miss Krenshaw," he said, "was never in the running. And how did you manage to wrangle a woman who herds kids for a living into looking after those two little Apaches of yours?"

"Alvira dropped by with a book she wanted to lend to Edrina. A thick one, with lots of pictures, likely to keep that child busy until school takes up again, after New Year's. Anyhow, I made tea." Dara Rose continued to walk, but she'd turned thoughtful. "Alvira sat down to talk and, well, there's something *about* tea, it seems, that causes a person to drop her guard, at least a little. The whole story—most of it, anyway—just poured out of me."

Clay suppressed a chuckle, knowing it would not be well-received. *Remind me to dose you up with tea first chance I get,* he thought. But, "Go on," was what he said, as they started across the street, his hand resting lightly at the small of her back now, barely touching, but still protective.

"I didn't tell Alvira about Luke, or even how it really was between Parnell and me," Dara Rose confided. "But I *did* say that you and I had had a disagreement and I couldn't stop thinking about where you might be or what you might be doing."

Even in the near darkness, Clay saw her blush. It had cost her, pride-wise, to make that admission, even to a good friend, and it was costing her still.

"I see," he said.

They'd rounded the corner now, and Dara Rose's house was just ahead, so she hastened to finish. "Alvira said I'd better come and find you, then, to settle my mind, while she looked after Edrina and Harriet."

"Is it?" Clay asked.

"Is *what?*" Dara Rose retorted, sounding a mite testy.

"Is your mind settled, where I'm concerned?"

They stood in front of her gate by then, light spilling

out of the windows into the darkened yard. The apple tree was a spare shadow, etched into the night.

"Where you are concerned, Mr. McKettrick," Dara Rose finally replied, "*nothing* is settled. I don't know what to think, what to believe—"

He kissed her then, deeply, the way he would have done if they'd had the whole world to themselves. Adam and Eve, in Texas instead of the Garden.

"Believe *that*," he said, when he'd caught his breath. "And the rest will take care of itself."

Dara Rose just stood there, looking dazed. Even in the poor light, he could see that her lips were swollen, still moist from his kiss.

Calmly, Clay opened the gate, held it for her and shut it after they'd gone through, Dara Rose and Chester and, finally, himself.

At the base of the porch steps, Dara Rose stopped and sort of bristled, about to make some delayed response to being kissed, Clay supposed, but she didn't get the chance, because the front door sprang open and Edrina and Harriet burst out, barely able to contain their glee.

"*Now* can we decorate the Christmas tree?" Harriet demanded.

Miss Krenshaw stood, smiling, on the threshold behind them, already buttoning her practical woolen coat, ready to leave.

"Yes," Dara Rose confirmed, fondly weary in her tone. "We can decorate the Christmas tree." Her gaze shifted to Miss Krenshaw. "You're not leaving, are you?"

"I have a few letters to write, back at the teacherage," Miss Krenshaw replied, sparing a polite nod of greeting for Clay. And with that, she was past them, down the steps, striding along the walk toward the gate. There, she turned back. "Don't forget about the party at the schoolhouse," she called, most likely addressing Dara Rose.

"What party at the schoolhouse?" Clay asked, as Edrina and Harriet beset him with hugs, in their joy at his return. Without missing a beat, he scooped them up, one in each arm, and the sight struck a deep and resonant chord inside Dara Rose.

She led the way into the kitchen, where she'd stowed a plate of supper in the warming oven, in hopes that Clay would be around to eat it.

"After the blizzard," Dara Rose explained, wadding up a dish towel to use as a pot holder and taking Clay's meal from the heat, "Miss Krenshaw decided to call off the Christmas program at school. Now, with all this springlike weather and Pastor Jacobs called away because of an illness in his family, so there won't be a church service, she's had second thoughts. There's no time for the children to memorize recitations and the like, but we can still have some sort of informal gathering on Christmas Day, for the community—sing a few hymns and carols...."

She paused, glanced back at him, felt a thrill as he set the girls down, then removed and hung up his hat and coat. His movements were easy and deliberate, and he looked from her face to the plate in her hands and back again.

"You must be hungry, after a hard day's work at the ranch," she said, suddenly and desperately shy.

"I am indeed hungry, Mrs. McKettrick," he said, in a throaty voice, letting his eyes move over her once before heading to the sink to wash his hands. Everything about him was so masculine—his stance, the movement of his powerful shoulders, the back of his head where his dark hair curled against the neck band of his collarless shirt. He turned, damp and handsome, his sleeves rolled up to his elbows, water spiking his eyelashes. "I am indeed."

"Eat fast!" Edrina urged Clay, as he sat down at the table. "We've been waiting *forever* to decorate the Christmas tree!"

"*Forever*," Harriet testified.

"For that," he said, "I do apologize." Clay looked down at the simple but plentiful meal Dara Rose had prepared—boiled potatoes, the last of the preserved venison and green beans she had grown in her own garden the summer before and subsequently put up in jars for the winter. He favored her with a slight, appreciative smile, and then spoke again to the children, who were fairly electrified with energy. "Settle down now," he said quietly. "We'll get to that tree, I promise."

They subsided, dragged themselves melodramatically out of the kitchen, portraying despondency, Chester tagging along, his ears perked up in anticipation of some new and wonderful game the three of them might play.

Clay ate at his own pace, the way he did everything, and seemed to savor the food Dara Rose had put aside for him, with no real conviction that he'd be around to eat it.

Once he'd finished, Dara Rose offered coffee, but Clay shook his head, said, "No thank you," and started for the front room. When Dara Rose lingered to clear the table, Clay shook his head a second time and beckoned politely for her to follow.

Edrina and Harriet had been busy, Dara Rose discovered. They'd taken every single ornament out of the boxes and laid them in neat rows on the settee.

Later, out in the woodshed behind the house, working by lantern light and supervised by two very lively little girls and an eager dog—Dara Rose spent the time fussing over her chickens—Clay cobbled together a stand to support the small tree and they all went back inside.

To Dara Rose, the thing looked more like a shrub than a tree, but both Edrina's and Harriet's eyes glowed with awe as one decoration after another was reverently added to this bough or that one. The homemade ornaments held their own against the store-bought ones, in Dara Rose's opinion, and she had to admit that, when finished, the effect was very nearly magical—especially when the porcelain angel with the wire halo and the feather wings seemed to hover over the whole of it, offering a blessing.

"Thunderation," Edrina breathed, reflected light from the colorful blown-glass ornaments shining on her face.

"It's bee-you-tee-ful," Harriet pronounced.

Even Chester, sitting between the children and gazing at the shining display, seemed spellbound.

"It's enough to make a person believe in St. Nicholas," Clay said quietly, for Dara Rose alone to hear. "Isn't it?"

"No," she said promptly, but without her usual conviction.

Only days ago, Dara Rose reflected dizzily, she'd been alone in the world, with two children to support, winter coming on and the threat of eviction hanging over her head. She might well have lost Edrina and Harriet forever, the way things were going.

But then Clay McKettrick had arrived by train, with

his handsome horse, and pinned on the marshal's badge, and turned her entire life upside down.

The man had even managed to turn a scrub pine into a more-than-respectable Christmas tree.

It was hard, under such circumstances, *not* to believe in magic.

Christmas Eve

THE CLOCK ON THE FRONT room wall chimed ten times, and the lantern light wavered as Clay came out of the bedroom, shaking his head.

"Not yet," he said to Dara Rose, who was waiting to fill the pair of small stockings she'd allowed the girls to hang from the knobs on the side table. She'd sent him in to see if Edrina and Harriet were really asleep, or just pretending. "Those two are playing possum, for sure."

Dara Rose had an orange to drop into the toe of each stocking, thanks to the box from Clay's people up north, along with a bright copper penny and the new mittens she'd bought at the mercantile a few days before.

These things alone would delight the children, she knew, but there was so much more; she'd splurged on shoes and ready-made coats for her daughters, and Clay's packages—still wrapped in their brown paper and tucked beneath the lowest boughs of the tree—contained numerous mysteries.

They retreated into the kitchen, Clay drinking luke-warm coffee left over from supper, and Dara Rose sipping tea. She'd felt downright reckless, spending Piper's ten dollars so freely, and it still made her breath lurch to think how she'd spent some of it.

Idly, Clay took a small package from the pocket of his shirt, and set it down next to Dara Rose's teacup.

She looked up at him, but she didn't—couldn't—speak.

"Open it," he urged, with that crooked grin tilting his mouth upward at one side, in the way she'd come to love.

Dara Rose hesitated, drew a folded sheet of paper from her skirt pocket and handed it to Clay. "This is for you," she said, so softly that he cocked his head slightly in her direction to catch the words.

"You go first," he said, holding the paper between fingers calloused from working practically every spare moment to prepare for the arrival of the Sears, Roebuck and Company house, all while tending to his duties as town marshal.

Dara Rose's fingers trembled as she opened the little packet, folding back its edges.

A golden wedding band gleamed inside, sturdy and full of promise.

"Will you wear my wedding band, Dara Rose?" Clay asked.

In some ways, it would always seem to both of them that *that* was the moment they were truly married, there at the kitchen table, in the light of a single lantern, on Christmas Eve.

She nodded, murmured, "Yes," all the while blinking back tears, and allowed him to slip the ring onto her finger. It was a perfect fit.

Clay sat watching her for a few moments, his gaze like a caress, and then, very slowly, he opened the sheet of paper she'd given him.

His eyebrows rose slightly as he read, and then a grin spread across his face, lighting him up from within.

She'd given him a receipt for a night's lodging at the Texas Arms Hotel—for two.

"Does this mean what I hope it does?" Clay asked.

Dara Rose had been blushing a lot since she met Clay McKettrick, but at that moment, she outdid herself. Her whole face caught fire as she nodded.

Clay still didn't seem convinced. "You're giving me a wedding night for a Christmas gift?"

She blushed even harder. As her legal husband, he was *entitled* to a wedding night, their bargain notwithstanding. Maybe she should have waited, given him socks or a book or perhaps a fishing pole....

Meanwhile, his golden band gleamed on her left ring finger, simple but heavy.

"Yes," she forced herself to say.

"Hallelujah!" Clay replied, and then he got up from his chair and pulled her into his arms—clear off her feet, in fact—and kissed her so thoroughly that she was gasping when he let her go.

Dara Rose dashed out of the kitchen, afraid of her own scandalous tendencies, and went to look in on the children.

Certain that Edrina and Harriet were at last asleep, she returned to the front room just in time to see Clay set the exquisite doll from the mercantile window squarely in front of the Christmas tree, next to a stack of storybooks that must have been meant for Edrina.

Dara Rose drew in her breath.

"Oh, Clay," she whispered. She'd hadn't dared think, or hope, that he'd been the one to buy Florence.

But he had.

He waggled an index finger at her and spoke gruffly. "Don't you dare tell me I shouldn't have done this, Mrs. McKettrick. I might not be Edrina and Harriet's real father, but I couldn't love them more if I were, and besides, after all they've been through in their short lives, they deserve a special Christmas."

Dara Rose was fresh out of arguments. She simply went to Clay, slipped her arms around his lean waist and let her head rest against his chest. She could feel his steady, regular heartbeat under her cheekbone.

"I love you, Clay McKettrick," she heard herself say.

Clay drew back just far enough to tilt her face upward with one curved finger. "Do you mean it, Dara Rose?"

"I never say anything I don't mean," she replied, quite truthfully.

He grinned. "I meant to be the first one to say 'I love you,'" he told her, "and darned if you didn't beat me to it."

"Hold me," Dara Rose said. "Hold me tightly, so I know this isn't a dream."

"It isn't a dream," he told her. His breath was warm in her hair. "I love you, Dara Rose. I think I have since I first laid eyes on you that first day, when I brought Edrina home on Outlaw and you were so riled up, you were practically standing next to yourself."

She clung to him, with both arms, and her body ached to receive his, but that would have to wait.

Still, it was Christmas Eve, and Clay was holding her, and in a few weeks, they'd be settled in their new house, with a room to themselves and all the privacy a married couple could want.

She'd waited a long time for Clay McKettrick, and she could wait a little longer.

ON CHRISTMAS DAY, in the early afternoon, members of the community began arriving at Blue River's one-room schoolhouse, some on foot, some on horseback, others riding in wagons or buggies.

Miss Alvira Krenshaw had done a fine job decorating the place with paper chains and the like, and everyone who could afford to brought food to share with their neighbors. Clay carefully carried in the huge ham, arranged on a scrubbed slab of wood and draped in clean dish towels, and set it on top of one of the bookcases, with the mounds of fried chicken and the beef roasts and various other dishes already provided by earlier arrivals.

Edrina, preening a little in her new coat and shoes, carried another of her gifts, a game of checkers in a sturdy wooden box, under one arm, hoping, Dara Rose supposed, to find some unsuspecting child to challenge to a game.

Harriet, also sporting a new coat and lace-up shoes—the first pair she'd ever owned that hadn't belonged to Edrina first—held Florence tightly against her side. The doll came with a small wardrobe, neatly folded inside a travel trunk, and Harriet had changed its clothes three times before they left home.

Everyone was there, including Dr. Howard, his wife, Eloise, and little Madeline, the newcomers.

People laughed and talked, often-lonely country

folks crowded together in small quarters, and eventually Miss Krenshaw sat down at the out-of-tune piano and launched into a lively version of "God Rest Ye Merry Gentlemen."

Just about everybody sang along; though, of course, some voices were better than others. Some hearty, some thin and wavering.

"Hark, the Herald Angels Sing" followed, and then "Silent Night."

Snow began drifting past the windows, and Ezra Maddox showed up, along with Peg O'Reilly, her two boys and little Addie, bundled warmly in a quilt.

Holding the child in his strong farmer's arms, Mr. Maddox looked around at the assemblage, as though daring anyone to question his presence.

"Come in, come in," Miss Krenshaw sang out, from the piano seat, "we're just about to start supper."

Dara Rose immediately approached Peg, though she gave Mr. Maddox a wide berth, and hugged her friend warmly. Peg had obviously made an effort to dress up, and the children looked clean and eager to share in festivities.

"Happy Christmas, Peg," Dara Rose said, smiling.

"Ezra didn't say we ought to bring food," Peg whispered, looking fretful, as though she might be poised to flee.

"Never mind that," Dara Rose assured the other woman. "There's plenty to go around. In fact, I wouldn't be surprised if we wound up with as many leftovers as the Lord's disciples gathered up after the feast of the loaves and fishes."

Peg managed a tentative smile. "Addie shouldn't be out—she's been running a fever. But the little ones were so pleased to have some kind of Christmas…"

Dara Rose couldn't help seeing some of herself in Peg O'Reilly. After her husband's desertion, and all the struggles to keep body and soul together, for her children and herself, Peg barely believed in good fortune anymore, or human generosity. If, indeed, she'd *ever* believed.

Putting a hand on the small of Peg's bony back, she steered her friend toward the part of the schoolhouse where the food awaited, helped her to fill plates for Addie and the little boys and find places for them to sit.

After that, everyone sort of stampeded forward, and there was much merriment and laughter as the people of Blue River, Texas, shared a simple Christmas.

Although she made sure Edrina and Harriet had supper, Dara Rose barely saw her husband for the rest of the evening. He was always on the other side of the crowded schoolhouse, it seemed, but each time she found him with her eyes, he smiled and winked and made her blush.

They finally converged at the cloakroom—Clay and Dara Rose, Edrina and Harriet—and the girls, probably exhausted, seemed unusually reticent.

Harriet tugged at Dara Rose's skirt and said, "Mama, bend down so I can speak to you."

Smiling, Dara Rose leaned to look directly into her youngest daughter's face.

"We have lots of presents at home," Harriet said, with a rueful glance at her lovely doll, which was now looking a bit rumpled from being clenched so tightly in her arms.

"And the O'Reillys didn't get anything at all," Edrina added, shifting her checkers game from one arm to the other. "They didn't even have a *tree*."

Clay had joined them by then, and he'd managed to collect their coats from the conglomeration in the cloakroom, but he didn't say anything.

"Do you think St. Nicholas would be sad if I gave Florence to Addie?" Harriet asked, her eyes luminous as she searched Dara Rose's face.

"And her brothers would probably like this checkers game," Edrina added.

Dara Rose's vision blurred.

She looked helplessly up at Clay.

He laid a hand on Edrina's shoulder, smiled down at Harriet. "I think a thing like that would make St. Nicholas mighty happy," he said.

Both girls shifted their gazes to Dara Rose.

She could only nod, since her throat had tightened around any words she might have said, cinching them inside her.

Edrina and Harriet raced off, beaming, to give away their Christmas presents.

Epilogue

December 26, 1914

Clay gave Dara Rose plenty of time to settle into their room at the Texas Arms Hotel that evening, making his usual rounds as marshal, tending to Outlaw in his stall at the livery stable and the chickens in the backyard at home. The children were spending the night with Miss Krenshaw, in the teacher's quarters behind the schoolhouse, and the thought made her smile every time it came to her. After all the times Edrina had played hooky, it was ironic, her being so pleased by the idea of sleeping there.

At her leisure, Dara Rose unpacked her tattered carpetbag, took a long, luxurious bath in the gleaming copper tub carried in, set down in front of the room's simple fireplace, the hearth blazing with a crackling and fragrant fire, and filled with steaming, fragrant water. She soaked and scrubbed and dreamed, and when she heard Clay's light knock at the door, she started.

She'd lost track of time. Meant to be properly clad in the lovely lace-trimmed nightgown and wrapper Clay had given her for a private Christmas gift, presented when the children were asleep and they were alone. Instead, though, here she was, stark naked, her skin slick with moisture, her hair still pinned up in a knot at the back of her neck. She stood, trembling, not with fear, but with anticipation, and reached for her towel.

"It's me, Mrs. McKettrick," Clay said, from the other side of the door. "May I come in?"

Dara Rose gulped hard. "Yes," she said.

His key turned in the lock, and the door opened, and Clay stepped inside. His eyes drank her in even as he shut the door again. Slowly, he took off his hat and then his coat, with its star-shaped badge, unbuckled the ominous gun belt he wore when he was working, set it aside.

"Do you really need that towel?" he asked, with a hint of mischief in his eyes, as he ran a hand through his dark hair.

Dara Rose, feeling deliciously reckless, let the towel drop.

Clay looked at her frankly, his gaze touching her bare breasts, rousing her nipples to peaks, gliding like reverent hands down the sides of her waist and over her hips and even to the silk thatch at the juncture of her thighs.

He swallowed visibly. "Mrs. McKettrick," he said, in a rumbling drawl, "you are unreasonably beautiful."

What did one say to that? Dara Rose didn't know, didn't try.

She simply waited to be touched.

Clay approached her then, lifted her out of the tub by her waist and set her in front of him. Kissed her until she felt drunk with the sensation of his mouth on hers, the radiant heat and hard substance of his body promising so much to her soft one.

"You have me at a disadvantage, Mr. McKettrick," Dara Rose managed, free to be the temptress she was at long last, and exulting in that.

"How's that?" he asked, arching one dark eyebrow and running his hands lightly up and down, along her ribs.

"You, sir," she replied, breathless at his touch, wanting more, so much more, "are fully dressed, while I am quite naked."

"Indeed you are," he agreed huskily, using one hand to loosen her chignon and send her heavy hair spilling down her back.

In the next moment, Clay lifted her again and, secret vixen that she was, Dara Rose locked her bare legs around his hips, tilted her head back with a slight groan when she felt the length of his shaft against her. That made him chuckle, and find her mouth with his, and kiss her into another, even deeper daze of jubilant need.

Suddenly, she landed, with a soft but decisive bounce, on the hotel bed, looked up at Clay as he unbuttoned his shirt, tossed it aside. Instead of stretching out beside her, though, he knelt at the side of the bed, gently parted her legs and kissed his way, very lightly, up the inside of her right thigh.

She gasped and arched her back when he conquered that most intimate place, and took her fully into his mouth.

Suckled, lightly at first, and then with increasing hunger.

Dara Rose, twice married, had never been so deliciously ravished, never felt so beautiful or so womanly, never known such a wild and frantic greed for pleasure.

Instinctively, she arched her back, and Clay slipped his hands under her buttocks, now quivering with the strain of making an offering of her entire self, and feasted on her until her body buckled and undulated in fierce spasms of celebration and she cried out.

The sound was low and long and husky, part howl and full of triumph that must have sounded, instead, like agony.

"That—" Clay chuckled against her still-tingling flesh

"—is why we need our own bedroom, Mrs. McKettrick. One with thick walls."

Dara Rose laughed, or sobbed, or both. She couldn't tell which, didn't care.

All that mattered, for the moment, was that she loved this man, and he loved her, and she could, at last, abandon herself completely to this one someone, leave behind her practicality and her fears and simply *be*.

How odd, she thought, that there could be such freedom in surrender.

Still soaring from that first shattering release, Dara Rose was only dimly aware of Clay rising, removing the rest of his clothes. But when he lay down with her, on the turned-back sheets, the deepest satisfaction she'd ever known instantly gave way to the deepest *need*.

It was primitive, urgent, that need. It rocked her.

Desperate, she tried to pull Clay on top of her, feverish to take him inside her. Hold him there, to please him and be pleased *by* him.

Her body, one with his.

Her soul, one with his.

But Clay was as deliberate about making love as he was about everything else he did. He moved with slow confidence, every kiss, every caress, backed with certainty.

He enjoyed her breasts freely, and for a long time.

She moaned, her nipples pebble-hard and wet from his tongue, his lips.

He teased her. He whispered in her ears, and nibbled at her lobes, and traced the length of her neck with the tip of his tongue, leaving a line of sweet fire behind.

And when he finally lay down flat on the bed, his hands strong, he set her astraddle of his mouth and devoured her all over again, until she was rocking on him, clenching the rails in the headboard of the bed, damp with perspiration, her head tipped back in a low, guttural cry of relief as he finally allowed her to crest the pinnacle and let go.

As she descended, he told her quietly that he had not yet begun to make love to her, that they'd be at it for a lifetime.

He told her all the places he would have her, all the times and ways. She reveled in the knowledge.

"Suppose someone hears?" she fretted, when Clay laid her down again and, at last, poised himself above her.

"Suppose they do?" Clay countered hoarsely, with a grin. And then, in one long, fiery thrust, he was finally inside her, deep, deep inside her.

Part of her.

And all the flexing and needing and carrying on started all over again.

Just as Dara Rose's *life* had started all over again, with

the arrival of this man, with his quiet, steady ways and his strength, so at home in his own skin.

It was the beginning of forever, for both of them.

And a fine forever it would be.

★ ★ ★ ★ ★

Sparkling Christmas kisses!

Bryony's daughter, Lizzie, wants was a *dad* for Christmas and Bryony's determined to fulfil this Christmas wish. But when every date ends in disaster, Bryony fears she'll need a miracle. But she only needs a man for Christmas, not for love…right?

Unlike Bryony, the last thing Helen needs is a man! In her eyes, all men are *Trouble*! Of course, it doesn't help that as soon as she arrives in the snow-covered mountains, she meets Mr Tall, Dark and Handsome *Trouble*!

www.millsandboon.co.uk

1112/MB391

Come home to the magic of
Nora Roberts

Identical twin boys Zeke and Zach wished for
only one gift from Santa this year: a new mum!
But convincing their love-wary dad that their
music teacher, Miss Davis, is his destiny and
part of Santa's plan isn't as easy as
they'd hoped…